Praise for Aramint

'Rare and very refreshing... a novel
are represented in all their wise, se
enjoyed it SO much'

'I loved it, right down to the utterly chilling final line'
Gillian Flynn

'A psychological thriller in the truest sense of the word: a thoughtful examination of the psyche of three credible women with baggage and flaws. So much will resonate, not least Hall's exploration of gender politics and motherhood. At points I was folding pages repeatedly. Deeply unsettling. Recommended'
Sarah Vaughan

'A propulsive and addictive study of the darkness of obsessive love. I was completely gripped from the first word to the last!'
Lisa Jewell

'Not only a deeply satisfying psychological thriller but an insightful and sometimes disquieting exploration of relationships, families and the challenges and pressures confronting women today'
Cara Hunter

'A tense, intelligent thriller that kept me gripped and guessing until the final page – and thinking long after that'
Erin Kelly

'A brilliant exploration of the secrets and hidden lives women create for themselves as they try to navigate their way through life. The friendships are real and touching, the relationships are consuming and passionate. I read this in no time and really enjoyed the pace, flow and insights Araminta writes about. A fabulous novel of modern love, life and people, with an excellent twist' **Dorothy Koomson**

'A dark, delicious thriller which holds the complexity of female friendship at its heart. I loved it' **Louise O'Neill**

'Addictive and disturbing – like watching a slow motion car crash through splayed fingers' **Tammy Cohen**

'As merciless a thriller as I've ever read. Astonishingly dark and sensationally accomplished' **AJ Finn**

'A cracking read' **Steph McGovern**

'A slow-burning, tense build to a furious conclusion. Female friendships and the compromises women make are explored in stark detail, and through three different perspectives the story develops to a pleasing and very just ending. It's great'

Harriet Tyce

'*Perfect Strangers* is a painfully honest, haunting portrait of friendship, betrayal, marriage and disappointment. While Hall is able to keep you on the edge of your seat (and awake much later than you should be) she can also make you weep, such is her insight and lack of judgement of the human condition. A beautiful book that will stay with me for a very long time'

Dolly Wells

'Beautifully written and expertly structured – a masterclass in psychological thriller writing' **Simon Lelic**

‘A taut, fascinating psychological thriller that explores timely themes about how society judges women and their sexuality. Be prepared for questions to linger in your head for quite a long time afterwards’ **Julia Heaberlin**

‘A stunning, dark novel about who women want to be and the reality of who they are. Beautifully written, thought-provoking and should not be missed’ **Samantha Downing**

‘A taut, nasty thriller about what society does to women who like sex. I loved it!’ **India Knight**

Araminta Hall has worked as a writer, journalist and teacher. Her first novel, *Everything and Nothing*, was published in 2011 and became a Richard & Judy read that year. Her second, *Dot*, was published in 2013, her third, *Our Kind of Cruelty*, in 2018, and *Perfect Strangers* published in 2020.

She has taught creative writing for many years at a variety of places, including New Writing South in Brighton, where she lives with her husband and three children.

Follow Araminta on Twitter @aramintahall to find out more.

Also by Araminta Hall

Everything and Nothing
Dot
Our Kind of Cruelty
Perfect Strangers

HIDDEN DEPTHS

ARAMINTA HALL

An Orion paperback
First published in Great Britain in 2022 by Orion Fiction
an imprint of The Orion Publishing Group Ltd
Carmelite House, 50 Victoria Embankment
London EC4Y 0DZ

An Hachette UK company

1 3 5 7 9 10 8 6 4 2

All the characters in this book are fictitious, and any resemblance to actual persons, living or dead, is purely coincidental.

A CIP catalogue record for this book is available from the British Library.

ISBN (Mass Market Paperback) 978 1 4091 9614 3
ISBN (eBook) 978 1 4091 9615 0
ISBN (Audio) 978 1 4091 9628 0

Typeset at The Spartan Press Ltd,
Lymington, Hants

Printed and bound in Great Britain by Clays Ltd,
Elcograf S.p.A.

www.orionbooks.co.uk

To my family, past, present and future,
both by blood and by design

'At present, moral responsibility is too weak an incentive in human affairs... The thing is a defect in human life of today – thoughtlessness for the well-being of our fellow men; and we are all guilty of it in some degree.'

Lawrence Beesley, The Loss of the SS Titanic

WEDNESDAY
APRIL 10TH, 1912

LILY

The funnels were surely too big. They were easily the biggest man-made things Lily had ever seen and they made her feel like she was floating, even more so than normal. They could, in fact, be bigger than the terrible, dreary hills she had to stare at out of one of the hundreds of windows at home, hills which only moved between the dankest of colour spectrums, from forest green to granite grey to coal black, only allowing a sprinkling of violet purple on the rare occasions the sun shone. Like the hills, the funnels were imposingly dark, all four of them standing so straight and true, as if there was nothing to worry about.

She turned her attention back into the dining room and focused on Henry, absorbed in his newspaper. She imagined telling him what the funnels made her feel like and the look of scorn he would give her, if he even acknowledged her words. She looked instead at what he was reading, but there on the front page was a replica of the ship she'd just been staring at through the window. *The Titanic to leave Southampton Today on her Maiden Trip Across the Atlantic*, she read, the words blurring in her eyes. Because the sensation of the two ships, of herself soon to be in one of them, made her feel dizzy, as if she was going to have one of her turns, but she forced herself away from the edge, desperate not to annoy Henry more than was necessary.

She concentrated instead on the laughter coming from the next table; two women and a man, excitedly discussing the crossing they were about to make, as if there were things to look forward to. Their voices were cut from glass and tinkled across the china, the toast, the kipper bones, the scraped bowls of porridge and cold cups of tea that had constituted their breakfast.

Her gaze involuntarily strayed back to the window, out of habit from home, but she forced her eyes downwards, away from the ship and into the street. It looked like a river of people streaming below, a palpable sense of adventure rising from them like steam, which tickled at the glass.

One of the women on the next table laughed again and Lily wished she could share in the joy around her, but all she could feel was a deep, lacerating fear, which speeded her heart and slicked her skin with sweat. And it wasn't really anything to do with the funnels looking too big; it was more because her life was joyless and loveless and graceless and had been for far too long. She folded her hands protectively over her raised skirt, wishing for things she could barely believe in.

Her mind tipped and swayed, but she forced it to steady by holding on to the thought that they were finally going home, or at least, back to *her* home. Once there, she was certain things would get better; her nerves would calm and the prospect of the baby wouldn't terrify her like a nightmare constantly stalking her thoughts. And, if she still felt this daily terror at home, perhaps there was some way she could refuse to board a ship back to England. She would appeal to May somehow and beg her for help, cling to her if necessary.

Henry snapped his newspaper so it made the sound of a whip

and Lily jumped in her seat. He allowed their eyes to meet for the briefest of seconds, although that was all it needed.

'Are you ready?' she asked, trying to pull her mouth upwards.

He looked pointedly at her untouched egg, the yellow yolk congealed against the side of the shell like blood, which made her wonder how she'd forgotten to eat again. He snorted his derision and stood, so she followed, knocking into the table, which made the china clink together.

'For God's sake,' he growled under his breath. One of the laughing ladies glanced quickly over at them and Lily worried that she would have dampened her happy day.

Henry strode before her through the dining room with all the confidence of his birthright, while she trailed in his wake. A few people glanced up as they passed, but she doubted any of them knew him because, strangely, they were not staying in the smartest hotel, where his set would be, but a smaller, cheaper one, not on the best road. She supposed some of the women might recognise him from the society pages, not that she knew when he'd last been in them, as she'd long ago stopped trying to track her husband's progress through the gossip columns.

Becky was in their bedroom trying on Lily's blue hat when they opened the door. She pulled it off her head too hastily, so her hair caught and her cheeks flushed as she met Lily's eye through the glass.

'You really should not touch my things, Becky,' she made herself say, the words sticking in her throat.

Becky bobbed her head. 'Sorry, Ma'am. I was just finishing off your packing. It was all a mess when I came in.'

'My wife always leaves everything in a mess,' Henry said, which made tears smart to Lily's eyes.

At almost her first society party in London, when she was still a fresh-faced, rosy-cheeked new bride, straining with love and passion, an older American woman, a duchess no less, had taken Lily to one side. 'You look like you are in love,' she'd said, in a voice which had reminded Lily so much of her mother's rich Southern drawl she'd longed pathetically for the woman far away across a long ocean.

'Why thank you. We are very happy,' Lily had replied, looking over at her new husband as he chatted to a group of men. He looked so fine, in his smart clothes with his thick moustache, that she found it easier to forget his greying hair and short stature.

'Well, be careful,' Consuelo Vanderbilt – as Lily, as every aspiring American girl would have known her to be – said. 'I have come to learn that the British upper-class male spends his formative years being hugged and kissed only by working-class maids and nannies, a taste which never leaves him.'

Lily had turned to the tiny, delicate woman standing next to her, but all she saw in her eyes was a flashing knowledge. 'Ours is a love match. Henry – Fitz – has been the perfect gentleman.' She hated having to call her husband by the nickname everyone used in London. His middle name was Fitzherbert, but she thought the diminutive made him sound insubstantial, like a cracker or a firework, which everyone knew shone brightly for only a few seconds before extinguishing entirely.

Consuelo had raised an eyebrow in a perfect arch. 'At least we knew what we were doing in my day. I mean, there was no pretence then, you swapped your millions of dollars for a title and thought it fair until you arrived on this wet island. I cannot believe you girls failed to learn our lessons.' She'd popped open her tiny, tortoiseshell bag and handed Lily a thick, embossed card imprinted with her name and address. 'You know Fitz was almost bankrupt before he met you?'

But Lily didn't see how that was possible, with his smart

London house and the castle they were going to visit in Northumberland in just a few days. His tailored suits, his gold watches, the beautiful ring he'd given her, the fine wines he liked to drink, the private railcar he'd hired to take them back to Newport to speak to her father.

'I – I think you must be mistaken,' she'd stammered.

Consuelo had leaned in closer so Lily could smell the violets on her breath. 'It's time to grow up, Lily, dear. You have to create your own life over here, you have to fight for it, because if you don't, it will consume you whole. Not that you have to do it alone; there are people who will be your friends if you let them. And, believe me, you will need them.'

Becky had been her friend once, her dearest friend, in fact. The person she'd confided in when writing to May had seemed like too much of an admission of failure, the person she'd laughed with when nothing was funny, the person she'd sat with on cold nights when home seemed a million miles away. The person who'd listened and held and comforted her.

'Organise the cases, Becky,' Henry said. 'Lady Elsworth and I will walk to the ship. Also, tell Dr Henderson to make his own way there.'

'Yes, Sir.'

Lily tried to catch Becky's eye as she hurried from the room, but she kept her head determinedly low.

'Have you taken all your medicine this morning?' Henry asked, as he gathered up his papers.

'Yes.'

'I'm so bored with reminding you.'

'But I never forget.'

He snorted, which made Lily wonder if she really had taken it. She tried to remember the sensation of mixing two drops from the glass bottle into her water and found it impossible had happened or not, if what she was remembering this morning or from all the other mornings she'd same thing. Her heart began to race, but then Henry was making for the door of their room, and Lily knew it would irritate him too much to find the bottle and check, so she simply followed him out and downstairs into the crowded Southampton streets.

They were very noisy and bright, which filled up too much of her mind, so it felt hard to fully believe in what she was doing, as if there were a veil in front of her face. She wanted to cover her ears and shut her eyes, but knew it would anger Henry, so concentrated on her feet on the ground, on placing one in front of the other. In that way she could move without too much consequence, without feeling that she was part of anything larger.

The quayside was even busier than the streets and the atmosphere was heavy with activity, the scents of sweat, smoke and rose mingling in an acrid mess that made her lift a handkerchief to her nose. She forced herself to glance up at the ship towering over the scene, but its hugeness spun her head so she had to immediately look back down, knowing that when she felt this way she had to take every second as it came. She forced her attention to the tiny buttons on the back of her gloves, made her mind wonder at the delicacy it would have taken to sew them, imagined the women bent over tables spending days at this work.

It succeeded in getting her to the bottom of a wooden gangplank where people were filing up into the ship, white ropes on either side to keep them safe. They had to stop and wait their turn, which she knew would irritate Henry and, sure enough, he huffed dramatically behind her. She turned and saw him looking up at a metal gangplank high above them, crossing over from a large metal structure, on which she could see people ambling serenely, looking down at the crowds below. It was an ornate, beautiful contraption, clearly the first class entrance, and it made everything feel wrong, because before today there would have been no scenario Lily could have imagined in which they weren't up there. Henry's face was red and contorted and she knew how slighted he would feel to be beneath, in every sense of the word. The unlikelihood of what they were doing knocked into her again so she couldn't catch her breath for a moment.

Her turn had come to ascend the much inferior structure which would transport them into the similarly inferior part of the ship and all she could do was step up. She held on to the thick rope as soon as she could, enjoying feeling its heft, as if it could support her. Henry was close behind, his hand on the small of her back, and she had a sudden desperate desire to turn and run, because it would be like this for the next week, this feeling of being enclosed and trapped, with no hope of escape.

Henry pushed into her back, the pressure mounting, even though she couldn't move any faster because there was a line of people in front of her. She tried to turn to him, but, before she could, he gave her a sharp shove and she fell forward, knocking into the man in front, who had to grab on to the rope to stop himself falling into the woman in front of him. He turned, his face moving from anger to concern when he saw Lily.

'My apologies, Sir,' Henry said from behind her. 'My wife is often unsteady on her feet.'

'It's quite all right,' the man replied, his cheeks reddening. 'I hope you're not hurt, Madam?'

Lily shook her head, her throat clogging with tears. But the man had turned and was already taking larger strides to catch up with his companions in front of him, who were all looking down at Lily, pity smearing their faces.

The baby was quiet in her stomach, so she thought it was

safe and, it was true, she was often unsteady. And she must have been mistaken because, even though Henry had never needed much of a reason to hurt her, there was no way he would have endangered the baby by pushing her on purpose. He'd told her too many times that a baby was all he wanted and her pregnancy had certainly been the most fervent wish for all the years they'd been married. Before this year, she'd long given up hope at the thought she would be able to do this for him, long accepted her uselessness as her body failed and faltered, so, when the unlikely conception came, she found she couldn't quite believe in it, couldn't quite make herself even desire what lay at the end of the nine months.

'Come on, then,' Henry said behind her and Lily had to make her feet move again because there was simply no other option.

LAWRENCE

Lawrence opted to walk from his hotel to the ship because it had struck him when he woke that it would be the last time his feet connected with the ground. He would obviously walk on deck, but that was different from the solid mass of earth which overlaid the planet he'd marched across for the past thirty-four years. He expected to feel a greater sense of sadness as he walked, but it took all his energy to make his feet move and so he let the moment pass and wondered why he'd expected otherwise.

There were streams of people making their way to the quayside and the streets had a holiday atmosphere from which he felt totally excluded. He wondered absent-mindedly if something had happened to his senses because nothing seemed very clear, as if he were existing inside a box or something, everything was muffled. But the thought didn't worry him because soon he would be dead and that was the only bit of comfort he'd been able to find in the past miserable year. People liked to say that time healed, but what Lawrence had learnt was that misery existed so physically it was like another presence, almost like an entity within his body.

He turned a corner and then he was standing at the top of the street which led to the ship. All around him, people were stopping and gasping and, it was true, she did rise up like an island before them. She reared out of the sea, her vast black body stretching upwards towards the white decks, topped by monstrous funnels and impossibly tall masts reaching skywards, with such an intricacy of lines and wires snaking off them. It made him wonder why he'd chosen such a dramatic way to end it all. Not that he'd really chosen, the opportunity had more sort of presented itself to him as he'd been walking back from an appointment down Leadenhall Street and seen the advertisements for the ships which carried people across the Atlantic to America.

He'd decided to kill himself a few weeks before that, understanding that a life without Cissy simply wasn't going to be possible. He'd given it his best shot for a year, but nothing was working and there seemed increasingly little reason to keep trying. Even Alec wasn't enough of a pull; in fact he was a propulsion, because any fool could see that Lawrence was contaminating his son with his misery.

After he made the decision, he'd felt such a deep sense of peace for the first time since Cissy breathed her last, that for a few days he was calmed, walking around as if in a dream. But then the practicalities started to sink in and he'd begun to realise that the need to die did not exist in and of itself, but came attached to so many other decisions, all of which could affect a young boy. It was obvious that he couldn't do it at home because what if Alec found him, or even heard the maid scream? But when he started to think like that, he also realised that even if he jumped in front of a tube train, or from a bridge into the Thames, still Alec would have days of confusion whilst the police looked for him and relatives were sent for. He toyed with the idea of taking Alec to stay at his parents' house and shooting himself in the woods, but knew he couldn't do that to his mother.

The plan had started to shrink around him, until sometimes he felt as if it were enveloping his body and he might die of suffocation, sparing himself the bother. But then his eye had been turned to the posters of a fleet of huge ships promising so much. He'd stood staring, his own face reflected over that of a boat in a picture, and an idea had started to form. If he took a trip, then Alec would have to be sent to relatives before he left, which would mean he would be safe and settled by the time news reached him of his father's death. And if he jumped from a ship and didn't leave a note, then no one would ever even be sure it was suicide, it could, after all, just be a terrible accident, and Alec wouldn't have to live with the knowledge that he wasn't enough to keep his father tethered to the earth.

He drank in that poster, looking at the hulk of the bow astride the waves, as if it owned them, as if it had defeated nature, and his idea had mutated into fury, which built into hatred. Hatred not just for the arrogance of the ship, but the fact that Cissy would never sail on the ocean, the fact even that she'd left him alone by so selfishly dying. And then he'd hated himself also for thinking like that and it all felt too big and too hot and maybe the sea was the only thing that could extinguish this pain. It was all too easy to imagine himself jumping, a tiny speck against the side of the ship, and it was the most exhilarated he'd felt since Cissy's death.

He knew that Cissy would be furious at his plan, but the truth was he was too furious with her to care. His death, in fact, would not just be about releasing himself from the daily pain of trying to live without her, but would also be a punishment for her for not taking proper care of herself and leaving him behind.

Lawrence had spun around in that moment, so furious he worried he might scream. Surely it was an affront to all decency that she had chosen to ignore all his warnings and let herself die? And surely the world needed to implode, to buckle and fall into itself so that nothing remained except for dust and ashes? Because, surely, the whole world recognised the futility of existence without Cissy?

His anger had propelled him through the door and up to a long, curved wooden desk, redolent with polish which made its surface glitter like a promise. The young man had tried to entice him with luxuries he could never have afforded anyway, but Lawrence had waved him away and told him his mind was already set, all he wanted was a second class ticket, one way. And now he was here, the moment arriving quicker than he'd anticipated.

The air of the quayside was full of noise and bustle, the sun illuminating streams of activity which seemed so futile to Lawrence that he wanted to shout at everyone to be quiet, there was no point in all this momentum, one day they would be dead and then none of this would matter. There were so many bodies, a mess of people jostling and bumping, that it took him a long while to reach the point at which he could board.

The stone of the pavement gave way to the wood of the gangplank and in the step he took he felt like he'd entered a new world. The ground now swayed with the water's undulation and so he looked down at the grey, frothing water of the harbour as he climbed into the belly of the ship. It was dotted with bits of debris and yellowing foam, reminding him of a weak soup, which turned his stomach.

LILY

As soon as the steward left after showing them to their cabin, Henry couldn't hide his disdain at the space, which Lily knew would be transferred to her, as if she was the reason they were there, which, she supposed, was true. Henry would never have been travelling to America if it wasn't where she was from. He vociferously hated their very infrequent visits, always complaining at how uncouth and backward he found the people, how tiresome her mother, how bland the food.

They hadn't made the crossing for five years and, when Dr Henderson had told her she was pregnant, Lily had pretty much given up the thought of ever seeing her homeland again. But then Henry had amazed her by saying he thought it would be good for her to give birth in America, near her parents, when never before had he shown any signs of caring that anything was good for her.

Dark clouds began to settle on his small features as he walked to the thin washstand and kicked his foot into its base, the noise slapping around the cabin, making Lily back herself against a modest sofa. The room was smaller than the smallest dressing room at Elsworth Castle, but it was lined in oak panelling and there was a porthole on the far wall, through which the sun streamed. Two beds stuck out of the wall like bunks, which made her cringe, although they looked comfortable and care had been taken to make them appear smart, with their bevelled edges and embroidered counterpanes. Not that any of that would be enough. Her hand involuntarily rubbed at the bruise on her upper arm from when she'd last irritated her husband.

'We could still change to first, Henry. I'm certain there will be space.' The mystery of why they were in second class circled Lily like a nightmare which refused to shift, because her husband was a man who expected the best of everything and had never stinted in his entire life. They even had friends making the crossing in first and she couldn't believe he'd passed up the opportunity to spend a week carousing with them.

His lip curled into a snarl. 'I've already told you it's too much money. What with us having to bring Becky and Dr Henderson because you are too fragile to travel without them.'

'But I never said that. I would be just as happy with an American doctor.' In fact, much happier, as she'd never liked Dr Henderson, who smelt of something tart and indefinable and never seemed entirely clean. She'd much rather have kind Dr Bushell, although Henry said he was a country quack and she hadn't seen him since before her pregnancy. It might even be better if Becky hadn't come, because to have her physically close but emotionally so far was like torture.

Henry snorted. 'You need consistent care and you know it.'

She found she knew less and less. 'But surely we have the money for first anyway?' The extravagance of their life made Henry's claim at penury ridiculous.

'Honestly, Lily, you have no idea what life costs. The tickets in first are a small fortune. Do not try to get involved with things you could never understand.'

There was a knock on the door which made her start. Henry

caught the movement and sneered, his face curling in disgust as if she smelt.

'Come,' he shouted and the door opened to reveal Becky in all her perky fineness, even more round and luscious than usual, reminding Lily of a peach.

'Are you just next door?' Lily asked, to which Becky nodded. Just six months ago, she would have wanted Becky as close as possible, but now the thought made her uneasy, which in turn made her ache with loneliness.

'Shall I bring your cases in, Sir?' Becky looked straight at Henry as she spoke and Lily thought she saw a flicker of a smile cross her husband's face.

'God knows where we'll put them in this hole,' Henry replied.

'They can stay in my room, if you would prefer.' Becky's mouth turned upwards as if it were trying to smile, but it lost its way, so all that happened was it revealed her slightly discoloured teeth.

He laughed. 'Good idea. But bring in our personal trunks.'

Becky returned with Lily's smaller case, the weight causing her to carry it lopsidedly across the room, wincing as it banged into her calves. A sheen of sweat broke out across her chest and her metallic scent filled the small space. 'Shall I unpack, Ma'am?'

But Lily shook her head because she couldn't watch Becky touch her things as if it was just her job.

'You're looking a little unwell, Ma'am,' Becky said.

The comment made Lily look at Becky to see if she really cared or if she was making fun, but the woman's face was almost expressionless and her eyes were flat. Lily glanced then at Henry, imagining what her father would say to a servant who spoke to her mother in that way, but it was useless to think like that. It had been nine years since she'd lived in her parents' house: nine long, torturous years which had felt like an endurance test with no end point, and she knew better than to expect her father's care.

'That'll be all, thank you, Becky,' she said, so the woman idled out of the cabin.

'God, do you have another fucking headache?' Henry asked and Lily felt like she was falling because his meanness still had the power to shock, which was silly, because it hadn't taken her long to work out what had happened to her after their marriage. She hadn't needed to hear the two women laughing on a balcony at a terrible ball she'd attended in her first few months as a married woman. 'She's ridiculously young,' one of them had said. 'I mean, I know you don't want them knowledgeable or anything, but she's a child. She could be his bloody daughter.'

'Apparently she's a bit of a hick,' the other had replied. 'But I've heard she has other attractions. Like her $4 million dowry and $100,000 a year.'

'So, they'll be broke by Christmas then,' the first one had said, their mirth peeling off into the night.

She'd been unable to stop her tears falling that night, realising what she'd begun to suspect as Henry's affections cooled almost as they stepped ashore in Southampton. But those words made it clear that she was nothing more than a commodity, traded so her father's money could make Henry's family seat, Elsworth Castle, gleam. And over the years it had done just that, transforming it from a leaking, crumbling wreck by installing bathrooms, electricity and heating, manicuring the grounds, mending the roof, building stables, acquiring a fleet of carriages and keeping it warm and full of food; all in all, glorious for visitors, none of whom she even liked.

Even on her first night at Elsworth, she'd dreamt of burning it to the ground, a fantasy which still loomed large in her mind. Too many times she'd imagined taking a match to the heavy curtains in the long room, tipping candles in the ballroom, or letting embers spray on to the carpet in her bedroom. Not one tiny part of the house felt like home and it never had, not since the first windswept, leaden grey day when tired horses had pulled them up a much too long drive, overhung by weeping trees that blocked out the sky, to the base of what felt like a small hill on the top of which stood a giant, stone monolith. A configuration of bricks and mortar that was, and always would be, her husband's first love.

'I'm going on deck,' Henry said. 'Are you coming?'

Lily walked unsteadily to the mirror. It felt as if they were already out at sea and she could barely keep her balance, but she focused on her reflection, which shifted and blurred before her eyes, as if she was dissolving. She forced herself to cling to the hope that when May and her parents saw the state of her marriage, they'd step in to save her, because, without Becky, she didn't think it would be possible for her to live the rest of her days in this way. 'I might have a rest,' she said, as she started to unpin her hat.

'Like the boring old maid you are.'

She stared at him through the wobbly glass. 'I'm twenty-nine.'

'And useless at it.' He turned and slammed out of the room, leaving her alone in the small, cramped space.

LAWRENCE

It was too loud on deck, but it was better than being alone in his cabin. Lawrence did many things to avoid being alone, even though the past year had taught him to hate most people. But sometimes the noise in his brain felt as if it were banging against his skull, desperate for any way to escape. He leant over the railings, feeling the push of bodies all around him, as the boat began to move, gliding off into the water miles below. Two sailors rushed towards where the gangplank was being pulled ashore, gesticulating at the ship, one even throwing his pack to the ground. People missed boats all the time, Lawrence thought, and in missing them who knew what opportunities leached into the sky, gone like puffs of smoke.

The sounds and squeals intensified as people waved and shouted at loved ones on the quay and it made Lawrence wonder at the reasons why all these people were on this boat. New lives were starting all around him, as if the ship was carrying not just bodies but was weighed down with hopes and dreams, so he imagined himself momentarily surrounded not by the watery sea but a sea of people looking for something new. The thought buried into him like a tapeworm, twisting his gut with a misery he'd long since become accustomed to because he knew that there would never again be a sense of newness or anticipation for him.

He'd accepted that the rest of his life would be coloured alternately by how much he missed Cissy and how angry he was with her for dying, and he didn't think it was a feasible way to live. If your memories of your dead wife are coloured by a white-hot rage, and if you miss her so much that you can't appreciate sunsets or birds singing or the taste of good food or even the smile of your son, then life is lost to you. And, more than that, he was tired of trying, tired of thinking that the feeling of desolation might lift, that he might see a point to life without the person he loved most in it. Or that he might stop hating a woman he loved with his whole being for the weakness of her body. He just wanted it all to stop and he could already feel the sense of peace that letting go would give him, like a velvet cloak wrapped around his shoulders.

He looked down into the water that was much further away than he'd anticipated, which meant jumping alone would probably break him. But still he thought it would be a pleasure to jump into the blackness and feel the water close over his head. To leave no trace, no hope, no room for anything apart from his memories.

And maybe when he was dead, his memories would only be good, if he thought at all, which he suspected was likely. It was one of the main reasons why jumping from a boat had seemed like such a good idea, because when his body finally succumbed to the ocean, he would leak out of himself into the water and that is where he would stay, all his being mixing with the vast ocean so that Cissy could travel across the globe.

After he'd so rashly bought his ticket, he'd studied the route the transatlantic liners took, trying to work out the best place to jump for the best distribution of his soul, presuming that some midway point would be where he would choose. But then he'd seen that all the routes took these ships through ice fields not far from the American coast, where giant icebergs rose up out of the sea like small islands. And the more he'd read, the more he'd realised that the ice in those bergs was magical, like a glittering, compact store of time and memory, holding on to all the moments of life. It was obvious that he could only jump there, so his essence could attach itself to an iceberg and be immortalised, so that Cissy could shine on forever.

A small part of him worried that it was a cold and lonely place to leave Cissy, but that was obviously not something that had worried her. He had begged her not to spread herself so thin, he'd warned her that her body couldn't take the long days and cold nights, but she'd pushed him away and said she couldn't, in all conscience, sit by a warm fire when women were suffering in every street across the land. And she clearly hadn't worried about leaving *him* encased in ice, so perhaps cold and lonely was what they both deserved.

'Why am I not enough for you?' he'd cried to her one night as she prepared to set off on another mercy mission.

'In many ways you are,' she'd replied, 'but you can't ask me to give up what I believe in to make you more comfortable.'

'Why not?' he'd said before he could check himself.

She'd looked at him with disdain. 'Because you are better than that, Lawrence. You didn't want a meek, obedient wife or you would have married one.' She'd pulled her hat low on her head. 'Besides, we cannot abdicate our whole selves to one person or we end up hating them.'

He hated her now, a thought so terrible he felt like he might be about to faint and had to push himself off the railings and make his way to the centre of the ship. His feet worked aimlessly, each stride taking him from one moment to the next, like he did at home, pounding the London pavements, sometimes all night, as if he could outpace his misery. He liked the vastness of the ship for that reason as it meant his walking could continue until the very last moment; he liked the thought of this endless circular route, meaningless in its lack of destination.

As he moved, his heart lurched and churned as it battled itself. Part of him loved Cissy so much he felt like his skin was being flayed from his body, and part of him hated her so much it felt like his organs might explode through his skin. She was right and he never would have stopped her from doing anything, but that didn't mean she shouldn't have stopped herself. It didn't mean that when her body ached with tiredness, or her lungs hurt, or the sweats came, that she shouldn't have looked at him and wanted to protect herself, for his sake at least. He loved her so much, he was prepared to lay down his life for her and she couldn't even stay in when the rain soaked her to the skin.

He had to stop and lean against a wall, shutting his eyes and turning his face to the sun in an attempt to burn away his feelings. But all that happened was that time fell from him and, momentarily, he was back in their childhood village of Wirksworth, running through the gardens at the Manor, on a hot July day, chasing Arthur, knowing that he was too old to be behaving in such a way and how angry Father would be if he saw him. He rounded a large azalea bush in his mind and, even though he tried to stop, tried to shy away from the image, his mind wouldn't let him and his youthful legs propelled him forward, almost on to the lap of the young lady dressed in white sitting under a large tree.

He'd skidded to a stop, aware of his untucked shirt and sweaty face, his hair dishevelled and hanging over his eyes.

The woman had looked up at him and laughed. 'Hello,' she'd said, 'and what are you running from?'

He'd felt foolish in her gaze and tried to stand straighter. 'I'm just chasing my brother. Sorry.'

She'd patted the ground next to her. 'No need to apologise. Please, take a seat?'

Lawrence did as she asked, resting his back against the gnarled wood of the tree as she was doing.

'Not that I would blame you if you had been running away. I hate these stupid garden parties Mother gives.'

Lawrence had felt a bolt of shame run through him. 'This is your mother's party? You mean Lady Macbeth?'

She'd laughed again. 'Yes. I'm Gertrude. But, please never call me that, I hate it. My second name is Cicely and everyone I like calls me Cissy.'

Lawrence had tried to smooth down his hair with his hand. The Macbeths were such mythical figures in his house, spoken about with such reverence by his father, that he knew it would be the undoing of him if his father ever found out about this. But a strange courage rose within him, allowing him to ask, 'Do your parents not mind?'

'Mind what?'

'That you have changed your name?'

She'd wrinkled her nose. 'The way I see it is this: if we do not have the right to call ourselves what we want, then what hope is there?'

He'd felt his heart hammering in his chest. 'So, in a way, you named yourself?'

'Well, yes, I suppose I did.' She'd inclined her head towards him. 'I like that idea, very much. And who, may I ask, are you?'

He had wondered for a moment if he could give her a false name in case this conversation ever reached his father's ears, but that was stupid. 'Lawrence Beesley.'

'And what are you doing here?'

'My father is the bank manager in Wirksworth. He handles all your father's dealings.'

'Oh yes, I thought I recognised your name. You have a hundred brothers and sisters, I believe?'

Lawrence had almost wished he could tell his father that his name had been mentioned in the Macbeth household, but he could hear the tone of mirth in Cissy's voice. 'Well, not a hundred exactly. I have six brothers and one sister, in fact.'

She'd bobbed her head. 'I stand corrected. Although, with my one paltry sister, that does sound like hundreds to me. What's it like, such a big family?'

Lawrence had never been asked such a direct question before and he couldn't work out how to answer it. He thought of his home in which there was never quite enough space, his mother and sister usually busy in the kitchen, boys tearing through the house, his father often pacing somewhere in a mood, and realised he often felt trapped. He imagined Cissy in the large, elegant house he'd seen when they'd stood in the garden earlier sipping on tea and eating sandwiches and he felt strangely angry at all the empty rooms which he thought were probably filled with books and musical instruments and opportunity. 'It is quite constricting,' he'd said finally.

She'd narrowed her eyes at him. 'Really? I would have thought it was the opposite, that you could get lost in the crowd.'

'Why would you want to get lost?'

Cissy had waved her hand in front of her face. 'Oh, I'm not very good at all this. Mother and Marion, my sister, are always plotting and scheming, organising parties or gossiping about who is marrying whom. But I find it all so boring, it sometimes makes me want to cry.'

'Well,' Lawrence had smoothed his hands down his legs. His father would be embarrassed at this conversation and he knew he would be better just saying something funny. But there was something in the paleness of Cissy's eyes that inspired confidence. 'I can see how that might be constricting in its own way as well. What I meant is that I want to do lots of things and big families make that hard.' He'd stopped, but Cissy didn't say anything, so he thought he could continue. 'Or at least big families where there isn't much money. I managed to get a scholarship to Derby School and I want to go to university, but Father thinks it all a waste of time. But I'm not sure I can stay here, in Wirksworth, forever, working at the bank, or wherever Father thinks I should.' He felt a little out of breath and shocked at himself when he'd finished speaking.

'How old are you, Lawrence?' She'd squinted sideways at him so her nose scrunched in a way that contracted his stomach. 'I mean, you said you are still at school.'

He had felt young then and wished he had on his jacket at least, so he didn't look so like a boy. 'Seventeen,' he admitted finally.

Cissy had nodded. 'I thought a bit older. Would you be very shocked if I told you I am twenty-two?'

Lawrence had turned then so he could look at her straight and be sure that he wasn't dreaming this conversation that meant so much more than the words they were speaking. 'I am very mature for my age.'

She'd laughed. 'Now that I can believe.' He forced open his eyes, feeling almost drunk, an odd sensation like waking from a vivid dream assailing him as struggled to ground himself, to remember that he wasn't in Derbyshire, that nothing he did or said could make it possible for him to see her again, that only misery endured and that his life was not just beginning, but ending.

LILY

She was surprised that she'd fallen asleep sitting up on the little sofa in her cabin, which she'd only sat on for a moment to gather her thoughts after Henry left. But Dr Henderson had told her that pregnancy made women very tired, and the rocking motion of the ship must have lulled her, because she woke confused and flustered, her heart hammering in her chest while her brain took a moment to catch up with her circumstances.

There was a knock on the door and then Lily realised that was what must have wakened her, so she stood too quickly and the blood rushed to her head.

Dr Henderson was standing on the other side. 'Lady Elsworth, I have come to see how you are feeling.'

She stood back to allow him in, even though she hated being alone with him. He was a tall man and up close she could see the pockmarks on his cheeks and smell the artificial scent that always emanated from him, as if he sweated ammonia. 'I am quite well, thank you. A little tired.'

'Well, it has been a busy few days for a woman in your condition. I should take your pulse.'

Lily extended her wrist, which he gripped between his thumb and forefinger as he consulted a watch on his lapel. She had to turn away from his fingernails, which were too long and slightly yellow.

'A bit fast,' he said, dropping her hand. He put his case onto the sofa and took out a small glass bottle. 'Drink this for now and we will see how you feel later.'

She unstopped the lid and drank down the bitter water, imagining it rushing through her and showering the baby. She missed Dr Bushell, who had been one of the few nice people who visited Elsworth. He'd spoken kindly to her and barely ever made her take anything, unlike Dr Henderson, who emptied potions into her like she was a witch's cauldron. And it wasn't as if she'd felt any better in the last year, although, it was true, he had helped her to get pregnant, which Dr Bushell had certainly never achieved.

He began to close up his bag. 'And you are well apart from the tiredness, Lady Elsworth?'

'I tripped on the gangplank and I am worried I might have damaged the baby in some way.'

Dr Henderson smiled indulgently. 'I'm sure it's nothing to be worried about. Your body is well designed to protect the baby. But perhaps I should give you a quick examination.'

'Oh, no, I am sure there is no need.' She wished then she hadn't said anything because she hated having his hands on and inside her flesh, which made her want to scald her insides with boiling water.

But he advanced towards her. 'Not a full one, just loosen your skirt.'

Becky had adjusted all her clothes so she was able to move more freely and all she had to do was pull on a string and the doctor could slip his clammy hand past the material and through her underskirt, resting it coldly on her stomach. They stood like that for a moment, her heart pounding through her blood, so she was sure he could feel it under her skin.

'All is exactly as it should be.' He smiled as he withdrew. 'You know, Lady Elsworth, pregnancy loosens women's minds almost as much as their bodies. It leaves many women unable to follow lines of thought, or thinking strange things. You are creating fears out of nothing.' He patted her hand. 'I will leave you to rest now.'

But Lily found she couldn't settle after he left. She needed to walk and breathe some fresh air, so went to the mirror to pat down her hair. She was surprised by how pale and drawn she looked in the bright sunshine streaming through the porthole, her eyes ringed in darkness and her lips slightly chapped. She rubbed at her cheeks in an attempt to give them a bit of colour and her skin felt rough. When they'd first met, Henry had marvelled at the smoothness of her skin and she remembered her radiance, the way she'd glowed, as if life sparkled from her. She leant closer to her own image, wondering why her beauty had ever mattered, surprised that she still felt sadness at its departure.

Her favourite blue hat was nowhere to be seen, although she was sure she'd hung it off the hook on the washstand when she'd removed it earlier. But Henry was always telling her how forgetful she was and it was easy to find the brown one in her case, which she pulled down to just above her eyes.

It was warmer than Lily had expected on deck, the sun strong in the bright sky which was full of whirling seagulls, shrieking and diving. It was busy as well, with people looking out, so Lily made for the rails and saw they'd stopped in what appeared to be a harbour, with a block of land in front of them. The sight disorientated her, because surely they'd just left Southampton, and yet she also remembered something about two stops before they set off across the Atlantic and she wished she'd paid more attention to their route.

She stopped beside a young man holding a large camera box. 'Excuse me,' she said, so he turned his head, keeping the camera trained to the land, his features ruffled with irritation at the interruption. 'Please, could you tell me where we are?'

His eyebrows raised up his forehead. 'Cherbourg, Ma'am.' His accent matched her own, which made her break out into a smile he didn't return. 'We are just taking on passengers and mail.' He indicated over the side, so Lily followed his gesture, where she saw tugs bobbing about beneath them as people and sacks were transferred over. They looked impossibly small from her vantage point, like nothing more than children's toys, which made a vertiginous feeling rush through her head because it was hard not to appreciate how far away from the sea they were when you looked down from the deck.

She stumbled backwards, her vision blurring with the tears that seemed to live so constantly in her eyes.

'Are you all right, Ma'am?' the young man asked, his annoyance receding for a moment. But she'd learnt not to trust men's kindness so pulled her face into a smile and walked away before he could question her any further.

The action calmed her a little and allowed her skittering heart to settle into an uncomfortable rhythm. It was a trick she'd learnt during her first year at Elsworth, when Henry had left her there for weeks at a time as he went to attend business she knew to be bogus in London. At first, she'd simply thought that she would go mad, stuck in the dilapidated house with surly servants and an increasing retinue of builders whom she hated beyond reason, because it wasn't their fault that her husband was a charlatan. But there was simply never anything for her to do, unless you counted deciding on what she might eat or wear, which took up only a few minutes of her long, relentless days.

She'd taken to walking around Elsworth itself, which was so large it could occupy hours of her day and often reveal places she'd never seen before. She'd climb the flights of thick wooden stairs and wander down acres of corridors panelled in dark woods, with displeased oil paintings staring down at her. But this had been in the times before her father's money had paid for electricity and heating and these tours had been cold and gloomy. She'd turned the handles on a few doors, but only ever been met by dark rooms with drawn shutters and furniture shrouded in sheets. In a room near the servants' quarters in the attic, the shutters had blown open and the windows had smashed and a family of birds had set up home, their shit splattering every surface. It was the one thing that had made her smile in those first terrible months, when the cold and desolation of her new home felt like it had seeped into her bones, so she thought she might die of misery.

At night, she would feel so lonely, she was sure she would go mad, like her mind might actually drop out of her head and run away from her. When they were courting in New York, Henry would sneak into her bedroom and wrap his arms around her and tell her wonderful stories about their life and all the things they would do. She knew by then that it had all been a performance, but still she would lie in bed and long for him to come and tell her the same lies. And on the rare occasions he did appear at her door, it was with neither love nor tenderness. In the end, she asked his estate manager to get her a dog, because she had to be close to another beating heart which cared about her or she worried she might shrivel up and die.

'The cracks run deep today,' Henry would say when she dared to express her unhappiness, and she'd feel like a barren earth, with deep fissures gouging out its rough surface. But then her lady's maid, a doughy, sullen girl, had taken sick and Becky had appeared and, over time, it had felt like it might be possible for her to survive.

Lily hurried then, because she felt suddenly too exposed out on deck, where anything was possible. She thought of the baby suspended so peacefully inside her as she trotted down the stairs towards her cabin and imagined her feet getting entangled and falling and, for a second, wondered how much she'd care. She was in her fifth month and had recently started to feel flutters, like bubbles popping somewhere deep inside her, which she imagined was the baby rolling and stretching. She'd heard women delight at this, but often the feelings made her worry that she was being pushed out of her own body and that, as the baby grew, it might overtake her until there was no room left for herself.

Becky was in her cabin, folding clothes and smoothing the beds. Lily smiled at her, but Becky ducked her head, busying herself with jobs that looked like they'd already been done.

'Have you taken a turn on deck yet?'

'Not yet, Miss.'

Becky's broad back was bent over her trunk and she longed to lay her head there and wrap her arms about her waist. The thought that such actions were now denied to her opened a hole in her stomach, as if the very marrow of herself was leaking away. The sky was large outside the porthole, which it never was at Elsworth, and it gave her a courage that had kept her silent for the last few months. 'Have I done something to annoy you, Becky?'

'What do you mean?' Becky's tone was sharp.

'I mean, we were such good friends and now I find I do

not even know what words to say to you. What has happened between us?'

'Nothing has happened.' But Becky's back was rigid.

'Stop that, please.' Lily crossed to the sofa. 'Please, come and sit with me.' She tried not to think that Becky only did as she asked because it was her job to obey Lily's commands. 'These past months have been like torture for me. Please tell me if I have offended you in any way. I cannot bear this.'

Becky tucked some hair under her cap and Lily saw the sweat on her brow. 'I really don't know what you're talking about, Miss.'

'And please stop calling me Miss or Ma'am. It is years since you have addressed me that way.'

Becky's skin was stretched tight on her face so she almost glowed and Lily wanted to run a finger across her cheek, she probably would have done just six months before.

'Is it the baby?'

Becky's brows contracted together. 'I cannot follow what you are saying.'

Sometimes Lily felt like her mind had deserted the situation she found herself in and she had the intense feeling of existing outside her body. 'I mean, you seem to have removed yourself from me since I have fallen pregnant. You must know I had no choice. You know what the last few years have been like, with Henry so desperate.'

Becky's hands were clasped tightly on her lap. 'I don't understand. The baby has nothing to do with me.'

'Yes, but…' Lily groped for what she meant, but her thoughts were skittery in her brain, as always. She wanted Becky's hand on her stomach, thought it might be the only thing that could ground her. 'Do you remember that infection I had a few years ago?' She blushed as she spoke with the memory of the fire inside her and the white pus which had oozed from her. 'And how Dr Bushell thought, well, that Henry's antics might have been the cause?'

'I don't remember him saying that exactly.'

'But you must remember.' She heard the rise of her tone, but it was surely impossible that Becky had forgotten how ill she'd been.

Becky stiffened. 'I remember you being ill. I remember how the stains would barely come out of your undergarments. But I don't recall Dr Bushell saying that. Are you sure you are remembering correctly?'

Lily rarely felt sure of anything any more and she placed her hand on the swell of her skirt. 'I just worry sometimes that there is something inside me which is harmful to the baby. It's not that thoughts of the baby have overtaken, well, everything else. I don't mean to be selfish and ignore our friendship, if that is what you think I am doing.' She glanced at Becky, but her stare was across the cabin, which made Lily feel desperate. 'This behaviour is so unfair of you, Becky.'

She saw Becky jolt, but at least she turned her attention towards her. 'Unfair of me?'

'Yes. If you don't tell me what I've done, then how can I make it all right again?'

Becky made a sound like a cross between a laugh and a grunt as she stood. 'You must try to stop overthinking things, Miss. Remember what Dr Henderson said about there being a strong heartbeat. And the fact you are carrying more in the back is a good sign, means it is more likely to be a boy. Now, if there is nothing else, I have much to be getting on with.'

'But that's not what I meant,' Lily said, leaning forward. 'I wasn't talking about the baby.'

Becky turned back momentarily. 'Oh, I think everything is about the baby now.' She hurried out of the room, her body so sturdy and fit it made Lily smart with a mean jealousy. It was almost as if, as she diminished, Becky enlarged and she longed for the strength of the woman who had been so much hers for these past years, the person who had emerged from the frightened girl fresh from her mother's kitchen to the one person she loved and relied upon in England.

The air was filled with a buzzing which made her completely aware of herself inside this mammoth ship, suspended in an ocean of water, just like her baby bobbing inside her. Except her body felt capsized, as if she had crashed and the baby was sunk into the deepest part of her, alone and vulnerable. Her muscles hardened and her limbs felt stiff and uncooperative and she worried that if she moved she might shatter and then it would be impossible to work out which were pieces of her and which pieces of the baby. She doubted her ability to recognise herself in the mess and thought she didn't want to be lost in another person, didn't want to feel like she might never again be truly herself, especially when she wasn't even sure who that person was.

LAWRENCE

Lawrence supposed the food was nice, although he didn't think he'd really tasted anything except chalk since Cissy died. Food had once been a great pleasure of theirs, but in her last year, it had become a battleground as he'd tried to cajole her with ever-diminishing morsels, which they both knew caused her pain to eat. He'd thrown many plates across rooms in her final months, his muscles vibrating with the desire to ram the food into her body. Once he'd even shouted at her that she could never expect to get better if she didn't eat. But she'd turned her head, as if she didn't care about getting better.

He pushed his curried chicken around his plate, watching the viscous orange sauce attach itself to the tiny shards of rice, imagining how he might chew and swallow them so they landed in his stomach and spread around his body. He tried instead to concentrate on the room, looking at the long tables and the white tablecloths, the bright lights burning above their heads, the red leather on the arm of the chair he was sitting in so smooth and shiny. But all he could imagine was what it would look like in years to come, how everything cracks and fades, how death is behind every curtain, decay under every table.

In a strange way, being a scientist helped him with the idea of ending his life, because he was able to see the body as a machine that he was simply deciding to turn off. Except this was also a misnomer, because he'd never seen nature in this way – in fact, he'd always been totally charmed and beguiled by its intricacy and fragility. And his was a fine body, he knew that much, a body which worked well and hard, a body that had pressed itself into and against Cissy, a body that had made her cry out, that she had rested her head against, that she had loved.

A woman walked past with two children, one being led by the hand and another balanced on her hip. The boy walking alongside her was probably about the same age as Alec and, as they passed, he could hear the steady stream of words spooling from his mouth, reminding him of the endless questions and observations that always fell from his son as well.

Thoughts of his boy defeated him and Lawrence let his fork fall against the plate with a metallic clang, which made the woman next to him glance over. He wanted to leave but worried that his legs wouldn't support him because he felt assailed by Cissy then, as if her lemony scent had filled his nose and her delicate hand was wrapped around his wrist.

He had to shut his eyes to stop his tears, but there was too much rushing through his body, so it felt as if he was moving, and then he was riding his bicycle along the lanes of Wirksworth, the tang of grass in the air, slats of sun hitting his face in quick succession between gaps in the trees. He slowed as he reached the gates of the Manor, allowing himself to stop so he could lean into the ornate metal and stare at the manicured grounds and tended plants beyond, the gravel drive leading up to the smart house, straining to see if by any chance the woman he'd met so briefly might be walking there. She never was, but it didn't stop her from marching across his dreams, as if she'd taken him hostage in the few moments they'd sat side by side on the grass exchanging pleasantries. But he would then feel the weight of his schoolbooks on his back and the coarseness of his trousers and remember the small house he was returning to and the impossibility of the situation would make him turn away.

'Did you ever think of me?' he'd asked her when he came home one day to find her chatting with his sister outside their house and they had walked together through the woods which backed on to his garden.

She'd laughed then. 'You do not really think I happened to be passing, do you? Or that I really thought Edith would like the book I just happened to have in my bag?'

They were back on the lane by then, nearly at the Manor, and he felt as if a thousand years had passed, that they were already old and grey and knew each other so well there was barely need for speech. She would walk through those metal gates he had leant against and the thought made him want to cry because he knew nothing was ever going to be enough. 'Can I see you again?' he'd blurted out, a terrible waver in his voice.

She'd stopped and turned to him, her arms crossed against her chest and her face serious. 'I do not think that is something either of us would be able to stop, even if we wanted to.'

He snapped open his eyes, aware suddenly of the assailing noise in the dining room, which had surely been turned up, so it sounded like the buzz of a swarm of insects. He almost wanted to look up and check that a million wasps weren't there, poised and ready to swoop, their stings sharp and pointed. He needed peace, to crawl into his bed and pull the covers over his head and maybe even sleep. His vision was jagged at the edges and he knew he was in line for a thick headache that would press down on him as if it wanted to kill him, although it never would, he should be so lucky.

He stood shakily, rocking into the table, causing a few faces to turn towards him before resuming their conversations. They would probably just think he was seasick, and anyway, he didn't care. He only had to endure this life for about forty-eight more hours and then the ice would save him. He could feel his body falling and longed for the moment it would just be him and the elements. It might even banish thoughts of Alec, so he would know what he was doing was right. The resolution calmed him and steadied his step out of the dining room.

THURSDAY, APRIL 11TH

LILY

Lily was woken by a rhythmic banging coming through the walls of her cabin. She lay still for a moment, looking at the motes dancing in the sunlight, trying to work out what was happening, because it almost felt as if someone were trying to break through the wall. Her mind felt as foggy as it always did on waking, or at least as it had done for the past year or so.

Her mother had often told her she was delicate when she was younger, a state she knew she'd been happy to embrace because it meant being taken care of. Although she wasn't sure now where the care was or how she was expected to pass it on to the baby in her stomach, if that was even what she was meant to do. It had anyway all become a self-fulfilling prophecy because she'd undeniably weakened more with every year she'd lived in England, the last one being especially taxing, so now she found it hard to read books, to retain cohesive lines of thought, even sometimes to stay awake.

A sharp noise rolled through the wall, which sounded like the retort of a hand against flesh. She turned on to her side, trying to blot out the images that rushed at her, but the truth was that Henry's gentle American lovemaking bore no relation to the lover he'd revealed himself to be from the moment they arrived back in England. He liked to contort her body, to mould and prod it, to dig his fingers into her flesh, to bite and leave marks, to pull at her hair so it sometimes ripped from the scalp, to push deep inside her. On the nights he visited, she would stumble from bed the next morning aching and bruised, often with a sharp taste in her mouth and disgust deep in her belly.

She sat up because where, in fact, was Henry? And the noises, she realised, were coming from Becky's cabin. She scrambled closer to the wall and cupped her hands around her ears. The sounds were indistinct, but there was a definite sense of movement and she thought she could hear a gasp or a shrill moan.

Always confront the worst, her mother used to say when she was young, *confront, make better and move on.* Except her mother had only ever been talking about not being invited to a dance, or serving a bad dinner, or the roses being hit by blight.

Lily had to stand because her blood was fizzing and what she was thinking could not possibly be what was happening. A memory rushed to her from the day they'd left: the way Becky had looked straight at Henry and, if she was honest, she'd seen those looks before, known that Henry's eyes often followed Becky out of rooms.

Her mind tipped against the thought, like it wanted to push it away and out, but the blocks crashed together, building and building until they towered over her. Because if what she was thinking was true, then that would explain why Becky had turned from her, why she refused to meet her eye, why she acted as if they had never meant anything to each other. Little pinpricks of realisation stuck into her, piercing her all over with the sensation that life was always capable of taking you lower.

Once, her dog Briar had found a dead bird and she'd watched her rip it apart, exposing all the blood and gore inside, unable to look away, even though it turned her stomach. She moved without really considering what she was doing, letting herself into the empty corridor with just a shawl thrown over her nightgown, and edged along the wall to Becky's door, pressing her body against it as if it were possible to somehow see through it. A deep laugh reverberated through the wood, a laugh she knew only too well. It was a thick, bass boom which announced itself proudly and unapologetically and, even though she had never produced it in her husband, she'd heard it across tables and through doors many times before.

A door opened along the corridor and Lily rushed back to her cabin, bending over her knees as she scrabbled to pull her breath deep enough. Henry always told her that she got everything wrong, and it was true, she so often felt confused it was as though she had a permanent fog in her mind. But the laugh still reverberated in her ears and she thought her legs might give way so she had to reach for the wall to stop herself from swooning, as her pores opened, leaking sweat on to her skin that dried instantly as her blood turned to ice.

Her whole body began to shake, so violently it was as if she was sickening for something, and all she could do was crawl back into bed, her hands trembling as she pulled the covers up to her neck. She tilted her head back on to the wall for support because her mind felt like someone had emptied a jug of water into it, washing away any sense of deduction.

A scream rose through her, making her clamp a hand over her mouth, but it refused to die, scraping so sharply against her chest she had to pull her legs up and bang her forehead against her knees to rid herself of the images crowding her brain. But Henry stood his ground, his naked body pumping into Becky, and Lily had to scratch the side of her head or she feared her skull would explode. And yet, strangely, she wanted to push Henry aside so she could look at Becky and see the expression on her face because, as she sat shivering and weeping in her bed,

Lily realised she didn't care what her husband got up to but that Becky's betrayal might actually kill her.

'My mistress is unwell,' Lily remembered Becky saying. 'Women's problems, Sir, nothing to trouble yourself with.' She had come back into Lily's bedroom at Elsworth with her eyes wide and her hand fluttering around her mouth.

'How did you think to say that?' Lily had asked, the relief she'd felt at Henry not coming to her that night like a warm bath.

'I'm sorry, Miss, I hope I didn't overstep. But you looked terrible frightened when he knocked and I hate how you get after his visits and it just came out before I'd had a chance to think about what I was saying.'

Becky's cheeks had been flushed and Lily had been struck by the courage it must have taken for her to say anything to Henry, how much she was risking by speaking for her mistress, all the things that Lily could do to ruin her life.

'It was very kind of you,' she'd said. 'And I do not just mean to say it, I mean to notice how I feel.'

'Of course I notice how you feel.' Becky had sounded almost annoyed and Lily had been struck by how pretty she looked with the fire lighting her features.

'Why don't you sit with me for a bit?'

Becky had hesitated, which made Lily realise that the girl had been working for her for a year by then and, even though she made her days brighter, she had never before asked her to sit with her. Becky had inched closer to the fire and sat right on the edge of the chair opposite Lily's, her hand worrying at the string of the apron tied around her waist.

'Tell me about yourself, Becky,' Lily had said, leaning back into her chair. 'I want to know all about you.'

Lily sat up to dislodge the memory because the noises from

Becky's cabin had made the past irrelevant and she needed to concentrate on her present. Henry's trunk sat solidly next to the bureau and she went to it because she had to do something concrete to help her understand what was happening. He kept his papers in the top-left compartment and she pulled them out, leaving little sweat marks as she leafed through them. None of them seemed remarkable until she saw an envelope addressed to her husband in her father's handwriting. Her hands were shaking as she pulled out a short, neat letter and she made herself focus on the swimming words.

Thank you, Henry, for all you are doing for our beloved Lily. Alva and I are truly grateful. We understand that Lily's mind has been failing for a while now and are so pleased that you have generously decided to let her have the baby near to home. It is a big sacrifice you are making and one I will not ever forget. Dr Henderson sounds like a fine fellow and, we agree, her treatment should not be disrupted at this critical stage, or the danger to her and the baby will be too great.

We have found a small, very secluded house outside Newport, just as you requested, which I think will suit your purposes, and have rented it for the next six months. I have to say, Alva and I are perturbed by your insistence that we refrain from seeing Lily, or hiring any servants for your stay. May will be hard to keep away, but we have firmly informed her that this is what must happen. I understand that Lily must not be shocked by another doctor being introduced at this stage, and even that our presence could excite her unnecessarily, but are you sure that the one maid you are bringing will be able to manage all the household duties, including the *cooking? Just say the word and I can employ a retinue of servants.*

It is hard to think of Lily so distressed and deluded and Alva, May and myself want nothing more than to meet you on the dock in New York and enclose her with our love. But your and your doctor's reasoning is sound and we shall abide by all you say. Please tell Lily we think of her always and cannot wait to be reunited after the birth of your child.

Lily looked up at the fixtures of the cabin she already knew well and the points of herself began to fray in her mind like a rip along a weighted seam. It was as if she'd fallen through her life into another world in which nothing made sense. Keeping her away from her family surely made as little sense as Becky lying with Henry and yet the words her father had used made her feel that she was hanging on to life by a thread, that her sanity was shot, that everything she thought she knew about herself was maybe false.

Her breath jagged in her throat so her head spun and she had to stumble back to bed, where she let her tears fall, blotting round stains on to the sheets like a marker of where she'd been. She sank further down the bed and put her hand over her heart, which faltered and leapt beneath her jutting ribs. She was nothing more than skin and bones, no match for anyone. The girl that Henry had married, fine and plump, full of life and vigour, floated before her, merging with an image she held in her mind of Becky and she couldn't work out what had happened, how she had lost both herself and a person so dear to her.

And the truth was, her father's words, and even Becky's actions, were all too easy to understand. She knew her mind was fragile, like a bird with a broken wing, and that she was trying to be around, and perhaps Henry wasn't being mean and solitude was what she needed. So much about life rushed at her, sometimes she felt as if she were racing in a carriage and everything was blurred. And, if she was honest with herself, the pregnancy was taking the last of her strength, so sometimes she wanted the baby gone, sometimes she just wanted her body returned to her, which could not be a natural feeling for a woman to have, which meant she was deranged and she did have to be careful and it was no wonder that her husband looked for comfort in the arms of Becky, who was so good at giving succour, and why was life so harsh and unfair, and who was going to care about her after she'd delivered the baby, what use would she be?

'We are happy, though,' Becky had said once, when nights by the fire had become commonplace, as Lily wept at Henry's meanness. 'These can be the real moments of our lives and we can pretend the rest is a dream. When I am scrubbing a floor or you are sitting at a boring dinner, we can remember this and it will carry us away from what makes us sad.'

'But there are so many sad moments, do you not find they threaten to overwhelm you sometimes?' Lily had answered.

'I suppose I was not brought up to expect much.' Becky had pouted her lips as she stared out of the dark window behind Lily's back. 'I never imagined I would ever sit by a fire with you and listen to what is in your heart, or tell you what is in mine. I suppose that seems so incredible to me, it is more sustaining than these moments are for you.'

'Oh no, I didn't mean that.' Lily had leant forward, which made Becky return her gaze and it was as though something had dropped through the atmosphere. 'These moments with you matter to me more than you can imagine. It is just that there are not enough and I want more. It cannot be that we are expected to live the majority of our lives doing things that make us unhappy.'

Becky had tried to laugh. 'Some might say it is a privilege to believe that. Some people feel happiness so seldomly they can count the times in a year on one hand. To some people, this would feel like a miracle.'

Lily turned the thought over in her mind as she sat on a monstrous ship, so far out to sea it just felt that she was stranded. Perhaps it had truly been a miracle. She certainly would give anything to go back to that time for just five minutes, which was a confusing and unsettling realisation because the baby should mean that it was the future which was calling to her, not the past.

She shook her head against her pillow to dislodge her thoughts, because, regardless of the rights or wrongs, it was all pointless, as, clearly, Becky didn't believe moments with her mattered any more. A chill rushed through her as she realised that, without Becky, she was alone and friendless, sailing across the deepest ocean towards a future that made no sense. She scrabbled about in her mind for someone she could appeal to, but a permeating blankness enveloped her, which felt as fearful as a nightmare. Because if you neither know who you are or where you are going, then no physical destination matters. They might as well be sailing to the coast of Australia for all the good New York was going to be.

LAWRENCE

Lawrence thought he might as well go up on deck as they came into their last stop before they set off properly, to a destination he would never reach. But as soon as he stepped into the fresh air, he felt an almost physical pain when he looked at the green hills of Ireland as they drew to rest just outside the harbour, waiting for the tugs to rush to them like supplicants to a king.

It hit him that this was to be his last sight of land, and the thought was unexpectedly distressing. His mind filled with images: running up the hills surrounding Wirksworth as a boy, lying on a bed of moss with Cissy watching the leaves dance above them, concentrating in stuffy lecture halls as professors explained scientific intricacies, breaking a twig in his own classroom and watching the boys he taught smell sap, the light on the bank of orchids in the botanical gardens in Cambridge.

A familiar, but forgotten, emotion of wonder at the magnificence of nature rushed into him, which also translated itself to the ship he was standing on. There was undeniably something so graceful in her movement as she rode up and down on the slight swell of the harbour, a slow, stately dip and recover, only noticeable by watching her bow in comparison with a landmark.

Seagulls screeched above and Lawrence looked up, entranced by their motion, noticing how they tilted as a whole from side to side, not by moving their wings, which reminded him of the Wright brothers and how new discoveries were always being made.

Cissy would be appalled to see how unambitious he'd become, not just for himself, but for life, because it was she who had always pushed them forward. He doubted in fact that he would have ever applied to Cambridge without her encouragement. And then it had been Cissy who suggested they marry after they'd missed each other too much in the first year. Cissy who had uprooted her life and come to live with him in their little house on Bateman Street, giving up all the wide-open spaces and luxury of The Manor. Cissy who had won her father round so Lawrence didn't have to give up his studying and start work. Cissy who had promised him that having a baby wouldn't interfere with the work he wanted to do and would actually bring him immense happiness. Cissy who had carried that baby, even as it ravaged her body, and Cissy who had loved Alec so fiercely that it had twisted his heart to see them together.

Except it was also that drive that had pushed her on so she didn't just get involved in the women's movement, but enmeshed. It was that determination that had sent her out in the middle of the night to the bedsides of sick women, that had made her feet march for hours chanting slogans, that had brushed away his concerns about the cold or the damp, that had ultimately been her undoing. He wished treacherously that she'd been calmer or even stupid or lazy, anything that might have kept her safe for him.

But the sun lighting up the hills refused to let his anger take hold as it reminded him of the first time he'd brought her to the little house he found on Bateman Street in Cambridge. As they'd entered the town, he'd watched her stare out of the carriage windows and worried that the banks of houses and long grey streets must have looked dreary compared to the views she'd grown up with. And then the house itself seemed smaller even than he'd remembered, just one of many, in a row of bricks and mortar.

'You don't like it, do you?' he'd asked in too shrill a voice, after their trunks had been unloaded and she'd walked into the sitting room, devoid of all furniture, so it looked barren and unloved.

She hadn't answered but had gone to stand in a patch of sunlight that was flooding through the windows at the far end and he worried that their little garden would seem absurd next to what she had left, which made him hate himself for ever presuming that he would be enough.

He'd followed her, his body tense so he stood stiffly beside her. 'I would not mind if you want to go home. Married couples do not always live together, and it is so different from anything you have known before. We could wait until after I have graduated and have a job and can afford a proper home.'

She'd turned to him, closing the gap between them so she could encircle his waist, reaching up on her tiptoes so she could reach his mouth. And then they'd been scrambling for each other in a way that only left them when the sickness took hold, as if they wanted to climb inside each other, as if nothing would ever be enough. They made love in the patch of sun, which warmed even the bones under their skin.

'I have never felt more at home anywhere,' she'd said afterwards. 'And I would give up anything and everything to be with you, Lawrence.'

And maybe what he was planning was not so very wrong when seen in that light? If she would give up everything for him, then surely he should do the same for her? Surely she could not expect him to wait around in this world, however beautiful and majestic it was, while she wasn't in it? And if she was angry with him, then he would meet her with his own anger because she had sacrificed everything they had as if it meant nothing and that was hard to forgive. If he met her again, the first thing he would ask, shout probably, was why their love hadn't been precious enough, why she'd allowed her stupid, weak body to succumb.

'Oh my!' a loud American voice said, so close that Lawrence was snapped out of his thoughts.

A large woman in a huge hat was being helped into a deck-chair by a worried-looking steward. For a moment, it looked as if the chair might not accommodate her backside, but it only sagged and groaned as she sat in it.

Once seated the woman took out a handkerchief from her purse and began mopping her brow. 'Oh my,' she repeated, 'I am so unsettled.'

There was only a small band of people nearby, of which Lawrence was the closest, so he felt an obligation to answer. 'I'm sorry for your distress, Madam. I hope nothing untoward has happened to you.'

He felt a few others stepping closer to the conversation, drawn by the woman's distress.

'Oh, but I wish I had not seen it,' the woman said, her voice now wobbling almost as much as her chins.

She made a play of waiting to be asked for more information, so Lawrence obliged, even though he cared nothing for the reply.

The woman sucked in her breath, as if the recounting were painful. 'When we were getting off the tender just now, a few of us looked up, so impressed were we by the sheer size of this boat, and there, clear as day, was a red-headed man looking down on us from one of those huge funnels.'

The steward, who had been hauling the woman's luggage up, turned back now. 'I have just heard word, Madam, and there is nothing to be alarmed about. It was one of the stokers from the engine room, who had climbed up that funnel to clear a blockage. It is just one that is used for ventilation, see. There is nothing sinister about it.'

'Nothing sinister!' The woman sounded like she might explode and she cast her eyes around the group gathered about her. 'Nothing sinister, he says.'

Lawrence was lost in what she was saying, but he also felt it would be too rude to back away now, as she seemed to be directing most of what she said towards him.

She waited for a moment to see if anyone would question her, but when no one did, she carried on. 'Are you really telling me that none of you know what incredible bad luck it is to see red hair before you sail?'

A young woman behind Lawrence gasped and he felt a building sense of irritation with the woman, which translated itself into a sharp tone. 'I, for one, did not know that.'

Her face flushed an unhealthy crimson. 'Well, there were several of us on that tug who were floored by the sight. *Floored*, I tell you. One woman had to be almost carried aboard, she was shaking and crying so much. Red is the colour of the devil and if you do not get a chance to speak to red-haired sailors before you depart, then you are doomed. And we are setting sail on a Thursday of all days. I said to everyone on that tug that it was a scandal they were asking us to sail on a Thursday. I have half a mind to get off this boat, however wonderful it is supposed to be.'

'Oh, I hate bad omens,' the woman behind Lawrence cried. He turned to see a young girl, probably no more than twenty, standing with an equally young man. 'Why is Thursday a bad day to set sail?'

'Because it's Thor's day, the God of storms,' the woman replied. 'We will have terrible weather on this trip, you mark my words.'

The young man standing with the woman tightened his grip on her shoulders. 'I am sure it is nothing to be worried about, darling.' Although Lawrence could hear the trepidation in his voice.

'But first that near miss when we were leaving Southampton, and now this.' The woman grabbed on to her husband's arm as she spoke.

'Near miss?' the American woman exclaimed. 'But we are besieged by bad luck then.'

'Come now,' an older man said, stepping forward. 'Please, no more talk such as this.' The American woman huffed, so the man turned to her. 'Madam, I am very sorry for your shock, but there really is nothing to fear. We do not have a predetermined path on which we all must walk and none of these signs, as you see them, have any real meaning.'

The man's words knocked into Lawrence because he was too well aware of their rightness. And yet, he also knew that he would have been swayed by superstition if it had even the smallest chance of saving Cissy. He'd have happily cut off his hand and burnt it by the light of the moon if it could have made her better. And, in a way, he had been swayed by his version of superstition anyway, researching and reading, sure he could find the answer if he just studied harder, if he just found the missing link between the words on the page and the knowledge in his brain. He would sit by her bed, cramming his head full until it felt like an overstuffed suitcase, in which you can never find what you're looking for. The days at work would pass in a blur and the nights would take on a ferocity which sometimes threatened to pull him under so every fibre ached and his mind dribbled out of his ear.

Very near the end of her life, Cissy had woken in the middle of the night as Lawrence knelt by her bed in the strange delirium he'd forced upon himself. His cheeks were wet with tears and his shirt soaked through with sweat, his whole body trembling with the effort of keeping his eyes fixed on the page. He was only aware that she'd woken when he felt her hand on his and he jerked his head up, the words he'd been reading fresh on his lips, for a moment convinced that he'd worked a miracle. But one look at her gaunt face, her sand-coloured skin, her cracked lips and her sunken eyes put paid to that.

'Be still, my love,' she'd whispered. 'Stop running at life so fast. All the important things are right here.'

'But I cannot stop,' he'd replied. 'I am going to make you better.'

She had attempted a smile. 'No, you are not. And I don't want the end to be like this. I cannot bear to think of you suffering after I'm gone.'

He'd collapsed forward on to the bed then. 'Don't say that, Cis. You can't leave me. This will work, I know, I'm nearly there.'

'Come here.' She'd patted the bed next to her, so Lawrence had pulled his shattered body up and laid it on the cool sheets next to her. She drew his head on to her shoulder and kept her other hand against his cheek. 'I love you, Lawrence. But you have to accept this is the end. Everything has an end, mine has simply come quicker than we would have liked.'

'But that isn't fair. It isn't how our life was supposed to be.' He'd worried he might never stop crying, that they might both drown. He'd felt her smile against his head. 'You know there are no rules, my sweet. Our love is proof of that, if nothing else. Promise me you will be a good father to Alec. That you will love him as well as I do and that you will tell him about me, even if you marry again and have more children.'

Her words were like pins being pushed into his skin. 'I beg you not to talk like that, Cis.'

'And I beg you to stop all this nonsense.'

He'd lifted his head so he could look into her eyes, which were still hers, even behind the pain and ravaging. 'Stop what?'

'The answer to my problem does not exist.'

'It does…'

But Cissy had stopped him with a crease of her forehead. 'Do you remember when I first got sick and Father wanted to take me to a sanitorium and you railed against him and said fresh air wasn't going to kill a bacterial infection?' Lawrence had nodded, so she smiled. 'Remember who you are, Lawrence.'

'But I am no one without you.'

'We are all ourselves,' Cissy had replied. 'Science is not able to save me. And I am not able to save you. Loving others is the greatest thing we can do as humans, but that should not be confused with thinking those people can save us, or us them. We are only ever able to save ourselves, which we must always do, if we have the chance. Life doesn't always follow a straight path and we must be prepared to step off and find new ways.'

He'd been going to argue with her, but she began to cough, the ferociousness racking her emaciated body, so he had to sit her up and then give her a handkerchief, which he watched staining with bright, vermillion blood as she retched into it, her eyes watering and her hands shaking. Death filled the room and Lawrence had wanted to rip the universe apart to banish its cloying, sour presence.

A sharp breeze returned him to the moment and he was surprised to find himself right up against the railings, the American woman long gone. He stared down into the choppy water so far below, but his memories refused to leave him, the pleasure and pain of Cissy conspiring against him. He was furious that there was any sadness to remember because their story should have only ever been one of love and joy, not sullied by a moment's unease, and yet all the goodness was being overtaken by misery, like night obliterating day.

He turned away from the side, but he could feel death at his back, as if she'd followed him on board and had him in her sights, refusing to give up because she never did.

LILY

'Why are you not yet ready?' Henry asked, as he came into the cabin, where Lily had been reading, or at least pretending to, because the words refused to settle.

'Ready for what?' she asked with as much calmness as she could muster.

'My God, Lily.' He ran his hands through his hair. 'Do you listen to nothing I say? Or is your brain too bloody soft for anything to stick to it?'

She felt desperate then but stood because she didn't want to anger him any further. 'Just give me a minute.'

She went to the washstand, where she adjusted her hair, before reaching for her brown hat.

Henry huffed behind her. 'Do you really have to wear that drab colour?'

She looked at him through the glass, her hand still on the hat. 'It's the only one I have.'

'Don't be ridiculous,' he snorted, pointing at her blue one on the stand. She was sure it had been missing before and, as she put it on, she wondered if maybe Becky had been trying it on again. It saddened her to think of Becky coveting her things and not having the courage to ask for them. She'd gladly have given her the stupid hat if she'd asked, but the fact that she'd taken it without asking made her feel like something fundamental had shifted.

'Come on then,' Henry said impatiently.

As they left the cabin, the words from her father's letter and the noises from Becky's cabin were keeping the baby company inside her, so she felt almost pushed out of herself.

They climbed some steps and then walked along a corridor towards a room from which Lily could hear the noise of chatter, overlaid by the tinkling of a piano. Henry opened the door and they stepped into a large dining room, with lots of oblong tables, covered with white cloths, surrounded by heavy wooden chairs. Each table could sit six or eight people and Lily realised, with a sinking heart, that there would be a communal aspect to meals. She had nothing interesting to add to discussions, as countless dinners with Henry's friends had proved. She could never think of anything witty or clever to say, never knew who they were all talking about and had seen men sigh when they saw her name on the card next to theirs.

'Ah, there are the Connaughts,' Henry said, striding off across the room, so all Lily could do was follow.

A tall, thin man stood as they approached and held out his hand, which Henry shook vigorously.

'Good to see you again, Charles, Mrs Connaught.' Henry bowed slightly to a plump woman sitting next to the thin man, and Lily was reminded of the nursery rhyme about Jack Sprat and his wife. 'My wife, Lady Elsworth.' He pulled out a chair for Lily as he spoke.

'Sorry to hear you've been under the weather,' the man said, as he sat opposite her.

Mrs Connaught leant conspiratorially across the table. 'Oh yes, headaches are the worst. I used to be such a martyr to them, but I found an amazing healer on Bond Street.'

Lily turned to Henry because she felt lost in the conversation. It was true she often had headaches, but she couldn't remember the last time she'd mentioned them to Henry, or him ever having expressed concern at them.

'How interesting.' Henry's voice was ladled with concern. 'If the question is not too impertinent, may I enquire how were you cured, Mrs Connaught?'

Mrs Connaught blushed. 'Well, it is most peculiar, but not in a conventional way. It was more through prayer and contemplation, you see.'

Lily knew how ridiculous Henry would consider such a statement, but he leant across the table as if fascinated. 'That sounds intriguing. I would be most grateful if you could provide us with the name of the man who helped you, Mrs Connaught.'

The woman giggled. 'Oh, please, I have told you to call me Emma. I must insist, Lord Elsworth.'

'And I must insist you call me Fitz, and my wife Lily.' Henry beamed around the table and Lily remembered how charming he was capable of being. 'But, please, tell us more.' There was a touch of scorn in Henry's voice which Lily knew would be because he didn't know something. Which was ironic, as there was so much he didn't know, despite his fine education that had assured him he knew everything.

'My healer is a Christian Scientist.' Charles huffed next to her and Emma playfully hit his arm in a gesture Lily simply could not imagine making. 'My husband thinks it all nonsense, but it is not, it is amazing. How else do you explain the total curing of my headaches?'

A waiter arrived just as Lily thought she was about to hear something interesting. 'Are you ready to order, Sir?' He directed his question to Henry.

'Pea soup, then roast mutton and baked potatoes with vegetable dumplings.'

Charles and Emma began to give their orders and Lily realised she hadn't even looked at the menu. She picked up the little card, but the words on the page swum before her and the idea of food was revolting.

'Madam?'

Lily was aware that the table had silenced and she felt as if everyone was looking at her.

'I … please …' But still the idea of food defeated her and she found it impossible to even articulate a request.

Henry put his hand over hers. 'My wife will have the pea soup and then a baked potato.'

The waiter looked relieved and began collecting the cards.

When he'd gone, Henry turned to her. 'I hope that is to your liking, darling. I know you cannot cope with too much food and I saw it had all become a bit much for you.'

'Thank you.' She wanted to cry, because Henry hadn't been this nice to her for so many years, and it didn't feel real. And maybe it wasn't real, or maybe she had everything wrong.

Henry turned his full attention to Emma. 'So, tell us about this Christian Science thing then.'

'They do not believe in medicine at all,' she replied excitedly. 'They believe in the divine power of God. They think illness is a defect of thinking because we are all in charge of our own destiny. They believe if you pray hard enough, then you never get sick.' She blushed with the telling, little red spots creeping upwards from her neck.

'I went to a spiritualist show once,' Henry said. 'Chap lifted a table right off the ground without touching it. Is that what you mean?'

'Not really.' Emma blushed, and Lily almost wanted to tell

her to stop because she knew Henry would be angry at being told he was wrong and she didn't want him to shout, not here.

But he didn't even frown and turned his attention instead around the table, to the other couple sitting with them, the man next to Henry and the woman next to Emma. 'And who do we have here?'

The woman smiled thinly, but Lily noticed that the man was having trouble with his food – she recognised the pushing around a plate of pieces of meat and vegetable, as if changing their place would somehow diminish them.

'Oh, how rude of me,' Emma cried. 'This is Daisy Arkwright. We have only just met ourselves, but she is travelling to relatives in America.'

'How intrepid,' Henry said. 'Does your husband hope to find work over there?' He looked at the man seated on his left as he spoke.

But the man spluttered slightly, his face reddening. 'Oh no, you are mistaken. We are not husband and wife. In fact, I have not met anyone here before. I just sat down to eat my lunch.'

Henry let rip a booming laugh. 'My apologies, I simply assumed. And what is your name, Sir?'

Lily noticed the muscles in the man's jaw clench before he spoke, as if words were an effort.

'Lawrence Beesley.'

'Why are you making this crossing then, Mr Beesley?'

He turned to Henry, but Lily didn't think he really saw him. 'Visiting my brother in New York.'

'And what is your profession?'

The man cringed slightly. 'I am a science master.'

'Ha,' Henry laughed. 'What, then, do you say to this theory Emma here has about being cured by prayer and contemplation?'

'I find it very interesting.' The man looked up and down the table for the first time and his gaze rested momentarily on Lily. 'It is true that medicine does not always provide the answers we want. And we are just beginning to discover the links between physical and mental health.'

'But what has the mind got to do with illness?' Henry asked.

Lily noticed Mr Beesley's face contract as if he had a pain somewhere.

'Well, I think it fair to say that harnessing the mind can help with curing illness, just as a slack mind can contribute to it.'

'Fascinating,' Henry said, turning pointedly to Lily. 'Absolutely fascinating. We must trouble you for the name of your healer, Emma.'

'If you will excuse me,' the man said, standing up, 'I have some letters that must be written.' He bowed his head to all three ladies and Lily attempted a smile back, but he wasn't looking and she didn't care.

The waiter appeared and a bowl of green liquid was placed in front of her. The others all began to eat, laughing about how serious the man who'd just left had seemed, but Lily found herself entranced by the bowl. She dipped her spoon into the soup, the liquid clinging thinly to the silver and smelling vaguely minty. Her stomach flipped and she wondered if the baby hated the smell as well. It seemed as if she'd been served a gallon, when the others were already halfway through, and she knew she would never manage a whole bowl. She imagined how she would swallow the liquid, how it would sink into her stomach and slosh around in there, unbalancing her.

'Come on, darling. You must be able to manage a couple of mouthfuls.'

Lily turned to Henry and he was smiling at her, a smear of green caught on his beard that made her want to retch. His bowl was clean and when she looked over at Charles and Emma, theirs were as well.

She lifted the spoon and, because her hands were shaking, some of it splashed back into the bowl. But she persevered; the spoon made it to her lips and then into her mouth, so then all she had to do was force her muscles to contract and swallow.

Henry was smiling at her, but Emma and Charles both looked embarrassed and she wanted to beg them to stop watching. But Henry kept his gaze firmly trained on her, so she repeated the process, this time managing to consume even less, her stomach contracting around the tiny morsels, and she worried she might be sick.

'My wife has to keep her strength up, you see,' Henry said. 'She is due to have a baby in the summer.'

'Oh my, how wonderful,' Emma exclaimed. 'I thought I noticed something, but I would never have presumed.'

It seemed grossly unfair to Lily that her body, which should have been private, was always so public. She felt all eyes on her and wanted to cry as she thought of all the violations it had suffered, all the prodding and entering, its refusal to grow another life, the endless discussions about this, the rough medical examinations. Then the strange life it was now hosting, the precautions she was forced to take to keep it safe, the stillness always required of her.

'Perhaps the soup is not to your taste, Lady Elsworth?' Charles said.

'Oh no, it is delicious,' she lied.

'I do love your accent,' Emma said and Lily saw she was still blushing. 'It sounds so romantic. I cannot wait to be surrounded by it when we arrive.'

'Just a few more mouthfuls, darling,' Henry prompted.

Lily focused on the bowl and the green soup, which almost

appeared to be rolling. To finish the bowl would be impossible, but she managed to force a few more mouthfuls down, whilst Emma tried to start a conversation with Daisy about her relatives. It was a little like what Lily imagined being in hell must feel like, the knowledge of a terrible task which had to be completed, because she'd never believed that hell was eternal pain, more likely she thought that it was the perpetual anticipation of pain.

Eventually, she must have eaten enough because the waiter returned and cleared their plates, while Daisy excused herself as well. Not that the ordeal was over, because all too quickly more plates were being put in front of them. At least Lily only had a baked potato to contend with, but the smell from Henry and Charles' mutton was thick and sweet and so real it was as though the sheep was standing between them. Charles laughed and Lily could see right down his throat, where tiny sinews of meat stuck to his teeth, and she had to raise her napkin to her lips until the nausea passed.

'Are you feeling quite all right, Lily?' Henry asked, and again Charles and Emma fell silent. 'You have turned awfully pale.'

'I do feel a little sick.'

'Perhaps the motion of the boat,' Charles suggested. 'I know the sea is very calm, but some people find just the sensation of being aboard a ship can make them feel ill.'

'Or the pregnancy,' Emma said. 'Mine all made me quite sick.'

Henry shook his head. 'I'm afraid my wife is quite weak.' His words sounded soft and padded and like he cared. 'She is often ill. In fact, if I may speak candidly?' He looked at Lily as if he were asking her permission, but she pretended not to notice because she knew he would say whatever he wanted anyway. 'That is why I was interested in what you were saying about your healer, Emma. And what that chap Beesley was saying about how physical affliction can be a manifestation of mental instability.'

Lily wanted to defend herself, but there was no point in contradicting Henry and his description of her was hardly unfounded. She probably did need a healer of some kind, and he was right, she was weak and pathetic and there could easily be something very wrong with her. Becky could testify to that and her father certainly seemed to believe in that version of her.

'It is certainly an interesting theory,' Charles replied. 'And while I'm not suggesting that Emma is unstable, she can be quite highly strung, which did lead to these terrible headaches. This healer chappy gave her these prayers and breathing exercises and they certainly have worked wonders.'

Lily looked over at bonny Emma and saw a little twitch at the side of her mouth which she hadn't noticed before. But she also saw Charles place his hand over hers and squeeze it in a way that looked genuine and she thought her regret might crush her.

'I think we must try something like that when we get back to London,' Henry said.

'How long do you plan to visit your family?' Emma asked.

'Until after the baby is born, so probably about five or six months,' Lily replied.

'And I expect you cannot wait to see them.' Emma beamed across the table and Lily thought she was probably perfectly well-meaning.

Henry pretended to suppress a laugh. 'Her mother is priceless.'

'I do not think I could bear to live so far from my mother,' Emma said and again Lily heard a genuine softness in her voice.

She nodded and forced in a forkful of buttery potato, even though it stuck to the roof of her mouth and burnt her tongue.

The men started chatting then about something to do with

the government and, because Emma was sitting diagonally across from her, they both stopped talking.

About a year after her marriage, on an enforced London visit, Lily had bumped into Consuelo at another terrible ball which Henry had made her attend, saying her continued absences were becoming rude. 'People are talking about you,' he'd said, which had been persuasion enough, as her mother had always hated that thought, unless they were saying you were the prettiest, or finest, or most wonderful, which Lily knew was definitely not the case.

The ball had taken place at a huge, lavish house in Mayfair, given by a Lady something and her young lover, although no one said he was her lover. It had a black-and-white theme which people had gone to town with, most using the excuse to dress up in huge powdered wigs and paint on ludicrous beauty spots. The lady and her lover had stood at the top of a mammoth flight of stairs welcoming people as doves fluttered in cages above their heads and a fake river trickled through the centre of the ballroom, encrusted with diamonds, between which huge goldfish swam. It had seemed preposterous to Lily, but everyone else, including the lady's doddery husband, had marvelled over it all.

Consuelo had sidled up to Lily as she'd been idly picking at food from a long table laden with sweetmeats and meringues, cakes and jellies.

'I had rather expected you to call on me,' she'd said by way of greeting.

Lily had in fact forgotten all about Consuelo's card, which had probably been lost the night she'd been given it. 'I am so sorry. I have been meaning to.'

Consuelo had arched an eyebrow. 'New wives are often busy.'

Lily had thought of the tedium of her empty days. 'Well, yes.'

'And how are things with Fitz? I read about him from time to time.'

She'd blushed at the thought of Consuelo Vanderbilt reading about Henry's exploits in the gossip columns. 'We are very happy,' she lied.

'I understand Elsworth is being made into a palace. I have never been, but I hear it is a beautiful building.'

'It is.' The awful castle had loomed up at Lily in her mind. She'd begun to see it as a sort of monster, satiated only by vast sums of money. Sometimes she felt that even she was part of the sacrifice, a young girl locked inside, slowly being eaten to death.

Consuelo had squinted her eyes. 'Well, I expect your money is paying to make it quite spectacular.'

That was the moment, Lily realised, as she sat listening to Henry pontificating about Asquith, that she should have told Consuelo the truth, maybe even asked for advice. But instead she'd said something bland and designed to halt the conversation, so in the end the woman had made her excuses and wandered off, although not before reminding Lily to call on her again. What a different world it could have been, Lily saw now, if she had taken up this offer, if she had sat at that woman's feet and wept into her expensively clad bosom.

But it was useless to think like that, because Consuelo had been dead for two years now and, instead, here Lily was, sitting at a table on a monstrous ship with no sense of who she was or who she was even supposed to be.

There was movement around the table and Lily realised that the plates were being cleared again. She looked down at her potato, still almost as whole as when it had been delivered.

'Oh dear,' Henry said, looking at it pointedly. 'I think maybe you should have some tapioca. I am going to have cheese.'

The thought of tapioca inching down her throat like frog

spawn was almost more than Lily could bear and she felt tears dart to her eyes. 'Oh, I think not...'

'No, no, I insist,' Henry said, waving the card at the waiter, who had somehow appeared again.

'No, Henry, really.'

'Tapioca sounds delicious,' Emma said, unhelpfully.

Henry clapped his hands together. 'I love a woman with a good appetite.'

She saw then the remnants of a picnic laid on the floor of one of the little copses that surrounded Elsworth, Becky lying back against the tartan rug, an arm draped lazily across her face. 'Lately, I find I am always hungry,' she had said from behind the screen of her arm. 'I've never had much of an appetite before, but when I went home last month, they all noticed the change in me. Mother said I must be happy because, she said, to love food you have to love life.'

Lily too had felt hungry in those days, but she now couldn't remember when food had last seemed appealing. Her shrunken arm rested like an accusation against the table, looking like nothing more than a stick, so easily broken.

She was disgusting and, of course, Henry loved Becky; it was so obvious that Lily wanted to shield her eyes. She felt Becky's arm link through hers and saw a smile play on her lips, heard the deep timbre of her laugh and the way her nose always freckled in the sun. It had taken time to absorb the whole of her and it had happened incrementally, so she was only aware of what she was losing now that she was slipping from her. A panic started to build inside Lily as she realised that Becky would be taken from her and change and she wouldn't be able to witness it. Her thoughts were messy and confused, but they struck at her like a blow and it felt ridiculously like she might not be able to survive Becky's absence.

Henry laughed, the same sound she'd heard through Becky's cabin door that morning, but when she turned to him, his face looked too large and the sound was distorting, as if they were in a cave.

'I'm convinced it is going to be a boy,' he said and she turned desperately to the others, but their faces were swaying and swelling.

'Oh, you must be so excited!' Emma shrilled.

'Too right.' Henry turned and smiled at Lily, his lips pulling apart so he looked like he was snarling and she expected him to growl in her face. 'I'm going to spoil the little rotter to kingdom come!'

What was happening began to unfurl before Lily then, like ribbon spooling from a present, and she felt as if it was her who was being unwrapped, her flesh falling from her so he could get to the baby faster. All Henry was interested in was the baby and her value existed only in the service she provided in carrying it: she was nothing to him, nothing more than a vessel. But after it was born she couldn't imagine him letting her have anything to do with it, couldn't imagine that he would want her instability rubbing off on his child, especially not when he had the comforting, wonderful presence of Becky. She saw then a faceless baby in Becky's arms and knew it was her baby and it was safer there and yet she wanted also to be part of the scene, wanted Becky to be smiling up at her as the baby cooed.

She turned to her husband and he looked back at her, his lip curling for a moment, before he was dragged back into the conversation. She knew then that this trip was a trap, her home nothing more than a lure, like cheese to tempt a mouse. The secluded house her father had written about loomed up like another hungry beast, waiting to devour her. And she knew also that she was right to be terrified because there was no way she was going to emerge intact. Henry was going to take Becky and her baby and there was nothing she could do about it because she was pathetic and powerless and probably deranged and everyone knew it. She had spent her whole life believing she was one person, set on one path, and yet she'd obviously been wrong. She was a stranger even to herself, her direction of travel as unknowable as if she had been thrown overboard.

Lily stood because she knew she was going to cry. The three faces turned to look at her with concern, but it was all too far gone and she could never hope to appeal to either of these people, so didn't think it mattered.

'Please, excuse me,' she stammered. 'I am feeling unwell, so I must take my leave.' Henry made to stand, but she waved him down. 'No, no, you stay and enjoy your cheese. I just need to lie down.'

He was still half risen. 'But what if you fall? You could hurt the baby.'

She attempted a laugh. 'No, I am fine. No danger of falling. Please, all I desire is to go back to the cabin and lie down.'

'If you're sure,' Henry said, his hand already wrapped back around his wine glass. 'Send Becky for Dr Henderson if you worsen.'

She nodded to the Connaughts. 'It was a pleasure to meet you.'

She didn't wait for their reply, but instead turned and left the bustling room.

Once back in the corridor, she felt irrationally scared at the prospect of returning to her cabin and being alone with her baby, who she knew now was her downfall, which could not be a good thing to think about your own child. It seemed safer to remain amongst crowds, so she climbed some stairs and walked on until she came to another public room, with tall ceilings and long white columns. Tapestry upholstered chairs were dotted around singularly and in groups in front of a wall of books, as the light streamed through a bank of long windows, outside of which was a covered walkway along which people were walking.

Her strength was ebbing, but she made it to a chair, where she sat as quietly as possible, trying to organise the thoughts racing through her head.

She remembered a day with Becky a few years before, when she hadn't yet given up the hope of becoming pregnant, but at the same time it was starting to feel increasingly far-fetched. They'd been walking through the woods, a sharp tang of bluebells heavy in the air, the ground a sea of purply blue that seemed like an illusion. 'Sometimes I wonder if I cannot get pregnant because no baby wants me. Or if it knows I might not be a good mother.'

'I don't think that's likely,' Becky had answered, her tone so soft it sounded maternal.

'Do you want children?' Lily had realised that she'd never asked Becky that question, even though they'd discussed her state for so many hours it must amount to days, weeks, months even.

Becky had paused before answering, so Lily could hear the snap of the bluebells as they broke beneath their feet. 'I do, but sometimes I feel like it would be the wrong thing to do.'

Becky's words didn't make complete sense and Lily had turned to take in the woman's strong profile, but she didn't return the look. 'But you would be a wonderful mother. Much better than I could ever hope to be.'

'Maybe, but I haven't much to offer my children. I would want more for them than I am capable of providing and that seems terrible to me.'

'What do you mean?'

Becky had tilted her head back, as if there was an answer in the branches above their heads. 'Sometimes it feels there is no point to people like me. Have I ever told you how much I hate my monthly day off?' Lily shook her head. 'Well, I do. I go home and I look around and it feels like we are all just existing. Since Father stopped working at Elsworth, things have been very pushed for us.'

'I forget what it is that your father did at Elsworth?' Lily had found it hard to imagine Becky anywhere other than with her and realised that when she had her day off, she thought of her as just being in another room.

'He worked in the gardens. But then his arthritis got too bad and so he had to stop and, well, I suppose at least we have been allowed to stay in our home. Although in other grand houses I think a pension is provided, or at least some food.'

'It must be nice for you to have them in Elsworth village, so nearby.' Lily had thought of the vast ocean separating her from her family and the time that stretched into years between visits.

'I still only see them once a month.' Becky had grabbed at a branch, snapping it between her fingers.

'But I do not understand why visiting them is a trial? I would give anything for just an hour with May.'

Becky had shot her a hard look. 'I'm probably not explaining myself well. It is not that I don't want to see them, but more that seeing them pains me.'

Lily had stopped, hoping that Becky would turn to her, but she kept her eyes on the ground. 'I'm sorry, but I still don't understand.'

Becky had begun walking again, so Lily had to run slightly to catch up. 'Well, every day, people like me do the same thing, every day is hard. Nothing gets easier or even achieved, and when I go home, that fact just becomes that much clearer to me because nothing is ever any different. Mother washes the same clothes, makes the same food stretch, digs the same earth in the garden, has the same conversations with her neighbours. And then one day she will die and by then I'll probably have married the blacksmith's boy and, if we have our own children, they'll go into service and the whole cycle will begin again.'

Lily knew there were soothing sentiments she should be offering, but the idea of the blacksmith's boy was consuming, as if he stood now before them, so all she could hear was the rush of blood in her ears. They'd reached a field and Becky climbed on to the fence, sitting across the top rung. She looked so free and easy, with the sun illuminating her in a way that made Lily wonder if it shone only for her. It was too easy to imagine others, the blacksmith's boy especially, thinking the same thoughts, and she was filled with the terror of realising that there were things about Becky she had no idea of, whole parts of her which were cut off.

'Do you have someone special?' She had hoped Becky hadn't heard the catch in her voice.

'Are you asking me if I am courting?'

'I suppose I am, yes.' The question had hung between them like a thick cloth.

'No, I'm not.'

'But what about the blacksmith's boy? There must be so many young men interested in you.'

Becky had turned to Lily then. 'There are, the blacksmith's boy included, but to be courting I would have to be interested in them.' She had raised her chin in a sharp movement. 'And have you ever considered, Lily, that maybe it is not that a baby doesn't want you, but that you do not want to be a mother?'

Lily knew she should have been shocked by the idea, spoken so openly, even though they were all alone, but she'd found she wasn't. 'Henry is desperate for an heir. I don't think I have a choice.'

Becky had jumped down from the fence. 'I suppose there is always a choice; it's just a question of whether or not we are brave enough to take it.'

LAWRENCE

Lawrence hadn't really had any letters to write when he'd left the lunch table, but knowing he only had a few days to live had focused his mind and made him see how much time everyone wasted on conversations that didn't matter, or worse offended. He wondered what would happen if everyone on board were told they only had a couple more days to live and no one was coming to rescue them. He wondered how quickly social conventions would disappear and how soon it would be every man for himself. He wondered in the end what would matter.

He went from the dining room straight to the boat deck, where cool, salty air enveloped him, and stood in a space between two lifeboats. The sound of bagpipes wafted up from below, which made him crane over to look down on to the third class promenade, where he saw a manic skipping game. Everyone was moving so fast, he saw them in a blur, a mass of frenetic limbs and red, swollen faces. If you'd told him he was watching a fight, he'd have believed it, but everyone was laughing and there were children standing at the side clapping their hands, and women holding up their skirts waiting to be allowed into the melee. The joy was too palpable, so he looked away and noticed a young man standing on his own, just apart from the group. He was probably no more than early twenties, dressed strangely in a tie and gloves, with a cane in his hand, his face screwed up in a sombre expression as if he wasn't sure how he found himself there.

Lawrence recognised that feeling too well, of never quite belonging, of always feeling like real life was happening elsewhere but that it was also impossible to penetrate. Cissy's love had smoothed all those edges, lulling him into a false sense of security, making him believe that life was built on possibilities. But it had also made him drunk with foolishness, the sense of rightness in their love blinding him to the impermanence of life, so he'd been swept along like the people skipping, a blur of mess and movement, forgetting that everything can change in a heartbeat and nothing is ever certain.

He looked at the set of the man's jaw and the grip he had on his cane and wanted to shout down to him to keep that vigilance forever, but it was no use thinking he could offer anything because his own life was a mess and he had nothing comforting or wise to impart. He forced his eyes away from another's pain, kidding himself that it was possible that young man might build a fantastic new life for himself in America, far away from whatever it was that dogged him in England. He might even find his Cissy, although that too could be a curse because it was unlikely to last and then his desolation would be worse than anything he was feeling at this moment.

He wondered then why so much of love was full of pain, even when you were right at its beating centre. Certainly, his and Cissy's passion had often flared and sparked, but their anger at each other had never felt real, or at least not permanent, as it did now. Love had made him brave, or perhaps foolish, allowing him an impetuosity which had felt wonderful because he hadn't realised it could ever vanish. Once, he'd climbed over the low wall at the back of the Manor on a clear, full-mooned night because they'd disagreed that afternoon about the nature of responsibility. Cissy believed passionately in a collective responsibility, in trying to help and change, whereas Lawrence thought that was a privileged view and that he had a responsibility to himself first.

The Manor had looked other-worldly in the dark, the moon so bright that it bounced off all the windows, the lawn coloured silver. His feet had sounded like an army on the gravel under her window and he was sure her father would fly out of a door, but the night stayed soft and silent around him as he picked up a pebble and threw it against her glass. Her curtains had moved very quickly, almost as if she had been waiting just on the other side, and momentarily she looked like a ghost with her hair hanging long and her white nightgown, so he had to look away as it felt almost like bad luck to see her like that.

But then she'd spotted him and threw open the window and she was returned to herself, as she leant on her arms, smiling down at him. She held a finger to her lips and then was gone, leaving her window open so he imagined the damp of the night covering her bed in a fine layer and felt jealous of the very air.

The long glass doors, which led to the drawing room, had opened in front of him and there she was, barefoot, with the moon flashing in her eyes and he wanted to tell her everything, know everything she had to say. He'd stepped towards her and pulled her into him, burying his face in her hair, which smelt of sweet lemon, as she wrapped her arms around his waist, squeezing him so he could have stayed like that forever.

'I'm sorry,' he'd said. 'I care nothing about anything other than you. I will be responsible for the whole world if you want me to be.'

'Maybe you don't have to take on the whole world, Lawrence.' She'd looked up at him then and he'd seen a flickering worry in her eyes. 'Try not to be so rash, think a little before you act or you might end up doing something you regret.'

His arms felt heavy, as if the fact that they would never again hold her left too heavy a weight. He could not spend any more time without her in his arms, so turned from the railings and made for the saloon, to consult the charts and see how far they were from the ice fields. He traced his finger along their progress line towards the tiny triangles poking out of the sea and the thought of his jump thrilled through his body like a bolt of electricity.

'I think we have done about 200 miles so far,' the purser said, coming up beside him. 'But we really only kicked into gear at about midday today, so it is what we do from now on that counts.'

Lawrence found that since he'd boarded he was surprised by the ordinary concerns of people, but he played along. 'Do you expect us to still arrive on Tuesday or Wednesday?'

'I don't think they plan to really push her this trip, but everyone wants faster and faster boats. I think in an ideal world they are aiming for Tuesday afternoon, not that you heard that from me.'

'I am not persuaded the quest for speed is always a good one,' someone said behind him, and Lawrence turned to see a short, rotund man. 'Reverend Carter.' The man held out his hand, which Lawrence took. His handshake was warm and firm and his face seemed open, topped by his greying hair.

'Lawrence Beesley.' The man smiled and Lawrence knew it would be impolite not to add to the conversation in some way. 'And I'm not sure I agree with you. I like the idea of speed.'

'Ah, we come from different sides of the argument then.' Reverend Carter tapped his dog collar. 'Please, can I tempt you to come and sit and have a cup of coffee with me and my wife? I would be most interested to hear your defence of speed.'

It seemed unlikely that there was much of a defence for speed, especially with no destination but death waiting for him, but Lawrence couldn't think of a way of refusing, so he let himself be led over to a low round table where a small, stout woman sat with much the same beaming smile as her husband.

'Where did you study?' Reverend Carter asked, as his wife began to pour out the steaming coffee from an elegant silver pot.

'Cambridge.' He waited for the usual surge of pride which followed that answer, that an institution which should have been closed to him had opened its doors, but nothing came and he wasn't sure it meant anything to him any more. Nothing did.

'What did you read?'

'The Natural Science Tripos, my specialisation was Biology.' And this time the answer stirred something in him, so he was momentarily surrounded by the smell of the laboratory, as he pored over a slide, his professor chatting at his elbow. 'I had an amazing tutor who really took me under his wing. We spent an incredible summer between my second and third year investigating an algae I discovered on Fleam Dyke. I had noticed that there was a green algae in the river and I thought it was worth investigating, so I took it back to the lab and we discovered it was a new species. In fact, it has since been named after me.'

Reverend Carter clapped his hands together. 'What a fantastic story.'

A trickle of excitement enveloped Lawrence for a moment, but then dissolved, as another memory sidled up to him, close on his heels like a snarling dog. Cissy had sung and danced when he'd shown her the algae bearing his name in a paper. She'd opened a bottle of champagne and they'd let the bubbles ricochet around their heads until they'd really believed that the world was theirs for the taking.

He looked up to stop his tears from falling and saw the extravagance of where he was sitting, the moulded ceilings and the fresh paint, the waiters weaving between the tables, their silver trays catching the light as the fine china tinkled into place. There was no point to any of it, no point in discovering anything new, without her to share it with.

'And what is your profession now?' the reverend asked, forcing him to return to the present.

'I have always been a teacher. Most recently, I taught Science at Dulwich College.'

'But not any more?'

'No, I resigned my post a little over a year ago.' Lawrence tried to return the reverend's smile, but his face felt tight.

'Are you travelling alone, Mr Beesley?' Reverend Carter's wife asked.

'Please, call me Lawrence. And, yes I am.'

'And I am Marjorie and my husband is William,' she smiled. 'Do you have you a wife and family at home?'

It was a question he dreaded because Cissy's death seemed like the most pointless part of her. 'My wife died of consumption a little over a year ago. I have a son, Alec, who is staying with relatives in Scotland at the moment.'

'I am very sorry to hear that,' Marjorie replied. 'How old is your boy?'

'Six.' Lawrence picked a napkin off the table because his hands felt suddenly useless.

'We all must grieve in our own way,' Reverend Carter said, but Lawrence wondered what he must look like to him, a man running from his responsibilities, letting everyone down again. He worried that it was no more than he'd done his whole life.

First taking his own ticket out of Wirksworth and not going back for any of his siblings, then failing to find a way to make Cissy well, refusing to ever acknowledge she was dying, so she didn't have anyone to talk to properly in her final days and had to endure her fear alone. And now leaving Alec with strangers, unable to hold his son or comfort him in any useful way, failing Cissy again in the one thing she'd begged him to do.

'You look as though you miss her terribly,' Marjorie said.

Lawrence had to clench his throat to stop his tears from falling. 'I do, yes. She was everything to me, you see. I fell in love with her the first moment I met her and she was the most wonderful person I ever met.' He clenched his mouth against the words that pushed at it, imagining what it would sound like to tell these good people that he also hated her for leaving him alone, that sometimes he doubted she had ever loved him.

'Oh, my poor boy,' Marjorie said, reaching across the table for his hand in an unwarranted act of kindness that made him want to pull away. 'I can only imagine.'

There was a throbbing tension in the air and, when he looked up, he saw a look pass between the Carters that reminded him of the way he and Cissy used to communicate, when one glance, even the smallest of movements, was enough. 'How long have you been married?' he asked, looking between them both.

Marjorie sat back, taking her hand with her. 'Well, my, it is coming up to fifty years now.'

Lawrence felt a stab of mean jealousy, but made himself smile. 'And I can see they have been very kind to you both.'

'We have been very fortunate to find each other,' Reverend Carter said. 'I simply could not be a good servant to my parish without Marjorie. And I mean that in every sense. It is not just that she is supportive to me, but she works so hard as well. It has been wonderful to share that.'

Lawrence recognised the description and felt compelled to reply, even though he knew it would continue the conversation and he rarely had the energy for that. 'That is one of the things I find hardest. Cissy and I were like that, in the way we shared things, I mean. I know some men like to think they control their wives, but it was never like that with us. She was involved in the Suffrage movement before she became sick and I know if she had lived, we would have created an equal life together. It makes me so angry that I was not able to save her.'

'Save her?' Reverend Carter creased his brow. 'You are not a miracle worker, son, the power to save rests only with God.'

Lawrence swallowed down his true reply because the Carters were kind and he didn't want to break the spell of being with them. 'But I worry that perhaps I could have done more.'

'It sounds as if you loved her very much and there is not much more than that,' Marjorie said.

'It is not always good to live too much in the past,' Reverend Carter said. 'As a man of science, you must know this.'

'Oh, but the past is where I am still with Cissy.'

'And the future is where you and your son are headed.'

Lawrence looked down at his clasped hands. 'I hate that word.'

'Which one?'

'Future.' Lawrence couldn't meet William's eye because he knew the man would see the darkness within him, how it shifted and pushed so that sometimes he felt removed from his own mind and body, as if you could cut his wrist and black tar would flow from him. Often he hated everyone and everything for not understanding that life had ended on the day Cissy died. It was hard to believe that the world hadn't folded over on itself, crushing and rending everything so life became nothing more than dusty rubble and bones.

'We all have a future right up until the moment we die,'

William said, very quietly, and Lawrence was frightened that he'd spoken his bile out loud.

'And you have a son,' Marjorie added. 'William and I have two boys, both grown now and with children of their own, but that is where your future rests, even if you cannot imagine it for yourself.'

Lawrence nodded, but he didn't think it would help Alec in any way if he lived. He had revealed himself to be selfish and useless and he didn't know what he could teach his son, how he could ever make anything better for him again, how he could ever be a person worthy of nurturing a child. He wouldn't even be able to tell him good stories about his mother because his anger was contaminating everything.

'The only person we can ever truly save is ourselves,' William said.

The words were almost an exact echo of the ones he'd been remembering Cissy speaking when she'd lain dying in their bed. He worried they were just platitudes, which made him want to lash out at the man, sat so calmly in front of him, his hands resting on top of his belly like a cartoon. 'But is that not bleak? Surely it means we are all alone?'

'Not to my mind. Because for most of us loving and helping others is how we save ourselves.' William smiled over at his wife as he spoke and Lawrence thought their love was almost visible, like a string that vibrated between them.

He turned from the sight, overcome by jealousy and rage that this feeling had been taken from him, which made him want to go and scream into the face of this man's God, who thought it all right to dangle his life over a ravine. The only thing Lawrence found possible to believe in was death, which was often hard and ugly, removed from peace and divinity.

'And I know what you are thinking,' William continued. 'That without your wife, there is no one for you to help or love, so you are doomed. Well, there is your son for one, but there will be many others.'

'But what if I do not want others?' The idea of falling in love again was revolting to Lawrence.

'I'm not talking necessarily about romantic love, Lawrence.' William smiled at him. 'Although there would be no harm in that if it were to come in time. But there is much joy to be found in friendships and in helping those who find it hard to help themselves, for whatever reason. There are many routes to salvation, you know.'

The words were meant well, but they felt heavy in Lawrence's body, so his skin began to itch and he knew he needed to move to stop from screaming. What William was saying sounded like a fantasy, like the sort of story he might tell Alec at night, awash with soothing words which ultimately meant nothing. The truth was that life was often brutal, filled with shit and blood, breath that couldn't be caught, fevers which wracked the body, despair and turmoil, fear and pain. Love always let you down eventually because it ended with one person leaving first and that was unacceptable.

He stood, worried that if he remained any longer he would be rude and the Carters were clearly good people who didn't deserve that. 'You have been most kind, both of you, and I have so enjoyed speaking with you. But please excuse me. I think I shall take a walk on deck.'

William dipped his head. 'It was a pleasure to meet you too. I hope we shall have a chance for more conversations before we arrive in New York.'

Lawrence forced a tight smile. 'As do I.'

'Take care of yourself, Lawrence,' Marjorie said, the sides of her eyes creasing with her genuine smile.

Lawrence turned before he could receive any more kindness and strode out of the saloon and back up to the deck. Despite the wind, it was quite crowded and his eyes were already blurring with tears, so he turned and walked quickly away from the direction of travel, hoping to find a deserted spot.

The crowds thinned out towards the back of the boat and eventually he came to a thin set of stairs which led up to what looked like another deck. He climbed the short distance without really thinking, but when he reached the top, he realised that he was now at the very back of the ship, on a smallish deck which was totally deserted. He strode right to the end, walking closer and closer to the huge expanse of sea, horrifying in its unrelenting beauty.

He craned over the railings, which only came up to his waist and meant mounting them would take no more effort than climbing a gate. He looked down at the water being churned away by what he presumed must be the monstrous propeller blades, parting the sea like an angry man forcing himself on a woman, with ferocity and arrogance. If he jumped from there, he might be caught in those blades, his body dismembered so entirely it could never be put back together, not by a benevolent God or a well-meaning doctor, neither of whom would ever understand his need to be rendered.

The truth was, he deserved to be annihilated because he wasn't even sure that he'd ever loved Cissy properly, or in the way she deserved. 'Why do you not ask me to marry you?' she'd had to ask him, when he'd returned to Wirksworth for the Easter break in his first year at Cambridge.

He'd just been a foolish idiot, because he remembered being shocked at her words, never imagining a life without her, but also never imagining the possibility of marrying her. 'I thought you knew we would be together forever,' he'd tried.

They'd been lying on the top of High Peak, watching the clouds scud past as it was one of those unusually warm April days which made the world feel like it was exploding, and Lawrence could remember saying something irritating like he could feel the grass pushing up into his back, which had made Cissy sit up and look down at him. The sun was behind her and her hair had escaped its bun at the base of her neck so it flared around her face. 'Women do not know anything, Lawrence,' she'd sighed. 'Or at least we know everything, but because we cannot make anything happen, it's as good as knowing nothing.'

He'd tried to pull her down towards him but she'd resisted. 'Come on, Cis.' He wanted to show her how much he loved her with his body, he wanted to travel through her, to read her mind for a moment like they said they did when they lay together. As if that had ever been enough, as if there was any glory to be found in the lover.

'No,' she'd said and, standing on the deck, he heard the exasperation in her voice.

'But you must know we will always be together. I didn't think your parents would let us marry.'

'Oh, so you think they would prefer for us to live together? Or perhaps you would like me to give up everything and follow you until you tire of me?'

'I will never tire of you.' His chest tightened now and then, the thought of losing her always physically painful.

'I wonder how many ruined women have believed those words. You know, Mother has made me go to a couple of stupid dances with Marion recently. Every time, she has made a point to steer me in the direction of a chinless wonder called Edmund, whom I have had to endure stepping on my toes as we spin around a room.'

'Why did you not tell me this?' Lawrence felt a rising nausea.

'Why did you not ask?' Her mouth had looked like a thin line, there were two red spots high on her cheeks and tears glistened at the corners of her eyes. 'You have no idea, do you? I mean, it's fine for you, waltzing off to Cambridge where you meet a hundred interesting people a day. After which you will get a degree and decide what job to do and go off out into the world, where there are lots of other interesting people. Life will unfurl before you, presenting you with all these options, whilst mine shrivels around me.'

Lawrence had sat up, but Cissy had turned her face away from him. 'Cis, what is wrong? How can you be worried about me? I might do all those things, but you will be with me.'

She'd spun round at that. 'Oh, how generous of you. Anyway, by the time you get around to asking me anything, I will probably have had to settle for Edmund, or the next oaf Mother puts my way, because I am twenty-eight, Lawrence, and that is interminably old for a woman.' She'd ripped at the grass by her feet. 'Do you have any idea what it feels like not to have any say in your own life, not to have any choices?'

His chest had contracted raw and tight, in the same way it was doing now on the deck of a ridiculous ship that he never should have been on because he should have been at home with her. The future should have been theirs, warm and safe, stretching on for years and years, and it was like being ripped apart to think that she had gone and would never return. He let a cry escape that was swallowed by the wind, whipped up into the sky.

They should be approaching the ice fields by Saturday night or Sunday morning and he would come to this part of the deck and launch himself into the abyss, hoping to be ripped apart by the blades but settling for being overcome by cold, deep water. He would take death in any form now, because there was nothing left for him in the world any more, even his son was not enough to keep him, and that meant the end had come.

Maybe he would meet Cissy where he was heading, but, most likely, Lawrence suspected he would meet nothing, there would just be an ending, a finality that would feel like a release.

He leant his head against the cold railing and let his tears fall in a slow, steady procession, watching them dart away as the wind carried them over the edge.

LILY

Lily found it hard to understand how she would move again, as she sat in her chair in the room she'd retreated to after lunch, with the books lining the far wall looming over her as if they were mocking her. In the early years of their marriage, she could have written herself a different story; she knew it would have been possible to draw a truce with Henry, if she had just consented to live by his version of what life should be like. Most of his male friends lived in the same way he did, so it probably wasn't even wrong, it was just that she'd never been able to accept it as her life, which probably did mean that she was deluded and unnatural.

Except her thoughts from lunch were still swirling inside her and what if she had only ever been told about one version of life? What if there were other realities waiting out there, other ways of living and being? Perhaps all those years she'd spent trying to shift her mind had been fruitless because maybe it wasn't wrong of her to mind the smell of another woman on Henry's skin, or to see him passed out from alcohol with urine staining his trousers, or to hear him laughing over gambling losses, or to simply avoid him when his temper was so bad that he could lash out.

She turned her head away from the books and all their

confusion and looked out of the window on to the covered walkway, the sun bright against a clear blue sky and the sea calm beyond the ship. It would be cool outside and the sharpness would get into her eyes, but still there were plenty of people unperturbed by this, women wrapped in furs and men with tall hats and long coats, all walking and chatting animatedly, laughing at jokes, many with arms intertwined.

So many people were so free with each other. Love and tenderness were easy for some to access, enveloping and enclosing them as though it was natural to feel this way. But love had always seemed like a slippery emotion to Lily, and she imagined it like a snake, sliding away from her into dark corners, its bite the only thing worth knowing about it. As a child, she'd felt the flinch under her mother's skin when she tried to hug her and she couldn't remember the woman ever telling her she loved her. May was much more demonstrative, always curling up against her in bed, or throwing her arms around their father, or pulling the dog on to her lap in a cloud of kisses. Lily would watch her sister jealously, longing to be that easy with her affections, but fear always held her tight, fear that her mother wouldn't be the only person who wanted to push her away, a slight shiver as she left room.

Henry had seemed like such an answer when he'd appeared, so confident and desired, so when he'd chosen her, she could hardly take it seriously. But he'd persisted, the need he said he felt for her was like a drug he couldn't shake, the presents he showered her with so thoughtful, the way she could feel his eyes on her in every room, even when other girls in pretty dresses were being put in his way. And her mother had noticed her then, primping and preening her, offering her bites of sweet chocolates, wondering if her hair looked better curled and loose or tucked under. 'There are fewer dukes to go round,' she'd said one night after too much champagne at a gaudy ball in which Henry had whisked her around the room until she'd felt like she was floating, 'but Countess sounds just as pretty.'

It would have been too disappointing for everyone involved if, in the end, Lily hadn't let him hold and kiss her, or fill her head with stories which never could have been true. Although she hated herself for being so fooled now, and should have known it was all a sham and no one would ever really care about her, no one would ever want good things for her simply because they liked her. She was drab and uninteresting and unlovable and all the other things Henry had since told her, which was at least something she could understand.

She was reminded how, just before she'd accepted his proposal she'd told May that he was the man of her dreams, expecting her sister to squeal with delight, the way she knew their Mother would. But May had looked very serious and said that dreams were flighty and maybe it would be better to wait for a real man, one with substance. At the time, she hadn't understood what May meant, but remembering the words now made her think only of Becky. She couldn't work out why she kept on thinking about the woman in such a way, but it was undeniable that, without her, she felt in danger of dissolving to nothing.

Becky and Dr Henderson walked past, simply striding into her vision, so it took Lily a moment to realise they were really there, and not a figment of her imagination. They stopped by a pillar a bit further along the walkway, so she had to crane her neck to look at them, perplexed because she hadn't realised they were friends, or even people who might walk together. Not that Becky looked comfortable; Lily recognised the tightness in her shoulders, which were drawn up too high to her ears, although it wasn't really even that which seemed off, but something else which floated just out of Lily's reach. Becky turned to

Dr Henderson so Lily could see her sharp profile as she started to speak.

Henry's love seemed then to encircle Becky like a force field, although she found she cared little about that and far more about what this must mean Becky felt for Henry. That Henry had taken her place filled Lily with a scratching terror. It was possible they would never smile secretly across a room, both knowing exactly what the other was thinking by the tilt of her eyebrow, or sit by a fire with warm cocoa in their hands and laughter on their lips, words pouring from them like a torrent. They might never again link arms easily or brush hands and the thought was surprisingly distressing, as if she might shrivel and die without that possibility.

Her heart seized with the terrible consideration that it was in fact possible that all her memories were false. She got everything else wrong and, watching Becky with Dr Henderson, it seemed entirely plausible that Becky had found her as hard to love as everyone else and that she'd only ever been nice to her out of necessity or duty. Or maybe it was even more simple and Becky, just like everyone else, only wanted something material from her and Lily had been foolish to interpret this as affection.

Becky pulled an envelope out of her skirt and handed it over to Dr Henderson, who tucked it quickly into his inside pocket. They said a few more words and then the doctor strode off up the deck, leaving Becky leaning over the railings. Lily could only see her broad back, but her shoulders were hunched and she rubbed her hands roughly across her face. She pushed herself off the rails and walked the opposite way from the doctor, passing right by Lily's window, so she could see Becky's red eyes and scrunched features. She reached out involuntarily for the woman and she was so close, she could have touched her if there hadn't been glass between them.

They'd stood by windows so many times, although they had always been on the same side, watching other people, and it pained Lily to think that glass now separated them and that what was happening was not something she could even guess at.

They'd once watched from her sitting room window as Henry and his supposedly best friend's wife ran giggling across the lawn. 'He's going to make love to her down by the lake,' she'd said, with a catch in her voice, which, in her memory, sounded overly dramatic.

She'd expected sympathy, perhaps even been fishing for it, but Becky had turned to her sharply. 'Oh God, and why do you care?'

The question had stumped Lily, making her realise that she didn't, which had felt wrong because surely proper wives had to care about such things. 'I do not really know.'

'If he doesn't make love to her, then he might try with you and that makes you cry as well, so, quite frankly, I do not know what it is you do want.' Becky had turned back into the room and walked to the chest, pretending there was some task that needed attending to. 'Unless you don't mind as much as you say you do.'

Becky's words had shocked her and it had felt desperately important that she refute them, so she'd followed her across the room and spun her round so they were close enough to feel each other's breath on their cheeks. 'You should not talk to me like that.' It hadn't been close to what she meant, but she couldn't think of another way of expressing herself.

Becky shook her arm free. 'I am just so sick of…' but she'd stopped and looked down, her chest heaving.

'No, say what you mean.' Lily had held herself still, even though it felt as if her whole body were shaking.

Becky had looked up, her eyes now glistening with tears. 'I just wish you would be braver, that is all.'

Sweat trickled under her dress and her heart knocked against her ribs then and now, so it seemed momentarily unclear if she was in Elsworth or out at sea. But wherever she was, Becky was right and she'd never been brave. Lily thought she'd used all her bravery up marrying Henry and moving across the Atlantic, and look where that had got her. A braver person would have fallen at Becky's feet and begged her to help her find her courage.

She looked back into Becky's eyes in that room and saw how they shimmered and sparkled with anticipation and knew that couldn't mean nothing. But the right words, she realised, had never been Becky's to say, so, naturally, she would have become bored with waiting for Lily to find her voice. Lily herself was bored with waiting, and yet, the right things to say and do still eluded her.

Dread circled her, lapping at her feet and oozing up her legs. The omens were bad and it was hard to ignore a suspicion growing inside her that the encounter she'd just witnessed was deeply ominous. A black cat had crossed her path in London and the housekeeper had complained about the milk curdling. In Southampton, the night before they'd sailed, she'd dreamt that all her teeth fell out.

They were clearly planning something, and the most obvious thing was that Henry and Becky were in love and intended to marry. But she knew also that Henry would never be parted from her money and the baby. Whichever way she looked at it, it seemed more and more obvious that they, along with Dr Henderson, must be involved in a plan to somehow dispose of her and take her baby.

Her father's words ricocheted inside her and she saw an empty house with locks on the doors and shutters on the windows, just three other people walking the corridors. She knew it was a trap, knew that it was simply a place to hold her until her body disgorged itself, until it squeezed out a life that would obliterate her own.

A mean, lacerating fear began to spread through her so it felt as if her blood was curdling and sticking in her veins. Soon she worried she wouldn't be able to move, as if her misery was going to overwhelm her and send her scrabbling to the floor. And then what would happen to the baby; the tiny, defenceless baby who didn't know that it was emerging into such a mean and loveless world? She wanted to cry for it and its motherless future and she hated herself for being too stupid, or slow, or whatever it was that was wrong with her, to work out what was going on. But it was just so hard to fathom, because nothing made sense and it felt like in stepping on board she'd fallen through reality to a place she couldn't navigate.

She stood and left the library in such a swift moment, grabbing her stupid blue hat and jamming it on her head so she knew it would look a mess. She climbed the stairs to the open top deck and walked away from the crowd, towards the back of the boat as it ploughed relentlessly onwards, although this time the action did nothing to dampen her fear.

The people began to thin out the further back Lily walked, until she came to a thin flight of stairs which led up to what looked like another deck. Nobody else was around, so she began to climb, a desperate desire to put as much distance as possible between herself and Henry.

At the top of the steps, she felt slightly out of breath and her vision spiralled nauseatingly upwards, as though she had completely left her body. She was keenly aware of herself standing alone on the deck of this hulking ship, itself just a pinprick in a vast ocean, the land so far away, salvation a distant hope. Lily had felt lonely for most of her life, but never had she felt so completely ungrounded, as if nothing she knew was right.

She caught sight of a movement right at the back of the ship, a man pushing himself off the railings, and a mad compulsion rushed through her to beg this person for help. He turned towards her and she saw that it was the man from lunch who'd been seated next to Henry, which felt like a connection, however tenuous.

She walked forward without letting herself think about what she was doing, even when she saw him stiffen as he realised she was approaching. But, when she drew level, she saw that he looked hardly any better than she did, his face drawn and his eyes red. At least he spoke, 'Can I help you, Madam?'

'We met at lunch.' She tried to tuck away her windswept hair and keep her voice even. 'You were sitting next to my husband, Henry. He asked your opinion on Christian Science, I think.'

'Oh yes.'

Lily had expected an introduction, or at least a jolt of recognition, but the man didn't say any more.

'My name is Lily Elsworth. I am sorry, I forget yours.'

'Lawrence Beesley.' She wondered if he might be sick, he looked so pale. 'Has something happened?'

It was an innocent enough question, but it landed on Lily like a blow and then she couldn't hold back her tears. Lawrence stayed very still as she snivelled, but she sensed his unease so pulled herself together. 'You are going to think me unhinged, but I'm in desperate need of help.' It was hard to know where to begin, or even what she was asking for. Lily looked into Lawrence's eyes, but they were flat, as if no life existed there. 'I need your help,' she repeated.

'I am not in a position to offer help,' he answered. 'If something has happened, I can take you to find one of the stewards.'

'No,' she almost shouted. 'I cannot speak to any of them.' She waited for Lawrence to say something, but he remained silent. 'Something very strange is happening to me and I feel as if I am losing my...' she hesitated because she'd wanted to say mind, but something stopped her, '...well, my grip on what is right, I suppose.'

She forced herself to meet Lawrence's eye, but he remained quite impassive. Finally, all he said was, 'I'm not sure I understand, Madam.'

'I don't know why I'm on this ship.' Lily looked out over the sea as she spoke, trying to catch hold of her thoughts, but the vastness of the view cowed her. 'I mean, I thought we were going home so I could give birth near my parents, but I'm not sure that is the case any more. I don't know what my husband has planned for me. He doesn't love me at all, you see. In fact, I think he is in love with my maid.'

Lawrence sighed and rubbed his hands across his face. 'I'm sure you must be mistaken. And, even if you are not, I do not see what help I can be. It would be better if you spoke to a steward. At the least, you need a seat and a glass of water.'

A rising panic fluttered through her. 'Oh no. Henry wouldn't like that and I cannot find myself on the wrong side of him any more. I have to be cleverer than that. He is always twisting my words. And maybe there are things which are very wrong with me, I cannot really tell, but I do not think they used to be and it scares me and—'

He reached towards her but didn't touch her. 'Slow down. I cannot understand what you are saying.'

Lily took a breath and tried to think of a way of appealing to this man. 'I think my husband is waging a campaign against me. For example, he only asked you about Christian Science because the other woman on our table, Emma, said she had a healer and he wanted to make out that he would send me to see him. Although it is all a lie, because he cares nothing for me.

I'm afraid he plans to steal my baby after the birth and start a new life with Becky.' She knew she was speaking too fast and incoherently again, but she also felt filled up by all she knew, as if there were too many words to find and she'd forgotten how to use them to make any sense.

Lawrence rubbed at the side of his head, as if he was in pain. 'You think your husband plans to steal your baby, which is yet to be born?'

She nodded, relieved that finally she'd made herself understood.

'And how do you think he plans to achieve this?'

'I don't know exactly. But he has told me that we are making this trip so I can be near my family when I give birth, but I found a letter in our cabin from my father which makes it clear they are not expecting to see me until *after* the birth. They have rented a secluded house and Henry is going to lock me up there with just the doctor he has employed and my maid until I've had the baby. And I don't know what will happen to me after that.'

Lawrence's eyes narrowed and Lily could see he wasn't taking her seriously. 'This plan sounds very… involved.'

She wanted to reach out and grab him physically, to shake what she knew into him. 'Because it is. I also just saw my maid give my doctor an envelope and I have no idea what was inside it. I'm sure they want to get rid of me somehow and marry.' She knew what she was saying sounded implausible, but it was also impossible to stop.

'My God,' Lawrence said, running his hands across his face again. But Lily could tell that the sentiment wasn't about her and what she'd said, but about himself. 'I really am truly sorry, Lady Elsworth, but you have come to the wrong person to ask for help. And you clearly do need help.' He glanced back over the sea and Lily was struck by the absurdity of her situation.

'I'm sorry for your plight, whatever it might be, but I am of no use to man nor beast.'

'So, you will leave me to my fate?' She still had no real idea what that fate might be, but she was sure it involved losing Becky and her baby and, if she was completely honest, she didn't know which of those would be worse.

'I do not think you are in any danger.'

It felt like life was closing in on her like a lion with its prey. 'You think I'm lying?'

'Not lying. Maybe mistaken.'

Lily choked on a sob as it rose through her. 'I am not mistaken, Mr Beesley.'

'Pregnancy is a strange time and it can shake even the most rational of minds.'

It was no good, Lily thought, as she looked at Lawrence. Men were all the same when it came down to it and she'd been a fool to think this one might help her. To him, she was no more than a hysterical woman with no grasp on reality. She wondered what he would think of her if she told him that she wasn't even sure she wanted the baby, that she would swap the baby for Becky, if that were possible. That she was scared mostly for herself, which must make her wicked and stupid.

'Let me walk you back to your cabin, or we could find a steward,' Lawrence said, offering his arm. 'I am sure this situation is resolvable.'

She ignored his gesture. Her hat felt too tight on her head and she pulled it off, which made her hair fly around her face. 'You do not understand. I am terrified, but with no clear idea even what I should be fearing. I cannot recognise any aspect of myself. I want to find out what is happening to me, but I barely even know what I think any more.'

'I am sorry,' he repeated and she perplexingly saw a real pain in his eyes. 'But I'm the wrong person to ask for help. Please, let me take you somewhere.'

She turned from him and began to walk back the way she had come, because it was all too bleak, no one was going to save her and she was powerless on her own. She felt Lawrence watching her as she left, but he didn't run behind her and say he believed her; he didn't, in fact, do anything.

LAWRENCE

Lawrence watched Lily rush off down the deck and knew, with absolute certainty, that he should follow her. While he doubted that anything she said was real, he'd seen enough of her husband to believe that she was probably miserable, and misery could do terrible things to the mind. His own felt like a piece of broken china, shattered and sharp, so penetrated by sadness that it was pointless hoping it might recover.

But thinking that Lily was unhinged and not helping her were two very different states, and it was impossible to ignore how Cissy shrouded him in her displeasure. He knew exactly what she would say and how disappointed she would be in him. When she'd first come to Cambridge after they were married, she had immediately announced her intention of doing something, as she put it. She said that she'd spent too many years delicately sitting on chairs, or sewing by fires, or deciding on meals, or taking tea, and that she never wanted to do any of those things ever again.

The sentiment had scared him slightly, if he was completely honest with himself, which of course he hadn't been. But he knew that in a horrid corner of his mind he'd wanted her to be still and safe, wanted to protect her physically from the world. Although he'd known better than to say any of that out loud.

And it was so confusing because he'd agreed with her when she'd said things to him like: 'Do you know how amazingly boring it is to be a woman? And, of course, that is only if you have money and kindness in your life. If you do not, then it is boring but also terribly hard work, all that cleaning and cooking and polishing, or also terrifying if the person who is meant to love you can harm you as much as he likes.'

Once, at Cambridge, he'd had a discussion with a group of men about the idea to admit women to the library. A man whom he'd quite liked had been astounded at the idea, saying that women could not sit quietly for any length of time and that within weeks it would become filled with chinking teacups and inane chatter.

'Do you think women enjoy domesticity?' he'd asked Cissy when he'd returned home that evening, but she'd snorted at him so he hated himself.

'I think you will find most women accept it, Lawrence,' she'd replied, holding his name in her mouth like a bomb. 'I know men like to say that women are more suited to these quiet, contained roles, but how do we know that to be true? Female experience is never documented, our opinions are never sought and our society hardly desired. It is just a clever nonsense to keep us in our place.'

'There is a woman in my lectures,' Lawrence had said, as a kind of peace offering, although it was true, there was a tall, quiet woman whom he knew to be called Martha who sat at the back of the room and never spoke. 'She cannot obtain a degree, but she is there every lesson. I have often wondered what she is doing.'

Cissy had sat forward, her hair falling over her shoulders. 'What she is doing, Lawrence, is very wise. She is educating herself for the future, not taking no for an answer.'

Cissy would be shouting at him to run after Lily. He could hear her voice vibrating through him, telling him that it was his responsibility to offer comfort, to listen, to help. Although that thought also refuelled his anger, because she had run so fast, she had left him behind.

Besides, Lily had vanished and the deck was darkening. The sun set at the front of the ship every evening and right now the golden ball was being cut in half by the horizon, its light flickering across the ocean as if the ship were following it. He knew it was a beautiful sight and yet the idea of this seemed lost to him, so he couldn't extract any pleasure from it. He barely even saw it, so consumed was he by memories.

Lawrence had invited Martha to supper and she and Cissy had hit it off exactly as well as predicted, so he would often find them sitting together when he arrived home in the evenings, a sight which scared him in a way he knew to be wrong because she made Cissy so happy. Martha was already involved in the women's movement and she began to take Cissy with her to meetings in the backs of cafés, where Cissy said she finally heard voiced the thoughts in her head.

'We are nothing more than property,' Cissy had remarked one evening, as she cradled a glass of wine. 'You know, if you chose, you could take all my money, you could beat me, you could have affairs, you could rape me. You could probably even kill me and get away with it because I am your wife.'

The thought of hurting Cissy in any way contracted something at the base of Lawrence's stomach and he'd leant forward so he could touch her knees, which were curled up under her. 'I worry at you exposing yourself to so much vileness.'

But Cissy had screwed her face up at him. 'What, because I am a woman, you think I am too delicate to hear such things?'

She'd pulled her knees away from his touch. 'Speaking like that does you no favours, Lawrence.'

He'd blushed with anger both at himself and also at her, for rushing forward without waiting for him.

'I'm sick of how long change takes. Why do some people think they're better than others just because of how or where or which body they've been born into? It makes no sense.' He could see tears dancing in her eyes. 'You know, we had a woman speak this evening who is blind in her right eye because her husband beat her so badly. Now she's living alone with five children, barely any money and no chance of getting any proper work because she has no education. But she's not even allowed to vote for the chance of change, whilst her husband, who is a brute and bully, can. We women might as well cut out our tongues, for the use they are to us.'

The sun was now nearly extinguished, its last remaining light wobbling above the sea, as if the water were putting out its flames. Men used to think the world was flat, people used to pray to the sun, women had been sacrificed to appease vengeful gods. Things had changed and moved forward without him and they would continue to do so after he was gone. Yes, he felt sorry for Lily, but he had just seen what was probably his penultimate sunset and he couldn't get involved, he didn't even think he was capable of getting involved. And besides, how can you save someone when you have given up on the idea of saving yourself?

Cissy would tell him to fight to the end. In fact, she would tell him not to accept the end, to be strong, just as she had been in her final months. Reverend Carter had told him we can only save ourselves, but that we do this by helping others. The sentiments knocked into Lawrence uncomfortably because he knew he was failing so many people. But the urge to die was strong. He felt like he had reached his ending and no amount of helping or praying or thinking was going to save him any more.

He turned back to the edge and leant as far over the rail as he dared, feeling it cut into his stomach. There was no way he could help Lily, however disappointed in him Cissy would be. It was probably true that to help others you had to have a confidence in yourself, but his had vanished with Cissy.

He pulled himself slightly forward and there was a moment of suspension, when he felt the shift of weight, the pull of gravity that would overcome his body if he just let it. It was dark and cold and he could hear the slap of water against the side of the boat as she continued forward.

He righted himself, his head spinning slightly. The ice was not far away and he didn't have long to wait now.

FRIDAY, APRIL 12TH

LILY

Lily woke with her heart skittering in her chest, her breathing already ragged, the light of the day harsh, as if it were trying to beat its way into her body. She sat up, but her head swayed with the movement so she had to lean it against the wall.

She tried to arrange her thoughts, although they felt insubstantial. Perhaps Lawrence had been right and she should talk to a steward. Although everything she thought of saying sounded unlikely: the only real expression she could make was one of fear, of her husband, doctor, even her baby. And now also Becky, whom she had never imagined it possible to fear. Besides, Henry's natural authority would override anything she could say. She imagined his loud, booming voice talking over her quiet one, the reasoning he would employ, the subtle nod.

Lily placed a hand on her stomach and tentatively prodded her flesh, which felt spongey, although she could also feel the jut of her bones and some alien nodules. She imagined the baby stilling at her touch and worried that maybe it too was sick of her. Other women claimed to love their babies before they were born, or to have known absolutely that it was a boy or girl by instinct. But Lily just felt a void, no sense of who this person inside her was. And if that were true, then how would she hold on to him or her when Henry tried to take it from her? How could you save someone when you didn't even know who they were?

She reached behind her shoulder to feel the raised skin on the bone of the blade and allowed herself to feel the water Becky had squeezed over it on the night it had happened. She shut her eyes against the clear day streaming through the porthole and let her mind fill with the fog from the heat of her bathroom at Elsworth.

Becky's ragged breathing had been close to her ear as she'd said, 'It's deep, Lily. I think it might scar.'

'I was stupid to speak to him tonight, I knew he had drunk too much.'

The tap had been dripping, a steady beat that was almost comforting.

'What did you say that was so offensive?' Becky's tone was hard, like a flat line.

'I asked why Clemmy was coming to stay again, so soon after last time.'

'But you know why. I don't understand why you care so much?'

Lily had stretched out the pain in her shoulder by pulling down on the back of her head. 'It is not that I care so much, but I cannot stand how open he is about his lovers. He had such a glint in his eye when he told me she was coming again and it is humiliating. I don't deserve to be treated this way.'

'I'm not sure any of us deserves anything,' Becky had said. 'Perhaps it is up to us to make sure that what we want to happen is the thing that does happen.'

She'd splashed her hand against the water. 'Sometimes I just want to run away.'

'Maybe that is what we should do then.'

The air had seemed to contract around them, so the atmosphere lay heavy. Lily had heard the sponge drop back into the bath and expected to feel more water dripping down her back, but when the touch came, it was without a barrier. Becky traced a finger along the length of the cut, her touch so light it felt like a dream. Lily's skin had chilled as soon as Becky withdrew, but then Lily heard the sound of a kiss and the finger was back, even softer this time, like tiny breaths, which made her shiver.

'I cannot bear that he does this to you,' Becky had whispered, her voice thin and drawn. 'I cannot bear to see you hurt.'

The tap was still dripping and the steam still rising, so the air had become warm and damp and the windows dripped with condensation. It had been almost possible to imagine that they existed only within that moment, that the rest of the world had fallen away and nothing else mattered. Lily had reached her hand behind her shoulder until it connected with Becky's so their fingers met, resting against each other in the still of the moment.

The door of the cabin opened and Henry came in, shattering her memories so succinctly that Lily jumped, a little cry escaping her at the thought that Becky could have chosen this man over her.

His eyes retracted into slits. 'You're finally awake, I see. Emma Connaught asked after you again.'

She didn't know that Emma Connaught had ever asked after her. 'What time is it?'

'Gone ten.'

'Really?' Her head felt muggy and her limbs were like lead.

'You were dead to the world when I got up.'

She hadn't seen Henry at all the previous night, wandering aimlessly after leaving Lawrence and then feeling too distressed to go in to dinner. Eventually, she'd gone back to her cabin and tried to stay awake, because she'd felt scared at the thought of what he might do when he returned. But, in the end, Becky had brought in her nightly cup of tea and after that it had felt impossible to keep her eyes open.

'Did you even sleep here last night?' She pulled the covers up under her chin.

Henry sighed, shucking off his coat. 'What on earth are you talking about?' He turned his back on her and started looking for something in his trunk, his dismissal making her feel desperate, as if she really had become less than nothing to him.

She stood quickly and the floor felt spongey beneath her feet. 'Henry.'

He looked back at her because she'd spoken with more force than usual, but she registered the curl of his lip.

'Please, Henry, it doesn't have to be like this.'

He stood straighter. 'Like what?'

'You do not have to hate me.'

He sighed. 'It is not that I hate you, Lily, but you are impossible. You must see what you have become.'

She looked down at herself and saw how thin her arms were, how almost translucent her skin. 'I'm sorry, I don't mean to be this person.'

He rubbed a hand across his face. 'I gave you so many chances.'

'Chances?' Lily's brain felt loose, as if she was becoming lost to herself.

'I opened so many doors for you. You could have been or done anything.'

She tried to grab hold of meaning in what he was saying, but all she could see was Consuelo. 'But that isn't true. I could only have been what you wanted. What if the things I want are different from the things you want?'

He made a snorting noise and threw his hands in the air. 'Oh, for God's sake, you have always been such a bore. Lots of women make a good go of this life.'

Tears spilled over and raced down her cheeks. 'Please let me keep my baby, Henry.'

'Your baby? What on earth are you talking about?'

She forced herself to meet his eyes, but he was holding them very still. 'I found the letter from my father. I know about the house we are going to when we dock. I know I will not be seeing my parents or May until after the baby is born.' She swallowed down a sob and forced herself to be brave. 'And I think you are in love with Becky. I think you want to abandon me and start a new life with her and our baby.'

Henry stood very still, but he let out one short, sharp sound like a bark. 'My God, you are completely mad. Dr Henderson warned me you were close to the edge, but I didn't realise things were this bad.'

Lily felt as weak as water. She'd been exhausted and having strange episodes for about a year now in which everything felt as though it was spiralling and her vision would blur and jag, but she didn't think she was completely mad, or that she couldn't trust what she'd heard.

'What on earth makes you think I love Becky? Or that I would want any kind of life with her? She's a maid, for God's sake.'

'I heard you in her room yesterday morning.'

'Don't be ridiculous.' Henry's eyes were bloodshot. 'So, now you're hearing things as well.'

'Henry, please,' she cried. 'I need to understand what's happening. What possible reason is there for you not wanting me to see my family when we get to America?'

He stepped towards her and put a hand on her arm. 'Come on, I think you need to get back into bed. This distress is no good for the baby.'

She let him lead her over to the bed and tuck her up in

the covers, only realising she was shivering as he pulled up the blankets.

'None of what you are saying makes any sense, Lil.' His voice was unnaturally calm. 'We are only making this trip for you. You cannot think I want my baby born in bloody America, but everyone has become so worried at your mental state that this seemed like the best course of action. Your father and I have been in communication for some time now and we are in agreement. So, yes it is true, we will not be seeing your family until after the birth, but it is not part of some conspiracy.'

'But I want to see them. It will make me so much happier.'

Henry rubbed a hand across his face and sat next to her on the bed. 'I wanted to avoid telling you this, but Dr Henderson is worried your pregnancy is weak. He thinks any form of overstimulation, including seeing your family after such a long time apart, could unbalance you to such a degree that you might lose the baby. He has been encouraged by hearing a healthy heartbeat, but we must be very careful about putting you under any undue strain or excitement.'

Henry's words were terrifying, but it was hard to tell if this was because she had put the baby at risk, or because it revealed something so dark about herself.

'Maybe I was wrong to take you on this crossing. I thought going home would calm you and I thought it would be nice for you to be near your family when the baby arrives. We are all worried about how you might take to motherhood as well, you see. But we do need to make sure everything stays as calm as possible for you until you give birth.'

Lily's brain felt full of jagged edges that pierced her thoughts. 'But what about Becky?'

'She is here for you. I thought you would be grateful.'

Lily turned her head to the light streaming in the porthole, but it was too sharp. The thought of being without Becky was torture, but that was the Becky she used to know, not the stranger who now occupied her body.

'Be honest with yourself, Lily. You have not been thinking straight for a long time. Everyone has been worried about your behaviour and delusions. The servants at home say you go out for hours, tramping across the fields in all weathers. You forget to reply to any invitation and take fright at the slightest thing; all our friends have noticed.' Henry sighed. 'Look, maybe I was mistaken not to tell you about these plans beforehand, but your father and I both agreed this is the best course.'

Lily was filled with an image of a whole world existing above her head, just out of earshot, forever denied to her. It reminded her of being locked into the nursery and she wanted to throw something because nothing was fair and it was hard to understand what was happening. Henry sounded so plausible, but she also had to trust in herself, or what was left. She screwed up the last of her courage. 'I know I heard you in Becky's room.'

He threw his hands in the air, but then he was walking to the door and she heard him call for Becky, telling her to fetch the doctor.

'I don't want any of his potions,' Lily said as he came back towards her. 'I don't like him. He smells and his nails are too long.'

'Shush now.' Henry's tone was sharp.

'Whatever happens, I will not let you take my baby.' And Becky, she wanted to add, or perhaps mainly Becky. But also all the faults Henry saw in her were true, so she wasn't surprised that Becky had abandoned her. She imagined watching Henry board a boat back to England with Becky and her baby and, even though she had no idea how he would manage it, she felt certain it was what he had planned. Becky waved to her from the deck and she knew it would kill her. 'I know you have never loved me, but I will try harder, I promise. I will try to be the wife you want, if you just let me return to Elsworth and keep the baby.'

He spun round then, his face puce. 'Do you know how unhinged you sound?' His fists were clenching and unclenching by his side and the air felt close and there was a moment when anything seemed possible, but then there was a knock on the door. Henry shouted, 'Come,' his eyes never leaving hers, even as Dr Henderson came into the room.

'What seems to be the problem here?' he asked, walking over to Lily, and she felt as if he was casting a shadow over her, that he chilled the actual air.

'Lady Elsworth is very distressed and ranting,' Henry said. 'I'm worried her hysteria will harm the baby.'

'Come now,' Dr Henderson said, 'lie back and we can check nothing untoward has happened.'

'No,' Lily cried, but the doctor was already pushing against her shoulders and then his hands were on her stomach, prodding and delving so she thought he might emerge on the other side of her and she flinched with the pain.

'Everything is as it should be, Lady Elsworth,' he said, straightening up. 'Really, you must stop worrying yourself in this way. Your husband is right, it is no good for the baby. You could do with some tea.'

Lily shook her head. She hated the brackish tea that Dr Henderson had her drinking every evening and couldn't bear the thought of it leaking into her days as well. 'No. Please, I am fine, really.'

'I have already sent Becky to make it,' the doctor said. 'It's very good for the nerves.'

His words made her cry, the problems she was facing

overwhelming. She saw Henry and Dr Henderson exchange a look that was hard to interpret.

'You're scaring me, Lil.' Henry advanced towards her, but she flinched as he approached, so he stopped, hovering by her bed.

'Please, Henry, stop this. I am the one who is scared.'

'But you have nothing to be scared about.'

'It is very common for women to become paranoid about their pregnancies,' Dr Henderson said. 'I've seen it many times, maybe not quite as severe as your reaction, but what you are feeling is not unheard of.'

'My fear is not about the pregnancy.' The words didn't sound entirely true, because she was scared of what was in her stomach, but it didn't feel like the most terrifying thing.

'I'm sure everything will be fine and he or she will emerge in good health.' Dr Henderson smiled, but it didn't suit his pointed face and she turned away from the sight.

Lily bit on her tongue to stop herself from speaking because she knew he would then fish around in his bag for a potion which would jumble her mind and pin her to the bed and she couldn't feel like that any more.

There was a knock at the door and then Becky was in the room, carrying the tea. Lily felt cold and nothing was making sense and the room was starting to fizz around her, so everything seemed too bright and her breath refused to push down into her.

'Here you are, Ma'am, sip it slowly,' Becky said, cupping her hand behind her head to raise it to the cup.

Lily stared up at Becky but she refused to meet her gaze and Henry was standing behind her, his arms crossed over his chest and his features scrunched tight.

Some of the tea spilled on to the white covers and mixed with her tears. The liquid felt like a living thing, rushing through her body, all through her veins, into her stomach, coating her baby.

Becky stroked her hair off her forehead and the tenderness of the movement made her lie back like a child. Her thoughts were beginning to run into each other and her limbs were thickening. She was so tired, so completely exhausted, the fight was leaching out of her.

Henry turned his back on her and she wanted nothing more than to sink into Becky's warm hand, to feel it travel across her whole body. She tried to remember what had been said, what she thought, why she felt so scared, but nothing came apart from the knowledge that there was no one to help her and she could not do this alone; she was lost.

LAWRENCE

It was strange, but Lawrence found himself looking out for Lily when he went into lunch. He hadn't expected the guilt to last, because of the weight of his grief, but she'd stayed with him over the course of the evening, now leaking into this next day as well. He was finding it impossible to rid himself of her pale face and pleading eyes, her hand worrying her throat and her body moving continually from foot to foot. Whatever the reason behind it, she was clearly deeply distressed, and he'd turned his back on her and refused to help, which ran contrary to all the ways Cissy had lived. And even through his anger, he knew that she'd been right and you had to help where you could, or what was the point? He'd woken in the night, enveloped by the sense that by helping Lily he would be helping Cissy by carrying on her work and, even though the light of day had burnt away much of this feeling, it still lingered uncomfortably.

He made his way towards a table that didn't seem too full. A young couple and single man were already sitting there, the couple arguing in a low, dispirited way while the man studied the menu. They all turned and smiled at him as he sat and the long rota of introductions began, which no one seemed that keen on.

'I'm not very hungry,' the woman, who had introduced herself as Hilda, said. 'I have never felt seasick before, but I feel very off balance on this trip, which is strange because it has been so calm.'

'I have felt the same,' the man on Lawrence's right replied. 'Almost like I am about to tip over. I think in fact we are listing slightly.'

Lawrence followed the man's gaze out of the porthole and it was true, the horizon did dip ever so slightly towards the stern.

The others exclaimed at almost the same time.

'Well, I'll be,' Hilda's husband said.

Hilda raised her hand to her mouth. 'Oh, I hope that is not a sign that something is wrong with the ship.'

'Oh no,' the man replied. 'I've noticed it before now and nothing has happened.'

Lawrence found he couldn't take his eyes from the sight of the tilt, as if the whole of nature were as unbalanced as he felt. He wondered if his grief was so powerful it had knocked everything off slightly, his misery permeating the atmosphere like a disease.

There was a steward walking past the table and Hilda's husband motioned him over. 'Have a look at this,' he said as the steward leant down to be of service. 'Look out there and tell me we're not listing to port?' The steward did as he'd been asked and Lawrence saw him recognise that what had been said was true in a slight movement in his face. 'How do you account for that, eh?'

The steward straightened. 'I expect you'll find the stokers are emptying coal from the starboard side first. That would certainly account for it.'

'But is it dangerous?' Hilda asked.

The steward laughed. 'Not at all, Madam.'

'And there are lifeboats in any case,' Hilda's husband said. Lawrence was struck by the tightness in his voice and felt nostalgic for a time when he'd feared death.

'They are simply a precaution,' the steward replied. 'I can assure you they will stay dry. You are on board the safest ship ever built.'

Everyone laughed, but the sound felt forced and Lawrence turned away from the false jollity of the conversation because the idea of safety was such illusory nonsense. We all end up as bones in the end and bones are uncaring and unforgiving.

He spotted Lily sitting about five tables away, next to her husband, wearing a glazed expression as she stared down at her plate, one of her hands fiddling with a brooch at her neck. Even from a distance, Lawrence could tell that Henry was speaking loudly, his movements those of a man happy to take up as much space as needed. Their table was full and he had everyone's attention, most people laughing along with his jokes. He looked, to all intents and purposes, a happy, jovial man, but Lawrence was more interested in Lily and how she shrank from him.

The woman opposite Lily addressed a remark to her, but Lily hardly lifted her head and her lips barely moved in response. Lawrence watched as Henry answered for her and then the slight shake of his head that he made to both the woman and the man sitting next to her, which made them turn away from Lily. She looked like a woman on the verge of collapse and it wasn't that he didn't pity her, more that he worried he couldn't even remember how to help any more.

'Have you ever considered how convenient it is that women are perceived as the weaker sex?' Cissy had asked him once when she'd come down with a cold after spending all night with a young girl caring for a sick baby on her own and he'd suggested that perhaps the fight was too big a strain on her. 'I know what you're implying,' she'd continued, two pink spots high on her cheeks, which he'd wanted to kiss. 'That I am only ill because my mind is strained by all I am hearing and experiencing.'

'And what is so wrong with me wanting you to look after yourself and not get sick?' he'd replied in a righteous huff.

Cissy had rolled her eyes. 'But you get ill sometimes and I do not immediately tell you that you're weak. I simply assume that you will get better.'

'My God, you can be so tricky. I was just trying to help.'

Cissy had looked at him out of the corner of her eye. 'The biggest help you can be is to get quicker.'

'Quicker?'

'In your thinking.' She'd sighed. 'Do you know what happens if you tell half the population that they're delicate and weak from the moment they're born? That they are destined only for small things? That this in fact is what will make them happy?' Lawrence could see the point she was making, but she was right that he needed to be quicker because her argument was going too fast. 'Imagine we one day have a daughter, Lawrence. In fact, imagine we only have daughters. Are you telling me you want only small, insignificant lives for them? That you will caution them against doing anything because they are delicate and precious? Will you warn them that the world is too dangerous for them to participate in? Or that their virtue is more important than their ambition? Will you be happy to see them denied the right to take a degree, or to vote? Perhaps there is no point in even educating them?'

'Oh, for goodness sake, you know I don't think like that,' he'd said, his voice slightly raised.

'So wake up then,' she'd replied. 'The world is designed for men and so women do find it harder to fit into. But that doesn't mean we are weak or delicate or wrong. It simply means we are different. I wonder how many women have been sent mad over the years just by being told they are mad, or by not being allowed to be themselves.'

Their food arrived, the plates clinking on to the table in front of them. Hilda said it looked delicious, but Lawrence found it hard to become excited by his baked haddock swimming in a lurid pink sauce. He cut a piece of the fish, aware of the fleshiness and that it had once been a living thing, that in fact they were, right now, surrounded by thousands of this species. He wished someone would hunt him down and boil his flesh, cut into him on a plate, chew him up and swallow him so he would be dissolved by stomach acid, so he was less than nothing, simply no more.

He looked back at Lily, who appeared to be having as much trouble with her food as he was, her fork barely making it from her plate to her mouth. And however much Cissy might hate the word, she did look delicate, like a piece of china, so you could imagine her breaking all too easily. He found himself willing her to eat something, because anyone could see she was in desperate need of sustenance, that her body was crying out for help. He remembered then how she'd said she was pregnant when she'd appealed to him, which made her need to eat even more pressing. It was hard to see the swell of her belly as she was sitting down, but her limbs were emaciated and he recalled something he'd read about how when starving women become pregnant every ounce of fat on their body goes to their babies, which strains their health.

'I am not ill!' Cissy had shouted at him when he'd tried to persuade her to rest more in pregnancy. But he'd seen the toll it took on her, which had made him worry, all through the nine months, that it would be impossible to love the creature inside her who demanded so much of her.

Henry leaned over Lily, cupping his arm around her shoulders, his face creased in a look of concern that certainly looked genuine. But Lily flinched as Henry said something to the others on the table and there was a general nodding of heads and a shifting and you could almost see the embarrassment rising from them like steam. The scene looked like a worried husband trying to comfort his neurotic wife, or trying to explain the situation to those around them, but something nagged at Lawrence, some feeling that refused to let him look away.

Lily swayed slightly as she stood and he worried that she might be about to faint, but she managed to turn as if to leave. Henry stood as well, but Lily pushed him back down with her hand, forcing herself to say something to the people on the table, so Henry sat back. Lawrence watched her bump into a couple of tables as she left, her distress coating her like a curse as her hands fluttered about as if she was desperately looking for something to hold on to.

Lawrence looked back at Henry and saw him deep in conversation with the couple opposite him, both of whom were nodding, their shoulders hunched forward. He looked so like he cared, except Lily did not look like someone who was loved, which was exactly what she'd said to him the day before. *Women always have a story*, Cissy said into his ear, *it is just that we're so rarely listened to.*

A strange sensation began to spread through his chest, like an expansion, a feeling he hadn't had for so long it was hard to define. It reminded him almost of excitement and, even though it felt so alien, it was also undeniably a feeling with a destination beyond the wish to die, not that he knew if that was a good or bad thing.

LILY

Lily made for the library again after she left the dining hall. It was still the last room she could imagine Henry coming to and so she presumed it would buy her a bit of time away from him. He'd tried to leave with her, once again playing the part of the concerned husband extremely well, but she'd managed to make him stay by pretending she wasn't really dying inside.

She took a random book off a shelf and made for a seat in the corner, from where she couldn't be seen from the window but could see the door, which might give her a modicum of advantage. She tried to sit back against the chair, but it was as though she was suspended, all her muscles tensed and wary, like a fox trapped by the hunt.

It was unbearable that she didn't have Becky when she needed her most of all, although more unbearable that Becky had fallen for Henry, whom she had always railed against. Lily tried to remember a moment, an argument, anything that might have caused this hostility, and a memory rose through her like a sickness, of finding Becky crying in her bedroom after her birthday the year before.

'What's wrong, what has happened?' she'd asked, but Becky had turned from her, wiping her eyes on her apron.

'Nothing,' she'd said, a huff in her voice.

'No, please tell me.'

'Oh, it was just Cook. She told me off for eating a slice of your birthday cake when it came back down from tea.'

Lily had opened her mouth to tell Becky that as she'd sat eating her cake with Henry she'd thought only of her, wished that it was they who were celebrating. But the words stuck somewhere in her gullet. 'That is ridiculous. You know you can eat my cake. I shall tell Cook not to be so absurd.'

'No, promise me you will not. It would cement my position with the servants, which is far from good as it is because they think you favour me.'

'But of course I favour you. We are always together, apart from anything else.'

'Of course,' Becky had repeated, her tone weary. 'It is just a matter of circumstances, after all.'

'Becky, please.' Lily had stepped forward but been scared to get too close. 'You must know you can have anything of mine that you want. You just have to ask.'

Becky had stilled at that. Lily could remember the atmosphere almost as if she was back there now, a sudden chill, a deadening of the air. 'And what if I don't want to have to ask?'

Lily raised her eyes at the sound of approaching footsteps and then it took her a minute to realign her reality and realise that Lawrence Beesley was standing in front of her and she was not really back at Elsworth.

'May I sit with you?' he asked as he reached her.

'Yes, if you like, Mr Beesley.' She felt herself blush as she thought she'd behaved badly the day before.

'Please, call me Lawrence.' He folded his body into the chair opposite, but didn't speak. Instead, he turned his hat around between his fingers. Lily looked at his profile, his bones all set like right angles in his face, which was thin and pale. 'Can I order you some tea and biscuits?' he asked, finally looking up.

She nearly laughed. 'You have come to offer me tea and biscuits?'

'I noticed you barely ate at lunch. I think you could do with some sustenance.'

'I find I cannot stomach anything at the moment.'

He ignored her and motioned for a waiter, which didn't surprise Lily because no one ever listened to what she wanted.

'How do you know I didn't eat? Were you watching me?'

'Yes.'

His directness was surprising. 'Why?'

'I do not entirely know.' His pale blue eyes were having trouble resting on her, but she held her counsel because he looked as though he had something else to say.

The waiter appeared with their tea, which he set on the table between them and Lawrence poured her a cup. She took a biscuit out of politeness but, as soon as she bit into it, realised that he'd been right and the sweetness was delicious, coating her mouth in sugar.

'You look like you could do with a few biscuits as well,' Lily said, as she ate. Lawrence's tea was untouched in his cup and he only seemed to notice it when she spoke. 'May I ask what you are doing sitting with me, Lawrence?'

He looked up and she could see real, glistening tears in his eyes. 'My wife died last year.'

'Oh, I am sorry.' Although she also felt a stab of jealousy that the death of a wife could produce that reaction in someone.

'I think she would have wanted me to help you.'

His words pulled her forwards in her seat. 'So, you believe me? About Henry wanting to take my baby?'

He was still for a moment. 'Not so much that. More that she

would have wanted me to help whatever the problem.' And Lily thought that was fair, because she didn't know exactly what she thought and her problem might easily spin and shift. 'I still do not believe I am the right person. Or at least, I mean, I do not think I am entirely capable of helping.'

'Then what are you doing here?'

She worried she might have offended him. But he barely seemed to have heard her. 'I suppose I am just trying.'

Talking to Lawrence was almost comforting, as he made as little sense as her thoughts, which softened her towards him. 'Tell me about your wife.'

He finally took a sip of tea. 'Oh, ours is not such an unusual story. We met and fell in love and became each other's worlds and then she died and left me heartbroken.'

'That sounds like a very unusual story to me.'

'In what way?'

'In every way.' Lily sighed, because even breathing felt painful. 'There has never been any love in my marriage and I do not think my husband would care too much if I died.' She spoke the words without considering them but, as she heard them, knew it was true and a fresh fear crept up through her from the floor.

He screwed his face up as if what she'd said was ridiculous. 'I feel like yours is the unusual story.'

'What was your wife's name?'

'Cissy.' He said the word as if it was precious.

'And why would Cissy want you to help me?'

He smiled then. 'Because she believed in helping people. Especially women. She was very involved in the women's suffrage movement.'

'Oh, yes, I have heard talk of that.' Snippets of information had reached Lily at Elsworth, although Henry had said that the women who chained themselves to railings should be left to rot. Sometimes it was discussed at the few dinners she still attended, but everyone made fun of the women. She'd heard stories of their beards and that they wore trousers every day, that they wanted all men dead, that they only wanted to lie with each other. She realised that she'd never considered the veracity of these stories, and yet, what had she considered?

'She would have been very annoyed at me letting you run off like that yesterday.'

'But, if you think that, then what do you mean by saying you cannot help me?' Lily felt a fizzing at the thought of how close salvation might be, almost as if she could see New York from the deck and May waiting there for her.

Lawrence shut his eyes for a moment and she saw in his still face the depths of his misery, as though it existed within him. But then he opened them again and looked straight at her. 'I cannot promise anything. But when I saw you leave the dining room earlier, I knew I had to at least speak to you again or Cissy would never forgive me.'

She wondered momentarily if he was unhinged, because surely a dead person could not offer forgiveness anyway. 'Speaking to me will not achieve much, I'm afraid.' Although she wasn't entirely sure what would achieve anything.

He sat forward, as if he was trying to concentrate. 'You said that your husband plans to take your baby from you.'

It sounded ridiculous in someone else's mouth and she put her hand to her head as if she could steady her thoughts. 'Everything is very confused,' she admitted, because there seemed little point in not being truthful. 'I have been unhappy in my marriage since it happened, which was nine years ago.'

'Unhappy how?' Lawrence looked like he cared, which loosened something in Lily's chest and allowed her thoughts to momentarily rest more calmly in her head.

'Henry has been a terrible husband.' She was flooded suddenly by a montage of awful images: Henry's raised hand, his face leering over her, spilt bottles of claret, women giggling in other rooms. It felt suddenly incredible that she'd let herself live this way, that she hadn't considered other possibilities. 'Oh, I feel so silly admitting this to you, a stranger, when I have never even told my own sister the truth. But Henry has never loved me, he has only ever been interested in my money, which I only worked out after we were married. He came to America with the express intention of ensnaring a rich heiress and my mother was desperate for a British title, so, you see, I never stood a chance.'

'I am sorry.' Lawrence dipped his eyes, as if her plight was embarrassing, which it probably was.

Her face felt hot and her throat was clogged, but it also felt strangely exhilarating to speak the words and she knew she was going to continue. 'At first, our problems were quite commonplace, mainly other women and spending all the money my father gave us on restoring his family estate and endless partying and gambling. But things got steadily worse as I failed to fall pregnant, because he is desperate for an heir. He is an only child, you see, and cannot stand the thought of Elsworth being left to a distant cousin, who is his nearest relative. It has made him very angry and he has spent a long time raging against my defectiveness, as he calls it. The last few years have been very dark.' Lily pulled in a breath as she worried she might cry. 'But then I finally managed to get pregnant five months ago and I thought things would improve. And they have in some ways, he is much less physically violent, but in many ways they are worse, so now I do not trust anything I think or do.' Lily paused, checking to see that she hadn't lost Lawrence, but he nodded her on. 'I think once this baby is born, he will have no more need for me.'

Lawrence ran a hand down his face. 'I am sorry your marriage has been so hard. But I still don't understand why you think he wants to take your baby? Or even how he would achieve this?'

Lily folded her hands into her lap as a reminder to herself to keep calm. 'I think he has fallen in love with my maid, Becky. Which I know sounds silly, but if you knew Becky, you would understand. And, I think I told you yesterday, I found a letter from my father in our cabin. I thought we were going to my parents' house when we dock and that I would give birth there, but this letter made it clear that my father has rented us a remote house, in which it will just be me, Henry, Dr Henderson and Becky until after the baby is born. Henry says this is because Dr Henderson thinks the shock of seeing my parents might be dangerous for the baby, but I do not see how that can be true.'

'Who is Dr Henderson?'

'My physician. He has been treating me for about a year now. He is the one who helped me get pregnant and he is the only person involved in my care.'

Lawrence raised an eyebrow. 'You have seen no other doctor?'

'Not since Henry hired Dr Henderson. And I do not like him.' Lily stopped herself from saying that he smelt sour or seemed unclean, because she knew how that would sound.

'And how did he help you to get pregnant?' Lawrence's voice was heavy with scepticism.

'He has been giving me potions and teas for about a year now and they must have worked, I suppose.' Lily put her hands on her belly as she spoke, the raised fabric a comfort.

Lawrence nodded. 'When are you due?'

'Dr Henderson says around mid-July.'

'And how are you feeling?'

'Most of the time sick and very tired, exhausted really.'

'Cissy felt sick often in her pregnancy, but you must eat as much as you can. We found little and often was good. She carried water biscuits with her and would nibble on them all day.' He smiled at the memory, but then remembered himself.

'I didn't realise you had a child.' Lily tried to imagine this stern man with a baby.

He nodded curtly. 'Yes, a son. He is six.' She wanted to ask more, but he continued speaking. 'You said your husband is in love with your maid. What makes you think this?'

'It is only something I have thought very recently, and is mainly just a feeling.' She saw the contraction on Lawrence's face and hurried on. 'But Becky and I have always been extremely close and over the last six months or so she has drifted from me almost entirely, so now she barely looks at me. I have been unable to work out why, but a couple of mornings ago I heard her and Henry together in her cabin.'

'What were they saying?'

Lily felt herself blush. 'No, I do not mean I heard them speaking. More, well, it was sounds, and I heard Henry laugh.'

'Oh.' Lawrence bobbed his head. 'But you have no actual proof?'

'And Henry denies it.' Lily felt deflated then, because everything she was saying sounded so flimsy.

'You know, even if they are having an affair,' Lawrence began, stumbling a little over his words, 'it does not mean that Henry intends to leave you. Men like him rarely marry maids. I think it more likely a phase that will pass.'

'Oh, but Becky is wonderful, lovable. And also very clever and wise, even though she is not educated. Once you know Becky you want all of her.'

'She sounds very dear to you.'

Sharp tears prickled into Lily's eyes as she realised the veracity of all she had said. 'She is. She has been my only friend the whole time I have lived in England. I was her first job, straight from her mother's kitchen, so we arrived at Elsworth at nearly the same time and she was as scared as I was. We helped each other learn and she became the only person I could talk to.' Her throat hurt with the effort of holding back her tears. 'Losing Becky is the worst part of this whole thing. Worse, I think, than if Henry does take my baby.' She looked up then, scared she'd gone too far, but Lawrence's eyes were filled with kindness. 'Did Cissy love your son before she gave birth?'

He nodded. 'She said she did, yes.'

'I'm not sure I feel anything.' Lily was shocked that she was speaking such words, but something about the fact that Lawrence was a virtual stranger made the confession seem safe. And as she spoke, she also realised that if she kept these things she had only just begun to admit to herself inside for much longer they would surely poison her. 'Sometimes it just feels like a void inside me. I cannot get any sense of the baby, I have no idea if it's a boy or girl. I don't daydream about names or nurseries, and I cannot imagine myself pushing a pram or singing nursery rhymes. The real truth is, I do not know if my life will be ruined if Henry takes it away or if it will be ruined if he lets me keep it.'

Lily expected Lawrence to walk away from her, but he didn't move.

'I felt a bit like that when Cissy was pregnant.' He hesitated and Lily found herself holding her breath because his words felt like standing under cool water. 'The pregnancy weakened her terribly, you see, and I could not help but blame the baby. The larger Cissy became, the weaker it made her and I started to see the baby like a parasite, almost as if it were eating her alive. I even felt jealous of it sometimes, as if I couldn't bear to share her love with anyone.' He had blushed a deep scarlet as he spoke, but his words gave her courage.

'I feel like I am just a host sometimes,' Lily whispered, amazed that it was possible to articulate these feelings which she hadn't even fully recognised until she'd started speaking. 'I don't know how you are meant to love something which makes you so subjected.' She glanced around the room, terrified that someone might overhear her treason. 'I am scared that I'm very unnatural, that I have no womanly instincts, which makes me frightened that everything will go wrong, that I do not deserve this baby and Henry will be right to take it away. Except that also feels awful. It feels like a nightmare, as though whichever way I turn I will be trapped.'

Lawrence sat forward slightly. 'I have no doubt that you've endured some terrible times for far too long. And pregnancy is a frightening time for many women. Fear can distort the truth in even the strongest minds.'

Lily shook her head, swallowing down a desire to scream because she could feel the panic rising. 'No, please do not say that. Henry says things like that to me all the time, as if everything that goes wrong is a defect in my thinking. But I know something is going on that I'm not party to and I'm scared. I might not know what I feel about the baby, or even myself, but it doesn't mean I want all the decisions taken from me.'

'But you do not know for certain that *anything* is going on. I'm not sure why Elsworth would be taking you to America to steal your baby, where you are surrounded by family. Would it not be easier in England?'

She shook her head to show him the force of the negative. 'No, no. He has to keep my father on side or he will lose my money and he simply could not let that happen. By taking me home to have the baby, he has made my father feel indebted to him, and made himself look like he is a caring husband. I don't know how he plans to achieve it, but I feel sure that Henry wants to leave me in America and start a new life with Becky, my baby and my money.' Lawrence had sat back in his chair as she spoke, which made her feel like he was retreating from her, so she continued. 'Nothing about this trip feels right. For example, it is very strange that we are travelling second class. Henry is a man who likes the best of everything and has never scrimped in his life. He says it's too expensive for all four of us to go in first, but I know that not to be true. My father gives us plenty of money every year and Henry has never baulked at asking him for more if needed.'

'I don't see how any of that proves that your husband wants to take your baby, though?' Lawrence said, his face creased with confusion.

It felt as though a bird was trapped in her chest. 'Oh, I am not explaining myself very well. I just know it feels wrong, everything feels wrong. These last few months have been so terrible, I have not felt alive half the time, as if I am seeing life from behind a veil or something. And now that Becky has retreated from me, the future feels completely terrifying without her.'

Lawrence nodded. 'I know that feeling.'

'I feel confused all the time and so tired. So tired and weak, I think I must be ill.' It was hard to explain how often she felt as if she were operating within a dream.

Lawrence pinched the bridge of his nose, as if he had a headache. 'But if you say you often feel confused, how do you know all you say to be true?'

The question was fair and it floored Lily because he was right. Her life felt like being trapped in a deep maze, high hedges on either sides, and she wasn't sure she had the words or the strength to find her way out. 'I cannot offer you any proof,

Lawrence. I can only tell you what I think, what I feel.' She looked over at him, but his eyes were trained on the floor and it made her feel as if something were stretching inside her, like her organs were splitting.

'I don't even know what you are asking of me,' he said finally and it made her want to cry, because nor did she. She supposed she wanted someone to swoop in and save her, to carry her out of her life, to tell her that everything was normal, that her mind was sound, that she would love her baby.

'Please think of Cissy and help me for her.' It was a desperate last throw of the dice and she saw the shock register on Lawrence's face.

'You must excuse me,' he said, getting up. 'I need to be alone and think about everything you have told me.'

'After we dock, I do not think anyone will be able to get near enough to help me. I do not have much time.' She tried to keep a whine out of her voice, but desperation swirled through her at the thought he might not appreciate the gravity of her situation.

But he shook his head brusquely. 'Nor do I, which is part of the problem.'

Lily couldn't understand what he meant, but he didn't give her time to ask another question, because he put his hat back on his head and turned and walked out of the library. She fancied for a moment that he left bloody footprints in his wake and she wanted to shout after him that her destruction would be on his conscience, but she had the sense he wouldn't care. Her life felt like grains of sand falling through a timer, as if they were dripping down her spine and rubbing against her bones.

LAWRENCE

Lawrence walked back the way he'd come without a real plan, not even really knowing what he was doing. He'd simply felt compelled to follow Lily when he'd seen her stumbling towards the exit from the dining room, almost as if Cissy had hooked her hands under his armpits and forced him to stand. He wondered if that was the compulsion Cissy had felt over the years and found the thought dampened slightly the intense fire of his anger, because it didn't feel like something you could ignore.

There was no doubt that Lily was a deeply distressed woman and he was sure Elsworth was the cause of that distress. He'd heard enough stories over the years about broke British aristocrats who went over to America to marry rich heiresses, desperate for a title. The women in these stories were usually painted as avaricious and the general consensus seemed to be that if they were treated badly they'd got what they deserved, but it didn't surprise Lawrence to hear that their husbands were capable of cruelty.

He stopped his walking and sat on a deckchair. The air was crisp, but the sun shone in a clear blue sky and the horizon stretched far away from him. There was a lump in his chest where his heart had once lain quietly and it twisted now against the idea that he too might have been cruel to his wife. Not that he would ever have done anything intentionally to hurt Cissy, but he wondered if he had been as supportive as he could have been, or as quick as she needed. It was clear that Lily was fighting against the things that were required of women by men like Henry Elsworth, which was what Cissy had been doing as well, the difference being that she had known she was doing that. Lawrence might not have told his wife she was mad for wanting something different, but he also hadn't made her feel as if she was entirely right. And, of course, a pregnancy in Lily's circumstances would feel terrifying because it trapped her even deeper in a life that must often feel horrific and relentless.

A gull screeched above him, transporting him to a cold passageway and a closed door, behind which he'd heard his own baby shout for the first time. He'd thrown open the door to see Cissy in a bed streaked with blood, as a wrapped baby was handed to her. A slithering fear had taken hold of his guts as he'd watched his wife, so ravaged she looked like she'd been in a fight, that he'd wanted to grab the baby from her and hurl it against the wall.

But then she'd looked up at him, her eyes sunk in dark pits. 'I just feel too lucky,' she'd said, her voice so weak he'd immediately crossed the room to her. 'One person should not have as much luck as this.'

'That is silly,' he'd replied, as the fear threatened to push up out of his mouth.

'But he is perfect,' she'd said, staring at their baby. 'And he is ours. He is like a perfect, living embodiment of our love.'

Lawrence leant back against the canvas of the deckchair and closed his eyes, turning his face towards the sun, but it refused to burn away his misery. He was a terrible, cowardly man who was abandoning his son and the last promise he had made to his wife, so what could be so bad about abandoning another woman as well? He had nothing left to give and no more strength, other than what it would take to haul his tired, worthless body over the side.

'Lawrence,' Cissy shouted over Alec's screams, 'Lawrence, can you help?'

He snapped open his eyes, because if he was quick, surely he would catch a glimpse of her through their bedroom door, as he raced the stairs, his legs heavy from fatigue. But the deck was empty and the sea still rolled relentlessly all around.

'Oh God,' he sighed out loud, raking his hands through his hair as he sat forward over his aching stomach. 'How were you not scared?' But his brain refused to let him walk away from his wife's bedside because it was suddenly so obvious. Love had never frightened Cissy, but it terrified him, in the same way it clearly terrified Lily.

He stood because something more than nothing was required of him. Even if it was his last act, he knew he couldn't get away with passivity, not while Cissy was watching. He had to prove to her that he wasn't really a coward, that he had learnt at least a few of her lessons, that he had, after all, been worthy of her love.

The saloon was smoky and filled with the loud noise of contented chatter and laughter, reaching up into its alcoves and mouldings. Groups of people were enjoying after-lunch coffees or brandies and the atmosphere was close and convivial. There was a large group towards the back of the room and when Lawrence got closer, he saw Henry Elsworth behind them, deep in conversation with a wiry-looking man with a highly waxed moustache. They were leaning close together and their conversation seemed intense and involved, so it was hard to look at them and not feel the sense of collusion and furtiveness which surrounded them, which made him wonder if this could be the doctor Lily had told him about. The same strange expansion that

Lawrence had felt at lunch began again in his chest, knocking into him and pushing him forwards.

He went to the charts to buy some time and made a play of checking the new information that had been put up since he'd last looked, absent-mindedly reading that they'd run 386 miles from noon on Thursday to noon on Friday, but he didn't know if this meant they were going slow or fast. On board, it was impossible to judge and in fact the movement he felt was simply that of being on a ship, not of any forward propulsion.

Elsworth and the man stood, giving each other quick nods before walking in opposite directions. Elsworth looked as if he was going to stay in the saloon, but the man was making for the door and Lawrence couldn't decide what his next move should be. But Elsworth was immediately absorbed into the large group, which meant any conversation with him would prove difficult, so Lawrence followed the man out of the saloon doors and up the stairs towards the boat deck.

The man stopped as soon as he got outside, where he lit a cigarette, before walking towards the railings, leaning on his elbows and looking out over the sea. Lawrence's plan only really formed as he approached the man, who straightened as he stopped next to him. 'I am very sorry to ask, but I have left my cigarettes in my cabin. I wondered if I could cadge one from you?'

'Certainly.' He reached into his inside pocket and offered Lawrence the packet. 'Annoying when you leave something behind, isn't it. All those steps.'

Lawrence cupped his hand around the cigarette as the man lit it and the nicotine rushed straight into his blood. 'I'm in D56 actually, so not too far to climb. Where are you?'

'Not so lucky, F43, so I have five flights to get on deck. And the damned lift is always busy.' His accent was overlaid with a slight roll that was hard to place.

Lawrence looked back over the sea. 'We have been very lucky with the weather.'

'We have. I was in the Navy and you would not believe some of the seas I've sailed on.'

Up close, the man's face was as weathered as you might expect from someone who'd spent years at sea. His eyes were also sunken in purple circles and his hair and moustache were too harshly waxed, so they looked almost false. 'You're not in the Navy any more, I take it?'

'No. Left about five years ago.'

'And what do you do now?'

He flicked his cigarette over the side. 'I'm a doctor.'

Lawrence's heart thumped against his ribs, but he kept his voice casual. 'That's quite a career change.'

The man laughed. 'Isn't it just? Funny what life throws at you. So, what's your story? Where are you headed on this fine ship?'

'Visiting my brother who lives in New York. And why are you travelling to America?' He tried to keep his voice casual; it was hard to tell if the conversation felt normal or not.

But the man didn't flinch. 'It's a strange story actually. I am in the employ of a man whose wife is pregnant but extremely delicate. She's an American and he's taking her back home because he hopes it will restore her somehow.'

'How fascinating.' Lawrence flicked his own cigarette and hoped the man hadn't noticed he'd barely smoked it. 'What's wrong with her?'

'She suffers from terrible delusions and paranoias. Women's minds are much less developed than ours so they find change almost impossible to process.'

Lawrence ignored the huff Cissy made in his ear. 'Have you been treating her for a long time?'

'About a year. He initially hired me because she was finding it impossible to get pregnant. It turned out there wasn't anything physically wrong with her, more a mental blockage, which I helped to soothe.'

'How sad.'

The man lowered his voice and leant in slightly. 'You're right, it is a sad story. She was apparently a great beauty when they married. You can still see traces of it in her now, although she has let herself go terribly, so she mainly resembles a ghost.'

Lawrence nodded, now just wanting to be able to go back to his cabin because he realised that he'd held out a small hope that Lily's story was real and he would be able to do something that might make Cissy proud. But it seemed unlikely there was anything tangible he could do to help a hysterical woman in the time he had left to him. Which would mean that Lily would just be another failure he left behind and that thought wearied him.

'They don't call women the weaker sex for nothing.' The man pursed his lips as he spoke. 'Can't imagine why any man goes to the bother of getting married. You're not, I take it?'

Lawrence forced his face into a rictus grin as Cissy changed her huff to a scream. 'No.'

The man laughed and clapped his hand on Lawrence's back. 'How wise of you.' He seemed puffed out by the success of his story. 'I'll tell you the strangest part. She's one of those American heiresses, you know, who are desperate to marry into the British aristocracy. My client's an earl, I'll have you know.' He bobbed his head in a strange gesture. 'They are rich as Croesus, but he's insisted on travelling second class because he doesn't want her to embarrass herself in front of all their friends in first. What a gent, eh?'

The last piece of Lily's jigsaw broke apart. 'Indeed. What an amazing tale. It makes you wonder at what other stories there are on board.'

The man sucked air against his teeth. 'Oh, wherever there's people, there's stories.' He pulled himself more upright. 'Now, if you will excuse me, I have some work to do in my cabin. It was a pleasure to meet you, Mr . . . ?'

'Mr Beesley, Lawrence Beesley.' Lawrence extended his hand, which the man shook. 'And what is your name?'

'George Henderson.' He touched the rim of his cap and then walked off, towards the door which led to the staircase.

The air was cold, so Lawrence made for the stairs as well, where he could hear the rush of feet and slamming doors, the ship filled with people with desires and destinations. He felt overcome by such exhaustion that the richly carpeted hall felt like mud beneath his feet and all the electric lights along the corridor were too bright, filling his eyes so nothing seemed real.

He removed his coat and shoes as soon as he reached his cabin, lying heavily on his bunk, with an arm draped over his eyes.

But sleep eluded him and Lily refused to leave his mind, taunting him with her misery. He wondered if Cissy had felt that way when she'd lain beside him at night, knowing that there were women suffering all around them, and he hated himself for not ever asking her about them, or trying to comfort her.

His watch told him it was just after three, which meant he only had about six or seven hours to wait until it would be completely dark. Maybe he didn't need to wait for the ice. Maybe he could jump whilst everyone was inside eating dinner, a thought which failed to excite much emotion in him.

He shut his eyes and pressed his fingers against his lids so little bubbles of colour exploded around him. Life was just hard and ghastly for so many people and you couldn't help everyone. *You can try*, Cissy said in his ear, but he rolled on to his side, pulling a pillow over his head, wrapping himself into the blank nothingness, cocooning his senses, obliterating feeling.

LILY

After Lawrence left the library, Lily found she couldn't stay sitting still. It felt as if she'd had a lifetime of sitting still, like she'd become a tiny, atrophied ornament placed inside a glass case. She saw large faces looming towards her, their breath fogging her view as they spoke in loud voices about her value, her rarity, her beauty. But ultimately they turned away from her, their voices fading, their large bodies casting shadows, their observations useless.

Her stomach contracted and she wondered if the baby was turning, but then she felt a deep dragging just under her pelvis, which sent a hot bolt of fear through her. It was a feeling that she'd only ever experienced at a specific time, once a month, for most of her adult life. Naturally, that had stopped since she'd become pregnant, although she'd had a bit of spotting at the beginning, as Dr Henderson called it, dark red marks on her undergarments, but not this feeling. The dragging worked its way around, pinching the small of her back and the tops of her thighs, which made her body break out in a sweat that smelt old even as it began.

She thought she might swoon as she stood, but steadied herself and managed to leave the library. The ground tilted as she walked, but her fear propelled her forward towards the only person she could think of to help her. She had to stop twice on her way to Becky's cabin, her heart too erratic to allow deep breathing, and then she found she couldn't remember exactly where her cabin even was. All the corridors looked the same and the numbers on the doors blurred so she couldn't be sure if she knew how to count any more. She had to shut her eyes and focus with her whole brain and then reason came to her in little bursts, so eventually she knew where she was headed.

When Becky opened the door, she seemed distracted, her hair loose and her cheeks rosy and Lily wondered if she'd been asleep. But her eyes widened at the sight of Lily. 'Are you all right? You look awfully pale.'

'I need your help.' Lily found her voice was shaking.

'Shall I come to your cabin?' Becky was already inching out of the door, but Lily stopped her, stepping forward.

'No, let me in.' The inside of Becky's cabin was almost identical to Lily's, although there was a tang in the air, like a sourness. She took off her hat to release the pressure cutting into her forehead and laid it on the washstand.

'Would you like me to make you some tea, Ma'am?'

She wanted to tell Becky not to call her Ma'am again, but the world bent and contracted, taking her away from the cabin as it seemed so intent on doing, and depositing her beside the lake at Elsworth, a warm sun on her face and a feeling of contentment swirling through her blood. They were lying on the bank, obscured from view by the tall trees which grew around the water, and she could feel little grains of sand under her fingernails and in her scalp.

'We should get back,' Becky said, propping herself on her elbows. 'Lord and Lady March are coming for dinner and I need to get you ready.'

Lily had groaned. 'Oh God, five more minutes.'

But Becky had stood, leaning down and pulling Lily upwards by the hands. Her limbs had felt fluid and languid and she'd resisted, so Becky had tripped. 'Stop it, Lily,' she'd said sharply. 'You might not care, but I will get in trouble if your hair is out of place, or your dress creased.'

'I'm sorry.' She'd stood quickly then and, as she did, her handkerchief had fallen from her sleeve, fluttering to the ground in delicate waves.

Becky had bent to pick it up with a flourish, handing it back to her with a bow, like a gentleman might make to present a bouquet to his lover. It had made Lily laugh as she'd turned to walk back towards the house.

'Come on then, we had better get me ready.'

'No thank you then, Ma'am?' Becky had said from behind, her tone as sharp as arrows, the word Ma'am as heavy as a stone.

Lily focused properly on the woman in front of her and thought that Becky's physicality had altered almost as much as her personality in the last few months. It was as if, as her nature had hardened, so her body had softened, the clean, muscular lines fattening and rounding, so she had somehow turned into a buxom, full woman who Lily barely recognised.

'Did you hear me? Would you like some tea?' Becky repeated.

'No. No, thank you.'

'Do you need to sit?'

'No, it's just...' Lily felt her betraying tears poking at her eyes again. 'I have a pain in my stomach. You know, that feeling when, well, when your monthly comes.'

Becky stepped forward, her eyes heavy with a concern Lily had missed. 'I think you should sit, come on.' Her hand around

Lily's arm was gentle and it made Lily desperate to pull her towards her so she could be enveloped by the whole of her.

On cold nights when the wind whipped through Elsworth and she was sure ghosts were walking the corridors, Lily would sometimes call for Becky to climb into bed with her and her arms had always felt like a place of safety. Although she had woken on those mornings with Becky long gone to start fires or find clothes and the world would seem terrifying again, just as it did every single minute of every day now.

'Let me help you remove your undergarments,' Becky said, reaching up under Lily's skirt without waiting to be asked. She felt her push up past her skirt and petticoat, then pulling on the lace at the edge of her undershorts. She raised her hips to help Becky and their eyes met briefly.

Becky held the shorts up and Lily could see the white lace spotted with little specks of what looked like rust circles, some as big as a penny. Her heart felt like someone was beating it. 'Oh God, Becky,' she whispered.

They looked at each other properly then and she saw the fear vibrating in Becky's eyes, the calculations whirling through her brain. But she also saw a tenderness that she'd missed so much and knew she would trade the baby for that love, which seemed like a dangerous thought to have at that moment and meant she was no doubt getting everything she deserved.

'I'll fetch Dr Henderson,' Becky said, dropping the underwear on the bed before rushing out of the cabin.

Lily lay back against the headboard. It felt now as if blood was gushing from her, that soon the whole counterpane might be stained and soiled, although she also knew that she often used to feel that way when she was wearing a white dress or attending a tea or anything where the shame of blood would be too much. Her mother had told her that the blood and pain was a punishment for Eve's transgression and she'd always hated the way it felt like her body was betraying her every month. But what was happening now felt too much, like her body had created a drama she didn't want to be part of but was completely trapped within.

She looked around Becky's cabin to distract herself, letting her eyes rest on the woman's few possessions, as if they might act as a talisman. The sight of her hairbrush, still trailing strands of dark hair, tugged at Lily's heart, and the photo she always carried of her mother, propped up behind it. Her own blue hat was sitting right by them, casually, so Lily allowed herself a moment's fantasy that she and Becky lived easily together, that everything about them mingled happily.

A bolt of sunlight shone dramatically into the room, illuminating a spark of gold just under the rim of her hat, revealing what looked like the rounded edges and small chains which made up a set of cufflinks. She sat upright and swung her legs off the bed, the movement jarring against the increasing pain in her stomach. But she forced herself to stand and shuffled to the washstand, like a magpie entranced by shiny objects.

They were indeed a pair of cufflinks, large golden ovals inlaid with two ornate black initials, H.E., and she didn't need to have seen them on Henry's wrists hundreds of times before, to know they belonged to him. The world shrank around her and all she could do was stumble back to Becky's bed, sitting probably on the sheets which had contained her husband.

She hoped then that she would leak all over the bed, that they'd come in to find her submerged in a pool of clotted blood. She wanted the baby gone, so she wouldn't have to look into its face and see her husband, so she wouldn't have to suffer the pain of its removal. Love was too dangerous, it took too much out of you, it was never steady and she couldn't bear to invest that much in something that might never really be hers.

The door opened and Dr Henderson strode into the room, followed by Becky, who was red-faced and panting. He went straight to her underwear, picking them off the bed and turning them inside out, holding them to the light so they could all see the blood and faint yellow lines criss-crossing the fabric. Lily had to repress an urge to snatch them from him, to scream at them to leave her alone, to let her be. She felt like a piece of meat, or a cadaver, spread and splayed on a block, all her workings on display for anyone who wanted to look.

'Lie back,' Dr Henderson said. 'I need to examine you.'

Lily did as she was told, but her whole body tensed against what she knew was coming. She pulled her legs up towards her chest and focused on a spot on the ceiling, a tiny circle of dirt that someone would probably get in trouble for not removing.

Dr Henderson snapped on some gloves and then his fingers pressed into her, pushing upwards further and further, leaving no part of her free of him. His eyes were on her face, but she refused to return his gaze. She gasped as he withdrew, catching Becky's eye over his shoulder, surprised by her expression of horror.

Two fingers of the glove were smeared in a pale, thin blood, but he pulled them quickly off his hands. 'The pregnancy is still intact. And, in fact, the bleeding is very slight. It is not an unusual occurrence, but you must rest with your legs raised until it stops.'

'It hurts,' Lily said, barely able to meet his stare. 'The way it used to with my monthlies.'

'I can give you something for that.' He turned to Becky. 'Fetch a glass of water.'

Becky left the room and the atmosphere seemed to close

around them, so Lily struggled to sit up. Dr Henderson licked his lips and smiled at her and she wondered if she screamed whether anyone would hear. But Becky was back quickly and then he got a bottle from his bag and squeezed a few drops into the water, before handing it over to her.

'All of it please,' he said, so she drank it down because there was never any other choice. She recognised the taste, herby and bitter, with a hint of lemon. He turned to Becky. 'Lady Elsworth must not move so she should remain here. I don't expect there to be much more blood, but it would be wise for her to lie completely still for a few hours. I'll go and find Lord Elsworth.'

Becky nodded, watching the doctor as he shut up his case and left the room. She closed the door behind him but didn't turn around, as if she were too tired to move. 'Has he done that to you before?' she asked in a shaky whisper.

'Do you mean examined me?'

'Yes.'

Lily was glad that they weren't looking at each other because she thought that would have made her cry. 'Many times.' Something like fear gripped her throat and she could have sworn she felt a heartbeat in the atmosphere. Becky was breathing heavily, her shoulders rising and falling and it felt like something had shifted and a small channel had opened between them, so she dared to ask, 'Why are you doing this, Becky?'

Becky turned, but her eyes were shut and she leant her head back against the door. 'You are asking me why?'

'Yes, I am.'

But when she opened her eyes, they were hard again. 'I don't know what it is you think I am doing?'

Lily let out a little cry. 'Oh, please do not make me say it. We both know what I'm talking about.'

'I'm afraid I don't, Ma'am.'

Lily banged her fist against the bed. 'I forbid you to call me, Ma'am, or Miss, or Madam.' Their eyes locked. 'I thought we were friends.'

'You certainly always treated me with kindness.'

She wanted to scream. 'I'm sorry, Becky, truly sorry if I have done something to upset you.'

Becky stood very still; she was a couple of inches taller than Lily and twice her width, which made Lily feel insubstantial. 'Like I said, you have always been a good employer. Dr Henderson said you should rest now.'

She had almost forgotten about the baby, which could be leaking out of her, which she wasn't even sure she wanted to retain, which certainly didn't seem as important as getting Becky to speak to her properly, which meant she must be some sort of unnatural witch. 'Henry's cufflinks are on your washstand.'

'What are you talking about?' Becky's tone was so sharp, it cut into Lily, but she moved quickly, holding them up. 'Did you put these there?'

The question was so strange that Lily couldn't answer for a second. 'Of course not. I heard you the other morning when he was in here with you. And it all makes sense, now, how you have withdrawn from me, and I have seen the way you look at him.'

'Please,' Becky said. 'Do not say such things.'

'I just cannot understand why you have chosen him, of all people. And I am truly sorry if I have hurt you in some way. I want to make it up to you. Please, can we start again?'

Becky's hand went to her mouth and Lily saw it was shaking. 'Please God, I beg you not to say things that you cannot, or will not, make happen.'

Lily felt as if she was slipping down a hole. 'But, Becky, you cannot really want to be with Henry. I mean, you know what sort of man he is.'

The door to the cabin opened and Henry walked in, so they all froze momentarily, their eyes flicking between each other. 'What in God's name is going on here?' he asked. 'I can hear you in the corridor.'

Becky stepped towards him, her tears finally falling. 'I'm scared,' she said, looking only at Henry.

'Please do not deny it,' Lily implored, looking between Henry and Becky as she spoke. 'Your cufflinks are on the washstand.'

'My apologies, Becky,' Henry said. 'Perhaps you could leave me alone with my wife.'

Becky nodded, rushing out of the cabin so quickly the door slammed behind her.

Henry turned his attention back to her. 'This has got to stop. Dr Henderson told me you have had a small bleed. You have to calm down for the sake of the baby, if nothing else.'

But her anger made her continue. 'What are your cufflinks doing on Becky's washstand?'

Henry strode across the room to the washstand. 'There's nothing here. But even if they were, my trunk is in here, in case you have forgotten.'

'You still would not leave your cufflinks casually on the washstand. And they were there, just a minute ago. By my hat.'

'Your hat is not here either,' he said and, when she looked, she saw it too had gone.

'Becky must have taken them,' she whimpered.

'Lie down,' he shouted, coming right over to the bed. He towered over her, the rage dancing in his eyes as he pointed a finger into her face. 'You were advertised as false goods by your social-climbing nightmare of a mother. You are totally unstable.

My God.' He shut his eyes and Lily watched him pull his anger back inside, waiting out the minutes until he was calm enough to look at her again. 'Dr Henderson has said you need to sleep, so that is what you are going to do. And when you wake, you will stop with all this nonsense about me and Becky. A common maid, for God's sake.'

He turned and stormed out of the room and she heard the clunk of the key in the lock. She stood and hobbled to the door, but, sure enough, it was bolted. A gnawing panic began to take hold of her, wobbling her muscles and distorting her vision. The walls appeared to be swaying in and out, almost as if the cabin were alive and wanted to eat her whole. It was far from the first room she'd been locked in; her mother had turned the key against her and May so many times when they were children, but it didn't mean it got any easier, didn't mean it stopped feeling as nightmarish as it did now.

She folded down towards the floor, her body simply giving up, until she was lying with her face against the soft carpet, her tears running into the fibres. Someone had made the carpet, someone had taken love and care over it. She thought then of all the miles of electrical cable, all the tanks of water, the rooms of food, the polished wood, the gleaming portholes, the tonnes of metal, the stacks of crockery, the women washing potatoes, the men far below shovelling coal, the stewards pouring drinks, everything going in to the creation of this ship. She knew then that it was not the vessel everyone loved, but the fact of it, the experience of being inside, of being delivered from one shore to another, transported in splendour and comfort, damn the effort that it took.

She rolled on to her back and pressed her hands against her stomach, wondering at her own passenger, sustained by the miles of intricacies inside her body, everything pounding and beating and working away to ensure its safe crossing. She knew then it was not her that anyone loved, but the fact that she could create an inside, that she could take life from one shore to the other, that she could transport, damn the effort that it took.

LAWRENCE

Lawrence woke with a start, his hands clasped tight across his chest and a dried line of spittle between his mouth and the bedsheets. He sat up too quickly so the blood rushed to his head and he had to wait a moment before checking his pocket watch.

It was five o'clock, but his sleep had been deep and he wondered if it was perhaps five in the morning. His cabin was in the centre of the ship without portholes, so there was no way of telling, which meant he'd have to venture out to make sure. Part of him hoped it was five in the morning and he'd simply slept through his last hours, because then he could go on deck and jump and it would all be over. He imagined the speed with which he would fall, how his body would break on impact, how his lungs would fill, and his mind claw and his chest clenched around the idea in a way that felt pathetic.

He forced himself in front of the mirror, hoping to see a steely resolve reflected back, but when he looked, it was as if the years had been stripped away and he'd reverted back to a young boy, his mother's tender hand pushing the hair out of his eyes. He cried then, because he felt sorry that he couldn't save that eager, excited child, who'd wanted so much and worked so hard to change his life.

But that boy had also become a man who had stood at the side of his wife's grave as they'd lowered the coffin down. Who had knelt on the hard ground and scrabbled for earth that had stuck beneath his fingernails. Who had thrown that dirt on to the roof of Cissy's coffin, as her mother turned her face into her husband's coat and her sister exclaimed, the sound like an angry bird. It had been a cold January day and Lawrence had looked up into the leaden sky which threatened an icy rain and known something in that moment. He'd known that all his striving, all his forward momentum, all his joy, all his passion were simply illusions designed to hide the truth from himself: which is that life is nothing more than a pointless hurtling towards death. He'd felt not just the end in that moment, but also a pulsing hatred for the person he loved most in the world, that she could have left him. And, however much he'd tried to fight it for the sake of Alec, it felt too hard, which meant he was a monster, unworthy of salvation.

Lawrence pulled on his coat and shoes and left his cabin, which was right outside the dining room, where he could see waitresses, in their black-and-white uniforms, busy setting up and organising, the clatter of cutlery tinkling in the air. There were also too many people in the corridors and on the stairs for it to be five in the morning, which meant he'd been asleep for less than two hours.

He climbed the three flights to the boat deck quickly, emerging to a still bright sun and brisk breeze, which felt disorientating. He decided to do a loop as he knew his skin would itch if he returned inside immediately and he didn't want to risk bumping into Lily in the library or saloon because he had nothing to offer her, so more conversation was pointless.

His walk felt overlaid by false purpose and he kept near the edge so he could avoid making eye contact with anyone, looking down into the grey-green sea, still calm, although pitted across its surface, making it completely opaque. It was all too easy to feel the giant snapping jaws below and Lawrence longed for a mammoth mouth to rip open the bow and save him from having to be brave, although he pulled away from that thought, because why should everyone else on board suffer because of him?

He heard the shouting before he realised where it was coming from, but then he saw a small group by the railings, a woman higher than the others, so it took him a moment to realise that she was standing on something and not levitating above them. A man was pulling at her coat and she was screaming, a high-pitched wail that made him want to turn away.

She toppled backwards, into the man's arms, and they collapsed together on to the deck as the small crowd pulled in around them.

A man's voice shouted, 'Please, stand back a bit, give her some air,' and Lawrence faltered because he recognised that rolling burr.

The crowd parted slightly and he saw George Henderson on his knees, pushing the people back with a motion of his hands. Lawrence looked then at the woman crumpled on the ground, a distinctive blue hat on her head, and Henry Elsworth leaning over her on the other side.

'I worried this might happen,' Henderson said. 'We need to get her back to the cabin and sedated. Do you think she can stand?'

'Oh, Lily,' Elsworth cried. 'Darling, I can't bear this.'

A few of the ladies around them gasped and some husbands placed an arm around their shoulders and turned them away.

Lawrence stepped forward, because he felt a tenderness then for Lily. Cissy had told him so many times that it was not that women were prone to hysteria so much as they had hysteria thrust upon them and he wished he'd tried harder to help, both of them. *Can you imagine*, she used to say, *if you had no purpose in life except to look after others, to behave well, to accept your place, to be ornamental? Can you imagine what that might do to a mind?*

But before he could offer assistance, Elsworth and the doctor had taken either side of Lily and were pulling her up. She looked pathetic, as if she had no strength in her body, her head lolling near her chest. They turned away from the group to make their way towards the stairs, but as they did, Lily tripped so her head jerked and raised slightly, which meant Lawrence could see under the wide brim of her hat. The movement was small and her head lolled again, but it was enough time for him to see that this woman had a full, bright face, with a large sharp nose, whereas the Lily he knew was all delicacies, like a doll. And, in fact, once he'd seen that, he realised also that the woman he was looking at was unmistakably taller and fuller all round, a good few inches taller and wider than Lily. He felt suddenly like a dog who gets the scent of a rabbit, all the hairs on his body raised from their roots. Because the more he watched, the more impossible it seemed that this woman and the person he'd sat across from in the library were one and the same.

The conversation he'd had with Lily flooded through him, all the implausibility, all the ways he'd dismissed her. He'd dismissed Cissy as well and that made him a fool because what he'd forgotten was that nothing about life was ever truly plausible. The very act of falling in love was surely the least plausible of all, the sensation of losing yourself in another, the world opening and expanding. Cissy had brought so much newness into his life and yet he still doubted too readily, still felt annoyed with her for having wanted to help others outside of himself. He cringed against himself as he remembered scoffing at some of the tales she told. *Stories always sound fanciful until we occupy them*, she'd said, *until we realise that nothing is stranger or more unpredictable than life.*

He tuned into the people around him as the group began to disperse and realised it was all they were discussing, expressing their sympathies for the poor woman and exchanging stories of mad relatives or acquaintances. The story would no doubt spread round the boat like an illness. His own sickness rose through him as he remembered all the meetings Cissy had returned from, filled with stories about women not being listened to. How, once, she'd read an article which had called the Suffragettes warmongers and he'd shouted at her that it was all they bloody talked about. He realised now that all she'd been trying to teach him was to look and listen and he'd been too selfish or stubborn to understand that until this very moment.

He rushed up the deck with an ease of movement which he thought long lost to him and followed the strange threesome through the door that led inside. He could hear them on the stairs a couple of flights below and slowed his pace so they wouldn't notice him.

'Come on, Lil, we'll be back in the cabin soon,' Henry Elsworth was saying.

'Watch your step, Lady Elsworth. Here, lean on me,' Henderson added.

'Can I be of assistance?' Another voice rose up through the stairwell.

'No, thank you, Sir. My wife is just feeling a bit unwell.'

Lawrence passed the man who had offered help on the next flight and he shook his head, his features contracted in pity. The little party turned off at F deck and Lawrence followed, keeping always a corner away from them, until they came to rest outside a cabin, where Elsworth fumbled for keys, while the woman leant heavily on the doctor until they went inside. Once they were inside, Lawrence walked to where they'd been, stopping momentarily to register the number on the cabin door. He could hear the murmur of voices from within, but didn't dare step any closer in case someone came.

A strange energy was fizzing through his body, like a thousand tiny bubbles had released into his blood, and it felt almost pleasant. He looked down the empty corridor and wished now that he knew where Lily was, but the ship seemed vast then, all the floors and rooms above and below him, all the people and spaces.

He knew he needed to think and so made for his cabin, his legs feeling looser than they had in ages.

Nothing had changed in there; the bed was still ruffled from where he'd slept earlier, his comb was still on his washstand, his books lying haphazardly on the sofa, his trunk half-open. And yet it felt different, more alive somehow. He paced across the room and back again, his body needing the movement.

He wasn't entirely sure of the meaning of what he'd just witnessed, but he was completely sure that the woman who had collapsed was not Lily and that Elsworth and Henderson had both been pretending she was. Little about it made sense, but it was obvious that Lily must be in some way right in all her accusations and that Elsworth was organising something ominous and dangerous.

The long fall into oblivion he'd planned for that night faded from his mind. He simply could not leave a wrong such as this unchallenged and the sea would still be there waiting for him tomorrow, or the day after. If he had a chance of somehow meeting Cissy again, then he was sure she would turn away from him if he neglected this chance to help. It might act at least part way as an apology for all the times he'd failed to understand her, failed to listen to what she was saying. Loving someone, he realised, was not enough, you had to also cherish them so they felt right and secure.

He went towards his door again and flung it open, because it now felt imperative that he find Lily as soon as possible.

LILY

Lily didn't own a watch and had lost all sense of time when she finally pulled herself up off the floor. It felt like she'd been lying there for hours, but it was still light beyond the porthole. Her whole body ached as she stood, as if her muscles had seized and her bones hardened. Her mouth was dry and she felt utterly defeated, but her mind was also strangely empty, the problem she was facing too huge to overcome. Her mother had once told her that nothing is hopeless, but she didn't see how that could be true, surely there were some situations without a solution.

A chill had settled in the cabin, so she wrapped the blanket from the bed around her shoulders and then sat with her back against the wall, her eyes fixed on the door. Sometimes she heard chatter as people passed by outside and she wondered about banging on the door and screaming for help, but it seemed pointless as Henry would say she was sick and everyone would believe him. At one point, she heard the door bang shut next door in her cabin and then the sound of low voices, but she couldn't make out what they were saying or who they were.

The pains and feeling like she was bleeding had subsided, but she had never trusted the sensations inside her body. She pulled a corner of Becky's white sheet towards her and worked it up between her legs, then pressed it into the tender space where she could still feel Dr Henderson's fingers. She hoped she would soil it, mark where she'd been like a reminder, but it came away clean and she couldn't work out if she was relieved or not.

The sun hadn't quite set, but the shadows in the room were lengthening when Lily finally heard the scrape of the key in the lock and then the door pushed open to reveal Henry. He stood looking at her for a moment in a way which froze her blood because it felt like nothing more than an assessment.

'How do you feel?' he asked, his tone businesslike, as if he were enquiring after one of his injured horses.

'What?' Her head felt mushy, as if she'd missed a whole section of the conversation.

He sighed. 'Are you still bleeding?'

'No.'

'Good. I think you could do with some food. Get cleaned up and then we can have a quick drink first.'

She stood, even though she felt shaky, and followed Henry to their cabin, where she went to the mirror. Her appearance seemed beyond repair, her hair a mess of feathery fluff haloing her shockingly pale face. But she forced herself to brush it out, twisting it round and repinning it at the base of her neck, then pinched at her cheeks and dabbed some red lipstick on to her chapped lips, although all that did was accentuate the redness of her eyes.

Henry came up behind her and smiled at her through the glass, so she involuntarily turned her own mouth upwards. He put his hands on either side of her shoulders and squeezed gently, and it felt like she'd forgotten something, or maybe this was a dream, or perhaps she was dead. It even seemed possible at that moment that she'd got everything wrong and she really was as difficult and troubled as he'd always told her she was and he didn't mean her any harm.

They turned to leave, but Henry stopped by the door. 'If people ask how you are, just tell them you've had a rest and are feeling better.'

'What do you mean?'

'Quite a few people heard that racket you and Becky were making earlier. A few have asked me if you are all right.'

She could barely remember raising her voice. 'What did you say?'

'That you had a bit of a turn, but were resting.' He smiled, which threw her off balance. 'I would never have mentioned it, but you know how gossip spreads and someone is bound to say something to you.'

The world outside the door seemed like a maze. 'Perhaps I should just stay in the cabin. I'm not particularly hungry anyway.'

'No.' Henry stepped towards her and took her arm. 'I think getting amongst people might do you good.'

Lily thought of the interminable weeks she'd spent alone at Elsworth since the beginning of their marriage. 'That never seemed to bother you before. In fact, I thought you liked me out of the way.'

A familiar flash of anger crossed his features. 'I think you'll find you chose that way of life, Lily.' He shook his head. 'You could have made anything of the life I gave you. But you chose to lock yourself away and look down your nose at the rest of us.'

The description felt totally alien to anything she'd ever felt. 'I didn't look down my nose. I just didn't want to live the way you did.'

He snorted. 'What, you expected me to consult you on how we lived?'

'But if you want a happy marriage, surely both people have to be in agreement?' Lily realised she was clutching her hands together so tightly they were beginning to throb.

'I wanted a functional marriage. But apparently that was too much to ask.' He pulled on her arm. 'Come on, I need a drink.'

They made their way up the flights of stairs to the saloon, which Lily could hear and smell before they arrived, the determined chatter and heavy smoke filling her with a creeping dread.

It felt as if all faces turned towards her as they came in, so she kept her head down and let Henry lead her to two chairs in the corner, only allowing herself to look around once she'd sat and Henry was beckoning for a drink. Most people were talking in groups, but there were two women a few tables away sneaking glances at her and bowing their heads together in conversation, which made heat rush to her face.

A small glass of sherry, which she hadn't asked for, was placed in front of her. She looked at Henry reaching forward for his tumbler of whisky and wondered how he didn't yet know that sherry made her gag, with its cloying sweetness. Or maybe he did.

Henry stood with a small sigh and she followed his gaze to see Emma Connaught approaching, her dress billowing around her as she speeded inevitably towards them. She stopped right in front of Lily's chair, her face a rapture of concern.

'Oh Lady Elsworth, I am so pleased to see you up and about. I heard all about what happened and I was so worried.'

Lily tried to arrange her face into an acceptable state, but found she didn't even know what that might be. A group of women were watching the proceedings and her head felt as if it was bulging again, that its heaviness could tip her over.

'Are you fully recovered?' Emma asked, her smile slipping against Lily's silence.

'My wife is feeling much better after a little rest,' Henry said. 'Aren't you, dear?'

It took Lily a moment to realise he was addressing her. 'Oh, yes. I am. Thank you for enquiring, Mrs Connaught.' Her words sounded heavy inside her, as if they were being dragged up through her body.

'Anyway,' Emma said, bobbing her head. 'I do not wish to keep you. I just wanted to check you were in no way hurt.'

'Hurt?' Lily looked between Emma and Henry, unsure if Emma knew about the blood, although that didn't seem possible.

'Thank you so much for your concern, Emma,' Henry replied, taking her by the elbow and turning her away from Lily, so she had no other choice but to retreat back across the room.

A tall, red-faced man approached Henry then and they started a conversation about diamond mining that Lily couldn't keep track of. Henry glanced over at her from time to time, as if he was worried that she might disappear, but there was nowhere for her to go, so she sat still, feeling as though the chair was growing around her and soon she would be lost in its cushions, making it impossible to move.

'Lily.' She looked up, her eyes taking a moment to focus. 'Do you mind if I sit here?' Lawrence indicated Henry's empty chair.

'What?' She was confused because she'd given up thinking Lawrence could help her.

He sat anyway and spoke in a lowered voice. 'I have been looking for you everywhere.'

'Well, I have been locked in Becky's cabin all afternoon. Not that you believe me, I'm sure.'

'That is exactly why I have been looking for you.' There was a stretch to his voice that made Lily lean into his words. 'I saw something this afternoon that has made me reconsider all you have told me.'

The words made her heart leap and her blood fizz. Her whole body strained towards him with something that felt very like hope, but the chair was spongey and she couldn't imagine standing from it. 'You believe me?'

Lawrence leant his elbows on to his knees so he could angle his body towards her and Lily felt jealousy at the ease of the movement. 'This afternoon I was on deck when I witnessed an hysterical woman trying to jump from the side of the ship, or so it appeared. I thought it was you because, when I got closer, I saw this person was being attended to by your husband and Dr Henderson; she was wearing that blue hat I've seen you in.'

It felt like ants were rushing across Lily's skin. 'But I was in Becky's cabin all afternoon. Henry locked me in.'

'I know, or at least, I did not know that, but I caught a glimpse of the woman in your hat and it wasn't you. She was much broader and taller than you and her features were plump, her nose very straight and angular.'

'That's Becky, my maid, who I told you about.' Something popped in Lily's chest and she wondered if she was dying.

'I thought as much. Lord Elsworth was crying and pleading with her and Henderson was acting as if this behaviour was not out of the ordinary. And they were both calling her Lily.'

Lily put her hand to her head, as if she could process the information faster by pushing it inside her.

Lawrence pushed down the air in front of him with his hands. 'Sorry, I'm going too fast. After we spoke in the library, I felt compelled to investigate your story, so I went to find your husband, with the idea of maybe speaking to him. But when I came across him, he was in conversation with a man whom I knew had to be your doctor from your description, George Henderson.'

Lily had forgotten her doctor's first name, not liking to think of him in any intimate way. 'You have spoken to Dr Henderson?' She was filled again with the restrictive feeling she'd had as a child when her mother had locked her and May into the playroom, of whole worlds existing beyond her reach.

'Yes. In fact, after I'd spoken to him, I had made up my mind that you were deluded and I should have no more to do with you.' Lawrence blushed with his words, but still they stung.

'Oh God.'

'But then I saw them performing the charade I just told you about with this woman who wasn't you, and it made me realise that something deeply suspicious must be going on.' There was no joy to be found in what Lawrence was saying, although perhaps a slight sense of vindication, but with this came also a flash of anger that her words should always be doubted. 'I followed them back to cabin 66 on F deck.'

'That is my cabin.' Lily remembered the murmuring she'd heard that afternoon. 'I was next door, locked into Becky's cabin.' Lily couldn't help glancing then at Henry because what Lawrence was telling her felt like a proper plan, a detailed one at that, like a richly woven tapestry, with Becky right at the centre, which made her want to give up.

'This is all very confusing. Tell me again what you think is happening.'

The spots of blood on her underwear floated into Lily's mind. 'I think Henry and Becky are in love and they plan to get rid of me somehow and take my baby. Henry would have left me years ago if it wasn't for my money, in fact he never would have married me, but he has persevered because having a child with me means my father will continue to give him money forever and Elsworth will stay in his bloodline.'

Lawrence nodded. 'I wonder where Henderson fits in.'

Lily shivered, the memory of his fingers still deep inside her. 'He is a horrible man. I expect you could pay him to do anything. When he was examining me today, he ...' But she faltered, unable to articulate what he'd done.

'Why was he examining you?'

'Oh, I had a little bleed this afternoon, after you left me in the library.'

Lawrence's face contracted. 'I'm sorry. How are you feeling now?'

'It has stopped. Apparently it was minor and there was little blood. Dr Henderson gave me a tonic and I had a rest. He said the pregnancy is still intact.'

Lawrence smiled gently. 'I'm glad, although really you should still be in bed.'

'Henry thought I needed to eat.'

'Well, that is true, I suppose.' Lawrence steepled his hands together, tapping his fingers against his lips. 'I know George Henderson's cabin number. While you are all at dinner this evening, I think I'll try to take a quick look, see if I can get inside.'

'You would do that for me?' Lily felt a rush of fear because what Lawrence was saying seemed like a trap. It seemed too unlikely that he would simply want to help her, without wanting anything in return.

But Lawrence looked so earnest when he met her gaze. 'Yes. If they mean you harm in any way, then I want to try to stop them.' She looked over at Henry, so Lawrence followed her gaze, and they both saw Henry ending his conversation and beginning to make his way towards them. Lawrence turned quickly back to her. 'Meet me tomorrow at 10 a.m. on that covered walkway that's become an unofficial children's playground, you know, outside the library, as I do not imagine we shall get another chance to speak this evening.'

'Mr Beesley,' Henry said, clapping Lawrence on the back, and

Lily saw him flinch. 'I thought it was you.' She looked at her husband, trying to work out if he'd heard their conversation, but his face was placid.

'Lord Elsworth,' Lawrence said, standing. 'I was just asking your wife if she's feeling better after her turn this afternoon.'

Henry laughed. 'My God, news travels fast on this damned ship.'

Lily saw a jagged vein twitch on the side of Lawrence's head. It was such a game they had to play, their hands so light, the stakes so high. She felt her aloneness then like a physical presence, like a stone around her neck, so heavy she wondered how she'd survived.

'Anyway, Lil, I think we should go in to dinner now. I don't want to tire you out by staying out late. It was nice to see you again, Mr Beesley.' Henry held out his hand and pulled her up and, even though her legs shook, she was able to stand.

Lawrence nodded first at Henry, and then Lily, before walking away. She watched him leave, filled with an incredulity that he was going to help her, concentrating on that thought as she followed Henry into the dining room, because she knew that she could only think about Becky when she was alone, when she could scream and cry. It was very clear now that Becky had made her choice and it was such a choice it seemed impossible that she had ever cared for her, a realisation that struck against Lily like a blow. She forced herself instead to think about Lawrence, right at that moment descending the stairs she knew well to F deck. It was almost as if she was making the journey, leaving behind her physical body and existing only in her mind.

LAWRENCE

He took the stairs two at a time to F deck, then followed the numbers round to 43, that strange sense of enlargement once again in his chest. It was quiet and he presumed most people were far above at dinner, but still fear gripped at him. Before he left the saloon, he'd checked that George Henderson was still standing in the corner of the room, his usually pale face flushed as he chatted to a group of men.

He tried the handle first, but the door was locked, as he'd expected. Different scenarios ran through his head, none of which seemed legal or moral, but Lawrence found he didn't mind the thought of that. Cissy had praised the women who threw lighted bottles through the windows of courthouses and he thought that the right thing wasn't always easy to discern.

Besides, he was planning on ending his life, so it didn't really matter if he was caught, or even if he was judged. He didn't believe in God, didn't think he'd be waiting outside the gates of heaven while Peter weighed up his virtues. He'd be found lacking anyway; suicide itself was a mortal sin and, besides, he'd had too many avaricious, mean thoughts in life to hope for salvation. The only judgement he cared for was Cissy's and he knew she would approve.

A steward carrying a tray turned the corner and Lawrence

thought fast as the man approached. 'Excuse me,' he said. 'I left my coat in my friend's cabin, but he is not in there. I wondered if you could open it for me?'

The man hesitated. 'I have to get this soup to a lady down the corridor. It cannot get cold.'

'I'll only be a minute. I can wait outside the door, if you like, for you to come back, so you can lock up again.' His chest tightened as he watched the steward make his decision.

The man fished a ring of keys out of his pocket and unlocked the door in one swift move. 'If you don't mind waiting until I'm back, Sir, I would be most obliged.'

'Certainly.'

Lawrence felt a little sick as he stepped into George's meticulously neat room, heavy with a close scent of pomade which caught in the back of his throat. There was nothing on show, apart from a Bible on the bureau and a trunk in the corner. He went first to the Bible, which was surprisingly dog-eared, with a broken spine, and opened it. A picture of an old, grey-haired woman, who looked uncannily like George, fluttered to the floor. He picked it up and hastily stuffed her back between the pages.

He turned then to the trunk, lifting the lid gingerly, to reveal many layers of neatly folded clothes. Lawrence did his best not to disturb them, feeling between them all, not knowing what he was hoping to find, until near the bottom he felt the smoothness of a large leather purse, which he pulled out and sat with, kneeling on the floor.

He pulled on the heavy brass zipper and removed a bulging envelope and two pieces of paper. The first was George's passport paper, his stern face staring out accusingly, dated, stamped and approved. The second was a letter from a Dr Samuel Graham, writing from the Kirkbride Hospital in Maine. Lawrence scanned his words quickly and a few sentences leapt off the page:

'the care of a mentally ill patient is extremely distressing', 'it does sound like she is approaching the time when hospitalisation will be necessary', 'the terms you offer are very generous'.

The envelope was bursting with cash, a quick count revealing what must be a thousand pounds, and he was reminded of how Lily had said something about Becky handing an envelope to George. But it was impossible she had this much money, impossible that any doctor, even the finest in the land, demanded this sort of fee.

Lawrence's palms were clammy and sweat had dried over his skin, making his shirt stick uncomfortably to his back. He replaced the purse and envelope quickly, his brain trying to make sense of the new information, as he shut the lid of the trunk. He stood and gave the cabin a final glance to check it looked as it had when he'd entered, but then saw the doctor's bag tucked in at the foot of the bed. It was too good an opportunity to miss, and he was opening it before he had time to think.

It was surprisingly empty, a stethoscope, a listening tube and a few bottles. He took them out carefully one by one, holding them up to read the labels: Valerian, Comfrey and Lady's Mantle. It was a confusing assortment which didn't make any real sense, but he replaced them quickly, then went to stand outside the door.

The steward appeared a few minutes later, red-faced and harassed and uninterested in Lawrence's bemusement that he hadn't found his coat. He locked the door with barely an acknowledgement, hurrying off up the corridor as soon as was polite.

Lawrence didn't know what to do with himself then. He was surprisingly hungry, something he hadn't felt for a very long time, as if a small hole had opened in his stomach. Dinner would be over though and he realised what he really wanted was a drink, his saliva glands releasing at the thought of the sweet liquid.

He'd stayed sober so far on board, for reasons which weren't entirely clear to him, but he thought were to do with witnessing the end of his life, owning the decision somehow. He'd spent much of the past year in a fog of alcohol, often waking with a rancid taste in his mouth, his limbs aching and his head heavy. The day would blur before him and Alec would ask things from him that sometimes made him snap, so the maid would appear and hustle him down to the kitchen. He'd promise himself that the evening he was approaching would be different, but as the night drew in and Cissy enlarged in his mind, the only thing that could stop him from tearing at his skin would be to down glass after glass. There was nothing pleasurable about the way he drank, nothing good in the absolution he was seeking, but he didn't care, didn't see another way.

He sought out a waiter as soon as he entered the saloon, asking for a large whisky, which felt like warmth running down his chest. He drank it quickly and then ordered another, only looking round the room as his senses began to smooth; George Henderson was standing in the same place, now ruddy-faced and swaying slightly, but Elsworth and Lily were nowhere to be seen.

Lawrence wandered over to the charts, not really sure why he was drawn so much by the progress they were making, when his destination was so final. Although that thought worried at him, because Lily's problem was enlarging and he couldn't work out how his death fitted into that.

'It seems like too much to accomplish,' Cissy had said to him one night as they'd lain in bed, her body curled into his.

'What does?' he'd asked, tipping between that moment of sleep and waking, knowing that Alec would come padding into them too early the next morning.

'There are too many women who need help. I think of it sometimes and it is like they stretch all around the world in a giant circle and I know I will never reach them all and that is terrifying.'

He'd felt exasperated at the ridiculousness of her statement. 'You cannot possibly help them all.'

'I know, I know.' She'd tried to laugh in the darkness. 'And, as Martha says, helping just one person is enough if you do it right.'

He had turned his back to her and he wished with all his being that he could go back and turn towards her, encircle her waist and kiss the top of her head. But he'd stayed rolled on to his side because he'd felt angry that she always wanted to help others, telling himself that he hated how she didn't let him protect her from harm. Although he wondered now if the person he had really wanted to protect was himself. He'd been a stupid fool, believing there was so much time in which he could pull her into him, unable to imagine that the woman who had changed his world wouldn't dissolve like everything else, succumbing, mulching, vanishing.

'The old girl's done well today, eh?' Lawrence turned to see Reverend Carter and his wife standing just behind him, both their faces split in wide grins that made him involuntarily smile back.

'I see you are as fascinated with the ship's progress as my husband,' Marjorie said.

Lawrence forced a laugh. 'Even though we disagree about the need for speed.'

Marjorie squinted at the chart. 'I have to say, I do not see the appeal. I prefer to take the time to look at what we're passing.'

'Marjorie and I like to watch the sun rise and set and sometimes it feels as if I cannot quite absorb the beauty of the scene, if you know what I mean?' William said.

Lawrence nodded his agreement; William's words reminded him of a feeling he'd forgotten, because he too had felt that incredulity many times himself, standing on the crest of the highest hill in Wirksworth, or wandering round the botanical gardens in Cambridge, or examining tiny details of a plant under a microscope. It often felt to him that his eyes were inadequate conductors of such magnitude and beauty and it would sometimes be hard to believe in what he was seeing. 'Nature is wonderous,' he said, surprised for a moment that he'd expressed this out loud, more surprised even that he still had the capacity to feel such a thing.

William beamed at him. 'God's gift to us all.'

It was strange to think of the sea as a gift, because since he'd boarded, he'd seen it as an enemy, knowing that if you jumped from the height of the boat it would break you like a twig in a gale. But William was right, and it was just as beautiful as clouds sweeping across a green hill, or the delicate layers of petal that made up a rose, or the interconnecting capillaries that ghosted paper-thin leaves.

'There are gifts everywhere, in the most unexpected places, if we just know where to look,' Marjorie said.

Lawrence looked up and around the magnificent room in which they were standing, every detail crafted to look like an expensive hotel, and it suddenly seemed like an illusion. He wanted, all at once, nothing more than to be standing in a forest clearing or on top of a hill so he could smell the wet soil and hear the birds chirping in the branches. Progress suddenly felt dangerous, because what if we don't know when to stop, or if in a constant forward motion we forget that some can't run as fast?

After they'd left, Lawrence felt so tired that even his face ached with the pressure of keeping all the conflicting parts of himself in check, so he went up to the boat deck to try to blow some form of resolution into himself. The temperature had dropped and it was dark, which meant it was deserted, so he walked straight to the thin steps and then up to the very back of the boat again, to the spot where he was planning to jump.

It was tantalising to stand there at a time when he could have so easily done it and that thought pulled at him, drawing him closer and closer to the side, until his body was pressed right up against the cold metal and he could have just climbed the rungs and let himself fall down into the blackness. He was filled with an intoxicating feeling of possibility, but also he shied away from it in a way that he had to admit wasn't just born from the situation he found himself in.

The moon was casting her silvery trail across the sea, pulling him forward in a way that made him wonder what Lily was, if she was an excuse or a reality. The answer seemed too complex and then Lawrence's mind just felt undone, like a piece of frayed material which has become more threads than whole.

'Look at me,' Cissy had said to him a few weeks before she died. 'You haven't looked at me for so long.'

'But I look at you always,' he'd replied.

'No, you look past me or through me,' she'd said. 'As if you're looking for what you want to see rather than what is actually there.'

He'd known what she meant, that she was dying, that there would be no improvement, that it was better to face reality than be slammed right up against it when the time came.

But, he realised now, he'd always somehow thought they'd be able to cheat death, that it wouldn't really stalk them as it did every living thing on the planet. As a boy, he'd collected tiny skulls, lining them up on his windowsill so the light shone through them and his mother would tut. He'd watched plants wither, performed dissections on small soft bodies, seen rocks crumbling and spiderwebs trembling in the breeze. He, more than most people, knew the impermanence of life, the fragility of being. He'd always known that the wonder, the beauty of existence, lay in its fleeting, translucent nature. But he saw now that he'd never absorbed this idea and it was Cissy who had lived with the truth of this knowledge, Cissy who'd been brave and faced up to their reality for them both.

A warm hand slipped into his freezing one and he whipped round. Of course, she wasn't there, but still his heart felt like it had been punched because it seemed suddenly so likely that she was still existing with him, just behind a screen or a veil, always a little out of reach, but maybe not completely gone. He wanted to rip through time to find her, to pull her out of the ground, to spin the world backwards, to beg and plead with whatever was out there to let him wake from this nightmare. His arms felt heavy with the sense of her in them and the space she had left was unbearable, unbridgeable, impossible.

His misery felt viral, as if it had invaded his body. His loss seemed too big to bear; he was just a man, unequal to such a task and he wanted to crouch and cower, to cover his head, because the world was falling in and he was terrified. There was so much he didn't understand, so much that weighed like a stone in his chest.

Lawrence turned his face to the moon and opened his mouth, hearing the desperate cry before he realised that he was the one making the sound.

crumbling and [illegible] [illegible] [illegible] the [illegible] [illegible]
[illegible] [illegible] [illegible] [illegible] [illegible] [illegible]
[illegible] [illegible] [illegible] known that the [illegible] the [illegible] of
[illegible] [illegible] [illegible] [illegible] [illegible] [illegible] [illegible]
[illegible] never [illegible] [illegible] and [illegible] [illegible] he had
[illegible] [illegible] [illegible] [illegible] [illegible] [illegible] [illegible]
and [illegible] up [illegible] [illegible] for them both.

[illegible] [illegible] [illegible] the [illegible] and [illegible]
[illegible]. Of course, [illegible] [illegible] [illegible] [illegible] [illegible]
[illegible] [illegible] because [illegible] [illegible] [illegible]
[illegible] [illegible] with [illegible] [illegible] [illegible] [illegible]
[illegible] [illegible] [illegible] [illegible] [illegible] [illegible] [illegible]
[illegible] [illegible] [illegible] [illegible] [illegible] the [illegible]
[illegible] [illegible] [illegible] and [illegible] [illegible]
[illegible] [illegible] him [illegible] [illegible] [illegible] [illegible]
[illegible] the [illegible] of [illegible] and [illegible] [illegible]
was [illegible] [illegible]

[illegible] [illegible] [illegible] [illegible] [illegible] [illegible] [illegible]
[illegible] [illegible] [illegible] he was [illegible] [illegible] [illegible]
[illegible] he [illegible] [illegible] and [illegible] [illegible] [illegible]
[illegible] [illegible] was [illegible] [illegible] he was [illegible] [illegible]
[illegible] [illegible] [illegible] [illegible] [illegible] [illegible]
[illegible] [illegible]

[illegible] [illegible] [illegible] [illegible] the [illegible] [illegible]
[illegible] [illegible] [illegible] [illegible] [illegible] [illegible]
[illegible] [illegible]

SATURDAY, APRIL 13TH

LILY

Lily was feeling unbalanced as she made her way to the covered corridor outside the library to meet Lawrence. Mornings had been like this for her for months now, this inability to focus, so she spent much of the day feeling like she was trying to escape from a dream. She thought it was a symptom of her pregnancy, and yet it felt like more than that, as if sleep enveloped her, dragging her down and under. She hadn't even dreamt for a long time, no memory lingering in her mind in the morning, only a sense that returning to the world was becoming harder and harder.

But this morning was worse than usual as she'd spent the whole night in a weird half-state of anxiety, trying to make sense of what Lawrence had told her. Because not only did it not make sense as to why Becky was pretending to be her, but also it must mean that she hated her, which made Lily feel like all hope was lost and there was no point to anything.

Lawrence wasn't in the corridor when she got there and she felt a stab of fear that he might have changed his mind. She worried that he had smelt the madness on her, that others could see things about her which were invisible even to herself. Without Becky's reassurances, it had felt harder and harder to cling on to the essence of herself, so sometimes she would be sure that her mind was damaged beyond repair, crumbling to nothing in her head. Henry had always told her she was unhinged and it was only Becky who had recognised the parts of her which no one else noticed. Without her true self being seen, she couldn't work out what the point of her would be, or even how that person was meant to continue existing.

The beginnings of a spiralling panic circled her, which felt like a whirlwind building in her body, a feeling she'd become used to in the last year at Elsworth, when anything and nothing could trigger an attack. Sometimes something as innocuous as walking into a room she hadn't visited for a few days could quicken her breath, a turn round the gardens might blur her vision, an unexpected question from the cook would spin her head. Even lying in bed, Lily's heart sometimes raced, making her call Briar on to the covers, where she would curl herself around her warm body and weep into her fur. Her instinct was always to turn to Becky, to ask her opinion, to solicit her company, but when she turned now, the space was always empty, which made everywhere feel unsafe.

'Apologies for my lateness,' Lawrence said, materialising at her elbow. He led her over to one of the open windows at the edge of the covered walkway. Deep purple bruises surrounded his bloodshot eyes.

'I worried you might not come,' she admitted, the heaviness of her panic easing slightly with his presence.

'You don't have to worry about that.' But he sounded exhausted, as if words cost him too much.

Lily followed Lawrence's gaze to two young boys rolling a ball between them a little way down the corridor. Their father was hovering over them, speaking in French, his eyes never leaving them.

'Where is your son staying?' Lily asked, as it was obvious what Lawrence was thinking.

'With some relatives of Cissy's in Scotland. I expect you're wondering how I can bear to have left him?'

'I don't know.' And Lily didn't really know what she thought. Her own baby felt like a judgement, although on what she was unsure.

'I think leaving your children is perhaps the hardest thing we ever do as humans. But, that said, sometimes it is also the kindest.'

'How do you mean?' Lily watched as the father of the two boys rested his hand on his youngest son's head.

'I have been a wreck since Cissy died. And not a good father. I realised that my misery was starting to contaminate Alec. You do not need to know about misery at six, it is too young. He's better off without me.'

'But surely you will have him back, at some point?' She had no idea what the right answer to this question might be.

'I think not.' Lawrence tapped his finger against his chapped lips as he spoke and Lily felt a chill.

'Would Cissy not want you to have Alec back?'

'Oh yes. She would be greatly annoyed at how I am behaving. But I find her impossible to recover from. She is my version of consumption, you see.'

Lily was struck by the extent of Lawrence's grief and it scared her in its completeness. Love was dangerous, except it was also so hard to work out what love was exactly. She'd told Lawrence that Henry had never loved her, but the truth was, she didn't think she'd ever loved him either. For him, she'd never felt those things that are meant to constitute love, no pulling towards him, no melting inside her, no pain at his removal. In fact, it was Becky who rose up in her mind when she thought about those feelings, but that was absurd, because they couldn't love each other, or at least not like that. She had to be mistaken, as she was about so much else.

Lawrence's eyes were glassy, staring into the middle distance. 'Cissy claimed the desire for a child felt like a compulsion, like something she wasn't in control of. But our friend Martha disagreed completely. They would argue about it for hours. Martha said that society has structured itself to make women believe all they want is children, because, naturally, it confines them. But Cissy said she thought our biology is different and that something happens inside a woman that's like an internal scream you know will only stop with pregnancy.'

The truth was Lily couldn't remember actively wanting to get pregnant, it was more what had been expected and then, as the years passed and nothing happened, everything about the process became hard and frightening.

She looked at Lawrence and saw he'd lightened, so fancied she could see what his life must have been like with Cissy, the way they must have talked and laughed, the friends they'd shared, the easy suppers they'd eaten. 'I wish I had met Cissy,' she said before she could check herself.

He laughed. 'She would have liked you. And she would be more help than me in this situation. I often think, in fact, that I should have died and Cissy lived, because she had so much more to offer the world.'

'Oh, please don't say that.' Lily felt a rush of fear at the casualness with which he spoke about death, because how could he be serious about saving her if he valued life so little?

'Cissy used to say that life is a series of choices,' Lawrence said and she could tell his mood had dipped again. 'She came from an aristocratic family, not as rich as yours, but still in a completely different league to mine. And she was five years older than me. Her life had always been laid out before her, you know, as in who she might marry and where she might live, all those things. After we married, she told me that she'd always known she couldn't live the life destined for her and I had set her free. But I'm not sure that's true, I'm starting to think it was she who set me free.'

Lily felt floored by the thought of a woman choosing a path and dictating her own happiness. Or of a love so strong that it gave freedom. 'But if Cissy is right about choices, then perhaps you can choose to be happy without her?'

'Oh, no, some things are just not possible.' Lawrence's tone was sharp and she knew she'd broken the moment. He forced a smile. 'Sorry, this is a depressing conversation.'

'No, it's nice. I like to hear about Cissy.' And it was true, the thought of Cissy was sustaining, in that it proved to her that it was possible for women to be brave.

'How are you feeling since your bleed yesterday? Have you felt the baby move today?'

She thought of the strange pops and rumbles which rustled inside her most days, hard to pinpoint, hard sometimes to attribute to anything more than wind. But she registered everything now and had become attuned to every shift in her being. 'I think so. Although I don't know what to expect.'

'The first movements are very subtle. They get more pronounced as the baby grows. Then by the end they are unmistakable. There were a couple of times we saw an actual outline emerge from Cissy's stomach.'

The thought of the baby enlarging and stretching her skin was unexpectedly disgusting and Lily didn't want to see the outline of tiny limbs pushing up through her stomach. 'Did you manage to get into Dr Henderson's cabin?' she asked, to change the subject.

'I did, and I still cannot make complete sense of everything I found.' He paused and his gaze intensified. 'Some of the things I am going to tell you are quite distressing, Lily, and I don't want you getting upset, it would not be good for the baby.'

She wanted, just once, for someone to think that she was more important than the baby, but she nodded. 'Please, just tell me.'

'Well, firstly, I found an envelope stuffed with cash, I'd say about a thousand pounds.'

One of the little boys in the corridor screeched and both Lily and Lawrence jumped, turning their attention outward again. The father scooped up his son, smothering him with kisses.

'A thousand pounds? I told you I saw Becky handing Dr Henderson an envelope, but it is impossible she has that sort of money.'

Lawrence shook his head. 'It cannot be her money. But we know she must be in on the plan, whatever it is, because I saw her performing that charade with them, so I would say the best guess is that it's your husband's money.'

'But why so much?' Lily thought of her father writing cheques, not realising where they were headed.

'It's hard to say, but I found a letter as well.' The way Lawrence said the words made Lily clench. 'There's no easy way to say this, Lily, but George Henderson is in communication with a Dr Graham from Kirkbride Hospital in Maine. Do you know of him at all?'

She shook her head.

He looked at her almost sideways, as if he were shamed by what he had to say. 'From what I read I think he runs an asylum, for women, and they are discussing having you admitted after you give birth.'

Lily's hand leapt involuntarily to her mouth and her eyes blurred. 'What do you mean? I don't understand.'

'I've been turning the problem around all night,' Lawrence said. 'Let us suppose that Elsworth does want to get rid of you because he has fallen in love with Becky, but he needs your father's money and he wants his heir. What is the easiest way to dispose of you without too much fuss or scandal or suspicion?'

She shook her head, her mind blank. Her breath felt raw in her throat and her diaphragm ached with the effort it was taking not to collapse in hysterics.

'Well, I would say an asylum is a pretty good place, somewhere where no one expects you to make sense and anything you say is dismissed as delusional ravings. And think about it, if Elsworth is taking you straight to a house where only he, Becky and Dr Henderson will be taking care of you, then they can say anything about your state of mind after you have given birth. Especially if this crossing is to be the last public sighting of you, complete with those little shows they're putting on.'

Lily's brain felt like it was running to catch up. 'I still don't see what you mean.'

'There's only one reason why they would be putting on their shows,' Lawrence said, resting a hand lightly on her arm. 'To make you seem unstable. And because this ship is a confined space, they're making sure that as many people as possible will witness you behaving erratically and can attest to your instability. It is never hard for a man to get his wife committed, but it would be especially easy in the circumstances they have set up, abetted by a doctor generously bribed to sign the papers.'

Lily gasped, tears leaking down her cheeks. Lawrence turned her away from the corridor and she was confronted by the vastness of the sea, imprisoning her on all sides. It seemed impossible that Becky could be part of such a terrible plan and it made Lily feel as if her skin was being ripped from her bones.

'I was also thinking about what you said about not being able to work out why you're travelling second class,' Lawrence added and, even though she wanted to know, she also wanted him to stop. 'Something George Henderson said made me think that I might have worked out the answer. Is it possible you have friends in first?'

'Yes, Henry mentioned a few.' But she couldn't remember who they were, although she wasn't sure it would matter as there would be no one she could appeal to.

'Well, it would be much harder for him to pull off this stunt if people who know you are about. You and Becky are too physically different for someone who knows you well not to notice that she is not you. The hat would not be enough of a distraction, whereas amongst strangers it works well.'

'He has thought of everything.' The realisation was so bleak, it dried her tears.

'How long have you been drinking Dr Henderson's potions?'

Lily turned to Lawrence because she couldn't quite follow the thread. 'About a year, I suppose.'

'Do any smell strange? A bit like stagnant water?'

'Yes, that's exactly how my nightly tea smells. I hate it.'

Lawrence let his gaze travel out across the sea and Lily had an urge to pull him back. 'I also found some tinctures in his cabin. One of them was valerian, which smells just like that. If you've been drinking that for a year, then it is no wonder you're feeling confused, it's quite a powerful sedative.'

Consuelo popped into Lily's mind, the woman's round face telling her to grow up and find friends that first time they'd met. But maybe she'd never grown up, maybe she'd simply let herself be passed from her mother to her husband, never stopping and thinking about who she was or what she wanted along the way. She had been such an idiot.

'The other two are lady's mantle and comfrey and I cannot yet work out what they are for. But, if you can, you should try not to drink anything he gives you from now on, especially not the tea.'

'But what can we actually do?' Lily felt a rush of desperation, because it was all very well to be believed by one person, but she was nowhere nearer to a solution. 'I don't think I can go to anyone in authority, because too many people have seen Becky pretending to be me behaving erratically. And, anyway, everyone always listens to Henry.'

'Oh no, that is out of the question. Also, if I can speak frankly, Lily?'

She nodded because she couldn't imagine hearing anything worse than what was in her head.

'I have been watching you and you do not help yourself. When, for example, was the last time you ate a proper meal?'

'Eating makes me feel sick.' She wanted to point out that Lawrence was not much more than skin and bones himself, but resisted.

'It does me too,' he said with that abruptness she'd grown quite fond of as it was so different from the hiding behind words she was used to. 'But we both must eat. Imagine we are going into battle, we need to keep up our strength and stay alert. Both things are impossible if we're starving. Also ...' He stopped and looked straight at her, his cheeks flushing slightly.

'Go on.' She smiled to show she wasn't offended.

'Well, also, you do come across as someone with a lot on their mind. You frequently act confused, which is just making Henry's job that much easier. And I know the tea has probably made you feel terrible, but you must try your best to seem as well as you can. I think the best bet is for you to stay as visible as possible on this crossing. And when you're with Elsworth act as normally as possible, especially if you're with other people. I will try to think of something more concrete, but, for now, this is a good start.'

She was struck then by just how many hours there were to get through until they reached New York, not that she was even sure it would get any better there. She'd waited out so many days, weeks, months at Elsworth, filling her time with nothing, but never had it seemed dangerous, never had there been this ticking clock in her head.

'Let's agree to meet after lunch? Say in the writing room? I'll get there for two o'clock, but come half an hour or so afterwards, so it looks as if we have just bumped into each other. My cabin is D56, if you ever need me, and I know where you are.'

There was a flurry of little footsteps and a young girl ran past them, bowling a hoop along in front of her. 'Jemima, Jemima, be careful, please,' her mother was shouting after her, as she hurried behind.

'We should separate,' Lawrence said. 'Keep moving and try to strike up conversations with people. Be confident and happy when you speak to them, talk about things you have planned for the future. The more people who recognise you, the less easy it will be for Elsworth and Becky to play their imitation game.'

Lily nodded, not trusting herself to speak because her tears were so close to the surface. She wanted to grab on to Lawrence and beg him not to leave her but knew that what he was saying was right. And then he was turning and walking away, this strange and unsettling man, who was also her only hope. Because she had to forget about Becky now, she had to erase the memory of what she'd thought they meant to each other because it could never have been true. All those looks and touches and unspoken words, which she had felt like a force, had clearly meant nothing to Becky. Maybe she'd laughed about it in the kitchen with the other servants, or more likely she'd felt silently disgusted, revolted that she had to play along with her mistress's stupid fantasy. Lily saw her, then, lying under the blacksmith's boy, under Henry, under any man who offered, and a sickness rose through her that felt as violent as a storm.

But the sea was calm and she forced herself to move, because there was nothing else to do, walking in the opposite direction from Lawrence, past Jemima and her mother and the French boys and their father, praying and longing for an answer that seemed too elusive to even exist.

LAWRENCE

Lawrence didn't want to go back to his cabin after he left Lily so made his way to the saloon. In truth, the desire to help Lily was an incomplete resolution because he had absolutely no sense of himself stepping ashore in New York. The thought of a long life without Cissy still felt like razors lacerating his skin, and yet he was beginning to wonder if even his grief had become selfish, if in fact he was like a child unable to accept her death. Worrying about Lily had implanted a tiny seed in his brain, the roots attaching themselves without him fully noticing, forcing him to look at the possibility that he was still capable of feeling something other than misery, which made him wonder if he might be acting on pure emotion when he jumped, if in the falling he might regret.

Elsworth was in the saloon, sitting on his own in a tall-backed chair, reading through a pile of papers.

Lawrence hesitated, but then something like weariness enveloped him. He and Lily didn't have a plan, they didn't really even know what they were up against, or even exactly what the man intended, which meant he had very little to lose.

'Lord Elsworth,' he said as he reached Henry's side.

Henry looked up over his glasses, his eyes heavy with

annoyance at being disturbed. 'Mr Beesley.' He made no attempt to stand.

'May I?' He indicated the chair next to Henry.

'Please.' Although the word was said without feeling.

Lawrence crossed his legs as he sat, looking over at Henry, who took off his glasses and began folding his papers. The man was very unattractive up close, with florid skin and a pot belly that stuck out of him like a ball. His forehead was also very creased, and his eyes yellow and bloodshot. 'I think I bumped into your doctor, George Henderson.'

An almost imperceptible twitch passed across Henry's face. 'Yes, he has been helping me with my wife.'

'I am sorry to hear she is unwell.'

Henry stared at Lawrence and it was unclear how he might take the statement, but then he just sighed. 'The last few years have been very hard. It has been nice of you to take an interest in Lily, Mr Beesley, but I must warn you that much of what she says is untrue. Or maybe that is unfair.' He rubbed at his face like a man with too many thoughts running underneath his skin. 'I don't think she even knows she's speaking untruths any more, I think she has come to totally believe her fantasies. I hope she hasn't said anything which might cause offence.'

Lawrence felt a flutter of doubt because it was still so much easier to believe in this version of a hysterical woman than the story Lily had told him. 'Oh no,' he waved the suggestion away, 'but I did see what happened on deck yesterday and I hope she is recovered.'

'Ah yes.' Henry stroked two fingers across his moustache. 'We are not having a good journey. We knew it was a risk attempting the crossing, but it seemed imperative to get her back home in case … well, in case things deteriorate further. But, if anything, her delusions have intensified since we boarded, which is most worrying.'

'Her delusions?' And despite all he had seen, Lawrence felt his heart beat against his ribs and his mind turned to the words.

Henry sighed like a troubled man, the sound rattling around his chest. 'If I'm honest, she was never really right, I just didn't notice it at first because I fell so completely in love with her when we met. And also, looking back, her mother was very conniving, reeling me in terribly. She was one of those dreadful American women absolutely set on her daughter obtaining a title and, stupid fool that I am, I fell for it completely.'

'How long have you been married?' Lawrence tried to push away the thought that Henry sounded entirely reasonable, when Lily so often did not.

'Nine years. I realised what a terrible mistake I had made almost as soon as we arrived back in England. I tried to make it work, but it has been very hard.'

Lawrence sat forward, his confusion swirling. 'What happened, may I ask?'

'Oh, it became apparent very quickly that she was a very troubled girl. She saw conspiracies everywhere. Refused to make an effort with any of my friends or family, and blamed me for everything. Said I'd locked her up in Northumberland, when really she hated coming to London and was so rude when people came to visit, I stopped inviting them. I tried to get her out and about a bit, but she always refused. And she did so many strange things, including setting up a sort of bird sanctuary in one of the unused rooms in the attic. It wasn't discovered for ages, by which time the room was ruined. And she would go on these long, solitary walks, and my groom would have to ride out to find her, often bringing her home filthy and bedraggled, with no memory of what had happened. And then she started to accuse me of having affairs and it became impossible for her to be at any social function as she would make a scene.'

Lawrence tried to read Henry's face, but it was set in a genuine concern that was hard to place. 'But she is pregnant now?'

Henry nodded. 'Yes. It is a blessing we . . . well, I at least, have longed for. I had pretty much given up on the idea of her being able to conceive in actual fact, but then I met George Henderson and he'd had some luck already helping a man I knew who also had a troubled wife. Within six months, Lily was pregnant.'

'That is amazing. I have never heard of such a thing.'

'No, nor had I. I think I remember you saying that you are a science master?'

Lawrence nodded.

'I'm not sure how strictly medical Henderson's treatment is, but it has worked, so I'm not questioning it.'

Lawrence thought of Lily's shiver as she'd said she hated Dr Henderson and doubted that would mean much to Elsworth. *That's what the suffrage movement is,* he remembered Cissy saying, *getting women heard, making our voices count.* He'd thought she must be mistaken, because surely it was all about getting women the vote. But suddenly he understood what she'd meant.

A fresh anger rose through him, but this time not at his wife, but at the reason she'd felt the need to fight. It was possible that all she had done hadn't felt like a choice, possible that she hadn't chosen it over him, possible that she hadn't abandoned him.

'Maybe the birth will settle her.' Lawrence kept his voice even, recognising he was dissembling, as Lily must have to do every day of her life. It felt as if it had left a film of grease on his skin.

Henry huffed. 'I hoped that as well, but I am far from convinced. She is frantic about the pregnancy, simply a bundle of nerves. She has become so deluded, you would be hard-pushed to separate fact from fiction.'

'What caused the episode yesterday?'

Henry shrugged. 'It's hard to know with Lily. One moment she is as close to fine as possible and the next she is desperate to die. We were walking calmly and suddenly she dragged a wooden chair to the side and tried to climb over. I think she meant to jump, but I wrestled her back and then she fainted.' He shook his head as if the memory pained him.

'The woman I saw barely resembled Lady Elsworth.' Lawrence stared straight at Henry as he spoke, his observation ambiguous enough but also loaded with meaning.

Henry coloured as he held his stare and his eyes narrowed. 'I know what you mean,' he answered finally. 'Sometimes when she is having one of her attacks, she is so distorted I barely recognise her myself. It is as if all her misery rises to the surface and contorts her features.'

Lawrence smiled thinly. 'The mind is a complex place.'

'Anyway, if you will excuse me, Mr Beesley, I must get back to Lily.'

Lawrence bowed his head, so Henry stood and clipped his heels together like a solider before heading out of the saloon. Lawrence sat back down after he'd gone and felt a sense of shame drip through him, almost as if Cissy were there, turning her back on him. Lily had told him what was happening and yet he'd needed physical proof before he'd truly believed her, which meant what he'd really done was minimise her feelings, dismissing them as if they counted for less.

He was filled with all the times he'd sighed at Cissy's obsession, as he sometimes shamefully called it, or all the small irritations he'd felt and probably communicated to her. And he had loved her, truly and completely, and still behaved that way, so what hope did women like Lily have against men like Elsworth? He wondered then if he was any better, or if he too only wanted women to bend to fit his needs, rather than considering what might be best for them. His shame felt toxic, like a pool of acid in the pit of his stomach which only the all-enveloping power of the sea could wash away.

LILY

Lily did as Lawrence had told her and went to the writing room for two thirty. She'd told Henry that she felt tired after lunch and wanted to lie down, which he'd accepted gratefully. She thought the performance they were both putting on was starting to strain him almost as much as her, and they'd both sat in silence for much of the meal whilst others had chatted around them.

Once, Lily had waited in a hallway at the end of a party given by one of Henry's mistresses, as he'd said goodbye to her enclosed behind a dark mahogany door. It wasn't that she hadn't known her husband was a philanderer by then, not as if she didn't hear the corridor-creeping whenever there was a house party at Elsworth, or read about different women on his arm in the society columns, or find countless love letters and bills for extravagant gifts. She just hadn't expected to ever be actually involved in the process.

It had been draughty standing on the cold flagstones, with the front door being constantly opened to allow people in and out and she'd been forced to pull her shawl tightly around her shoulders, which made her feel like an old maid. A few of the passing guests had nodded at her or stopped to enquire after her health, but everyone had moved quickly on, as if they were as embarrassed by her situation as she was. After a while, the servants had started to cast surreptitious glances at her, until finally a footman asked if she needed any assistance. The humiliation she'd felt was so fully formed it was as if it existed alive within her, as if she stood no chance of ever escaping, as if everyone at the party, everyone in the whole of London, maybe even England, was laughing at her. She had wondered if the whole thing was a joke, if Henry had fetched her over from America as a dare, or a piece of entertainment for everyone. She had thought maybe she was on a stage and that she'd forgotten her lines, or that her mother would one day jump out from behind a potted plant and they'd all laugh. Finally, she'd banged on the door and Henry had emerged red-faced and dishevelled and marched her out of the house as if she'd been the one being rude.

'Are you feeling well?' Lawrence asked as she sat opposite him. 'I'm sorry to ask, it is just you are quite flushed.'

Lily's heart was still racing from her memories, but she didn't have time to entertain them any more, so she nodded. 'I have been thinking.' And it was true, she had spent the morning lost in active thought, which was very different to the passive daydreams and reminiscence with which she usually filled her time. 'I think I should write to my father.'

Lawrence raised an eyebrow. 'I'm not sure what good that would do. Nothing will be posted until we dock.'

But she'd considered this already. 'Yes, I know. But I was thinking earlier, my father has already agreed that we are to go straight to the house he has rented, which makes me wonder if Henry has been filling his mind with my weaknesses for ages. I mean, this plan is clearly intricate, so I'm presuming it has been a long time in the making. And that means my family will not be at the dock to meet us, so I won't get a chance to speak with him. If I write a clear and concise letter explaining what

Henry is doing to me, with all we know, then surely he will at least investigate what I have to say.' As Lily spoke, she wondered how her pride had stopped her writing to her father, or even May, about her marriage before. She felt a surge of annoyance with herself then, because she'd been so foolish, so silly and self-absorbed, such a bloody child when all was said and done. Consuelo had been right, it had been time to grow up nine years before, a lesson she hoped she hadn't learnt too late.

Lawrence was sitting quite still, his hands resting calmly on his knees, which made her want to shake him, because he always acted as if they had all the time in the world.

'Well, do you think it is a good plan?' she pressed.

'If it makes you feel better.'

She felt tiny tears smart to her eyes because he'd made her feel foolish and maybe she still was that petulant young bride refusing to come down for dinner. She spoke before she'd really considered what she was saying. 'When I was a child, my mother used to lock my sister May and I into our playroom when she thought we'd been naughty. It didn't take much for her to think that either, and usually had something to do with us not behaving like proper young ladies. May has a wicked sense of humour, you see, and she would often say inappropriate things and I would laugh and Mother would go all red and tell us to get upstairs and we would know what that meant.' Lily paused, hoping Lawrence would say something, but he just continued looking impassively at her. 'I don't know why I'm telling you this. Maybe what I'm trying to say is that I feel like I have been locked away for a long time. Well, forever really. In a funny way, it is as though there are always keys being turned against me. And I am starting to think that has made me quite, well, naïve, I suppose, and stupid. I understand that probably sounds ridiculous to you, especially with Cissy and how amazing she was, but not all of us are like that. So, I am sorry if my plan sounds foolish, but that is probably just because it comes from a foolish mind.' Lily felt a little out of breath when she'd finished speaking and knew a red blush had extended across her cheeks and down her neck because she could feel the hot itch on her skin. She couldn't bring herself to look at Lawrence, but she could feel him shift next to her.

'Lily,' he said finally, which made her look up and into his creased face. 'I'm sorry if I sounded harsh. It's not a foolish plan, it's a good idea.' She allowed herself a small smile. 'And please do not call yourself foolish or stupid. If you are those things, then so am I because Cissy taught me all the important lessons I know. Or, at least, she tried to teach them to me, but I was too pig-headed to learn. You know, I had this supposedly fine education, but she had more knowledge in her little finger than I will ever hope to have. We should always listen to those we love, which sounds so simple, but has been a late lesson for me.'

He fell silent after he'd spoken, his face contracting in on itself, but his words had reminded Lily of lying in her bed, almost delirious with a fever that had made her insides leak out of her. She felt the coolness of a cloth on her forehead which dampened the heat for only minutes, before it all rose through her again, so every part of her flesh ached, right up to her teeth.

Becky had wobbled in and out of focus, her sight so distorted it had been hard to make out if there were tears on her friend's cheeks. But she was sure her hand had been held, that the mopping of her brow was as gentle as it could be and that Becky kept up a low dialogue: 'This has to stop. You have to act now, this cannot continue. We can go away together. Life can be different.' But when she'd woken the next morning, the fever broken, it had all seemed like a dream and she hadn't felt brave enough to ask Becky if she'd spoken those words, too weak to even consider acting or leaving.

Lawrence sat forward slightly. 'When I was trying to sleep last night, I remembered how Cissy used to say that she was fighting for female agency.'

'In what way?' She wasn't even sure she knew what the words meant, which made her feel useless.

'She said that, more than anything, she wanted women to have the right to be who they wanted to be.' Lawrence's gaze was fixed on a point over her shoulder. 'She said that women always denigrate themselves, even when they're talking about things that have been done to them. She said that almost every abused woman she ever spoke to said that she'd been stupid to let it happen, or she'd been annoying to live with, or foolish with money, or a hundred other inadequacies. She said they never let themselves make actual decisions, even about the smallest things, but would prefix everything with the word might, as in I might take a walk, or I might leave him, or I might have soup for dinner. She said we live in a world in which women are made to feel stupid and unworthy for so much of their lives that it is impossible for them to think of themselves any other way and so cannot trust their own decisions. And that makes them childlike and vulnerable and it all becomes a self-fulfilling prophecy.' He looked back at her. 'Cissy would tell you not to listen to any stupid men like me, but to trust what you feel and to do what you think is right.'

Lily found she didn't know how to respond to what he'd said. She'd never heard words used in this way and never thought about the things his words enclosed. His, or really Cissy's, ideas felt alive and vibrant to her, like a hothouse plant, bursting with colour and scent.

'Come on,' he said gently. 'I think you should write that letter to your father.'

She felt emboldened by the confidences they had exchanged. 'Perhaps I could give you the letter and you could deliver it to my parents if Henry takes me straight to the house. You could even speak up for me.'

But she saw Lawrence wither as she spoke, so all the joy that talking about Cissy had brought to his face vanished, and he was left looking like the troubled man she'd first met. 'I want to help you as much as I can, Lily, but I do not know how much I can promise.'

She felt foolish again and then angry, because she didn't think she would ever learn how to behave. 'I'm sorry if I asked too much of you.'

'It's not that.' His eyes were filled with a desperation she knew only too well. 'I promise I will help you as much as I am capable. I just do not want you to rely on me too greatly, or to think I will always be here.'

His words scared her. 'What do you mean? Are you planning on returning to England soon after we dock?'

He dropped his eyes from her. 'No, not necessarily. Forget what I said, it is of no importance. But . . .' he hesitated for a moment, 'is there really no one else who could take care of you, if I was not around?'

'Well, I know my parents and May would if they could, but I'm not going to see them and I fear they will be persuaded by Henry.' She felt herself heat at the thought of the other person and then remembered what Lawrence had said about bravery. 'And, well, a few months ago, I would have trusted my whole life to Becky. But I think I must have been mistaken about that, or maybe I ruined our friendship in some way.'

A crease formed between his eyes. 'What makes you say that?'

She squeezed her hands together to stop herself from crying. 'I don't know exactly. I think, maybe, I have relied on her too much and not been a good friend in return. Or perhaps I never let her know how much I valued her?'

He smiled gently. 'She is very dear to you?'

'Oh yes, as dear as anything.' She knew her whole face was flushed and dropped her eyes to her feet.

'I will fetch some paper and you can write that letter.'

Her embarrassment only allowed her to look back up when she heard him leave and then she tried to make sense of all his words, even her own. She was used to not knowing what to think, but the conversation had made her feel like there was something fundamental deep in her very core that she was failing to understand. Cissy's thoughts echoed through her and it was certainly true that she felt as if she had no agency in life, but surely Becky had even less.

She watched the steward hand Lawrence a sheaf of papers and it reminded her of a letter Becky had received about a year before, brought up to her along with Lily's letters, so she'd watched her open it and then seen her face collapse and the tears leak from her eyes.

'What's wrong?' Lily had asked desperately, her hands feeling useless in her lap.

But Becky had swallowed down her tears. 'My sister is ill. But then she is often sick. She has weak lungs and our house is very damp, so this time of year is hard for her.'

Lily had tried to imagine Becky's home, but realised she'd never asked about it; she didn't even know which house it was in the village. 'Is there nothing that can be done for her? What does the doctor say?'

'The doctor?' Becky had grunted. 'We can't afford the doctor's opinion.'

That evening over dinner, Lily had asked Henry if there was anything that could be done to make Becky's family home more comfortable, or if they could send a doctor to her sister. He'd laughed at her stupid sentimentality, as he'd called it, which had fired an unusual anger in her breast so she'd pushed where she would normally have stopped. 'Please, Henry. Can we not help at all? Becky is desperate.'

He'd looked at her over the rim of his glasses, eyeing her as if she had for once said something interesting, but when he'd spoken, it was with his usual disdain. 'My God, Lily, you have been in this country for eight years and still you do not know the basic rules. Servants hate it when you interfere in their private business. You have probably mortally offended Becky even discussing it with her.'

And when Lily had returned to her rooms later and watched Becky through the glass as she removed her dress and unfastened her corset and unpinned her hair, she'd seen how white and drawn she looked, her mouth set in a thin line, and she'd thought Henry was right and wanted to kick herself for her insensitivity.

She rested her hand on her skirt, but the baby lay still, even though she directed all her attention towards it, trying to imagine it suspended and contained within her belly. It still felt like an enigma, but she had her first hope for it as she watched Lawrence walking back towards her with the white paper fluttering in his hands. She shut her eyes and wished for it to be a boy, hoped that once released from the confinement of her body, it could branch out and stride forth, using its voice and privilege in ways she could only dream. Having a daughter would be terrifying, like being forced to feed your child to the lions, creating something that you knew would one day be destroyed.

It seemed likely that she had failed not just herself, but Becky as well and maybe that was why this was all happening now.

Maybe it wasn't that Becky had never cared for her, more that she had given up waiting to be cared for.

Lawrence coughed as he sat, so she opened her eyes to see him putting the paper on the table in front of her and smiling softly. She pulled off the lid of a pen and let the nib touch the fresh white page, so a blot of ink was the first marking she made. But it didn't matter; what she had to say was messy anyway. She began to write and, for the first time in years, an odd calmness enveloped her, because there was something cathartic about watching herself unfurl from her hand. It was time to start owning the words which constituted the story of her life.

LAWRENCE

Lawrence felt exhausted by the time he returned to his cabin to dress for dinner. He'd sat with Lily while she wrote her letter to her father, so filled by his memories of Cissy, it was as if she was occupying him. He felt desolate at the thought that he hadn't been as good to her as he'd thought he was, or had wanted to be. It made him wonder if the real tragedy wasn't her death, but his reaction to it. If he had, in fact, always had the wrong responses to a woman he loved more than life itself. And if that was true, then he needed to find a different way of telling her story, one that didn't involve making himself the central drama, one that gave her the ending she deserved.

He was finding it hard to articulate his limbs into his clothes, which made him worry that even with wanting to make amends to Cissy he would still always be drawn to jumping. He was glad for Lily then, because he'd grown fond of her and wanted to help her. He should probably agree to deliver her letter, although what that meant for him was nebulous. Everything was confused, no path seemed straight or concise, every action had a consequence and he wasn't at all sure which way to go.

As Lawrence left his cabin, he was struck again by the jollity in the corridors, as if the whole ship were engaged in a party. People were constantly laughing and chatting and there was a collective air of exuberance, as if no one could quite believe their luck at being on board. Although the joy was lost on him and his heart sank as he walked into the clamour and heat of the dining room, the energy needed for participation leaching from him with every step he took.

A hand grabbed on to his arm, making him stop and turn to see William Carter beaming up at him. 'Marjorie and I were just talking about you. Please, join us.'

There was no reason not to and so Lawrence sat next to the reverend and opposite Marjorie.

'How has your day been?' Marjorie asked, as she buttered a roll.

Lawrence thought about his strange day, which he almost felt as if he'd spent with Cissy. 'I spent most of it thinking about my wife, so it has been a mixture of pleasure and pain.'

He noticed a glance pass between the Carters and thought he'd probably been too candid.

'I can see how that might be bittersweet,' Marjorie replied.

William placed a hand on Lawrence's arm, which made him turn to look at the man and his round, open face. 'Something my profession has taught me is that death is so much harder for those left behind.'

'Does your son talk about her much?' Marjorie asked.

'Not an awful lot.' Although, as Lawrence spoke, snapshots invaded him of Alec hovering at doors, his quiet eyes watching, his little hands twitching.

'I always found that our boys understood so much more than I gave them credit for when they were little,' Marjorie said. 'Children are very perceptive, I find.'

He'd shouted at Alec to leave him alone when his grief had felt like a building toppling him, he'd sometimes not gone to kiss him goodnight when he'd already drunk too much, he'd removed all of Cissy's pictures into drawers, he cringed when Alec used the word Mummy.

'Children pull us forward,' William said. 'I love to watch the children play on this crossing and imagine all the life awaiting them. I always think of them as like little markers of the future.'

'What did you and your wife wish for Alec?' Marjorie asked and Lawrence saw a deep intelligence in her stare that he hadn't noticed before.

'I suppose happiness mostly.' But that wasn't the whole truth, they'd also wished for a wide, inclusive life for Alec that he wouldn't be getting in Scotland with Cissy's cousin, who was a kind, good woman, but very traditional. 'But also, Cissy was very keen that our children be taught about equality, that they should go out into the world and do good somehow.'

'How very noble,' Marjorie said. 'And what a wonderful legacy for you to pass on to your son from your wife.'

'I wish I'd been a better husband and father,' Lawrence heard himself say, knowing he was giving too much of himself away.

'Ah, I wish for a wish,' William said and Lawrence wondered who he was quoting. 'Wishes are a little like prayers, I find, good for the moment, but not something to be hung on to.'

Lawrence turned to him again. 'I'm sorry, I do not—'

William smiled. 'Too many people waste their lives on wishes, Lawrence. Marjorie always used to say that to our boys when they wanted something impossible.' Lawrence looked back at Marjorie who was smiling still. 'But wishes cannot feed you, or make anything better. I mean to say, I'm not advocating giving up dreams, they're essential for the soul. I'm just saying that if you spend too much time longing, you don't spend enough time living.'

Lawrence's throat felt scratched when he spoke. 'But if I give up my longing, I am turning my back on Cissy.'

'Not at all.' Marjorie's tone was sharp and urgent. 'You yourself have just told us what Cissy dreamt for your son, so fulfilling that is akin to helping her live on. And perhaps she had other dreams as well you could help her achieve.' She reached across the table and surprised Lawrence by touching his chest through his shirt, pushing against his breastbone. 'Because she will always live on in there.'

'There are always people who need our help,' William added.

Lawrence looked between William and Marjorie and found he couldn't think of the words needed to reply to them. And then it was as if Alec was in his arms, his chubby limbs wresting from his grasp, his talc scent wafting up his nose, his gurgling laughter filling his ears. Except the words also reminded him of something William had said to him before, something about how we can only ever save ourselves, which sounded so bleak and lonely. Although hadn't he also said that we save ourselves by helping others? And then Lawrence was sitting once again on Cissy's bed and she was telling him that she couldn't save him and begging him to take care of Alec. And he had failed her in every way. He hadn't done anything right, it was all hopeless and pathetic and pointless.

He stood abruptly, his chair scraping against the floor, so both William and Marjorie looked up at him, their faces creased with worry. 'I am sorry,' he stammered. 'I feel a bit unwell. I think I shall take a turn in the fresh air.'

'Shall I accompany you?' William asked, making to stand.

But Lawrence waved him down. 'No, please. Please finish your dinner. I have bad sea legs, it is nothing to worry about.' He knew the excuse was lame considering the crossing had been nothing but calm, but it was the only thing which came to him.

He turned to go, but Marjorie called him back, so he was

forced to turn around again. 'You know it is a fact that you cannot stay seasick forever,' she said.

'No, I did not.' Lawrence could feel sweat breaking out under his clothes and he longed for fresh air like a drowning man.

But she continued speaking. 'Yes, it can take years, so you might not regain your balance on this voyage. But the more you stand on the sea, the closer you get to it vanishing.'

Lawrence couldn't work out what she meant and doubted even that it was true, but he smiled and bobbed his head, before turning again and leaving the room. He felt better almost as soon as he'd left the dining room, but his legs were weak and there was a tremor in his hands, so he made his way upwards and on to the boat deck. The sun had set, although a faint brightness was lingering along the horizon, contrasting with the deep blackness above his head and the thousands of glittering stars. A few people were on the deck, which he was pleased for because they limited his options.

He walked to the seductive edge and stood staring down into the darkness of the sea, broken only by little trails of white as they cut so confidently across its surface. He'd left his greatcoat in his cabin and was soon shivering as the air had cooled dramatically, which he presumed must mean that they were approaching the ice fields. When he'd boarded, the time it was going to take to reach them had seemed like an eternity, but now he felt like they'd rushed to meet him and he wanted everything to slow down.

He turned to go back to his cabin, but was so absorbed in his thoughts that he walked straight into a steward.

'I'm sorry, Sir,' the man said, extending a hand to Lawrence.

'No, no, my fault,' Lawrence answered. 'I should look where I'm going.'

'Can I assist you with anything?'

'No, no, thank you.' But then Lawrence remembered something. 'Oh, perhaps I could ask you one question?'

'Anything, Sir.' Lawrence thought the steward was young, perhaps mid-twenties, and he sparkled with a preposterous youth that didn't seem entirely real.

'Someone just now told me that you cannot stay seasick forever and I wondered if that is true?'

The steward laughed. 'My, that's an old saying I have not heard in a long time, but yes, I believe it is.'

Lawrence was surprised. 'What happens then? I mean, do you wake up one day and it has just gone?'

The man stepped a little closer to Lawrence. 'I started working on ships at sixteen and I cannot tell you how sick I was on my first voyage. Barely left my bed. I was so embarrassed, but my officer was really nice about it, told me all the boys have at least one voyage like that, but it would get better each time I went to sea. I didn't believe him at the time and vowed that when I got back on to dry land, I would never set foot on a boat again. But when I got home, I found I missed the sea something terrible, all that movement and life and uncertainty right beneath my feet. I met an old sailor in a pub one night and we got very drunk and I told him my problem, and he ended up taking me to a tattoo parlour and said he'd make sure that I had to get back on the sea.'

The man held his hands out to Lawrence and in the dark it wasn't clear what he was meant to be looking at. But then the man angled them towards the light of the moon and Lawrence saw dark letters inked across the backs of each of his fingers: HOLD FAST.

'You'll find those words on lots of sailors' hands. And they don't just mean literally hold on tight, although that's useful advice on many crossings. They mean hang in there, it will get better.'

'Hold fast,' Lawrence repeated and the words sounded sweet in his ears.

'You'll feel better in a bit,' the steward said and Lawrence wasn't sure what they were talking about any more. 'Anyway, I must get on, if there is nothing more you need?'

'No, no.' Lawrence watched the man as he was swallowed up by the night, finding tears pricking bizarrely at his eyes at the thought of that young man holding on, holding fast.

The words reminded him of Cissy and how she kept on going, always asking questions and pushing beyond where others might give up. He remembered then how Lily had shone as she'd spoken about Becky and realised that he had never even considered her voice, when it could easily be integral to the story. Cissy had always sought out the stories that weren't usually heard and she would have wanted to hear Becky, a realisation that shamed him in how long it had taken him to work out. There didn't seem any point in delaying, so he made his way straight to F deck, remembering the cabin he'd seen them go into the day before and how Lily had told him that Becky's was next door.

Becky looked surprised to see a strange man outside her cabin, but Lawrence was struck by a sense of weariness also that seemed to envelop her. Hers was definitely the face he'd seen under Lily's hat, but up close he thought it looked puffy, so her features were almost lost in the expanse of flesh.

'Can I help you, Sir?' she asked, tightening her grip on the door.

He felt suddenly scared that he had acted too rashly because there was no doubting how involved Becky was with the plot.

But at the same time he felt they had little to lose. 'I am sorry to bother you. I'm a friend of Lady Elsworth.'

Becky's brow furrowed. 'I wasn't aware she had any friends on board.'

'No, no,' he waved a hand in front of his face. 'What I mean is, I have met her on board and we have become friendly.'

Becky kept her gaze fixed, her mouth set in a tight line.

'She has mentioned a few things that appear to be very worrying and, as she has spoken of you in such high regard, I wanted to ask your opinion of them.'

'She says many strange things.' But Lawrence noticed Becky's grip on the door had loosened slightly.

'She said you are, or at least were, very close.' Lawrence watched the words land on Becky in a slight softening of her features, so the line of her mouth turned gently upwards.

'I've been her personal maid for nearly nine years now, so we have spent almost all our time together.'

'But would you call yourself friends?'

Becky shifted her weight and her eyes filled, although she was quick to swallow down her emotion. 'She has been a good employer.'

'Is her husband cruel to her, in your opinion?'

Becky looked at her feet. 'I really cannot discuss that with you, Sir.'

'She claims you and he are in love.' Lawrence held himself still and the air felt alive, as if all the atoms were whizzing past them. 'My wife was an aristocrat,' he said, impetuously, 'and I am very far from that. So I know what it's like to always be looking in, to never quite feel that your place is secure, or that you know what is right, or sometimes even what things mean.' He remembered interminable dinners at the Manor, in which he'd feel Cissy's mother tense as he picked up his cutlery. Cissy had told him to ignore it, but he'd never been able to, because you can only really ignore something when you know what that something is.

Becky's cheeks had flushed. 'Was yours a love match?'

Lawrence nodded. 'Absolutely.'

'Well, you are very lucky then.' She swallowed again, her chest heaving. 'It is unusual for people like us to be able to rely on love. I think you have to be rich to be able to afford emotions, or lucky, or loved by someone brave.'

Lawrence couldn't really remember what they were talking about and he took a small step backwards, away from the door. 'My wife was brave,' he said and then Becky was swimming before him as his eyes filled with tears.

Becky's expression drew down, as if she was zipping herself up tight. 'Like I said, you were very lucky. But there's not much luck in life, I find. I'm going to close the door now, Sir.' It swung towards him and Lawrence was left looking at the brushstrokes on the wood reflected in the light, reminding him of all the ways we are all only ever versions of ourselves, forever changing and adapting.

His steps dragged as he made his way back to his cabin because everything felt murky, as if he had already jumped and was right now in the water, thrashing around in the darkness, unable to work out which way was up, if that was even the direction he wanted to travel.

LILY

Lily lay very still in her bunk, trying to regulate her breathing so it sounded as if she were sleeping, when really her nerves felt as if they'd broken loose from her skin and were skittering about inside her body. It was, however, imperative that Henry believed her to be sleeping because she was sure he would then sneak out to Becky's room, which would leave her free to find Lawrence.

Her evening had been dreadful, spiralling her down into a pit of fear and speculation, and she couldn't wait until morning to find out if Lawrence had forsaken her along with everyone else. She'd looked for him in the dining room and then the saloon after dinner, but he'd been nowhere to be seen and she'd grown quite frantic with the thought that he'd changed his mind about her. The only good thing about the evening was that she'd managed to pour her tea into a corner under her bed when Henry went to the bathroom.

Henry's bunk creaked with the sound of him sitting up, so she held herself as still as she could, shutting her eyes against the darkness. She heard him lower himself down and tiptoe to the door, which he opened quietly, and then she heard the click of the latch as he shut it behind him. She opened her eyes and it was as if the sea had found its way into the cabin as blues and greens swirled before her. There was a faint bump from next door and she sat up, her whole body alert. It was madness to attempt to get to Lawrence, and if Henry came back and found her gone, she had no idea what she would say. But she had the sense that Henry never slept in their room and, besides, she didn't think she had anything to lose because her situation could hardly deteriorate.

She dressed quickly without fastening herself in or wearing one of the protective skirts, letting herself out of the cabin as noiselessly as possible. The corridors were almost deserted and she knew it must be late, probably gone midnight, which made her heart race because what she was doing was absurd and she worried what Lawrence might think she meant, appearing at his door in the middle of the night. But she wouldn't have a chance to question him in the daytime, surrounded by people, and if he'd decided to abandon her to her fate, she had to know, she had to prepare herself.

D deck was two floors above hers and she took the stairs quickly, emerging outside the dining room, where a few women were clearing up the last of the evening's meal. The numbers on the doors led her round to Lawrence's cabin and then she knew all she had to do was knock. But standing in the corridor, with just the faint clinking of china accompanying her thoughts, she felt indescribably foolish.

She leant her ear against the door, but there was no sound from within and no line of light that she could make out from under the door. It was nearly enough to make her go back to her cabin because fear seemed preferable to embarrassment, but their conversation from earlier dragged up a modicum of resolve.

The knock, when she made it, sounded so loud, Lily was surprised that all the doors along the corridor didn't fling open. But in fact nothing happened and then she wondered if perhaps he was still upstairs in the saloon, or if he'd asked to move rooms so she couldn't bother him.

She knocked again and this time there was a muffled sound from behind the door and then she could hear uncertain footsteps and finally the door was opened and Lawrence was blinking out at her, his hair mussed and his eyes blinking against the light.

'Forgive me,' Lily said. 'I have woken you.'

He rubbed at his eyes, which seemed to return him a little to life. 'Has something happened?'

'No, no. I'm sorry.' She realised she was repeating herself and knew her face had flushed because she felt the heat on her skin.

He opened the door wider and retreated into the room. There was a click and then it was light. 'Come in,' he said.

It seemed absurdly intimate to step into Lawrence's space, especially with the knowledge of his sleeping vulnerability still heavy in the air.

He flicked the covers up over his bed, which had looked as naked to Lily as if Lawrence himself wasn't wearing any clothes.

'I'm sorry,' she said again.

'Please stop apologising.'

'But I've disturbed your rest.'

'No matter. Would you like to sit?' He motioned behind her to the sofa, so she made herself bend and sit, although there was nothing relaxing in the movement. He leant against the washstand, crossing one foot over the other.

'I feel foolish,' she heard herself say, which reminded her of Cissy's complaint that women always denigrated their experiences and served at least to make her feel a little angry. She forced herself to look up and meet his eyes. 'It's just when I didn't see you this evening I became convinced that you must have changed your mind about helping me.'

He shook his head. 'No, it's not that. I'm sorry, I should have found you and explained. I just felt out of sorts tonight, and rather strange.'

'Are you ill?' He did look peaky, pale but with blotches of red across his cheeks.

'Not physically.'

She couldn't for a moment think what he meant, but then she thought of the terror which so often accompanied her and how her brain fizzed in her scalp and how her limbs could tingle and her heart race. 'Is it about Cissy?'

He nodded and tears welled in his eyes which embarrassed her until she realised that he didn't mind that she'd seen. 'Oh Lawrence, I'm sorry.'

He shrugged. 'My thoughts are very jumbled.'

Lily clasped her hands together because she felt useless against his misery. 'What did you love about her?'

His response was instantaneous. 'Everything.'

'No, tell me specifically.'

He looked up. 'I suppose what I most loved was her passion. I have never before or since met anyone who knew their own mind as she did and who then acted on all the things she thought. But I'm not sure I ever told her that, or made her feel that she was wonderful. Sometimes I felt as though I was just a passenger on her craft and I think I resented her for that. I have even felt furious with her for dying, which is absurd and so selfish of me. She deserved someone so much better than me, someone who understood and appreciated her, someone who realised that what she was doing was important and gave her complete freedom.'

'I think you are doing yourself a disservice, Lawrence. You once told me that she said loving you set her free.'

He waved a hand in front of his face. 'But it wasn't enough. I didn't do enough.'

Lily wondered what on earth could ever be enough, which made Becky rear up in her mind, so she felt a sickening regret. 'It must be amazing to be loved as completely as you clearly love her. I cannot imagine it. And I know that must make losing her feel indescribably cruel, but also, well, you had that time with her. And that feels like a gift to me.'

Lawrence covered his face with his hands and then his shoulders started shaking and he was making great heaving noises.

Lily stood, worried that she'd caused him pain, but knowing also that it had nothing to do with her. She recognised that feeling of powerlessness, that thought that you were all alone and no one was coming to help and you'd got everything wrong and every corner you had to turn from now till the end was terrifying. But she also knew how, in those moments, all she ever wanted was for someone to put their arms around her and hold her until the feeling that she was going to dissolve passed.

She moved before she'd really considered what she was doing, striding towards Lawrence, where she wrapped her arms around his shaking body. Because he was half sitting on the washstand, they were pretty much the same height, so he was able to rest his head against her shoulder and soon she felt his tears soaking through the cotton of her shirt.

As she stood holding him, Lily realised that it had been too long since she'd touched another human. She'd grown too used to reaching for Becky and there'd been the nights she'd been forced to lie with Henry, but neither of those things had happened for a while now. But she'd missed this contact, the heat from another body, the feel of bones and flesh under your hands, the pulse of another's heartbeat. Although it was more than that as well, she realised, she'd missed the giving of comfort as much as the receiving and that thought made her feel strong and useful in a way she could barely recognise.

Eventually Lawrence shifted beneath her embrace, so she pulled back and saw his face was creased and rumpled, which sparked a spike of pure tenderness for him and his broken heart. The truth was, they were both so broken, her and Lawrence, which was a terrifying realisation, because she didn't know how they were going to put themselves back together, or if it was even possible.

His pain was like a living thing in his body, as if it might push through his skin in the same way as her baby would eventually. 'Can I tell you something, Lily?' The break in his voice sped her heart.

'Please, you can tell me anything.'

'Can we sit?'

She followed him back to the sofa, which felt more comfortable this time.

Lawrence sat forward, his elbows resting on his knees. 'I have lied to you about my reason for being on this ship.' He faltered, but she held herself still, waiting for him to force out the words she could almost see building in his chest. 'My plan, in fact, was to wait until we are in the ice fields and then jump.'

The words shocked her so profoundly she felt them like electric currents. 'Jump? You mean into the sea?'

His eyes were like two little stones. 'Yes. I mean to kill myself.'

Her hand shot to her mouth in an involuntary movement. She had heard his use of the present tense and it wounded her. 'But you cannot do that. You must not.'

'It is not that I want to die. It just seems the only sensible course of action left to me.'

'Because you cannot recover from Cissy?'

'Yes. But also, on this crossing, I have started to realise that I failed her in ways I hadn't realised. I don't think I can live with the knowledge that I didn't love her well enough.'

Lily felt a keen desperation at the thought of losing this man. 'Lawrence, please, look at me.' She waited until his eyes were once more trained on her. 'You cannot kill yourself, do you hear me? Think of Alec for a start, but also I feel confident in saying that it is the last thing Cissy would want you to do.'

He sighed as if the very air was painful to him. 'I have resolved to help you and I shall do that to the best of my ability, but I feel very confused. I don't think I can step ashore in New York, but I cannot work out what that means for you.'

'That is not what I meant.' Lily heard the sharpness in her voice and saw the shock on Lawrence's face. 'I didn't say any of that for me, but for you. I don't care for myself, but for you. And for Alec.'

'Please,' he said, holding his hand up. 'Please do not talk of Alec. He is better off without me. And there is no other course of action open to me. Life without Cissy feels like an anathema, like a betrayal.'

'Oh, that is nonsense.' Lily hadn't felt so sure of anything for such a long time that the feelings rushing through her were making her tingle. 'You would betray Cissy by giving up, Lawrence, you must know that. From what you've told me about her, she would want you to do all the things she is unable to do. Forgive me, but it doesn't sound like you're going to jump because you can't live without her, but because you can't live *with* your memories, which, you are right, is very selfish.'

Lawrence leant forward over his stomach as if it ached. 'But I don't know what to do. It feels like choice was taken away from me when she died.'

Lily's body felt washed through with heat. 'But that's not true. You have the choice to honour her memory. My God, don't you dare give up when you have the possibility of change. Look at me, trapped by everything, even my biology. In fact, if what you say is true, then I should jump with you. I am loveless, forsaken, powerless and now you, my only friend, are telling me you are going to leave me alone.' It was too easy at that moment to imagine herself staring out of barred windows. She stood to dissipate the fizzing energy in her body and walked to the washstand, but her agitation made her clumsy, as it always did, and she tripped, falling into the wooden stand, the hard edge cutting into her belly, so she let out a little scream.

Lawrence jumped up and rushed to her, helping her right herself. 'Are you hurt?'

'No, I think not.' She held her hand to her stomach, willing the baby to give her a sign, but it felt strangely flat and still in her nightgown and she wondered again if it was teasing her, if it couldn't wait to be rid of her. 'Oh God, I am such an idiot. I knew I should have put on my protective skirt.'

'What protective skirt?'

'For the baby.' Lawrence looked blank. 'Becky has sewn padding into all my skirts. My pregnancy is delicate, you see. Oh God, do you think I have harmed the baby?'

'No, I'm sure it's fine. But you do need to take better care of yourself. You probably should not be wandering around a ship in the middle of the night.' He almost smiled and Lily returned the expression.

She wanted to laugh suddenly, because everything was so ridiculous and nothing made complete sense.

'You cannot kill yourself, Lawrence,' she said finally. 'I would miss you too much.'

'But I hardly exist as it is. Sometimes I just feel like a shell, like I have been all scraped out.'

'You can recover, I know you can.'

He rubbed a hand across his face. 'I want to help you, Lily. I will help you. I just have to figure out a way of doing both.'

She let out a little cry. 'We all have to learn to survive, Lawrence. It isn't easy for any of us. And if I can survive being abandoned by Becky and examined by Dr Henderson, then you can survive your grief.'

'What do you mean? What examination?'

She felt embarrassed then. 'Nothing. I'm being silly and we're not talking about me.'

'No, what do you mean?' There was an urgency to his tone that made her chest tighten because, since Becky's reaction at witnessing her examination, she'd begun to question the incident herself.

'Just all the humiliations that women have to suffer, really. I did not realise that pregnancy would be so invasive.' She forced herself to continue. 'Dr Henderson says he cannot get an accurate idea of what is going on with my pregnancy unless he, well, unless he is inside me.'

Lawrence flinched. 'What are you talking about? He puts something inside you to feel the baby?'

She shut her eyes for a second. 'His fingers.' She felt them, ripping into her.

'My God, Lily.' Lawrence had reddened and his jaw was clenched. 'Does Henry know about this?'

She saw Henry then, in the corner of rooms, his breathing heavy. 'Yes, he has watched it many times.'

Lawrence rubbed his hands across his face. 'We have to get you out of this horrendous situation.'

She shook her head because it felt like her fault, that she should have known better, and she was ashamed in this man's eyes, ashamed she'd let herself get into this position and done nothing about it. She sat on his bed, letting her head rest in her hands so she didn't have to reveal herself any more. The bed dipped as he sat next to her and then she felt the weight of his arm around her shoulders and she let him pull her head down so she could cry silently and privately, and she thought it was one of the kindest things anyone had ever done for her.

In the end, she stopped because there was nothing else to do, sitting straighter and pushing the hair out of her eyes. 'I am so stupid.' She felt terrified of herself then, as if her body and mind were no more connected to her than the lamp on the wall. She could trust nothing about herself and every single thing was a mystery.

'I promise I will help you, Lily. I cannot let them treat you like this.'

She grabbed his hand. 'But will you promise me that you will not kill yourself, either? Ever. Not that you will stay alive just long enough to help me, but that you will meet my baby, that you will still be in my life in years to come, when we are old and grey.'

He sighed so deeply it was like she could hear the air travelling through him. 'I cannot imagine growing old without her. I think love made me selfish, like I wanted to possess all of Cissy, every atom of her mind and body, so I can't imagine missing any part of her. But I see now that if you truly love someone you have to let them be themselves. You have to listen to them and try to understand them, if you want them to know they're loved.'

The words filled Lily to the brim, pushing out everything but the sure knowledge that that was how she felt about Becky. But, also, it was how she had failed Becky.

Lawrence stood and picked his watch off the washstand. 'Goodness, it's two thirty, Lily, and it would be unwise for you to be discovered out of your bed. I should get you back to your cabin and you should try to sleep.'

He was right, so she stood as well, knowing she would get no more assurances from him. She followed him out of the cabin and along the corridor, past the dining room, all laid for the morning, but completely empty, and the sight made her shiver.

'Are you cold?' Lawrence asked.

She paused at the top of the stairs and looked back over her shoulder at the static scene. 'No, it just looks strange, all quiet like that.'

'Like a ghost ship.'

She wondered then what it was all for, all the glitz and glamour of the crossing, wondered if she was no different from the ship, a magnificent creation amounting to nothing much. It seemed so unlikely that Becky had looked at her life and wanted to have it for herself because she'd never been enticed by trinkets and trappings. But perhaps it was simply that Henry was offering her something, as opposed to Lily's nothing.

When they reached her cabin, Lawrence told her to check that Henry wasn't there, so she inched open the door, spilling the warm light from the hall across the darkened room. His bunk was still mercifully empty.

'Goodnight, then,' he said as he stepped away from her. 'I will see you in the morning.'

The night felt terrifyingly unresolved and she wanted to run after him and beg him not to do anything stupid, although she also knew there was no point because he was not a man who would make promises he might not keep.

She shut the door of her cabin and then went to the wall which separated her space from Becky's, pressing her body right up to the cold wood. Lawrence had called his love selfish, but hers had been the same, so selfish, in fact, it had never even announced itself. A bolt of shame ran through her as she realised that she'd acted as if simply being in Becky's life was enough, as if confiding in her or constantly needing things from her amounted to something. It was entirely probable that Becky had needed things from her as well, things she could have provided if she had just been braver and made the right choices. Although she wasn't even sure that the things she wanted were a choice.

Her body felt raw, as if it were breaking open and tiny parts of her were fluttering away. In truth, she understood Lawrence's desire for obliteration because, without Becky, she too didn't feel whole and that feeling was as terrifying as any she'd ever had. Lawrence had talked about jumping into the ice fields and she shut her eyes and imagined the ship approaching those frozen seas. The cold would soon be all around them, encasing them in ice, slowing their movements, numbing their whole selves.

SUNDAY, APRIL 14TH

LAWRENCE

It had been stupid of them not to have made an arrangement for the morning, but Lawrence thought they'd both been too dislocated by what they'd told each other. His mind felt shredded, as if the problems he faced were impossible, which they probably were. The need to die was still alive inside him, existing as physically as Lily's baby, taking up space and pushing him out of himself, but, at the same time, Alec's little face was never far from his mind and he couldn't abandon Lily to the secluded house and probing fingers, with nothing but an asylum waiting at the end.

It was on Lawrence's second lap of the deck that he spotted her, walking on her own, wearing her blue hat, her head moving in a way which suggested she was looking out for him as well. He speeded up and drew alongside her, feeling the relief drain through her at his arrival. But she kept her composure as she turned to him.

'Good morning, Mr Beesley.'

'Where is Lord Elsworth?' he asked, as they fell into step. He hoped if they walked to the back of the ship it might be quieter and they could talk more freely.

'I told him that I have a headache and am returning to our cabin.'

He smiled as if Lily had just said something funny. 'How wise.'

The crowds did thin the further back they walked, so by the time they reached the steps that led up to the lonely deck, Lawrence was able to lead her over to the side, where they could talk without being overheard. But when they stopped, he saw that she was shivering, her lips a pale blue in her porcelain face.

'Are you cold? We could find somewhere inside if you would prefer?'

She gave her head a determined shake. 'No, I'm fine. I just cannot stop thinking about what you told me last night. I have barely slept.'

Lawrence wanted to touch her in some way, because she needed comfort so badly, but the deck was too public and, besides, he thought she'd been touched by men too many times in too many ways. 'I'm sorry. For what I told you and for what is being done to you.'

'I feel very peculiar.' She looked behind him as she spoke. 'I cannot bear to think of you gone from this world and I still do not understand fully what they have planned for me.'

Lawrence felt furious with Henry then, a rage which was hot and potent in his stomach. 'I refuse to let him get away with this.'

'But I'm not sure what we can do. No one is going to doubt Henry's word over mine, or even yours, especially when I've been witnessed as being a hysteric on a seven-day crossing.'

There was a movement over Lily's shoulder which made Lawrence jump because, for a second, he could have sworn that he'd seen a woman with messy hair and rosy cheeks, her hands on her hips as she stamped her foot. It felt like the fabric of life had split and Cissy really was there, reaching out across time and dimensions. Life seemed compressed to him then, as if all his moments had been flattened, so he could see them clearly.

But Lily went on speaking. 'I thought about your grief all night and I want to say something to you. I know it sounds like a platitude, but you are so lucky that you got to love Cissy at all, for any time.' She flushed and looked down at her hands.

'What do you mean?' Her words felt urgent and he wanted to understand them.

'Just that some people never get to love the people they love, or to be loved by them. Some people never find their person and some people find them but cannot be with them. And, I am not meaning to diminish what you are feeling, but I think that might be worse. To be wretched because of yourself rather than circumstance.'

Lawrence stared at Lily as he absorbed her words and they made him consider something he'd never thought before, which was that love was both never-ending and finite. You can always love someone, but the way you love them, or are loved by them, has to change as people are never static. His heart speeded up as he understood that death fells bodies, but can't kill love. And, if that were true, then maybe Lily was right and the time you spend with another person was immaterial, as it will always end, but this corporeal ending doesn't have be an emotional one as well. A small gap appeared in the fog in his mind, parting to tempt him with the idea that there were different ways of loving, in the same way that there were different ways of dying, different ways of living.

He looked up, at the smoke trailing from the monstrous funnels which rose up from the deck, and then down at all the people and life on board. It was almost impossible to comprehend what allowed this hulking steel monolith to stay afloat, just as it was hard to understand what constituted love, how a feeling could alter the structure of your body.

Lily was struggling to keep her emotions in check, her skin taut on her face, and he felt a rush of affection for her. 'Thank you for saying that, Lily. But, for now, our first task is to find a way to keep you safe. I still think your best bet is to act as well as you can around everyone, so they will find it harder to cast you as hysterical. Talk about future plans, anything that makes you seem present and in your right mind. There are still three days until we dock, so we have a bit of time to figure things out.'

Lily bit down on her bottom lip. 'Does that mean . . . ? I mean, have you decided not to jump?'

'I haven't decided anything,' he said, which was as close to the truth as he could get. 'But I will help you. If that means not jumping, then so be it. But I cannot promise that I will not take my own life at some point.'

She nodded. 'I can ask for no more than that at this time. But I will make you a promise as well, Lawrence. I will do everything in my power to persuade you not to kill yourself. If I get through this, then I will stay your hand if that's what it takes.'

He felt his mouth turning upwards involuntarily, because her passion was so vibrant it was as if it glistened on her skin, and he hadn't seen that for a long time, not since Cissy had left him. Life rocked into him like a falling tree and he knew it was both beautiful and tragic and that others could stand this, but he still wasn't sure that he could.

LILY

Lily went from her meeting with Lawrence straight to Becky's cabin. The permanence of Cissy's death was terrifying, but she also believed what she'd said and it was more terrifying not to try. She knew she should feel angry with Becky for what she was doing and it was possible that there was nothing she could say to make her stop, but also she was beginning to see that she'd spent so long, all her life really, doing the things she was supposed to do and all that had done was leave her miserable, with a bleak and uncertain future. Whereas Cissy and Lawrence had seized a chance which must have felt like a gamble and tasted pleasures she could only imagine. She was starting to see that life presented many paths when she had only ever believed there to be one.

Becky looked tired when she opened the door, but Lily strode forward, so she was forced once more to let Lily into her space. She'd felt so sure of what she was going to say on her walk to the cabin, but something about Becky's physicality stopped her tongue and a silence opened between them.

But then Becky spoke. 'Can I help you with something, Ma'am?'

'I'm sorry, Becky.' Lily wanted to step towards her, but it felt as if there was a wall between them.

Becky narrowed her eyes in a way Lily recognised. 'What for?'

'For everything. For not being a good friend.'

Becky stepped back, as if Lily had pushed her. 'Why are you saying that?'

It wasn't the reaction she'd hoped for and it made Lily fearful. 'I've been thinking and I don't think I was kind to you. I cannot remember ever helping you properly or even doing anything for you. You spoke to me once about your family and I never tried to make things better for them. I never considered all the things you have to do and how hard it is. I am sorry.'

'Stop,' Becky said, holding up a hand. 'Do not say things you don't mean.'

'But I do mean them.' Lily closed the gap between them and tried to reach for Becky's hand, but she pushed her away. 'Becky, I have been a fool. I've spent so much time thinking about my own plight and never considering yours. I should have been braver.'

A single tear dripped from Becky's eye and she swiped at it as if she wanted to hurt herself. 'It is unfair of you to say this now.'

'But I cannot stay quiet.'

'Yes you can. You are good at that. Staying still and quiet.'

Lily knew then that Becky's anger was potent and that she wasn't wrong that she was the cause. But there was also hope because anger was not a passive emotion. 'You cannot love Henry.'

'What has love got to do with anything?' Becky's tone felt like a slap.

'Surely everything.'

Becky half laughed. 'Only in a world where you are secure in other ways. And only when the person you love loves you back.'

Lily wasn't sure if they were still talking about Henry and she tried again to reach for Becky, but again she was pushed away and then Becky turned, a little cry escaping from her.

'Please, just leave me alone. It is too late.'

'Don't say that, Becky.' The floor was opening beneath Lily's feet and she knew she was the cause of all the pain, but she had no idea how to put it right. She longed then for Cissy, which was ridiculous as she'd never met the woman, but she was sure she'd know the right words.

'Just go,' Becky said again, her voice so pure and hard that Lily felt she had no choice and stumbled from the room before her tears could fall.

She went back to her own cabin and stood in the centre of the room, trying to regulate her breathing. It felt like there was a herd of horses rushing through her and she wanted to beg them to slow down so she could understand what everything meant. Her feelings felt too big and scary and as though they could overwhelm her if she let them. Her biggest fear, she realised, was that she had lost Becky; it outstripped any fears she had about herself or the baby. She could endure almost anything if it meant Becky was returned to her, and yet that seemed so unlikely she wanted to scream.

She placed her hands back on the raised fabric of her skirt because it seemed like the baby was at the centre of everything and yet she still couldn't work out why or how. The easy thing to do would be to lie on her bed and weep into her sheets and there was an allure to that thought, but Lily knew it was time to start fighting for her place in this story.

It was coming up to lunchtime, so she forced herself to make her way back up to the dining room, where she waited outside until she saw Henry approaching.

'Where on earth have you been?' he asked as she joined him,

his voice slightly raised, so the people near them turned to look. 'I have been looking everywhere.'

'Oh, I'm sorry,' she answered innocently. 'I took a stroll around deck as the weather is so pleasant and then read in our cabin.'

'But I looked in the cabin.' His eyes narrowed.

'We must have missed each other.' She smiled brightly. 'Oh look, there are the Connaughts, shall we sit with them?'

'I do not think—'

But Lily pretended she hadn't heard and set off in the direction of Emma, who had already started waving. She fixed a smile on her face as she approached their table, clenching her stomach to try to give her strength for what the next hour held.

Charles rose and Emma attempted a ridiculous half-stand, half-curtsy.

'Are these seats free?' Lily asked.

'Yes, please sit,' Charles replied, as Emma flushed with pride, not being able to resist looking around to see who had clocked that Lord and Lady Elsworth had chosen to sit with them.

Lily could feel Henry bristling next to her, but she sat and so he was forced to copy.

'How are you feeling, Lady Elsworth?' Emma asked as soon as she was settled, contracting her face into a look of deep concern.

'Much better, thank you,' Lily replied. 'I am feeling well, in fact.'

'Well,' Henry shifted next to her. 'We still need to be careful, don't we, dear. Things can be rather up and down.' She caught the look he gave Charles as he spoke, eyes widened and brows slightly raised. Charles nodded briefly, one tiny movement an acknowledgement of all that was wrong with the female race, a thought which Lily was surprised to find herself having, but then she thought of Cissy and it made her feel better to think that other people had already had these thoughts, that in this very dining room there were probably other women feeling the same things.

'The weather has chilled remarkably,' Emma said. 'When Charles and I were walking this morning, I saw ice in the sea.'

Charles nodded enthusiastically. 'I'm so looking forward to seeing the bergs. I hear they are very beautiful.'

'I hadn't realised we were already that close to the ice fields,' Lily said, her mind immediately going to Lawrence.

'We should be right in the middle of them tonight,' Charles replied.

'He's so excited,' Emma laughed. 'He's planning on sitting up late so he can watch us pass through from the deck.'

'I am indeed,' Charles said. 'I only wish I had a camera, or some way of recording them.'

A waiter approached, pad in hand, so Lily quickly scanned the menu. There was nothing she felt like eating, but she wasn't going to make the same mistake as the last time they'd eaten with the Connaughts. She heard Emma and then Charles order and was just turning her eyes upwards when Henry spoke, 'My wife will have the consommé, followed by the eggs l'argenteuil and I—'

'Actually,' Lily said, not meeting Henry's eye, 'I will have the cock-a-leekie, followed by the fillet of brill.'

There was a moment of silence around the table as the waiter wrote on his pad, unaware of the tension.

'I have a large appetite today,' she said to Emma.

Henry slammed the menu on to the table, which made Lily cringe because she knew how rich his anger would be at having been contradicted. 'Unless my wife wants to order for me, I will have the cock-a-leekie as well and then corned beef, with vegetables and potatoes.'

'You certainly look much healthier, Lady Elsworth. And you are eating for two, after all,' Emma said as the waiter retreated.

'Maybe it is the baby who is hungry.' Henry sighed loudly next to her, but she still refused to turn to him.

'Do you know, I don't believe I have asked where you live, Emma.'

The woman visibly inflated in front of her. 'Cheltenham. I believe I have read about your home in Northumberland?'

'Yes, that is correct.' Lily heard Henry falter in his conversation with Charles, no doubt as he heard mention of his one true love. 'It is a rather large house for my tastes, if I'm honest, but I have great plans for the gardens. I want to do some planting when we return home.'

'Ooh, do tell,' Emma squealed. 'I adore our garden, which would look like a postage stamp to you, I'm sure, but serves our needs.'

Lily had spoken without real thought, simply remembering what Lawrence had said about making it seem as if she was thinking about life beyond the ship. She in fact knew nothing about gardening and knew the names of almost no flowers. 'I was thinking of a rose garden.'

Henry drummed his fingers on the table. 'Roses do not grow on our soil.' She could hear how hard he was working at keeping his voice mellow. 'I have told you that before, Lily. You must have forgotten.' He turned back and spoke to both Emma and Charles. 'My wife has these fanciful ideas from time to time, about the garden, but nothing ever comes of it.'

It was clear now that Henry meant to play the game and Lily felt a ripple of excitement mixed in with her fear. 'I do forget how unforgiving the climate can be in Northumberland. I have lived there for nine years and still I think it cannot really be as cold and dismal as it is.'

Their food arrived, so the conversation stopped as plates were laid before them. The mixture of smells from all the dishes turned Lily's stomach, but she grabbed her spoon and dove into the thick liquid, forcing herself to taste and swallow.

'It's not dismal,' Henry said.

She pretended to be surprised at him continuing the conversation. 'My husband's patriotism runs deep.' She addressed Emma and Charles in the way Henry had done, 'but I think it's stretching credulity to claim that the weather in Northumberland is anything but dismal. Have either of you ever been?'

'No, but we would love to, dismal weather or not,' Emma replied much too quickly.

'Well, you must come and stay when we are all returned to England.' Lily felt every muscle in Henry's body tense next to her. 'Since we have been married, the whole of Elsworth has been renovated. You should see the ballroom, Emma, you would love it. Henry went to such great lengths to have it restored to its original glory, so it positively sparkles now.' She turned to Henry. 'We should have a ball this winter to celebrate the birth of our baby. And the Connaughts must come.'

'Oh, but we would love to,' Emma said, her cheeks now flushed a deep purple.

'But you hate balls.' Henry's face was crumpled by confusion that Lily recognised only too well.

'I should like to give one this winter,' she said resolutely.

The waiter returned to clear their plates and Lily was surprised by how easy it had been to finish the soup. The new dishes were laid in front of them and this time the smells didn't catch at the back of her throat and her stomach didn't contract against the idea of the fish on her plate.

'We shall have to see how well you are,' Henry said, as he

cut into his sinewy-looking corned beef. 'In fact, I must get the name of that healer chap you mentioned, Emma.'

'I'm not sure—' Lily started.

But Henry laid a hand over hers. 'I think it wise, darling. You know how you always feel almost invigorated whenever you recover from a turn. But things can spiral down just as quickly. And we must be careful not to underestimate how delicate you might feel after the birth.'

The Connaughts both had tight smiles on their faces and Lily realised they were embarrassed. She saw also the fear in their eyes that was directed at her and not Henry. Trying to get people to hear her over Henry was going to be like screaming into a storm and the thought made her weary and desperate. And, if Henry got her to the secluded house, she could scream as much as she liked and no one would even hear. But then Lily thought of Lawrence, and Cissy, or at least the women like Cissy who she knew now were out there, and that calmed her enough to take a mouthful.

Charles then asked Henry a question about the hunting around Elsworth and Emma took the opportunity to engage Lily in a long and boring discussion about plants, so the rest of the meal passed without either her or Henry being able to land any significant blows.

When their plates were cleared again, Lily felt sure that Henry would order pudding and she planned to take the opportunity to slip away and find Lawrence, but Henry surprised her by pushing back his chair and taking her elbow.

'Thank you for a most enjoyable lunch,' he said to the Connaughts, 'but I must take Lily back to the cabin for her rest.' He increased the pressure on Lily's elbow until it began to sting. His eyes were dancing with a terrifying anger, and there was no way she could refuse him.

'I am fine,' she tried.

'No, no, Lily, you know how you get if you don't rest enough. And we must think of the baby.' He began to stand, pulling Lily with him so she was forced to rise.

She cast her eyes desperately around the room in search of Lawrence, but it was too crowded and loud for her to see anything properly.

'I hope to see you this evening,' she said to Emma as a last throw of the dice.

'I shall look out for you,' Emma replied, which was at least something.

Henry directed her out of the dining room, his hand pressing too hard into the small of her back, which made her want to cry, although she forced herself not to in front of all these people who might soon be being asked to believe in her instability. His jaw was set hard and he refused to look at her as they began their descent of the stairs, his silence more menacing than if he'd shouted. The small victory she'd felt at lunch began to dissolve as she wondered at the point of believing anything so paltry could be significant. She thought then of Cissy and all her work in the women's movement and how it had ultimately amounted to very little because nothing had changed and here she still was, a woman totally at the mercy of a man.

Henry opened their cabin door as though he wanted to rip it from its hinges, pushing her inside so she stumbled. He came in behind her, shutting the door, which he leant against for a moment, his eyes closed, trying to regulate his breathing. 'What the fuck was that, Lily?'

'I don't know what you are talking about,' she stammered.

He crossed the room in three large steps and leant into her face so she could smell the meat on his breath. 'That performance you put on over lunch. A rose garden? A goddamned ball?'

He half-laughed. 'Christ, if you'd shown that much spunk before now we might not be in this mess.'

It seemed amazing that he might think it plausible to blame her for everything he was doing. 'You're not making any sense, Henry.'

'I have no damned idea what you're playing at, but do not think for a moment that anyone on this ship is fooled by you. They all think you mad. They have all seen the way you act and heard the frankly deranged things you say.'

The words cut into her as they always did, opening those well-riven seams of doubt and confusion in her body, so she felt undone. 'Oh Henry, please.'

'You disgust me.' He raised his hand, so she cowed again, ducking her face behind her hands. But the blow when it came was only on the top of her arm, a splintering pain that spread through her muscle and into the bone. 'And now look what you have made me do,' he shouted, so shrilly he sounded like a schoolboy. 'Forcing me to strike you when pregnant.'

Lily backed herself into the corner, battling her tears because she knew they would anger him more. The resolution she'd felt only hours earlier had dissolved and she wondered then if it would be kinder to take her baby from her because it would be such a curse to be burdened with a mother so weak and pathetic. She imagined the sterile white walls and bedsheets in an asylum, the peace and quiet, the locked doors, the sense that nobody was coming, and it almost felt like a release.

Henry snorted and turned to leave the room. But as he reached the door, he grabbed her blue hat which she'd discarded on the washstand. He didn't bother to explain or even look at her again before leaving, locking the door behind him.

Lily made her way shakily to the sofa, where she sat, clutching her shaking arms around her body. The day was still bright outside the porthole, the sun projecting a golden spot on to the floor in the middle of the room. There were thousands of people on the ship having fun, living lives, forming attachments, feeling excitement and anticipation for when they arrived.

There was a gentle knock on the door, which made Lily jump to attention. She crossed to the door and leant against it, calling out, 'Hello?'

'Lily, it's me.'

She wanted to cry at the sound of Lawrence's voice and put her hand against the wood as if she could draw him into her space. 'I'm locked in.'

'I saw you and Henry leave the dining room and he seemed angry. I was worried he might have hurt you in some way.'

'He hit me, but only on the arm.'

'I'm sorry.' Lawrence sounded so sad, she worried she'd disappointed him by being too weak. 'Are you all right?'

'I don't know.' Her legs felt weak and she sank down to her knees, turning her back to the door and leaning her head against the hard wood. 'Becky hates me and Henry means me harm and perhaps I am too weak to retain my own baby.' Her head was throbbing with the enormity of her problems. 'What would Cissy say? If she were in my situation.'

He was silent for a moment and, when he spoke, his voice was very quiet. 'I think she would tell you not to give up. In the whole time I knew her, I never saw her give up on anything, not one person, not one idea, nothing.'

Lily sucked in a breath. 'Can you hear what you are saying, Lawrence? Do you not think that advice applies to you as well?' He was silent, so she carried on. 'You know we will be in the ice fields tonight?'

His voice was brisk when he spoke. 'I saw Henry go into the

saloon before I came here, so I will go back there now and see what he gets up to.'

She knew there was no point in pushing him. 'He took my hat, so he's probably planning a show with Becky.'

'Yes, that sounds likely. He's bound to let you out for dinner, but if he doesn't, I will ask him where you are. Also, I have just bumped into a couple called the Carters whom I seem to have befriended, and they are organising a sing-song in the saloon after dinner this evening. I think we should go as it's bound to be crowded, so a good opportunity for more people to see you behaving normally. I'll find you this evening and invite you to come. And remember not to drink anything Dr Henderson gives you.'

Lawrence's plan was fine, but it was also incomplete, because life, Lily was starting to see, was fragile and unpredictable. The ice was coming and she felt it like a presence, as if its chill was going to infect them all so they would be paralysed and frozen forever in their terrible realities.

LAWRENCE

Lawrence made his way back up to the saloon, where Henry was still sitting on his own, nursing a glass of what looked like whisky. His face was set hard and he appeared to be staring at something on the floor, so Lawrence wandered over to the charts, where he could keep an eye on him. He hadn't needed Lily to tell him that they were approaching the ice fields because he'd felt their pull since he first stepped on board and it still didn't seem possible that he was going to simply watch them pass by. He had no impression as to what might happen after that. There would probably only be thirty-six hours until they arrived in New York, and then he wasn't entirely sure how he could help Lily, or himself.

Henry stood, so Lawrence braced himself, hanging back as he left the saloon and then following as quickly as he could without drawing attention to himself. He caught the back of Henry's coat descending the stairs and skirted in behind him, watching as he trotted down the flights until he reached F deck. He turned in the direction of his cabin, and Lawrence raced down the stairs, almost tripping.

He slowed his pace as he turned on to Lily's corridor, just in time to see Henry and Becky emerge from her room, the blue hat on her head. They were making for the stairs, so he quickly turned into a door and pretended to be fumbling for a key because the corridors were too narrow for them to pass him unobserved. He felt Henry look at him, so bent lower to the lock as if it were bothering him, his heart thumping richly in his mouth. But they passed without stopping and Lawrence was able to glance at them before they turned the corner to the stairs. They were both dressed for outside, so Lawrence presumed they were going up to the boat deck.

He stalled for a minute, looking back along the corridor to Lily's door; it was strange to think of her locked behind it and it seemed absurd that she was right there and yet they were both so helpless, so constrained by the actions of one man whose position of authority amounted to nothing more than an accident of birth.

Cissy used to say that the women's movement wouldn't just help women but would help to bring about a more equal society all over, which would help so many men as well. Misery dragged at his coat then, stopping his progress, because he wished he could tell Cissy he now understood so many of the things that she'd been trying to teach him. He wished he could see the pride in her eyes, or hear her exclaim with joy one more time, or kiss him with excitement. His longing felt sharp and angry and then he heard William Carter's voice saying, 'I wish for a wish,' which returned him to the present. Henry and Becky had disappeared while he'd been wishing and, William was right, there was life not only to be lived, but to be saved, the responsibility of which felt like the only solid thing within him.

Lawrence jogged up the stairs towards the boat deck, agitation running in his veins, because if he lost Henry and Becky, then it would be entirely his fault, and William was right, what would be the point of sacrificing what was happening now for what had gone before? He emerged into the bright day slightly out of breath and had to tug at the crisp air, which burnt his lungs. It spoke very clearly of how freezing the water would be in these temperatures and he knew it would be a terrible way to die, like an animal taking chunks of flesh from your body until there was no more of you left. Except wasn't that also the point, to replace his mental pain with a physical one, so he had a tiny moment of peace before the nothing.

The thin steps and deserted deck were calling to him, but so was Lily's desperate voice, so he walked away from the temptation towards the front of the boat. It wasn't long before he spotted three people sitting on a bench, two men with a woman between them, Lily's blue hat on her head. Lawrence stopped and drew in behind a lifeboat, noticing that everyone who passed was also drawn to the spectacle. The shaking woman was folded over her knees so her face was entirely obscured by the hat and the two men, who were of course Elsworth and Henderson, were bent over her, whispering soothing words.

Lawrence had expected them to provide a bigger show, but he was impressed by how much cleverer this was, this silent misery speaking of something much darker and deeper than simple hysterics. He felt a clench of fear then at the intricacy of Elsworth's plan, embedded as it was in a structure that gave weight to everything he did, that gave right to wrongness, that had never played fair.

The men stood and then helped Becky to her feet. She leant into Henderson's arm and kept her head low, which hid her face, although there was no disguising her sturdy frame. They turned and began a slow shuffle up the deck towards the door that led inside, whilst Henry stayed staring after them. He rubbed his hands across his face and clenched his jaw, as if trying desperately not to cry. Everyone passing looked at him and Lawrence saw a few shaking their heads at his plight. When the doctor and Becky passed through the door, Henry walked to the edge, where he stood looking down into the sea, as if searching for an answer. Lawrence slipped behind the lifeboat and came to the edge, right next to Henry.

'I trust you are not too affected by what I just witnessed,' Lawrence said.

Henry's grip on the railings was tight, the leather of his gloves straining. 'Ah, Mr Beesley, here you are again. Lily's doctor is accompanying her to her cabin and is going to sit with her until she sleeps. I needed a moment to gather my thoughts.'

'That woman barely resembled Lady Elsworth.' Lawrence kept his gaze out to sea.

He felt Henry turn to him. 'That is the second time you have said that and, if I may say, it is an unhelpful comment.'

Lawrence met his gaze and they stared at each other for a moment, each allowing their disdain for the other full dominance on their features. 'I trust your wife will be recovered enough for dinner. I will look out for her.'

Henry reddened. 'You know, Mr Beesley, I don't know what Lily has told you, but you do her no service listening to her ramblings.'

'I enjoy talking to her. And she has never appeared rambling to me.'

Henry threw his hands into the air. 'For God's sake, man, you saw the state she was in just now. You even know she tried to throw herself over the side of this bloody boat.'

'But whenever I speak to her, she doesn't seem like the same person who would do those things.'

They were both quiet for a moment and then Henry leant in closer, positioning his mouth by his ear, his voice low but insistent. 'Mr Beesley, I advise you to stay away from my wife and my business, if you know what's good for you.'

Lawrence had once watched Cissy leafletting, her missives usually dropped as soon as they were taken. But one man had come right up to her, snatched a leaflet and then screwed it up in her face before throwing it into the gutter. His anger had shimmered off him and Lawrence had been about to cross the road and lay into him, when Cissy had calmly bent down and picked up the scrunched-up paper, smoothing it out with her hands and replacing it in her pile, before turning her back on him.

Lawrence smiled at Henry before replying. 'I have always known what is good for me, thank you, and it has nothing to do with staying away from situations that I know to be wrong.'

'I could be the death of you,' Henry snarled.

Lawrence shrugged. 'And the reason that I am dangerous to you is because that is not a concept which scares me.'

Henry took a small step backwards, his brow furrowing. But Lawrence simply touched the brim of his hat and turned, walking back along the deck towards the stairs. He was sweating by the time he turned inside and began the descent, because Henry's anger was potent and his threat so real. Lawrence thought about Becky's pantomime on the railings, how high and vulnerable she'd seemed. He thought about himself up there, pushing off and barrelling downwards, and knew it would be a terrifying and terrible end. He'd told Elsworth that death didn't scare him, but that was a lie. Nothing in his life had been more petrifying than Cissy's death and he felt suddenly confused about how his own death could ever atone for that.

Lawrence stopped at the bottom of a flight, unsure where he was going or what he was doing, feeling a lightness in his head. His had been a life filled with forward momentum, all his actions, his thoughts, his learnings, they all strained to the horizon, just like the boat he was standing in now. Cissy had loved him for precisely those reasons, and so how could turning his back on all that be the right thing to do? He thought then of Alec, nature pulling him upwards, how his body would strain and stretch, how his mind would expand and his ideas grow and sharpen.

He shut his eyes and felt a soft hand brush the length of his cheek, so he wanted to cry out for her, wanted to ask her what he should do, how he was expected to carry on walking through a world of grief and pain without her there.

LILY

Lily woke to the sound of the key being turned in the lock. Her body felt stiff and cold and her arm had gone numb beneath her, so for a moment she thought sensation was lost to her, feeling eradicated.

'This was found in the corridor,' Henry said as he came through the door, holding up her blue hat. 'A steward returned it to me just now because he knew it was yours. He said he tried knocking this afternoon, but there was no answer.'

Dr Henderson followed Henry into the room, his medical bag ominously in his hands.

She felt ungrounded, not just because Henry's tone was soft and untroubled, but also by what he was saying. The light had dimmed outside the porthole, which added to her sense of dislocation. 'What do you mean? You took my hat with you when you left me here after lunch.'

He raised an eyebrow. 'What are you talking about? Why would I do that?'

'I saw you pick it up. Just before you left.' Henry always made Lily feel so unsure of herself that even knowing all she did, even as far along as they were with this game, she still wondered if perhaps she'd been mistaken and she really had dropped her hat and somehow dreamt Henry picking it up.

He snorted. 'What on earth would I want with your hat? Anyway, I haven't time for all this nonsense now. Dr Henderson is going to give you a quick examination before we go to dinner.'

'I do not think that is necessary.' She stood quickly, her head taking a moment to catch up with her body.

'Of course it's bloody necessary. Lie back down.'

'No, please,' Lily said, as Dr Henderson advanced towards her. 'There's no need, I'm sure I felt the baby move today, so all is as it should be.'

'Even so,' Dr Henderson said, 'an examination is still a good idea. After you have drunk this.' He held up a small unstopped bottle.

He was so close to her by then that she could feel the bed against the back of her legs and had no choice but to sit and accept the bottle. No one spoke, but they were watching her so intently all she could do was tip the liquid into her mouth and swallow down the bitter lemony water.

Dr Henderson motioned for her to lie down as he opened his bag and pulled out his gloves, tugging them over his disgusting hands. 'Raise your legs.'

She looked past him at Henry, who had sat on the sofa and was staring without blinking, totally absorbed by the scene. He must have felt the force of her stare, as he met her gaze just as Dr Henderson pushed a finger inside her, probing and pushing. He then inserted another, widening and tearing her flesh so she felt as if she'd been stung. She winced, a tear leaking from her eye, as her husband watched.

'Make sure you go deep enough,' Henry said, his mouth turning up into a smile as he kept his gaze fixed on hers.

She wanted to beg, but didn't know what she was even asking for, apart from them all to leave her alone, to return her to her body, to let it rest, to expect nothing more.

There was a knock on the door, which made Henry jump. 'Who is it?'

'I have come to dress Lady Elsworth.' Becky's voice was muffled through the wood.

Henry rushed to the door and leant his weight against it. 'You will have to wait a minute.'

Dr Henderson pulled out of her so sharply she gasped. 'All is well.' He spoke to Henry and not her.

'Get up,' Henry said, flicking a hand at her.

Lily did as he asked, feeling as if she was moving in slow motion, her skin running with shame and disgust.

He opened the door and Becky stepped into the room, her eyes dancing between all three of them. She was a strange colour, her skin almost yellow and her eyes ringed in purple, and she seemed nervous, her steps uneven. She was holding the dress that Lily was clearly meant to wear that evening, a green shot silk, with lace ruffles around the bust and at the end of the sleeves. Becky had told her many times that it brought out her eyes and made her look prettier than any other dress, and the memory spun her head because it was so incongruous with what they were doing to her.

Dr Henderson shut his bag and made for the door. 'Have a pleasant evening,' he said, as he let himself out.

Becky crossed the space and began to ease Lily out of the dress she'd been wearing, as Henry turned to his trunk. The fabric pooled around her feet as it dropped down and then Becky offered her hand so Lily could step out and into the green silk. She was puffing with the effort of bending and straightening and kept her eyes down, but still Lily thought she could feel her heartbeat pulsing through her hot hand. She watched through the mirror as Becky began to fasten the tiny pearl buttons which ran all the way down her back and Lily could feel the tremor in her hands. But there was something else, something which nagged at her as she watched this woman she knew so well, whose body was no secret to her, but who had changed so much and become so removed. She had the sensation that Becky was filled with a secret that was giving her strength and power and supposed love did that to you, gave you a sense of place and purpose which made you confident in taking up more space, and then she just felt desperate that she hadn't been the one to inflate Becky.

'Thank you, Becky,' she said, allowing a real tenderness into her voice. Cissy would understand Becky, would probably, in fact, feel more sympathy for her than Lily herself. And whatever happened, she pitied Becky the life she'd been forced to create for herself, because, even if Henry loved her, he was also mean and mercurial and nothing would change that fact.

Becky raised her eyes to meet Lily's in the glass and they sparkled full. 'You look beautiful.'

She was aware of Henry standing straighter on the other side of the room, but she kept her eyes locked with Becky. 'If I had my time again, I would do things differently.'

Becky nodded almost imperceptibly, bending her head to hide her tears.

'Stop your blathering,' Henry said sharply, coming towards them. 'We'll miss dinner if we don't get a move on.'

The moment shattered around them as if he'd put his fist through the glass and then Becky was scrabbling about on the floor, picking up the discarded clothes, and Henry was taking Lily's arm and steering her out of the cabin. She felt like she was floating, unable to focus on anything other than the look in Becky's eyes, which she knew she wasn't mistaken in thinking had strained towards her, so she wanted to run back to the cabin and fall at her feet. She imagined turning to Henry then and offering him the baby in exchange for Becky, a swap which she knew she would make willingly, which terrified her in what it revealed about herself.

Although maybe she wasn't wrong not to want those things. Cissy had lived a different life to the one Lily had always thought was proscribed for all women and the world hadn't fallen in. She'd taken a different path, allowed her route to be dictated by desire and circumstance, so it had to be possible that others could do the same. There were choices to make and chances to be taken, which was scary, but also wonderful.

Henry was careful not to sit anywhere near the Connaughts and instead they shared a table with a tedious couple who talked at length about their children, retelling boring moments in minute detail. There was too much in her head for Lily to play the game nearly as well as she had at lunch and so she failed to speak up or convey a sparkling impression. George Henderson was sitting only two tables away and his gaze often rested on her, which felt a little like a knife being run down her skin. By the end of the meal, she was sure the walls were closing in, the noise in the room bearing down as if it could crush her skull.

But just at the moment when she felt like she couldn't sustain anything any longer, she felt a presence next to her and looked up to see the tall, thin form of Lawrence standing over her, making her heart rush with relief.

'Lady Elsworth,' he said. 'I was wondering if you would like to accompany me to a sing-song in the saloon, organised by Reverend Carter and his wife?'

'Oh, I...' She glanced back at Henry because her behaviour felt not her own. But his glowering face gave her courage. 'I would love to.'

Lawrence looked over her head. 'You would be most welcome as well, Lord Elsworth.'

Henry waved his hand dismissively. 'A sing-song is not my idea of fun. But I will be waiting for you afterwards, Lily. We do not want you tiring yourself out.' He kept his eyes trained on Lawrence for the whole time he spoke, even when he was addressing her.

Lawrence crooked his arm and Lily stood, not daring to look back at Henry as she left the dining room. It felt as if there was a bird trapped in her chest and her breath refused to travel past her throat, but her ever present fear was also tempered with an exhilaration the further she walked from Henry. She gripped Lawrence's arm even tighter as they made their way up to the saloon. It felt as if they were buying little snippets of time, which, with any luck, they could sew together to form a magic carpet that would carry them to a place of serenity, where they could possibly both discard their tattered old selves and start again.

LAWRENCE

The walk to the saloon was short, but Lawrence held his breath the whole way, half expecting Elsworth to accost them or demand Lily return to the cabin. And the truth was, he didn't have much of a plan if this should happen. Cissy had always said that the most important determiner of any woman's life was luck, which had annoyed him, because he thought that did a disservice to her mind and ambition. But he saw now that, even though she'd made choices, she'd also taken her luck where she could find it. Because she had been lucky to have a father who didn't insist she married for status and a husband who didn't want to control and debase her. And he also had been so lucky to meet her, because she'd changed the whole course of his life, which surely also meant that he could change again now, that perhaps he didn't have to jump.

The saloon was warm and full by the time they stepped inside, filled with noisy chatter and peals of laughter. William and Marjorie were standing near the piano chatting to a large group, so Lawrence simply raised a hand to them before steering Lily towards the back of the room. They settled against a wall, looking out over the proceedings.

'Do you have faith?' Lily asked, worrying at her bottom lip with her teeth.

He thought of Cissy dying in their bed, her face sheened in sweat, her body racked by coughing so she was too weak to sit up. 'Not really. Do you?'

Lily furrowed her brow. 'I'm not sure. I always thought of myself as a believer, but I think that is just because of how I was brought up. I suppose the truth is I didn't know there was an option not to believe.'

'Cissy said that life was all about understanding you have options,' Lawrence said, remembering their wedding night when he had marvelled at the fact that they really were married and she'd laughed at him and told him it was only because she'd grabbed at the chance. He felt himself leaning over her in the bed in the hotel, her warm breath against his mouth, and once again the idea of grabbing chances amazed him.

'I'm starting to see that she's right,' Lily replied. 'I think I may have been travelling down the wrong path all this time without realising it, without even knowing there were other routes. I've been like this ship, Lawrence, blindly following its course. But suppose we suddenly changed direction and avoided the ice fields altogether? Then you couldn't jump.' She smiled at what she'd said.

He tried to return her smile. 'I expect that would add days to the journey.'

'Which is not necessarily a bad thing. I wish I had taken more time to think about what I wanted.' Lily ran a hand absent-mindedly across her face. 'Maybe it's all a bit like free will. Supposedly God gave us all the knowledge to be good, but what we do with it is up to us. I've always thought goodness was the most important thing. But it has made my life so full of fear, the thought that I am going to disappoint or get things wrong. It has constrained me to such an extent that I worry I have not been true to myself, which means I have never even recognised my options, let alone had the courage to take them.'

Lawrence looked over the building crowd as he absorbed Lily's words. 'I'm glad you think like that. But my problem is I'm not sure I want options or chances. I can't forgive myself for not understanding Cissy better, which must have made her life harder than it need have been.'

Lily stood on tiptoes so she could whisper into his ear. 'I think we are all allowed to make mistakes. I've never thought that before this moment. I thought I was set on this one, immovable path, the only one that could possibly be right. But if I can change course, then so can you. I don't believe that Cissy's death means you have to set sail on this path of self-destruction. I think there is another way.'

His heart felt stretched by the contradictions it contained. 'But I did not do right by Cissy. I neither saved her nor loved her right and that feels unforgivable.'

'But I don't think that's true. You loved her as best you could with the knowledge you had and you could not have saved her because the science is not there. Surely the responsibility you have now is to keep learning, not to give up? Just like I should learn to be brave.'

Lawrence thought of Martha sitting in a lecture hall of male students, ignoring the looks she got, concentrating on the knowledge being imparted. It reminded him how much he'd always loved learning and how Cissy was always trying to teach and help. 'It's a lovely sentiment. And maybe learning and helping is the answer, it certainly was for Cissy.' He looked at Reverend Carter standing at the front of the room, a wide grin on his face, and an idea struck at him. 'Maybe that's what religions are trying to do, at their best, giving people that space to find out who they are.'

Lily beamed at him. 'I'm so glad I met you, Lawrence. And Cissy, which I know is a silly thing to say, but she seems so alive when you speak about her. Whatever happens, I want you to know how much you both have helped me.'

He wanted to hug her. 'As am I.' And, as he said the words, he realised they weren't platitudes. Because Lily had helped him to remember Cissy calmly and solidly; she'd forced him to really look at her, to stop and consider her, to understand her fully and completely. And, in that, he had fallen in love with his wife all over again, been filled up by her passion and intelligence and started to truly see the world through her eyes, started to understand the nature of his responsibility to life. It was both a wondrous and terrifying feeling, because, as it grew inside him, he retreated further from the edge, which meant it would take him longer to get to her, but also maybe when he arrived he would be all the better for what the future had to offer.

William had told him that we can only save ourselves, which was perhaps not that different from the sacrifice made by Jesus, if that's what you chose to believe, or soldiers who died for their country, or women who chained themselves to railings, or men who went down mines to feed their families, or doctors who walked miles in the snow to treat a patient.

For the first time in his life, Lawrence understood that sacrifice didn't mean giving up, it meant showing up and standing firm, it meant believing in something and seeing that through to the end. Cissy had understood this before she died, when she'd told him that she couldn't save him. And then he began to see what William meant when he'd said that we save ourselves through helping others. Because surely we can only do that if we know ourselves, if we have taken responsibility for who we are and what we want.

Life, Lawrence thought, ultimately owes us nothing. Lily was right, it wasn't like a ship travelling along a predetermined path. Sometimes we get lost along the way, sometimes we crash, and maybe sometimes that is the only way to find the right direction. You can only really make decisions moment by moment, crawling forward in the darkness and hopefully emerging a better person on the other side, like a continual rebirth.

He looked down at Lily next to him, noticing how her hair curled into the nape of neck and knew clearly and completely who he was, who he'd always been. He was a fighter, a man with a brain and a belief in what was right. It was why Cissy loved him and why also he was capable of helping Lily now.

LILY

Reverend Carter clapped his hands together and the room fell quiet, so Lily switched her attention from Lawrence to the front of the hot, crowded saloon.

'Marjorie and I are thrilled that so many of you could join us,' Reverend Carter said, beaming out across the crowd, as Marjorie stood solidly next to him. 'I thought it would be nice to have a little sing-song to mark this Sunday as we sail across God's wondrous ocean.' He clapped a hand on to the shoulder of a nervous-looking young man sitting at the piano. 'This is Robert Norman, who has very kindly agreed to accompany our singing. He's an engineer who is going to join his brother fruit farming at the foot of the Rockies.' A murmur of appreciation flowed around the room. 'We are all making this crossing for many different reasons, so it is most heartening to see so many of us united in the pursuit of glorifying God. It just goes to prove there is always common ground if we choose to look for it.'

Lily glanced at Lawrence with the thought of their conversation still prominent in her brain and saw he was smiling at the reverend. It was hard to associate goodness or common purpose with all the things Henry had planned for her and the truth was she felt abandoned by divinity as she had always known it, although she hoped that didn't mean it wasn't there to be found.

She had to keep hold of Cissy's options and believe they could still apply to her.

'Anyway,' Reverend Carter continued, 'can anyone suggest a hymn to start us off?'

'"There's a Wideness in God's Mercy",' a man shouted in front of Lily, then another voice said, '"Lead Us Heavenly Father",' whilst a few others chimed in with '"Eternal Father Strong to Save".'

'I see we are going for a nautical theme,' Reverend Carter laughed. 'Shall we save "Eternal Father" for the end, seeing as it's the Naval Hymn? Let's start with "There's a Wideness in God's Mercy", which I believe was written by Frederick William Faber.'

Robert fumbled to the right page in his hymn book and then the first notes sounded out on the piano, firm and reassuring in the way Lily always found hymns to be, almost as if they were all composed of single, meaningful notes.

She drew in her breath and sang out with the others, trying to catch hold of them, as if they could save her somehow. But it wasn't her own plight that rose through her, but Becky, who filled her so completely it was almost as if she were standing there, her image swelling with the sound. Lily's heart was keeping time with the music, opening and expanding and, even when she shut her eyes, all she could see was Becky and it was as though the singing made what she was feeling seem possible. She remembered Lawrence telling her that Cissy believed love set you free and the idea was so simple and obvious she wanted to laugh.

The music thundered around them, so loud she was sure it must be resonating around the whole ship, and she imagined the sounds reaching Becky, imagined her turning her face upwards towards them. She pushed her voice out into the air, hoping that it would rise above the others and reach her, that she would hear the message in the words, that she would at the least know she was loved. Because that is what Lily knew she felt, as she stood singing in the hot room, love in all its wonderous magnificence.

'And now for the Navy Hymn, "Eternal Father Strong to Save", or "For Those in Peril on the Sea", as most of us know it,' Reverend Carter said and Lily realised that they must have been singing for an hour and it would soon be over. The resolve she'd felt only minutes before tightened around her because, in truth, there was no telling what would happen; life wasn't like a song, with one line following on from the other so you knew where you were headed. To take a different path would be frightening, but it couldn't be worse than how she had been living. The time had come to capsize her life and start again, if only she could find a way to make that happen. 'Written by John Dykes and a favourite of sailors everywhere. As we raise our voices, let us give thanks that there has been no peril on this voyage, that it has in fact been a calm and joyous privilege to cross the ocean on this magnificent ship. Let us all look forward to arriving in New York in two days' time and continuing on in a happy, peaceful fashion.'

Reverend Carter raised his arms like a conductor as the first note struck, beating his hands together in time with the music, making everyone raise their voices louder still. Lily began to sing with the crowd, 'Eternal Father, strong to save, whose arm hath bound the restless wave, who biddest the mighty ocean deep its own appointed limits keep. Oh, hear us when we cry to Thee, for those in peril on the sea.'

The fear wrapped tighter around her with the words because they reminded her of all the obstacles in her way. She might be able to speak to Becky, she might even hear back similar words, but it wouldn't matter, because ultimately both their fates were in Henry's hands. No one was going to hear her when she cried out and, even if they did, they wouldn't believe her.

She scanned the faces all around, red-cheeked from the heat and the exertion, and felt a building panic because they didn't appreciate the words they were singing; none of them were in danger, she alone was at peril and not just on the sea, but everywhere.

Her gaze swept across the room to the glass doors, where she saw Henry and the doctor both staring in, faces set firm and their lips unmoving. Her heart skipped tightly in her chest and her body slicked with sweat. There was no other way out of the saloon and their intention was clear, they had come to find her and take her away, to another ghastly examination, or worse, and she couldn't do it any more, she couldn't stand it.

She spun round to Lawrence, but he was singing loudly, his eyes focused on something that was clearly not within the room, and she knew all of a sudden that he wasn't going to be a match for Henry. She felt cornered then and terrified, the way she imagined the fox must feel at the end of one of Henry's hunts, shivering and weakened in a burrow, easily torn apart by dogs with sharp teeth, as men looked on laughing, no one thinking that anything was wrong in what they were doing.

LAWRENCE

The hymns had moved Lawrence in a way he hadn't been expecting, filling the space where he knew his heart beat, so when Lily tugged on his arm, it took him a moment to return himself to the room. She was saying something that he couldn't hear because the crowd seemed as stirred as he was and were all chatting animatedly now the singing had finished.

He bent down so his ear was near her mouth and heard her frantic words, all running into each other. 'Henry and Dr Henderson. They're standing just outside the door, waiting for me.'

Lawrence straightened, his height allowing him a view over most people's heads to the door, where he saw Henry and George Henderson looking in, scanning the room. There was something very poised in both their stances, a bit like how he imagined lions looked before they leapt.

'They've probably come to take you back to your cabin. Henry did say he would, and I doubt they want to give you the opportunity to speak to me too much.' Lily had made her lip bleed, a red drop glistening in the light. 'Are you all right, Lily?'

Her eyes were shaking when they met his. 'Dr Henderson examined me again just before dinner, with Henry watching.

He was rougher than before.' Her voice caught. 'I cannot do this any more, Lawrence, it all feels impossible.'

He rubbed the side of her arm as her tears spilled down her cheeks, which made nausea rise through him. 'I think you should come to my cabin. We can get through the doors in a throng if we stick with the crowd.'

'Henry will find out where your cabin is and look for me there.'

'I know, but we need to buy some time.' Lawrence felt a building sense of dread as the warmth of the singing fell from him, so he wanted to scrabble about on the floor for it and shove it deep into his pockets. Happiness was such a fleeting friend, whereas misery clung so hard it shaped itself to your body and became integral to who you were.

A section of the crowd started ebbing towards the door, but lots of people were still standing around chatting, many making their way over to William, Marjorie and Robert to thank them, so there wasn't a mass of people to lose themselves in. But, on the other hand, if they didn't move, then the room might disperse gradually and they would run the risk of becoming exposed. He pulled Lily over to the side of the room so they'd exit as far away from Elsworth and Henderson as possible, directing her into the middle of a group of people.

He could feel Lily shaking as he took her arm and she stumbled slightly. He glanced at Henry and the doctor and saw they were watching the group heading towards the door, so kept his head down and angled his body to shield Lily. The group was jolly and making quite a bit of noise, and every step felt like a mile, but the door was close and he could almost taste the sense of freedom they would feel once they'd rounded the corner.

They were about to step out of the room when the woman in front of Lawrence stopped suddenly, raising her hand to her mouth and laughing loudly. Lawrence was forced to stop as well or bump into her, but the people on either side kept moving, exposing them, and he knew without looking that the noise would have attracted Henry.

'Lily!' Henry shouted as they reached the edge of the room.

Lily gasped, but Lawrence didn't turn, pushing her elbow so she walked on through the door, directing her along the corridor.

'Lily!' Henry shouted again. 'Lily, stop!' Then a hand was on Lawrence's shoulder and he was yanked round to see Henry's red face leering up at him, Henderson just behind him. 'Mr Beesley, what are you doing making off with my wife? Did you not hear me shout?' He looked then at Lily. 'Lily, you must have heard me.'

Lawrence was aware that it had gone very quiet around them, so he felt as if they were part of a show. Which is what they were, after all. A show which Henry had written and directed and was now playing his part in very well.

'I told you I would be waiting for you after the sing-song,' Henry said to Lily, who looked as if she'd shrunk, her skin pale and her eyes trained on the carpet at her feet. 'What do you mean by running from me like that?'

A few women sucked in their breath near him, the sound like a vacuum closing.

'I was not running,' she stammered. 'I didn't hear you call.'

Henry rounded on Lawrence then. 'Mr Beesley, I have asked you time and again not to interfere between myself and my wife. She is very sick and needs help and you pandering to her like this is putting her treatment back significantly.'

Lawrence forced himself to hold Henry's stare. 'I do not believe your wife is sick. I believe you mean to do her harm.'

Henry sighed and pinched the bridge of his nose between a finger and thumb. 'I know that is one of Lily's more outlandish fantasies, Mr Beesley, but really I would have expected a man like you not to be taken in by such foolishness. She has been saying this for some time and I can assure you if I meant to do her harm, I could have done so in many more private places than this.'

A small ripple of amusement rolled through the watching crowd and the noise sank Lawrence, because Henry had created the perfect set-up and it seemed unlikely that anything he or Lily could say would make the slightest difference. It was so easy for men like Henry, whose path was not just set to accommodate only them, but tilted forever in their favour.

Henderson stepped forward. 'Mr Beesley, as Lady Elsworth's doctor I can confirm that she is suffering from some serious mental delusions, which have increased significantly since she became pregnant.' A woman gasped somewhere. 'She needs to be returned to her cabin with some urgency so she can be given her medication.'

'No,' Lily shouted, 'please, no!' She spun around and Lawrence knew she was trying to find an ally in the crowd, but also that it was completely pointless. 'This is all a farce. My husband means to steal my baby and send me mad.'

Henry leapt towards her, enfolding her in his arms. 'For God's sake, stop this, Lily. It is no good for the baby.' He turned to the doctor. 'What in God's name is happening to her?'

Lawrence almost wanted to clap the performance, but then he caught Lily's eye and her expression was one of such total desperation it was like a kick to his gut, so he felt winded.

'Lawrence, please,' she cried, 'please do not let them do this to me.'

'Come on, dear, you will feel better after a rest. I knew it was a mistake to let you stay up this late,' Henry said as he started to lead her away.

She looked back, which made her trip, and there were tears coursing down her face and Lawrence knew she looked completely and utterly undone and that no one would ever believe a word she said. They had been out-maneuvered and the knowledge silenced him.

'I'm sorry you've been so fooled,' Henderson said as Henry and Lily turned the corner, his voice still loud enough to entertain the crowd. 'Lady Elsworth is very credible, I know, but she's also completely deluded.' He gave a small laugh and Lawrence saw some of the men in the corridor nod sagely. 'Let me accompany you back to your cabin.'

'I don't need accompanying.' Lawrence felt totally dejected, as if everything he'd felt so convinced by in the sing-song had been an illusion and he was no further forward in understanding than he'd been when he boarded.

'No, I insist,' George said, touching Lawrence on the elbow.

There didn't seem any other option than to walk then, which Lawrence did, past the staring people who seemed to have multiplied in numbers and all would bear witness to what they'd seen, none of whom would doubt Lily's kind husband for a second.

Henderson was silent all the way to Lawrence's cabin, but just before he stepped inside, he whispered, 'I'd stay in there for the rest of the voyage if you know what's good for you.'

Lawrence didn't bother to look at him or respond, simply going inside and shutting the door. He didn't turn on a light, but went and sat on the sofa, staring into the shifting, bluey darkness as the ship thrummed around him, vibrating up through his feet in a steady rumble. He imagined the story of what had just happened spreading through the passengers like a fire, the words multiplying and carolling so they became alive and vibrant.

He leant back against the hard back of the sofa, tilting his head until it connected with the wall and wondered how he'd ever thought that there was a way out. Wondered how Cissy had kept going against so many brick walls and closed minds. Wondered how it was ever possible to see a clear path and if he even wanted to find it. The thought of jumping began to creep over him again, teasing him with her icy fingers, because, without Cissy to teach him, he was devoid of ideas or plans or even knowledge.

Lawrence shut his eyes, a terrible weariness overtaking him.

LILY

Henry's arm wrapped tight around Lily felt like a vice and he was pressing almost his full weight on to her, which made it hard to walk, so she knew she would look as if she was faltering and staggering to anyone they passed. He kept up a low monologue about how they were almost there and she was doing so well, which she knew was not for her benefit, all the while his nails digging through the material of her dress. Little spots began to appear before her eyes and she could taste salt when she licked her lips.

Once they were in the cabin, she expected Henry to shout at her, especially as his eyes were hooded and his breathing ragged. But he surprised her by attempting a smile. 'We need to get you into bed. I'll call Becky to get your tea.'

'I don't want any tea.' She knew she'd spoken too shrilly, but her heart was thick and fast in her throat and it felt like she had no resource to calm.

'Please,' Henry said wearily as he left the cabin.

She heard him knock on Becky's door and for a moment she thought he'd gone inside, so she crept towards the door to try to make an escape, but before she was halfway across the room he was back.

He noted the fact that she'd moved with a raised eyebrow. 'I told you to get ready for bed.'

She didn't have any option other than to do as she was told so began trying to pick at the buttons on the back of her dress, although it was hopeless because her clothes had always bound her in a way that made movement hard.

Henry strode over and began fumbling with the delicate buttons that were too small for his fat fingers. He huffed behind her and she felt a couple ping and fall to the floor, not, she supposed, that it mattered any more.

He'd undressed her on the first night they'd ever spent together, taking such time and care over the removal of every piece of her clothing, kissing every bit of her skin as it was revealed. She'd felt consumed by love that night, as if every part of them was in communication, so she'd truly believed that their future was as dazzling as he promised. But she could see now that was just what she'd been taught to believe and how false that emotion had been. He'd no doubt been lying even then, taking advantage of an innocent girl whose head had been filled with romantic tales and beautiful flower gardens. A girl who'd been cossetted and protected and put in a glass case to stop her from believing in options.

There was a knock on the door and then Becky appeared. She was very pale, with red, swollen eyes, and her hand carrying the cup of tea was shaking so the china tinkled.

'Let me help, Sir,' she said as soon as she put the tea on the washstand.

'Why do they make the infernal things so damned hard?' Henry huffed, standing back. 'And hurry up, we don't want the tea getting cold.' Lily was surprised at the gruffness heavy in his tone and the way he barely even looked at Becky.

Her body felt limp and detached as Becky undid the last of

the buttons and began pulling at the dress, but, as the sleeves slid past her hands, she felt Becky's hand squeeze hers for a fraction of a second and then she felt the imprint of a folded piece of paper in her palm, which she quickly closed her fist over. Becky helped her into her nightgown, not meeting her eye, her movements brisk and businesslike so Lily would have thought she'd imagined it, except there was a tiny piece of paper held fast in her hand, which speeded her heart.

'You can leave us now, Becky,' Henry said, so Lily had to watch the door close fast behind her without the sustenance of a glance. 'Now, get into bed and drink your tea, Lily.'

The paper in her hand gave her an unfamiliar courage. 'I said I don't want any tea.'

'Oh for God's sake. Drink the fucking tea.'

'I think it's drugged.'

Henry advanced towards her so she was forced to sit on to the bed. 'I've had quite enough of your madness. And you are going to drink that tea if I have to pour it down your throat myself.'

The space seemed to almost contract around them, as if the walls were closing in and the light dimming. He leered over her, there was no other word for it.

'Henry, please. There are other ways around this. I can give you a divorce and I promise to make sure Father gives you a good settlement. I even promise not to make a fuss about returning to England so the baby can be brought up at Elsworth.'

He pounced, his feet leaving the floor, and she cringed, thinking he was going to hit her or pin her to the bed, but in fact he just ended up sitting right next to her, one of his arms encircling both of hers so she couldn't move. He reached for the cup with his other hand and brought it to her lips so she could smell the brackish, mouldy scent she'd grown familiar with. 'Open your mouth,' he hissed in her ear.

She shook her head, biting down on the inside of her lips to clamp them together.

He kept his mouth close to her ear, allowing his words to shoot into her like tiny arrows. 'It's going to be so much worse for you if you stop drinking this.'

She inched her head round to look at him and his eyes were swimming in hatred, like a fog drawing in across a sea, which was strangely relieving because at least she hadn't been wrong. It was almost enough to make her open her mouth and accept the absolution, but then another thought overtook her as she realised that she'd been told to sit still and be quiet and accept, accept, accept for the whole of her life. 'You have to make it easy for them,' her mother had said on her wedding day, not knowing that Lily and Henry had already lain together. 'You have to just let them do what they want and get it over with.' She'd smiled behind her veil, but that night Henry had unexpectedly stuck his penis in her mouth for the first time, clamping his hands around the back of her head as he pumped himself into her. She'd gagged against the sour stench and choking sensation, tears filling her eyes as her mouth filled with a salty, cloying liquid.

A sob rose through her which made her gasp and Henry took the opportunity to tip the cup to her lips so she tasted the bitter, milky tea. She spat out against it, turning her face away, and it spilled on to her cheek. Henry roared, flipping her round and pinning her to the bed with his legs, forcing her mouth open, with two fingers pinched around her jaw. But the paper in her hand gave her an unexpected strength which convulsed her body. She thrashed against the hard bunk, making Henry topple so the cup smashed into the wall, streaking the wood with a dark stain.

The noise shocked them both into stillness and they locked eyes, both panting in the foetid atmosphere. Lily saw a flicker in Henry's eyes, a moment of humanity that seemed to acknowledge the awfulness of the place they'd arrived at. He let go of her arms and stepped off her. He stood at the side of the bed, brushing down his jacket and readjusting his collar and tie, smoothing a hand across his hair. She stayed still, unable to take her eyes off him, feeling almost hollowed out by what had happened.

He shook his head at her. 'You always were too stubborn for your own good.'

'The baby,' she gasped, as her stomach heaved with her breath.

He waved a hand in front of his face. 'It'll be fine.'

'How can you say that?'

'My God, you are so stupid.' He fished a cigarette out of his inside pocket and lit it, his hand wavering slightly.

'I'm not stupid, Henry, I have worked it all out. After I give birth, you plan to take my baby and marry Becky. That is the real reason you're keeping me from my parents when we dock, so you can spin a tale about how I lost my mind and cannot care for a baby.'

He laughed then, a proper sound of mirth which she didn't think she'd ever produced in him before.

'What's so amusing?'

He wiped a tear from his eye. 'Just that you really think I would marry a maid. Or that your mind isn't already lost, for that matter.'

'But if that's not what you want, then I don't understand why you're imprisoning me. You don't have to take away my baby. We could come to some arrangement?'

He squinted down at her through the smoke. 'You are a very mentally unwell woman, Lily. Your nerves are shot and your mind is useless and you never make any sense. My priority now is to make sure that I come out of this situation with a healthy baby, sired from my blood, who can inherit Elsworth. Nothing else matters to me, so you might as well stop speaking, as it's extremely grating.'

It was like a bright light was being shone into her eyes, so all she could see was the periphery, and when she opened her mouth to speak, nothing came out. She thought of the captain on the bridge at that moment steering them through the freezing night, the spray and the darkness hiding their route.

Henry hovered over her for a second, little droplets of spittle at the corner of his mouth. 'You are nothing and you should never forget that,' he said, before turning and slamming out of the cabin, locking the door behind him.

She found she couldn't move after he'd gone because the world was spinning too quickly around her, or maybe they were moving too fast. Either way, there was too much speed inside her body so she felt as weak as a rag doll. But then she remembered the note.

She opened her fist very slowly, revealing a small square of paper in the palm of her hand, folded over many times so it was now like a little stone. She opened it with shaking hands, lying it flat on to the bed and smoothing it out. The words were very small and ran together so she had to squint to read what they said.

> Lily, I cannot tell you all that is happening in a note, but you are in grave danger. The tea will make you feel very sleepy so bang on the wall the second Henry leaves and I will come to speak to you.

She ran to the wall connecting her cabin to Becky's and used her fist to beat three large raps, then rushed to the door and, even though she'd known it was going to be locked, still it made her want to cry.

There was a tap on the door and then Becky's voice saying, 'Lily,' so her heart felt like it was being stretched.

'I cannot open the door. Henry has locked it.'

'Oh God, I don't know what to do.'

The panic in Becky's voice was dreadful, but Lily refused to let herself be scared. 'I think I know what's happening. I think Henry is drugging me and you are pretending to be me, with the idea of making me appear unhinged. And that you and him are in love and want to return to England without me, but with my baby and my money. I think he plans to have me committed.'

There was a strained silence and then Becky asked, 'How do you know all that?'

Lily's heart was so high she could taste it in her mouth. 'So I am right?'

There was no reply from the other side of the door, which filled Lily with a sudden rage that made her bang her fist against the wood.

'At least do me the decency to tell me I'm right.'

'Oh, Lily, I can't bear it.' Becky's voice was thick with tears. 'You must hate me with all your being.'

The adrenaline left her body in a rush so she had to sink against the door. She wanted to hate Becky, but all she could imagine was Becky's body pressed right up against the wood on the other side. 'I could never hate you.'

'But it's so much worse than you can imagine. You will hate me when you know the truth.'

'That is impossible.'

'You're right in much you have said, but before I tell you everything, you must believe me when I say I do not love Henry. That nothing, in fact, could be further from the truth. That every moment I am with him is like torture and my skin runs with shame. You must believe that.'

It felt as though the baby was gouging out her insides with its nails. 'But why then have you done all this?'

She heard Becky's ragged breathing through the door. 'Henry said he would evict my family from their house on the estate unless I did as he said. And my father has no prospect of finding another job and my sister is sick again. They would end up in the poorhouse, or worse, which I could not let happen.'

A deep nausea rose through Lily. 'But why did you not come to me?'

'Oh, I nearly did, a few times, but I lost my nerve and thought perhaps I was mistaken about how much you cared for me. I spoke to you about my family once, when my sister was last ill, but you did nothing. You always did whatever Henry wanted and, in the end, it seemed like I didn't have a choice.'

It felt as if the whole world was spinning. 'I am sorry.'

'But what I have done. Oh, Lily, it is unforgivable.'

'Becky, listen, there will be time for this later. For now, you must tell me what is planned for me.'

'I feel like I need to see you when I tell you this. I want to look into your eyes when I say the words, because it is worse than the worst thing you can imagine.'

'Bend to the keyhole.' Lily knelt as she spoke, squinting one eye into the tiny opening. The light shifted and blurred, but then she saw a flash of white and knew she was being seen, against all the odds. 'Oh God, there you are.'

'And there you are. Oh, Lily, I have missed you.'

'And I you. Nothing you can tell me will change that.'

There was a bang in the corridor and Lily knew Becky had stood, so she did the same. 'There are too many people out here milling about. I cannot tell you this through a door,' Becky said.

'Can we meet tomorrow, first thing after breakfast, and I will tell you everything, I promise.'

Lily felt a searing desperation at the thought of waiting all those hours. 'Please, I want to hear it now.'

'But Henry could come back at any moment and if he sees us talking like this, I worry it will endanger you further. I have an idea: straight from breakfast tomorrow, tell Henry you feel sick and need to visit the bathroom. Ask him to send for me and I will come to you immediately. Even if he waits outside, he cannot come in and we will have time to talk.'

'All right.' Lily let her forehead fall forward so it was touching the door. She heard Becky move away as she tried to make sense of what had just happened because it was hard to marry the ideas that Becky did care for her with what she'd already done. And she also didn't see how anything could be worse than what she knew or what she was going through.

Her mother had once told her that it is a woman's job to get married, no mention of love. It had angered her at the time, but perhaps her mother had actually been trying to be kind by imparting the knowledge that just about the only agency women have is in deciding whom they will marry, going from the house of their father to their husband. Her mother, she saw now, had made the best business decision she could when putting her in Henry's way, securing what she supposed would be a marvellous future for her daughter.

It was possible that Becky had acted no differently. Perhaps Becky had simply done the best thing for herself in a world in which the opportunity to change things rarely presented itself to women, especially when that woman doesn't have the supposed protection of titles and wealth. Lily had been an idiot to have believed in the fairy tales of her youth, to ever think that love was enough, that you could sit still and let yourself be carried along by the current without trying to navigate a path.

She put her hand on her stomach and thought that maybe the baby could belong to her and Becky, maybe they could escape Henry in some way. Although that thought was also enough to sink her. The love pooled around her as meaningless as the sea they were crossing, because the baby meant Henry would never let her be and she was a fool to think that adding the voice of a maid to her own would make any difference. The conversation with Becky in the morning would be wonderful in many ways, but ultimately it would be tragic, because the truth was that there was no real path open to them, no possibility they could ever live the lives they desired. She thought then that the asylum might be the best place for her because what is the point of living if you cannot be the person you want to be?

LAWRENCE

Lawrence moved from the sofa to the bunk, turning on the light and taking a book with him to try to drown out the thoughts of Lily. The muffled sounds of people milling about and chatting in the corridor seeped through the door, but they felt so far from him, as if they existed in another world that he would never reach. *Ultimately we are all alone*, he thought, as he let the book drop on to his chest.

His mattress heaved unexpectedly beneath him, the movement playing against his spine, so he thought he might be having a fit, his misery leaping out of his body. Another followed, which felt like the back of a sea monster pushing up against the bottom of the ship. Or maybe it was Lily's distress, rising up through the floors to remonstrate with him because he was weak and let everyone down.

The dancing motion stopped as abruptly as it had started, his mattress stilling, although now he could feel his heart hard and fast through his chest, and was assailed by alternating images of his pumping heart and the ship's engine. But stillness was so rarely an option in life, so he sat up and placed his feet on the floor. The constant vibration he'd felt throughout the crossing had vanished, like being in a room when a clock stops ticking and you realise that a sound you barely registered was actually very loud. He felt sorry for the ship then because, if she felt as tired as he did, he understood why she'd given up, understood the desire to stay still and let the sea carry you wherever without any unnecessary effort.

A strange invigoration made him stand because the stillness of the boat felt like a reminder. They'd been moving forward and now they'd stopped and he recognised the drama of that feeling, the desolation on the other side, as if it was flying to them across the sea and he had to hold it back or it would overwhelm the whole ship. He pushed his feet into his shoes, tying the laces quickly and rushing into the corridor without even putting on his jacket, aware that his shirt was trailing him as he ran towards the stairs.

A steward was leaning against the wall by the dining room, a bored expression on his face as he no doubt waited for the last people to come down from the smoking room.

'Why have we stopped?' Lawrence asked as he turned to the stairs.

The man shrugged. 'No idea, Sir, but I don't suppose it is of any concern.'

'Well, I'm going on deck to see.'

The steward smiled indulgently and motioned to Lawrence's thin shirt. 'As you wish, Sir, but it's mighty cold up there.'

His amused attitude made Lawrence feel foolish, but the steward didn't know about the desolation and the monsters, the edge and the cold. He raced at the steps, taking them two at a time all the way up to the boat deck, where he exploded through the door. The air cut into him, scalding the inside of his nostrils and penetrating his skin down to his bones, immediately sending a violent shiver through his body. Still he strode to the edge and looked down into the black, still waters, but there was nothing there, no monster, no desolation, no drama, no tragedy, not even the swell of a storm. He bowed his head because perhaps this hopelessness did just belong to him and he'd been a fool to think a ship was capable of sympathy, a fool to think that anything about himself mattered in the great scheme of things.

The stillness spoke to him of arrival and he hoisted his weight into his arms, trying to find a place on the smooth surface of the metal edge for a foothold. It was clear that the ship had stopped to let him off, bored by his indecision and his misery, which cast a heavy weight in the world. But just as he was finding purchase on the smooth edge, footsteps clattered behind him and Lawrence turned to see three men approaching, one the young engineer, Robert, who'd played the piano as they'd sung their hymns so hopefully a few hours before.

'Can you see anything?' one of them asked, as they drew level with Lawrence.

He shook his head, dropping his weight back to the deck, his mind now bulging and contracting. The sea mocked him in his cowardly fear, but the thought of falling once again seemed terrifying and he was filled with shame at the idea of abandoning Lily so easily.

'I'll go down to the smoking room, see if anyone knows anything there,' Robert said.

'Let me accompany you,' Lawrence offered because he didn't want to be alone on the cold deck any more.

They went back through the door and down a flight of steps. Through the smoking room windows, they could see a game of cards taking place between five or six men, so they went in and over to the group, where Robert asked if they knew what was going on.

The men all looked up, some with cigars clamped between their teeth.

'We felt a heave and then the engines went off. But no idea

why,' a man with a big nose said, as he slapped a card on the table in front of him and a general groan went up round the table. 'Probably something to do with the engines.'

'We did see an iceberg pass pretty close,' another said, pointing to the deck on the other side from where Lawrence had been moments earlier, which made him realise they had arrived without him noticing, those monstrous blocks of water memory he had so admired. Maybe they were calling for him, maybe they wanted him to sink past them and merge with them, maybe they longed for him.

'About fifty feet, I'd say,' the man was saying now.

'More like a hundred,' another countered. 'My guess is that we got a little close and scraped it and the Captain doesn't like to go on until she's all painted up again.'

'I'll bet there's ice on the deck. Maybe someone could run and get me some as I need more for my whisky,' an American man said, which made everyone laugh.

'But isn't that dangerous? If we've scraped a berg, I mean?' Robert asked, a tremor in his voice.

'Don't be ridiculous,' the man answered. 'We're on the unsinkable *Titanic.* The safest ship ever built. Sit down and have a drink with us while we wait to get moving again.'

Lawrence looked between the men, all so confident in their assumptions, and it felt like he was plummeting, as though life was falling through him. He saw everything all at once, Cissy dying, Lily crying, the sea far below, the cold air, his own body breaking, the ice, the ship. He knew then that nothing and no one is invincible, that no course is ever set, and that we are fools until we stop believing in this.

He stumbled away from the group, the jollity following him out of the room, but as he came to the top of the stairs, he had an odd sensation of being off balance, as if where he was going to place his foot had lost its place in the world and he had to grab on to the handrail to stop himself from falling. He took a breath to try to steady himself, but still the stairs seemed to tip very slightly away from him and the sensation made him think of Lily and how scared she must be all alone, no doubt locked into her cabin. And he couldn't just leave her – if Cissy had taught him anything, surely it was that.

Three shrill ladies in dressing gowns were being assured that everything was fine when Lawrence reached his corridor and he had to inch past them, the steward who was talking to them raising his eyes as he passed. But just as he came to his cabin, the door next to his opened and a man came out shucking on a coat.

'Anything fresh?' he asked.

'I can't work out what's happened,' Lawrence replied, because it was hard to tell if the tilt he was feeling was internal or real.

'Look at this.' The man pushed wide the door of his cabin so Lawrence could see the shape of a man curled up in his bedding on the top bunk, his face to the wall. 'He's refusing to budge.'

'You won't catch me leaving a warm bed to go up on to a freezing deck in the middle of the night,' the man in the bed said. 'I know better than that.'

'But the boat's stopped,' the other man laughed. 'That not worth investigating?'

'Not at all, let me sleep.'

Lawrence let himself into his cabin, where he pulled on some thick trousers and a Norfolk jacket. He was shaking as he did so and couldn't work out if he felt excited or frightened, but the night suddenly felt alive, as if the whole boat was filled with a common purpose. But the truth was, he didn't know what that purpose was. It might simply be that he had to go on living without Cissy, which felt as terrifying as anything that had happened to him in the past year.

A sense of pure exhaustion washed through him and he sank downwards, until he was squatting, his head held between his hands. The moments were arriving and soon he would be asked to act and he still had no idea what was the right thing to do.

He shut his eyes and she was right there, as she always was, painted on to the inside of his eyelids. 'You can do this,' she'd said to him in one of her last lucid moments, when the weight of losing her had pressed him so out of shape there was no hiding his fear from her. 'You are strong and capable and bright and fine and I love you and that will never change.'

LILY

Even though she had been lying in bed for a while, Lily was nowhere nearer to sleep when she started to hear noises from the corridor and, even though she didn't know the time, it felt too late for there to be so many people about.

She tiptoed to the door and pressed her ear against the wood, where she felt a sense of movement and excitement from the other side, doors opening and shutting and footsteps moving purposefully. And then she realised that this activity was at odds with the ship itself, from which there was no sense of movement at all.

She put her hands on the walls and was shocked by how still they felt, filled with a silence she recognised too well and which made her want to cry for this monstrous boat and all the lives she contained. Lily only contained one little life and it felt too much for her, too heavy a weight, too complicated a burden. Mothers were meant to be a place of safety and yet this was not something she could offer her baby.

And it was worse for *Titanic*, who had been advertised as the biggest and the best. It seemed likely that she had felt as unequal to the task as Lily felt about becoming a mother. Lily would forgive *Titanic* for wanting everyone to leave her alone, for wanting to disgorge her cargo, squeezing everyone out of her in the same way Lily would have to when the time came to give birth. She saw then all the passengers bloodied and naked as they emptied into the sea, her own body contorted in agony, and she wanted to scream for help, but knew if she did, everyone would presume she was having another attack and she'd end up back where she started.

She'd told Lawrence how she always felt that she was listening to life from behind a locked door, but never had that been so literal as it was now. She could have been a young child again, her mother stalking off down the corridor and May twirling behind her and the thought produced a deep longing for her sister, always so much braver and stronger than she'd ever been.

Lily turned back into the cabin, a panicked fluttering in her throat because the thought of May believing all the things Henry would say about her if he was able to execute his plan was unbearable. She turned on the light and went to her chest, digging around until she found the little album in which she kept the photos of her family, flicking over until she came to the picture of her and May standing on the beach in Newport, dressed as perfect little ladies with lacy white parasols above their heads. They must have been standing in front of the sun because their hair danced around both their heads in a way Lily's mother would never normally have permitted, May's naturally wilder than Lily's because it was filled with curls and fire.

She brought the photo closer to her face because she felt like she was missing something that wasn't just the freedom and vigour of those two young girls, it was more than that, it was as if May was trying to tell her something, that she was reaching out to her through the paper, straining to be heard.

And then May's voice exploded into the air. 'Oh bugger, if I'd done as Mamma said and kept my hair pinned back I could pick the locks now.'

Lily spun around because it seemed impossible that she wasn't back in the nursery in Newport, May stamping her foot and laughing at their predicament all at once, her hair completely loose, the reason in fact why they'd been locked in that time, because their Mamma said they looked like common street urchins. It was so obvious then, as Lily realised that even her own sister had found the courage to tread her own path.

There was a shout from the corridor, a man's voice telling everyone to put on their life jackets and make their way up to the boat deck. She ran to the door and banged her fist against it as she shouted for help, but the noises outside had intensified, so she knew her voice was being drowned out.

'Becky,' she tried and then a feeling of desperation overtook her and she felt her body cracking and breaking in a way that meant she needed to lie very still. But she stopped herself from sinking completely because, in all likelihood, no one was coming and that meant she had a clear choice: to lie down and give up while life sped up on the other side of the door, or to open the door herself.

She stood quickly and rushed to the washstand, overturning boxes so powder leapt into the air, filling the cabin with a scent of dried roses that tickled her nose. Her hairpins were mixed in with some jewellery, which clattered on to the floor, as Lily grabbed a handful. She took them over to the door, where she knelt in front of the lock, a strange feeling overtaking her that felt a bit like a lift arriving, the jolt as all the mechanics worked in time to suspend it in place. She used her teeth to straighten out a pin, which she jammed into the lock.

LAWRENCE

Lawrence opened his cabin door to the sight of a full corridor and people hurrying towards the stairs, even though the stewards still looked unperturbed. Cissy loved him and he held on to that as he joined the slow procession upwards because the boat deck would clearly now be the best place to find Lily, as he couldn't imagine Henry keeping her locked in in this situation.

As they climbed, a strange sound began to permeate the chatter going on all around him, like a scream, except magnified a thousand times, so it was more like a high-pitched shriek. It was winding its way down the stairs and he knew it was looking for him, knew a hundred harpies awaited him on deck, ready to whisk him away and tear at his flesh, so he wanted to cower on the floor with his hands over his head.

The screams were deafening as they filed out on to the boat deck and his eyes were drawn upwards, where he saw a rush of steam shooting from one of the funnels, a white stream against the dark sky, which looked like a flock of ghosts rushing from the scene. And it wasn't just the noise which was disconcerting, but also the fact that there was an officer in every lifeboat, throwing off covers and barking orders at stewards, who were untying ropes.

Lawrence looked out into the blackness, expecting to see

rough waves, but the sea was still completely calm, as if mocking him, as if reminding him that the unexpected is around every corner.

He was aware of a press at his back and saw that the deck was filling up, which meant he needed to find Lily urgently. He stood on his tiptoes and began to scan the faces of his fellow passengers, all of whom were standing stoically still, trying hard not to let trepidation into their expressions.

He spotted Henry first, standing quite near the edge, his arm wrapped around Becky's waist, who was crying quietly, as they watched the preparations being made to the lifeboat nearest to them. Henderson was on the other side of her, his hand on her elbow, which gave the impression that she was being kept in place by them both. He scanned the crowd around them, but Lily wasn't there, which sent a rush of fear through him, so rich and deep it tasted meaty in his mouth.

He pushed further forward so he was standing almost next to them when the officer in the lifeboat started calling for women and children.

Henry immediately raised his hands as he pushed Becky forward.

'Please take my wife,' he shouted up at the officer, 'she's pregnant, she needs to get on a boat.'

Lawrence looked behind Henry, because he must have missed Lily, but she wasn't there and it was Becky that Henry was pushing forward towards the boat. Momentarily, the noises all around ceased as he looked between Becky and Henry, their faces swaying and distorting as the meaning penetrated his thick skull.

'Hey, there,' Henry shouted again, 'I said my wife is pregnant and she needs to get on to your lifeboat.'

Everything danced before Lawrence then: Lily, Becky, Cissy,

and he wondered if they were all the same person and no one needed his help and nothing was wrong and everything was an illusion.

'Come on then,' the officer said, holding out his hand to Becky.

She shrank back. 'I'm not leaving without her.'

'I've told you I'm going to get her,' Henry hissed. 'But I want the baby safe first.'

'Hurry up,' Henderson said, pulling at Becky's arm, but she scratched his hand so he jolted away from her.

'I can't leave her.' Becky's face was streaked with tears.

'And I can't risk something happening to my baby,' Henry snarled. 'I advise you not to thwart me in this.'

Lawrence thought they were all blind, they all had been fooled by what was right in front of their faces. He scanned Becky's frame and saw how her stomach protruded, her chest heaved and her skin was tight and knew he had failed to see because no one had told him to look, in the same way that *Titanic* had fooled them all with her absurd promises. This had never just been about him, he understood finally, but about them all and their failure to see what should be so obvious, which is that nothing is preordained and no path is straight.

'I'll start screaming if you make me get on that boat,' Becky said. 'I'll tell everyone what you have planned. I'll not get on without her.'

Henry threw his hands in the air. 'You are a little idiot and you will regret this ridiculous stunt.' He looked at the doctor. 'I'll go and get Lily, you stay with her. Make sure she doesn't do anything stupid.'

Henry turned and began to push against the crowd, which roused Lawrence to follow, because he didn't want Lily to have to face what was happening alone.

A steward stopped him just before the door. 'Please, Sir, everyone is to remain on deck.' But he brushed the man's hand off his arm and dived into the people coming up the stairs, finding any gap he could to make his way down, avoiding all the looks of confusion as he passed.

The crowds began to thin out the further into the ship he travelled and he became aware of a different attitude in the stewards he encountered, more focused and busier. The steps were now undeniably off balance, every movement he took lurching him forward in a strange desperate momentum. The movement jolted into him, as if reminding him that there is always something more you can do; until the last breath leaves your body, there is always hope, or why else had he sat by Cissy's bed until the very end, why else were people right now scrabbling on to lifeboats. Hope might sometimes come to nothing, but trying was everything. He had not lost his hope, he realised as he reached F deck, and that alone could be worth living for.

LILY

Lily had learnt the intricacies of the lock through the pins she'd used, coming to recognise how their delicate structure could in fact be manipulated to tease around and pull at the mechanism. Her palms were slick and she was aware of heat in her face and tightness across her shoulders. She caught the larger piece of metal she'd identified what felt like a hundred times already, wrapping the little knot she'd made at the end of the hairpin around it. Steadying herself with a deep breath, she supported her wrist with her other hand, willing strength and precision into her movements. She pulled gently but firmly and felt a movement in the catch, a giving that made her heart speed, inching it further and further back until it gave and the lock clicked and she fell back on to the floor, laughing because it seemed so absurd that she'd done it.

Her head was spinning slightly and she dropped it between her knees to catch her breath, where she saw a crimson stain blotted like an inaccurate circle on her white nightgown. She scrambled to her feet and felt the stickiness on the insides of her thighs and the dragging back in her pelvis and knew this time the flow could never be dismissed as light.

Dr Henderson would tell her to lie down with her legs raised and she made for the bed to do just that, but she stopped her feet halfway across the room because surely that was madness. She wasn't a hunk of metal like the ship she was standing in, she wasn't just a vessel carrying a life, she was a life herself and she mattered, she counted.

Lily flung open the door, hesitating for a minute because there was something glorious about the empty corridor and she hoped *Titanic* could feel it too. But the silence was broken by the clatter of footsteps before a man sped around the corner and then she almost wished she hadn't unlocked the door because it was Henry, his face tight and angry.

'Hurry up,' he said as he ran towards her. 'We need to get on deck.'

'What's happening?'

'God knows, but they're putting everyone into lifeboats. Come on, hurry up.'

More footsteps sounded into the moment and they both looked towards the corner as Lawrence rounded it, his face red and his eyes glassy.

'What the fuck are you doing here?' Henry shouted at him.

'I came to check that Lily was safe.'

Henry stepped towards him. 'You think I can't look after my own wife?'

'Stop,' Lily shouted. 'I am bleeding.'

Both men turned to her and she saw them take in the mess on her nightgown. Lawrence stepped past Henry towards her and she reached for him. He was crying, she saw then, which seemed so unlikely.

'There is no baby,' he said, his voice shaking.

'Shut up, you fool,' Henry shouted from somewhere far away.

'I'm sorry, Lily,' Lawrence said, so she kept her eyes fixed on his face to stop herself from fainting away. 'I saw Becky on deck just now and I heard Elsworth say that she is pregnant. And it's obvious when you think about it, I have just been slow to work it out.'

'Oh God,' Lily's mind was filled with Becky and her sturdy, enlarged form and her voice through the door saying that what she had done was worse than the worst thing. She ran her hands down her flat stomach, which had only ever swelled because of the protective skirts, and was filled with a sense of shame that she had been so taken in by what she was supposed to be, she had been fooled by even her own body. Although mixed in with the shame was also the beginning of a sweet relief, that her body had always been her own.

Lawrence was sweating and he almost looked as if he had been dipped in the sea. 'I have realised also what those others tinctures that I found in Dr Henderson's cabin are for. They both help to regulate a woman's flow when it's too heavy, but in you they could easily have stopped you from bleeding, or at least reduced it to almost nothing.'

She felt empty. Hollowed out by the shock. The blood continued to drip and she thought she could feel its progress from inside her body, as if it was drawing down and out, cleansing her with every drop.

'Shut up,' Henry shouted. 'Get your coat on, Lily, we don't have time for this.'

She went back into the cabin and pulled on her boots and wrapped her coat around her before fastening her life jacket. Her hands were shaking and she tried to push away everything she'd just heard because if she thought about it too closely, she might not move again. But Becky must be waiting for her on the deck and she thought she was the only person who could properly explain what was happening to her.

The stairs were eerily empty, apart from the odd steward rushing, but the deck was crowded when they emerged into the night and she started to prise her way between the bodies, looking for Becky.

'Where is she?' she asked Henry, desperation swirling through her.

'I expect she got on a lifeboat and you're a fool if you think she cares about you.' He curled his lip as he spoke and she wanted to claw at his face, because if Becky had left her, then she was done for, like *Titanic*, a useless vessel emptying her cargo into the abyss, never strong enough to support life.

A hissing roar made her jump and she turned her face upwards with the crowd to watch the tail of a rocket climbing higher and higher into the millions of stars which twinkled above them. Lily knew an explosion was coming, but still, when it did, it was so loud it felt as if it had split the night in two, so everyone around her gasped as they watched a shower of stars fall back down towards the sea.

Lawrence was standing solidly next to her and she wanted to ask him what it meant because she wanted him to tell her that it didn't really mean they were calling for help, but there was no point because she wasn't a child and she understood.

Another rocket then flew into the air, closely followed by a third, both of which illuminated the huge funnels and tapering masts, as well as all the upturned faces beneath it.

There was a cry, which made Lily turn back towards the lifeboats in time to see the stewards on the ropes straining as they began to lower one jerkily towards the sea. The crowd surged and Lily felt herself being sucked away from Lawrence, as Henry grabbed on to her arm.

'Men to be saved from port side,' a voice shouted, which Henry jerked his attention towards. He pulled her with him across the deck, his movements so sure and sharp that she tripped and fell with a thud, the impact reverberating through her into the empty space inside her body.

'Get up,' Henry shouted, but she found she couldn't move, that all she could focus on was her hands pressed on the wood of the deck. He yanked at her arm. 'I said get up.'

She looked up at him. 'Just leave me alone, Henry. You don't need me. Becky has your baby.'

'Don't be an idiot.'

He dragged her to her feet.

'George,' he shouted, so Lily followed his gaze to see Dr Henderson pull up beside them, a nasty scratch down the side of his face. 'Where's Becky?'

'I don't know. She got away from me.'

'Well, find her then,' Henry whined.

But Henderson didn't even answer as he turned back to run with the crowd of men.

Lily jerked away in a sharp movement that meant Henry lost his grip on her arm and she used the momentum to run up the deck, now undeniably at an incline, towards the back of the boat. The thin steps which had first led her to Lawrence glinted in the moonlight, so she scrambled up them, feeling Henry at her back. But, once on there, she knew she'd made a mistake; there was nowhere to run, because *Titanic* was a trap, designed to glitter and distract, like everything else in her life. She made for the edge as the only place left, but Henry caught up with her as she reached it, slamming her into the metal rungs and spinning her round so his face was very close to hers.

'What are you doing, running from me, you stupid woman?'

She could hear the men shouting below them as they waited for their lifeboats. 'I don't understand what you want from me, Henry.'

'My God, you are a total idiot,' he spat, droplets landing like sea spray on her face. 'You still haven't worked it out, have you?'

'What are you talking about?' The metal railings were digging into her back so it felt like it might break.

'Your father is hardly going to pay for Becky's baby to live happily ever after, is he?' He shook her so she felt like a rag doll. 'For God's sake, Lily, wake up. *We* are going to have Becky's baby, my blood heir, who will one day rightfully inherit Elsworth. I've told the little fool that we will say you have lost your mind and leave you behind in America and she will be employed to bring up the baby, but you can tell a maid anything and she'll believe you.'

She gasped at the cold air. 'No, no, I know that isn't true. I know that is what you're really planning, because I know Dr Henderson has a letter in his cabin from an American doctor and you plan to send me to an asylum.'

'How on earth?' But Henry shook his head. 'You're right, we do have a place waiting at an asylum, but it's not for you. It's for your poor maid who has fallen in love with me and is suffering a phantom pregnancy. Sadly, after you have given birth, she will become convinced that it is she who gave birth and that the baby is in fact hers.' He laughed, his little white teeth glinting in the moonlight. 'It is not you who will end up in that asylum, Lily, but Becky, once she has delivered our baby.'

Life was crashing around her, whole chunks of her being, acres of her memory, sections of her future, all spinning and flying through the night in a whirlwind, diving into the sea, sinking to the bottom, cracking and splintering, rending and disintegrating.

'I will never let you do that,' she cried.

He drew his lips away from his teeth. 'Oh, I think you will agree to anything after four months locked in that house your father has so kindly rented for us, with Dr Henderson and I doing everything in our power to persuade you. I hope you realise that the examinations you've had up until now are very mild. They can and will get much worse, much more invasive. Although I feel sure we will be able to come to the right agreement without that being necessary. Now, we need to stop this stupid chatter and get into a lifeboat, as Becky no doubt already has done.'

Lily looked into Henry's eyes and they were as black as the night all around them. 'You are mad.'

He leant in closer. 'Stop being so sentimental. The Beckys of this world are unimportant. They do not have the same sensibilities as people like us. All you have to do is accept what I have proposed and we will return to England a happy little family. It is a simple choice I am offering you, Lily.'

She nodded then because he was right. Even at this bleakest of moments, she still had a choice. Both she and Becky, all the women Cissy had helped, every woman when it came down to it, had bodies that were under threat, occupied, used. It so often felt like there was no choice, that your path was predetermined, but that was as illusory as the thought that any ship could be unsinkable. Life came down to a million simple choices, it always had; she just had never realised before that she had the power to make them.

LAWRENCE

Lawrence had become a rock in a river, the men streaming past him being pulled to safety by the current. He felt a strange sucking in his gut and a whispering in his ears that could have been the sudden, quick movement all around him, but he knew were words. 'Stay still, Lawrence,' she whispered into his ear, so he shut his eyes and then she was right there, in their bed again, as he paced and worried around her. 'Stay still, my darling,' she repeated, louder this time. 'There is no need to rush at life so. All the important things are right here.'

He snapped his eyes open, because surely, surely, she was there this time, but he was met by an empty deck, redolent with an eerie calm, as if everyone had vanished. He spun around and even Lily had gone, which made him feel entirely lost.

A movement caught his eye on one of the benches and, when he looked closer, he saw two people sitting there, their arms wrapped around each other. He started towards them, and William and Marjorie, because naturally it was them, stood as he approached, warm smiles still on both their faces.

'Oh, I am pleased to see you,' William said and they could almost have been meeting in the saloon, as they'd done so many times already on this trip.

'I am lost,' Lawrence said.

'I think we all feel like that,' William replied. 'But the way often becomes clear only at the very last moment.'

'Have you seen Lady Elsworth?' Lawrence asked, remembering at least part of what he needed to.

'No,' Marjorie answered, 'but we shall help you find her because then, I expect, you also will find yourself. We need to get you two on to a boat.'

'As do you,' Lawrence replied.

'Oh yes, yes. But first, I wondered...' Lawrence saw that Marjorie was holding two letters out in front of her. 'Just in case, I wondered if I could give you these.'

Lawrence held out his hand to accept the letters, looking down to see one addressed to a Tom Carter, the other Alfred Carter. 'I don't understand...' He turned his face upwards towards the stars and their brilliance blinded him.

'Our sons,' William said. 'Their addresses are on the front. Perhaps you could see that they get them.'

Lawrence felt a tightness begin to spread across his chest. 'No, I cannot promise that. You must give them yourselves.'

'I forgot to say something in those letters,' Marjorie said, ignoring his words. 'Perhaps you can say it for me.' Her eyes were wobbling and Lawrence felt the weight of the task, the weight of all tasks, the way life continually conspired to force him to carry on. 'I forgot to say that if they had been younger, I would have got on a lifeboat.'

'She refused,' William said, his voice low.

'The thing is,' Marjorie went on, 'I have loved William for nearly fifty years now and I am too old to start again. I do not even want to. If the boys had been little, I would have gone to them, but they are grown, with their own families, and this is the right way. Will you tell them that, will you tell them that they have always been first for both of us?'

'Please tell them yourselves,' Lawrence tried, a sob reaching his voice.

'No.' She placed a hand on his arm. 'I am entrusting you with the most important messages of my life, Lawrence, and, after you have delivered them, I want you to hug your son tight for me.'

'Now we must find Lady Elsworth,' William said, as if something had been decided. 'Marjorie and I will walk towards the back and you go towards the front. She cannot have gone far.'

Lawrence felt a spinning in his body then, a sense that time was running down faster than he'd anticipated, that things still needed to be done. But as he rushed down the deck, he also felt a slippery panic at the precariousness of it all, at the way things seemed to be sliding from him.

LILY

Lily only caught a glimpse of Becky over Henry's shoulder as she launched the full weight of her body against him so he stumbled to the side, falling and knocking his head against the railing. A thin line of blood began to trickle from his forehead and he raised a finger to it, as if he couldn't believe such a thing were possible.

It seemed so unlikely that Becky was real, so hard to trust anything about her, but she was undeniably there, her eyes wide and her chest heaving. They knew each other so well in that moment, in every moment really, and a communication passed between them that felt like the real choice, like the one she'd spent all this time searching for. Because sometimes it is the things we never consider which are the answer after all.

Henry scrabbled to his feet and ran at them, his face so contorted by anger that Lily knew he wouldn't be thinking about the baby and his only aim would be to hurt them. She felt her body fill, as if all the pain and fear and hatred of her marriage had been building inside her, waiting for a chance to explode in this unrecognisable strength. The muscles in her stomach contracted, pulling into the centre of her being, squeezing the blood and the fear and the disappointment out of her.

She met him with her own force, ramming into him to stop

him from reaching Becky, a scalding pain erupting through her shoulder as they made contact. He lashed out, his hand connecting with her cheek, and her head cracked backwards. But then Becky ran into him as well, clawing at his face. They both pushed into him so they were right at the side again, against the thin railings which were tipping now ever so slightly towards the black sea, which made her feel as if *Titanic* cared, as if she understood and wanted to help them.

Henry shrieked, but it was a night filled with confusion and fear and no one could hear anything other than their own heartbeat. She felt the tip in his body as his balance began to shift and he reached out for her, his hands scrabbling at the air. Her hand moved involuntarily towards his, but Becky grabbed on to her arm so she turned and saw the fear rampaging in her eyes. The moment evaporated into the drama of the night, one of so many, and then it was too late and he was falling, spinning and spiralling down into the blackness.

'Oh my God,' Becky cried, hunched over the railings, her body shaking and her teeth chattering in her head. 'What have we done?'

'The only thing possible,' Lily replied, with more resolve than she felt. She reached for Becky's solid form to steady her, drawing the woman towards her, enfolding her in her arms. The hard roundness of her belly pulsated between them and she drew back. 'So, it is really true?' she said, placing a hand on Becky's stomach which undeniably contained life, and she felt ashamed that she'd been fooled by her own body. Although it also made a strange kind of sense because her body had never belonged to her before this moment.

'I'm so sorry,' Becky gasped. 'This is not what I wanted. Henry had a plan to pass my baby off as yours, but to say you'd lost your mind and leave you in America in an asylum and then employ me to bring up the baby in England. I begged and pleaded with him not to make me do it, but he promised he would ruin my family if I did not. I still refused, but he forced himself on me every night until we knew I was with child, and then he said if I didn't help with the plan to unbalance you, I would lose both my family and my baby. And then, since we have boarded, he has been forcing himself on me again because he says there'll be no one else for the next four months and if I complain he says he'll send word to England and my family will lose their home anyway.'

Lily drew Becky back towards her and smoothed her hair. 'You do not need to apologise. He has used us both. He has made us feel that we have no choices, but we have proved him wrong.'

'I could never have gone through with it. I wouldn't have let him put you in the asylum,' Becky whimpered, her voice muffled by Lily's shoulder. 'I've known that for a while now, but I didn't know what to do. I thought maybe to appeal to your father, or May, when the time came.' She pulled back and her face was streaked with tears, so Lily used her thumb to wipe them away. She tried to imagine all that Becky had gone through and all that she didn't know, all that Henry would have still done to her if he'd had the chance, and how simply falling through the night might have been too good for him.

The moment was strangely beautiful, not just because they were standing on the deck of a wondrous ship with the stars above their heads, but because Becky had come back for her without knowing what Henry had really planned. Becky had chosen her and the thought was like a summer's day in her brain.

Lily closed the gap between them and moved her hand to the back of Becky's head, drawing her closer and closer until there was no space between their lips. She pressed into her and it was like nothing she'd ever felt before, like nothing she'd ever even imagined, like her blood had found its way through every fibre of her body and she knew, with all of herself, that this moment, even if it were to be their last, was what her whole life had been building towards and it would all be worth it, every second. The route of her life opened magnificently in front of her, as clear as the brightest day.

'Lily!' a voice shouted from far away and it made her draw away because she knew who it was and she knew he would never save himself without her and she wanted him safe.

'Come on,' she said to Becky, pulling her by the hand so they could go back down the thin stairs, even if it meant leading her away from the salvation of the men's lifeboats. 'We have to go this way.'

LAWRENCE

First he had lost Cissy, then Lily and now the Carters, which filled him with an acute desperation because he was incapable of saving anyone. He was nothing like the sailors who had acted and triumphed and it was fitting that he should be left alone on this ship, which was nothing more than a contrivance anyway. He would let many people down again, never able to deliver the Carters' letters, or hug Alec, or help Lily, or even honour Cissy's memory, but that was maybe the story of his life and he had been an idiot before, chasing impossible dreams. Finally, finally, he understood that Cissy had always been showing him the way, even in death, and he'd just been too foolish to understand that, so now surely the best thing to do was lie on the deck and look at the stars as he waited for the water to lap around his ankles and absolve him of all his ineptitude.

Figures were racing towards him now and, as they exploded out of the gloom, he saw it was Lily, trailing Becky behind her. The sight made him laugh, a genuine burst of pleasure that knocked through his chest.

'We must have become separated,' Lily said as she reached him. 'I've been looking for you.'

Lawrence looked between the two women, both out of breath, and he was aware of something burning between them which was glorious to see. 'Your cheek,' he said, noticing the raised, bleeding welt on Lily's face.

But her answer was swallowed by a sharp cry from the side, so Lawrence ran to the railings and looked over and there was a lifeboat launching from the deck below, just beginning its precarious descent towards the sea, rocking against the angle that *Titanic* was now undeniably set at.

The steward looked up as he let the rope out through his hands. 'Any more ladies up there, Sir?'

'Yes, two,' Lawrence replied.

'Can they jump?'

A bolt of exhilaration shot through Lawrence because it didn't seem possible that he should be given this second chance and that he didn't have to abandon Lily, that in fact he could watch her being saved. She'd come up behind him and he pulled her forwards, leaning her over the railing.

'You'll need to jump, Miss,' the steward said. 'Be quick.'

'One of them is pregnant,' Lawrence shouted.

Becky was crying and shaking, but he and Lily managed to manoeuvre her up on to the side. A man was now standing in the prow of the lifeboat, reaching up for her, so Lawrence and Lily hooked their hands into her armpits and lowered her at least part of the way before she dropped into the boat.

'You have to come with me,' Lily said, turning to Lawrence, her face streaked with tears. 'I refuse to leave you here.'

'But you must.' He lifted her even though she pushed against him, putting his arms under her legs so he could sit her on to the edge.

'No,' she sobbed, pushing against his arms. 'You don't understand, Cissy was right about love being a choice and how that sets you free. I don't think either of us understood that there are so many different ways of living out there and we can choose to take them. I would have done anything to stop you jumping only a few hours ago, but now I see it's the only way or it will all amount to nothing.'

'Please, Miss, I can't hold her much longer,' the steward shouted.

Lawrence touched the small of Lily's back just enough for her to topple, falling the few feet to land in the bottom of the boat.

She scrabbled quickly to her feet. 'Please, Lawrence, please jump,' she shouted, turning to the steward, 'please can he come as well, please.'

'You might as well, Sir,' the steward shouted, 'we're not full and we aren't going to be making any more stops.'

'Wait, there's more people here,' Lawrence said, turning back for the Carters. But the bench was still empty and, even though he knew they'd made their choice as well, he couldn't leave them.

'Lawrence!' Lily shouted from below.

He ran back to the bench, but they were nowhere in sight, even though he spun with the effort of looking, as if momentum alone could make them appear. He could still hear Lily shouting for him and what to do felt unfathomable, like the absence of choice. Although Lily's words rang in his head and he knew she was right, knew that they were the exact same ones Cissy would have spoken to him in that moment.

'I can't believe we have done this,' Cissy had said the morning after their wedding, as he leant over her in a messy bed as the sun streamed through a window and everything felt new and perfect. 'We have to remember always to take our chances because look where it can lead us. To the happiest day of our lives.'

'Lawrence!' Lily screamed again, her shouts dragging him back to her. But, as he crossed the deck towards the edge, he was stopped by a scraping noise and then a shadowy figure appeared out of the darkness, hurrying along, his coat flying behind him as he pulled a cello along the deck, not caring that the spike at the bottom was gouging a deep rivet in *Titanic*'s perfect wooden floors.

The man disappeared up Lawrence's thin steps and then some halting music started up, which strengthened as he listened and he recognised the hymn they'd sung only a few hours earlier, 'Eternal Father Strong to Save'. And it made him want to cry, this ability man had to chase beauty in even the worst places.

'Lawrence, please,' Lily shouted again, so he was forced to complete his progress right to the edge and look down at the dangling lifeboat and the darkness beneath it.

'If you're coming, you need to jump now,' the man holding the rope to the lifeboat shouted.

Nothing was as it seemed. Lily was not pregnant, but Becky was. *Titanic* was not unsinkable, wealth and power counted for nothing, a calm sea was still deadly, time marched, everything changed, salvation was perhaps possible. Cissy had died but still remained.

The music behind Lawrence was clear in its message: if he jumped now, this way, he could never look back. He could not take this salvation and ever reject it again. This was more than a decision to live, it was a decision to thrive. He sucked in the cold air, feeling it deep in his lungs, so pure and innocent. He wanted to see Cissy sooner and yet there was Lily screaming in the boat and the Carters' letters in his pocket and his own son waiting all those miles away.

He shut his eyes and then she was right there again, her whole body next to him, pressed so close that there was no denying it. She leaned in closer and closer, her form weighing into him, her shape soft against him. And then it was more than closeness, he felt it first in his belly and then it spread through his arms and legs, so he knew she was pushing into him, merging with him, that his blood was now running with her. Her memory was precious and he would do anything to save her.

He swung himself on to the edge, letting his feet dangle over for a second, understanding how different everything could have been, how different life always was, how many possibilities existed everywhere, even in the worst moments. He pushed off and for a second he was flying, the wind whipping his coat around him and the decisions and chances rushing past him so there might be a lifeboat beneath him and there might be the roiling sea. It was the choices he had made that were important, he realised as he hovered, suspended over an abyss, those were things that marked out who he was, they were the moments to grab on to and be proud of. He had never made a better decision than to love Cissy and the knowledge smacked into him as he landed with a thud in the lifeboat.

LILY

They were ushered on to a thin wooden bench, Lawrence next to a woman, then Lily, then Becky. She felt for both their hands in the dark, not daring to let go, not daring to yet believe they were safe, because she'd seen the distance they had to travel to reach the sea, which surely must be like being lowered from the top floors of Elsworth.

Their descent was slow, jerking and creaking, so, as they passed down the ship, Lily was able to look inside, all the rooms alight and shining, all the furniture solidly standing firm, as if nothing was wrong, as if just waiting for the people to return. And she wanted to shout at *Titanic* that it didn't matter any more, she could stop pretending she could be everything to everyone, appearances were always deceptive and soon no one would be looking.

Lily tilted her head and saw another lifeboat swing out above them to begin its trip to the sea, and she could imagine the same happening all over the ship, on the other side as well, and the thought that Henry could have been saved swelled in her brain.

Lots of lifeboats were already on the water, some already quite far away, their little lights marking them out on the black sea like a puzzle waiting to solved.

'Stop, wait. Please save my son.'

Lily strained around the woman in front of her and saw a man leaning out from the covered walkway outside the library, the books visible in the lighted room behind. She had a vertiginous feeling of herself in that room, trapped behind the glass, looking out as she had done for much of the voyage, and it seemed equally likely that she was still there, so her physical body fizzed with the effort it took to believe that she was really in the boat. The man was holding the baby out over the sea, like an offering, and she gasped at the thought of it falling, this tiny human.

A man at the front of the boat reached out for the baby and the bundle was exchanged and passed back and back along the rows as the mother and father were also pulled across the gap, slithering on to the floor of the lifeboat as if they too had just been born.

The baby came to rest on the lap of the woman next to Lawrence and Lily looked into its scrunched-up face and thought that it was oblivious, that it was powerless and defenceless and totally reliant on the mercy of others. Except there was also unmistakably life behind the baby's eyes and Lily realised that one day soon the baby inside Becky would arrive and it would bring with it a responsibility. And then she knew that the blood leaking from her was not an ending, but a beginning, a chance to be different, to break through the surface and emerge as the person she should have always been.

They landed on the sea with a bump, right by a stream of water gushing out of *Titanic*'s side, so they could immediately feel an urgent pull and rush all around them.

'Start rowing!' the steward by the tiller shouted, and it was clear that he'd taken control of the situation. 'Get as far away as possible, quickly!'

Lily hadn't been aware that some men had oars, but she heard them now clanking together as they began to pull away from

Titanic's side, each beat like a strained heart. The spray splashed into their faces and it felt like a baptism, as if they were all being reborn into a different world.

'Why do we need to be quick?' she whispered to Lawrence, thinking of Henry hunting them down, across the icy sea. She saw again the anger, then surprise on his face as he realised he was falling, his arms and legs barrelling as he went. Her stomach contracted as if she was going to be sick and it was impossible to feel like she'd done the right thing, that there was even a right thing to be done.

'I think because when she sinks the suction could pull us down with her,' he whispered back.

She couldn't take her eyes from the ship as they rowed and the further they travelled, the more defeated she appeared, like nothing more than a wounded animal which had given up the fight, settling down to the blow it had taken without a murmur of protest. She was still putting on a good show, with light streaming from every porthole and the funnels and masts illuminated by the stars which didn't just shine, but dazzled, giving the ship an outline that looked like a child's drawing. But there was no denying that *Titanic* had also been fatally wounded, that something had gone catastrophically wrong and she'd had enough.

A man on the bench in front of them turned, his face blackened and lined. 'She's done for,' he said. 'They all thought they could push her and push her, but nothing is invincible.'

'Do you know what happened?' Lawrence asked.

'We hit a berg. I was in the stokehold and saw it cut right through her side like a knife through butter. The water rushed in and knocked me off my feet, which was lucky because it swept me through the compartment doorway just before the watertight door came down. They operate them from the bridge, so they must have known what had happened pretty quick.'

Lily noticed then that he was shivering, his teeth actually chattering in his skull, which wasn't surprising as he was dressed only in a singlet and cotton trousers. She began to wriggle her arms out of her coat. 'You're freezing.'

But he waved his hands at her. 'It's hot as hell down in the furnace and I didn't get a chance to go to my bunk before I went on deck. But nothing would make me take your coat, Miss.'

'Have one of mine,' another woman said. 'I'm wearing two.'

'Oh no, please no.' The man started to cry then, which was almost more shocking than what they'd just gone through, the sight of this gnarled man weeping, his tears streaking coal dust down his face in black rivers. 'There's lots of men who didn't make it through the door before it shut, so I'm not going to start complaining about the cold now.'

Becky gasped next to her and Lily felt a dropping through her stomach. She felt her weight against Henry again and the strength within and how she had withdrawn her hand, which had been a choice, there was no denying that. But she also knew that she would do it again and again, a million times, if it always meant saving the woman next to her. Many would see her actions as unconscionable and the law would probably hang them if they ever knew, but what she would say to them all was that life isn't fair and she had played by rules she didn't even know, with every card staked against her. That she knew what she had done was wrong, but that injustice came in so many forms, it was sometimes only possible to follow your own morality, which itself was surprising and ever-changing.

She thought then of the young boy, surely no more than sixteen, who'd operated the lift and how he'd look out when they reached the boat deck and wished he could take a turn.

Or all the faceless people who'd served her dinner, or opened doors, or made the deck sparkle every day. She squeezed Becky's hand tighter.

'Bert,' the steward at the front shouted. 'Come here.'

'But I need to row.'

'You're in no state, man. Come here.'

Lily was amazed by the tenderness so evident between these two hardened sailors, the steward at the tiller's voice warm and soft.

The crying man stood and made his way shakily towards the back, collapsing at the steward's feet, letting himself be covered over by a blanket and lying on the floor under a bench.

She looked around the disparate group of people in the boat and thought they were all there by chance, accidents of fate, which she supposed was really true of the whole of life. You just had to understand this and seize your moments. Because there was no set path and all it ever came down to was luck and chance, good and bad, all twisting and turning until you arrived somewhere.

LAWRENCE

They came to rest once they were about a mile away from *Titanic*, in a raggedy line with the other lifeboats, although none near enough to see beyond their beacon light. Lawrence couldn't tear his eyes away from the ship and knew every focus was on the picture before them, that every living thing could only be looking at the scene in front of them, which was in fact incongruously beautiful.

It was quite simply one of the most stunning nights he'd ever witnessed: the sky without a single cloud to mar the perfect brilliance of the stars, clustered so thickly together that in places there were more dazzling points of light than the background of dark sky itself. And each star seemed, in the keen atmosphere, to have increased its brilliance tenfold and to twinkle and glitter with a staccato flash that made the sky appear as nothing more than a setting for them in which to display their wonder.

Lily was very still next to him and he worried she was cold with just her thin nightgown under her coat. There wasn't a breath of wind, but the air was bitter, a strange sort of motionless cold that appeared to have no origin, to simply exist in permanence all around them.

'What will happen to us?' a woman a few rows in front asked.

'We'll be picked up by another ship,' the steward answered.

'The wireless operator will have sent out lots of distress signals and I guarantee there'll be ships racing across the ocean towards us right now.'

'How long will it take?'

'A few hours at most. And you don't have to be frightened because I've been at sea twenty-six years and have never yet seen such a calm night.'

'But surely it is impossible for her to sink?' the woman persisted. 'Surely we'll all be able to get back on board when she's been mended?'

The steward didn't answer, but there was a tightening in the muscles around his jaw.

Lawrence looked back at *Titanic* and knew what the woman meant because it was hard to imagine anything terrible happening to her, still looking as fine as she did, with all her lights blazing and her funnels and masts so definite against the sky. But there was something also very troubling about the image, which took him a moment to figure out but, as soon as he noticed, knew was all wrong. The illuminated portholes formed dotted rows, one on top of the other. They should have been parallel with the sea, but now they met it at an angle, so the lowest portholes in the bow were already underwater and the ones in the stern raised just above.

No one spoke any more and everyone who'd been rowing laid down their oars, so that even the steward on the tiller was forced to turn towards *Titanic*. They watched together as she sank lower and lower, the tilt Lawrence had noticed becoming ever more pronounced.

It was hard to tell how much time was passing because it seemed irrelevant in those moments, as if it had slowed and speeded up all at once, so it began to seem like a strange concept. The idea that he couldn't swim through it, like the sea beneath him, and hold on to Cissy, or stand once again on *Titanic*'s deck, seemed preposterous and unlikely. Life seemed only like a series of moments then, like photographs strewn across a floor, which could be arranged and rearranged for all eternity until you came up with the right structure. Because Lawrence found it hard to fully believe in what he was witnessing, hard to understand that this was just a moment, no different from the one in which Cissy had died, or Alec had been born. No different even from a moment in which you eat your lunch, or wash your face, or walk across a meadow catching the first spring in the air. No different from a moment spent tripping on your shoelace but saving yourself from falling down the stairs, or stepping back from the kerb just as a bus thunders past, or catching your child's arm before they hurtle around a corner. All just moments, ticking endlessly onwards, dividing and subdividing around a trillion possibilities to make up the whole of your life.

'Moments count,' he heard Cissy say from far away, as she stood in their living room in Cambridge, a pile of leaflets in her hand as she prepared to go out into the rain to distribute them. He cringed now at how he'd told her it wasn't the moment to do so, making her turn her back on him as she'd headed for the door, but still he'd heard her say, 'But what you make of those moments counts more.'

It was possible that this was *Titanic* making her own moment count. Her refusal to be seen in only one way, her reminder that it is not all about show, that substance counts, that life is capable of capsizing you, but also pulling you back up. He looked down at the sea, which was now so close he could see the tiny choppy undulations on the surface, so, for a moment, it was as if the rules of life had vanished and he was looking at broken water. The thought made him smile because it was important to remember that nothing is ever as it seems and the unexpected, which can be wonderful and can be tragic, or even a combination of the two, is around every corner.

Titanic tilted slowly upwards before them, revolving in a way Lawrence couldn't understand until she came to a perfectly vertical upright position, the water now covering so much of her frame, it reached nearly up to the captain's bridge.

'My God,' the steward at the tiller said, standing up and taking off his hat. 'I never thought I'd see the vanishing angle.'

'The what?' Lawrence shouted because he felt a desperate need to make sense of what he was witnessing.

The man didn't turn but spoke over his shoulder. 'When a ship tilts past its point of central gravity. It's the point of no return.'

All the lights which had still so gamely shone went off suddenly, flashing back on for a brief second, then extinguishing altogether. A tremendous crash sped at them across the sea, and he felt Lily and Becky cling to each other, as some people began to cry. But Lawrence held firm, forcing himself to bear witness, staring straight at the stricken ship, absorbing the howl of her last moments, imagining all the fixtures and fittings, all the boilers, all the furniture, all the engines, all the crockery, all the everything coming loose and falling, falling, through the walls and floors and out the other side, spinning down through the ocean, lost forever.

The minutes ticked inextricably onwards as *Titanic* remained sticking out of the sea, prolonging a moment they all knew was coming, in the same way Lawrence had been forced to witness all of Cissy's end, knowing she was leaving him, powerless to stop it. It seemed obvious then that he was no more responsible for her death than he was for *Titanic*'s, that nothing he might have done could have prevented either thing, that he had never called desolation to his door. He was a part of both tragedies and he had the power to pass on these stories, to not just understand in the telling, but to be understood. He'd spent the past few days speaking of Cissy to Lily and it had made them both understand things so long denied them, which seemed like a wonderful legacy. He wanted to speak of Cissy to Alec then, to give her moments permanence, to breathe life into her with the words he would use.

'It's OK, if you need to go,' he whispered to the stricken ship, so his breath whitened the freezing air in front of his face. 'It's OK, Cissy, I finally understand.'

Titanic rocked back slightly, as though she was allowing herself a final sigh, and then she started to slip downwards, as gracefully and quietly as a ballet dancer, letting the water close over her, sending barely a ripple towards them in a final generous gift, until she was completely vanished.

The sea looked as if nothing had ever graced its surface and yet it also contained her calmly, as if it knew what it had taken Lawrence so long to learn: things do not have to exist to be real, nothing lasts forever, and vanishing does not have to mean ending.

LILY

At first, Lily couldn't make sense of the noises she was hearing, a terrible keening which sounded like it came from another world or, more accurately, the depths of hell. She lifted her head from Becky's shoulder and looked around the little boat, because she couldn't even be sure where the sounds were coming from, they could have been right next to her or from the other side of the world.

The others in the boat sat straighter as well, a few women clasping hands against their mouths, or around their throats. There were three young girls behind Lily and she could hear them all crying quietly, their voices clogged and muffled.

'How can there be people in the water?' someone said from somewhere behind her.

'Oh, God,' Becky moaned next to her.

'Shush,' Lily whispered into her ear. 'It wasn't a real choice, you must remember that.'

The steward who'd taken on the position of captain of the little boat turned back towards them, his face completely ashen, as if he'd aged a hundred years in the last ten minutes. He opened his mouth to speak but floundered.

'There was time for everyone to get into lifeboats,' the same voice said. 'How come not everyone was saved?'

Lily looked around their little vessel and estimated there to be about forty people on board. It was full, but it could have been fuller, and there were empty spaces between some people which suddenly looked terrible.

'I don't know,' the steward answered finally. 'I simply don't understand.'

'There weren't enough lifeboats,' one of the men who'd been rowing said. He was dressed in a white chef's jacket which shone luminous against the night.

Lily noticed the steward slump backwards on his bench, his hand uselessly grabbing for the tiller.

'I'm from Belfast,' the chef said, stating the obvious because of his thick, lyrical accent. 'I know lots of men who worked on the building of that ship and they all said there weren't enough lifeboats.'

'But how was she allowed to sail then?' Lawrence asked.

'Apparently they didn't want to put any on board because it went against their unsinkable claim, but Ismay thought they should have a few or it'd look bad.' He made a sound that came somewhere between a grunt and a choke.

'What happened to the men who went to be saved from the other side?' Lily asked. 'There was a call that there were more boats there?'

'Only one boat came down after us,' the steward said, partially rousing himself. 'I knew there was only one left, but I didn't realise so many people were still on board.'

Lily thought of the throng of men she'd seen on the other side, Dr Henderson amongst them, and it was impossible to think of all those lives screaming now in the sea. She knew then that Henry and the doctor would be remembered as heroes, two of the many men who had stepped aside to save others, history as fallible as it ever was.

'We have to go back,' a woman near the steward said, reaching for the tiller. 'We could save some people.'

'No,' the steward answered. 'That's not the cries of a few men. If we go back, there'll be a scramble to get on board and we'll end up being tipped over and then we'll all die.'

'But you said ships were coming for us,' the woman insisted. 'Maybe they'll get here in time.'

The steward shook his head. 'The water's too cold. No one could last for long in there.'

The cries were already beginning to subside, the plaintive wailing reducing, the people, Lily realised, succumbing.

Becky was warm beside her, the heat of her body seeping into her and she longed to touch her again. She shut her eyes and saw her own face again in the library window, watched Lawrence falter before he jumped, held her breath as the baby was passed across, and she understood that the threads which bind us to life are as thin as a spiderweb and as delicate as the petal of a flower.

LAWRENCE

The cries lasted a pathetically small amount of time and then Lawrence just felt stunned. Stunned that he should have survived when only a day before he hadn't even known if he wanted to. His mind offered up the image of Hold Fast tattooed on to fingers and he wondered if they were clinging on, wondered if the words meant anything to a young man losing his life in a freezing sea, if the sailor regretted having them inked on to his hand, his path written on to him. But then he remembered how he'd spoken about missing the feeling of uncertainty beneath his feet and thought the only real regret was in not doing because there is no stability in life and the trick is surely to stand until you fall.

The baby in the woman's arms next to him cried out, the squally sound piercing the quiet in a way which almost felt barbaric after all they'd just heard. Lawrence looked down and saw the baby's little feet kicking out of his blanket, turning blue in the icy air. He reached out for them instinctively, wrapping them back into the warmth and holding on to them with his hand.

The cries lowered and the woman rocking him smiled and said, 'Thank you.'

'My wife always said babies hate having cold feet,' he replied, before considering his words.

'Is that the woman you jumped with? I wondered who she was.' The woman cast her eyes around the boat.

'No,' he turned to Lily and she smiled weakly at the woman, 'no, this is Lily, my friend.'

'Oh no, I don't mean her.' The woman nodded at Lily. 'I saw her and the other lady jump first, before you. I meant the woman who jumped at the same time as you. Right next to you.'

Lawrence felt a shiver from the top of his head to the soles of his feet, not from the cold or the situation, but because something moved through him. 'No one jumped with me,' he answered finally. 'It was just me. I was alone.'

'But... I mean, well, where is your wife then?'

'She died, a year ago.'

The woman parted her lips to speak, but must have thought better of it.

The baby's feet felt warm and snug in Lawrence's hand and it had stopped making any more sounds of distress; his eyes were closed, his lashes resting peacefully against his cheeks. Cissy had been right, all those times she'd covered Alec's feet. He felt Alec then, like a presence in his arms, and remembered what William and Marjorie had said about his future. He had Cissy there, at hand, in a little boy who was too many miles away across an ocean. And he had Cissy with him always, in the beat of his heart and the thoughts in his head. Just because something vanishes, it has not ended, his blood chanted as it thrummed through his veins.

It was as clear as the stars above his head that some people remain. That there are those we meet who touch us so deeply they leave fingerprints on our souls. Cissy had left a whole handprint, but he knew that William and Marjorie and Lily also would have left their mark, that there are people whom we meet who change everything. He too wanted to leave his fingerprints, a knowledge which pushed into him on that small wooden boat miles adrift from anything he'd ever known.

There was no breeze at all, the sea as calm as a lake, the sky as cloudless as a dream, but still he felt a wind stream past his whole body, across his whole body, through every hair, even under his nails. He looked out across the sea, expecting to see all the souls rising and rushing upwards, because there was no other explanation for the sensation. He knew that Cissy was with them, knew that she was finally free to leave because he had realised that she would never be gone. It was a fanciful and absurd thought, but he hoped that she'd found William and Marjorie and that they held her hands on her final flight.

My God, he loved her, and my God, love was a wonderful thing. Impossible to suppress even as a mighty ocean rolled over you, penetrating every aspect of your being so you became convinced that a bleak nothing was better than what you were left with. Although there was never nothing, he saw now, there was always something more. Our paths are not written, because life is extraordinary, and that is a wonderful thing.

He looked over at the scattered lights of the lifeboats strewn across the pitch-black sea, all holding tight to those who had been saved, and then along to the space where *Titanic* had simply vanished, all the hopes and dreams and sweat and toil built into her beauty like a false promise.

He knew then that there would be other *Titanic*s, because that's what humans do, pushing and striving forward because it is the only way. And that meant there were things to look forward to, not least the fact that in a few short hours, the earth would revolve far enough to allow the sun to peek up from the horizon, casting light and hope across the sea, revealing them all back to themselves, whoever they were, whoever they would become.

LILY

Lily laid her head briefly against Lawrence's shoulder because she'd heard what the lady next to him had said about the woman jumping with him and knew what it meant. Not that she'd ever doubted it, really.

Lawrence's whole body pulsated next to her, as if it was still filled with the vibration she'd felt every time she'd put her hands on *Titanic*'s rails, which were gone now, probably already resting on the ocean floor, the sand rising around them, the salt beginning its corrosion, all the splendour and beauty cracking and breaking, so her mind could hardly comprehend the loss.

Becky shifted next to her and she inched her hand towards her, placing it on to her belly, holding it there. She lifted her head then and looked into Becky's eyes, eyes which she knew so well and would never either doubt or let down again. Something rolled beneath her hand, which felt like a fish swimming through water, and it seemed incredible that she had forgotten we all begin our lives sunk deep inside a woman. That our waters break, but we do not. That a woman's destiny is inside not just her body but also her mind. The life force undulated towards her, and it made her want to laugh with a giddy happiness.

Becky smiled and placed her own hand over Lily's.

She leant towards Becky and whispered into her ear. 'I hope it is a girl.'

She would tell Becky all about Cissy. She would fill her head in the way Lawrence had filled hers and they would create a new life together, a girl who was fine and fit and fearless. Who would be confident and sure in her body, who would never let anyone in who wasn't invited, who would stand tall and strong. And she knew the perfect name for this wonderful new life.

She was completely exhausted and yet also strangely exhilarated. She cast her gaze around, trying to take in every detail: more stars than she'd ever witnessed, beating their way out of the black sky like millions of diamonds; a sea so still and calm it looked like an oil slick; the lights from the other lifeboats flickering like a promise of home; the unnerving silence after the screams, just the gentle lap of water against the side, as if they were all enjoying a peaceful day out; and the rolling beneath her hands, promising hope in the midst of death.

Life was full of contradictions. So many lives had been lost that night and it was as if a great line of people stretched behind every single one of them, because every death is the end of so many possibilities, so many future people, in the same way that every life is the beginning of so much, so many future people. The spiderweb shimmered in her mind as she leaked her own blood and the baby rocked beneath her hands. She felt truly responsible for perhaps the first time ever, aware of the burden and the honour of survival. It was not a thing to be wasted, this time they all had, and she had done too much wasting. Lily knew then with a cold, hard certainty that never again would she settle for a compromised, controlled existence for either herself or those she loved.

She squeezed Lawrence's hand in the cold darkness as she realised that Cissy had been right all along; the world was filled with possibility and it was worth fighting for, this thing, this living, this precious, precious life.

Author's Note

This book is a work of fiction, but the story of *Titanic* is obviously true. This particular story, however, has more truth in it than just the historical facts. Lawrence Beesley was a real person, a real survivor of *Titanic*. He was also my great-grandfather. A man who boarded *Titanic* in Southampton on 10 April, 1912 in the hope of outrunning the grief he felt at the untimely death of his beloved wife, Cissy.

I have been researching this book for many years, talking to his children and grandchildren, including my grandmother and mother; reading his notes; looking at his photographs; and studying the book he wrote, *The Loss of the SS Titanic*, about that fateful night. This novel is a version of what happened and what might have happened, some based strongly in truth and some complete fiction.

The survivors were picked up from their lifeboats at about 8 a.m. the next morning, by the ship *The Carpathia* – the first ship to arrive in response to *Titanic*'s distress calls. They landed in New York four days later, engulfed by a raging media storm, fuelled only by gossip. Lawrence was incensed at the largely false accounts he read of mass hysteria, of officers shooting passengers and Captain Smith committing suicide. The only way he could see to remedy this was to write an account himself, which he began immediately and, only a month later, *The Loss of The SS Titanic* was finished. It quickly found a publisher and went on to become a bestseller on both sides of the Atlantic. I have been as accurate as I can with all the details about *Titanic* and its sinking in this novel and much of that has been taken from my great-grandfather's book, which I find a wonderful mixture of fact and contemplation. For anyone who reads his book, you will notice I have even lifted a few of his lines clean from the page, as I love the idea of his words travelling across time, of still telling their story.

Only 14 men from second class survived and Lawrence only did by chance. As in this novel, he was on deck when the call went up that men were being saved on the opposite side. He, however, always said that he was filled with the sense that he should stay still, something he talked about in an article he wrote for *The Christian Science Sentinel* in 1913: 'A rumour went around that men on the top deck would be taken off on the port side and, although subsequent events proved it had no official origin, this report seemed at the time to be authentic, and was accordingly acted upon by nearly everyone. But it seemed more in harmony with the spiritual sense of the ninety-first psalm, more in tune with the teachings of Christian Science to "be still and know that I am God," to avoid the crowd and remain quietly on the starboard side until some opportunity of escape presented itself.' Lawrence rarely spoke privately of his experiences on *Titanic* and yet this idea of being still, of something stopping his arm, is one that many family members remember him saying. I like to think that Cissy had a hand in this and that all he had gone through with her death gave him a calm sense of perspective.

As in the novel, Lawrence leant over the railings in response to a call for women from a lifeboat leaving the deck below.

When he said he was alone on deck, the steward told him to jump, as the boat wasn't quite full. The boat he jumped into was 13 – the second-to-last lifeboat to leave *Titanic*. It is hard to imagine now, but almost no one on board, including most of the crew, had any idea that there weren't enough lifeboats. Lawrence hauntingly describes in his book the moment when the people on the lifeboats began to hear the screams of the dying and realised that not everyone would be saved.

Survivors' guilt was not a concept that people would have been familiar with in 1912, but just on the horizon of history were two world wars, in which this idea would start to materialise. Lawrence certainly suffered from this – he was a man always interested in helping others, but this intensified after *Titanic* and remained central to how he spent the rest of his life. All his children and grandchildren spoke of the depressions into which he could sink, right up to the end, and his obsession with accidents, that could see him chasing fire engines and ambulances through streets to see if he could be of assistance. My grandmother told me that whenever they stayed in a strange house, the first thing he did would be to lead them all on a tour of the fire exits, even if that meant climbing along roofs and shinning drainpipes.

He never left the UK again, which my grandmother said was deeply frustrating to him, but he couldn't make himself step foot on board a ship and, when they lived near the coast, he would sometimes take a chair and sit on the beach for hours on end, staring out across the sea. Right at the end of his life, fifty or so years after the tragedy, the family employed a housekeeper to look after him. She recalls how Lawrence only ever once spoke of the night *Titanic* sank, coming into the kitchen without knocking, which was very unusual for him, sitting down with a glassy, faraway expression in his eyes and saying, without preamble, 'I just can't get over how calm the water was.'

A few months after the tragedy, Lawrence returned from New York to London. He had a bit of money in his pocket from the sale of his book and a fair amount of celebrity, so was asked to speak and write quite regularly. He was always a forward thinker, a man, in fact, I think born slightly out of time and, eventually, he decided to open a business as a Christian Science healer. Lawrence definitely believed in Christian Science; he remained distrustful of medicine all his life, but I'm not sure how completely he believed. From what I have read of his work and from what he did, I think that he saw it as a way of helping women in a time when female complaints were so often dismissed as hysteria.

In 1917, Lawrence was called to the house of Fred Greenwood, who told him that his wife was confined to her bedroom with a nervous complaint. The woman was called Muriel and Lawrence spent the next six months treating her. He learnt that Fred was a mean and violent man who drank too much and treated his wife and their two daughters, Vera and Dinah, with contempt. Now we would recognise this as an abusive relationship and Muriel's illness as a nervous breakdown, but at the time the problem was seen to lie with the weakness inherent in all female minds.

Lawrence, however, understood what was going on and as he and Mollie, as he always called her, spent more time together, they fell in love. Within six months, he had taken her and her daughters to live with him in London and, later, Mollie became one of the first women in England to petition her husband for divorce for unreasonable behaviour.

They were married in 1919, but not before the birth of their two daughters, Laurien and then my grandmother, Waveney. My grandmother was born very premature, at just seven months, and the doctor told Lawrence there was no hope of survival. He, however, refused to believe this and lined a drawer with layers of fleece and blankets, insulating and protecting her in the same way as a modern incubator. He made sure she was fed every two hours, before being returned to her womblike state and, after two months, she was declared fit and healthy by an astonished doctor.

Right at the end of my novel, as Lily is sitting in the lifeboat watching *Titanic* sink, she thinks about how precarious life is, how we're all attached to it by such thin threads, which she sees in her mind as a shimmering spiderweb. Researching this book and learning a little about my own history, I have felt the presence of this spiderweb often. My great-grandfather so nearly died on *Titanic* and then, years later, my grandmother so nearly died simply by being born too soon in the wrong time. And without them, there would not have been my mother, me, my children – the list is endless and makes you realise there are people lost on every corner. As Lily says, it really does make you understand that it is a privilege to be alive and not something to be wasted.

Lawrence and Mollie's final child was a son, Hugh, born in 1921. Lawrence's first child, Alec, had also been returned to them for a few years by then and so, in his early fifties, Lawrence found himself with a large, young family, living in Harrow and working as a Christian Science healer from his offices in Marylebone. Over the next few years, Lawrence and Mollie worked on plans to open a school, which they both wanted to be progressive in its thinking. In 1934, they moved to Bexhill on the Sussex coast and opened Normandale, a preparatory school for boys aged 5–14, (although all their daughters attended lessons), where they lived happily until midway through the Second World War, when living on the South Coast became too dangerous. After selling Normandale, they returned to North London, where Lawrence tutored pupils at home, with students often ending up living with them for months at a time.

Their life was, however, not without terrible tragedy. At the age of twelve, Vera had died from bone cancer, which my grandmother cited as her first memory, saying Vera would cry out in agony at night and their mother slept on her bedroom floor for months. Hugh also died young, shot down off the West Coast of Africa, whilst piloting a plane during the Second World War. And then, finally, Mollie developed breast cancer and died in 1948, at the age of sixty-eight, leaving Lawrence a widower once again.

There were, however, so many happy times, recalled by all the relatives I have spoken to over the years. Lawrence was undoubtedly a maverick, with a deep love of knowledge, his children and life. He didn't like wasting opportunities or time and all his children recalled him as being fun and encouraging. His daughters were very well-educated for the time and encouraged to go to university and work. And the whole family was mad about golf – Lawrence played in the British Open for a number of years in the thirties, and Waveney won the Craig Cup in 1933. They all remembered his deep love of reading, especially crime novels, the plays he wrote with them every Christmas, the games he devised and the sense of self that he instilled in them all. My grandmother once told me that he had two fundamental beliefs: he made it seem that nothing was impossible and refused to see distinctions between people. It wasn't just that he was fair or equal-minded, she said, he genuinely could not understand how it was that people were discriminated against because of external factors like class or race or gender.

Lawrence's final year was spent in a nursing home in Lincoln, very near to where his daughter Dinah lived. He died aged eighty-nine on 14 February 1967, with Dinah and Waveney at his side, alert and peaceful at the end, according to both sisters.

Alec, Dinah, Laurien and Wave all married and, apart from Alec, had children, grandchildren and great-grandchildren. Alec moved to California for a while after marrying the novelist Dodie Smith, author of *I Capture the Castle* and *A Hundred and One Dalmatians*, before settling in the Essex countryside. Dinah lived in Lincoln, Laurien in London and Waveney in Kent. All four siblings are now dead, but all remained close and lived to ripe old ages, leaving behind large and happy families.

In this novel, I have stuck very closely to historical facts, but have taken many liberties with the emotional states, because who are we to ever know what another is thinking? I have no reason to believe that Lawrence planned to kill himself on *Titanic*; in fact, with everything I know about him, I think it is highly unlikely. But I do know that he was low and despondent when he boarded, finding it hard to rouse himself from the misery of Cissy's untimely death.

The details about Cissy are true – she was five years older than him, an aristocrat and involved in the woman's movement. They met in their home town of Wirksworth when he was seventeen and she was twenty-two and she did seem to have changed his life, so I can only imagine how desolate he felt at losing her. I think he hoped for a change when he set sail on *Titanic*, but, of course, what he encountered on that trip was more than he could have ever have imagined.

Lawrence details some of the people he met on *Titanic* in his book and some of them have made it into this story, including the Carters, who really did lead a sing-song on the last night. Also the baby and his parents saved at the very last moment are real characters, as is Lawrence's covering of the baby's cold feet in the lifeboat.

However, Lily is a work of fiction. But women like Lily were not unusual. In the years leading up to the *Titanic* disaster, there were a number of marriages between broke British aristocrats and eye-wateringly rich Americans. Many of these marriages have been documented and, unfortunately, many were deeply unhappy. Plenty of the situations Lily finds herself in are, sadly, not exaggerated. So, while maybe Lily herself wasn't on board, many other Lilies would have been, their experiences diverging so markedly from women like Cissy who were trying to tread a new path.

Lawrence's story has always been part of my life, not just in the book he wrote, but also in the fabric of our family, as one of those legends that whispers through the generations. Everyone has their own tales to tell, their own memories, their own snippets. I love stories and for so long I've wondered how to tell this one, if at all, because, of course, it is not mine to tell. But then again, who owns any story? As writers, we don't even own our own stories once we've set them free into the world.

Dinah told me quite a few times that Lawrence loved reading crime novels and so I like to think he would enjoy this reimagining of a small part of his story. I do know that he was always happy to speak about *Titanic* to newspapers and film-makers and that it was a fascination that never left him. In his eighties, he was asked to be a consultant on the film *A Night to Remember*, which took some of its research from his book. He loved being part of the process and was invited to attend filming on one of the days, to which Dinah accompanied him. They were filming sinking scenes and a replica of the deck had been built in a studio on which the actors had to play the parts of people who knew all was lost and they were not going to be saved. Dinah recalls asking her father if he really wanted to watch that, but he said he didn't just want to watch, but to be part of it, convincing her to sneak 'on board' with him.

When she asked him why he'd want to do that, he said he'd survived once, so might as well see what it was like to sink. Again, she asked him why, to which he replied, 'Because it's interesting to see the other side of the story.'

It is undeniably strange to write a story about your ancestors because it is hard not to feel the weight of responsibility that we owe to memories, or the relentless passage of time. As humans, we move forward, we learn, we repeat, we judge, we teach, we repeat. Sometimes it can feel a little pointless, as if even great tragedies become nothing more than tales. But at other times it feels important, as if we remember because we must. Sometimes it feels true that the telling of stories fulfils a fundamental human need, without which we would be lesser. If I have learnt one thing from my great-grandfather's story, it is this: we cannot change history, but we can tell it well and, in the telling, we can learn how to make the future better. I think that is a legacy Lawrence would believe in and I think, and hope, this story is one he might enjoy.

had he made that scary [illegible] but of the part of the meaning he [illegible] the total attention.

When she asked [illegible] had done that, he said he [illegible] a point, so he might [illegible] see what it was like for [illegible] again, she asked [illegible] why, to [illegible] he replied, 'Because it's interesting to see the [illegible] of the army.'

It is unfortunately [illegible] to write [illegible] about your [illegible] because it is hard not to feel the weight of responsibility [illegible] we [illegible] of the references [illegible] all [illegible] within [illegible] we are [illegible] we [illegible] we [illegible] [illegible] but [illegible] a little [illegible] of [illegible] our [illegible] become nothing more than [illegible] of [illegible] it [illegible] important as if we [illegible] must [illegible] is true that the telling of stories [illegible] fundamental [illegible] need, without which we would be lesser. If I have learnt anything from my [illegible] candidature [illegible] it is that we cannot change history, but we can tell [illegible] in [illegible] we can learn how to make the future better [illegible] that's [illegible] we [illegible] in [illegible] I hope this story [illegible] one [illegible].

Acknowledgements

More than any other book, thanks are due to my family. Lawrence's story is one I've grown up with and thinking about and then researching this book has taken years. So many people were generous and helpful with their advice, but especially my grandmother, Waveney, my great aunt Dinah, my mother Lindy, Dinah's son David Quilter and Laurien's son, Nicholas Wade. It has been such a joy to hear their stories and memories, and it has taught me that families should always go on asking questions. Thanks also to my dad, David, who is always amongst my first readers and always full of advice and encouragement. And always to my husband Jamie and our children, Oscar, Violet and Edie, who don't complain (too much), when my mind is otherwise occupied.

Thanks also to my friend Lizzie Enfield, who is also always one of my first readers and whose advice is invaluable. And all the rest of the Brighton writing community, notably Dorothy Koomson, Kate Harrison and Laura Wilkinson – we can discuss books and plots for hours.

Huge thanks also to my agent Lizzy Kremer who has helped me shape this book and turn it into a proper story and been endlessly patient and encouraging. And also to my editor Francesca

Pathak, who has loved this story from the beginning and been such a wonderful champion of Lily and Lawrence. And finally, to everyone at DHA and Orion because, as I've said many times, it sometimes feels unfair that only my name is on the cover, considering how many amazing and talented people contribute so much to each and every book.

Credits

Araminta Hall and Orion Fiction would like to thank everyone at Orion who worked on the publication of *Hidden Depths* in the UK.

Editorial
Francesca Pathak
Lucy Frederick

Copy editor
Jade Craddock

Proof reader
Kati Nicholl

Audio
Paul Stark
Amber Bates

Contracts
Anne Goddard
Jake Alderson

Design
Debbie Holmes
Joanna Ridley
Nick May

Editorial Management
Charlie Panayiotou
Jane Hughes

Finance
Jasdip Nandra
Afeera Ahmed
Elizabeth Beaumont
Sue Baker

Production
Ruth Sharvell

Marketing
Katie Moss

Publicity
Francesca Pearce

Sales
Jen Wilson
Esther Waters
Victoria Laws
Frances Doyle
Georgina Cutler

Operations
Jo Jacobs
Sharon Willis
Lisa Pryde
Lucy Brem